A BANISHING OF KINGS

A BANISHING OF KINGS

REALM BREAKER • BOOK TWO

JASMINE YOUNG

DRAGONFYRE
BOOKS

KDP Paperback ISBN: 978-1734993240
KDP Hardback ISBN: 978-1-7349932-8-8
IngramSpark Paperback ISBN: 978-1-996804-07-9
IngramSpark Hardback ISBN: 978-1-966804-08-6

Cover art and interior chapter illustration by Ertaç Altınöz
Photography by Steven Deisig

Published by Dragonfyre Books

www.jasmineyoungauthor.com
jasmine@jasmineyoungauthor.com

ALSO BY THE AUTHOR

Also by the author:

Realm Breaker

#0.5 *A Descent of Dragons*

#1 *A Breaking of Realms*

#2 *A Banishing of Kings*

#3 *A Building of Empires*

#4 *A Battling of Continents*

Short Stories & Novellas:

#1.5 *A Quest of Rangers,* #3.1 *A Bond of Brothers*

Four Kingdoms: Origins

#0.5 *The Morrow Fall*

#1 *Stormfire*

#2 *Winter's Blade*

#3 *The Olden Spire*

THE DE
THE NAUTHE
THE ALFVINDOR ALPS
THE LONGCOLD
DELLFAST
LYSMARK
CITY-
OF EL
FJORLAND
SVENNANDIA
BERETH BETHEL
FEL TIR
GHEALE'AD CITY
OLD GRAVEN
NHON'S MIREA
EBRENNIA
THE SUNDERE
NEW SER
HAL MAELIN
CAER I'LEON
LOGATHIA
AELIN DO
NARENNOR
CRIDAM
THE WEST REACH
MIRIESWEN
ERAUWIEL
FARIN'S CROSSING
SAANPORT
PENTAR
TYROS'S LANDING
THE SOUTH FENS
ZALYRIS
VELOSBAN
THE FIVE FREEHOL
BAURON OCEAN

NORTH
ELENWËA
BELFAINE
BLIC
TAR
BERIA
RHAENNÖRIAN EMPIRE
DHEL LORIEN
STES
THE DIVINE REPUBLIC OF ARANOR ELONDRIS
DRAGONMOUNT
ELONDRIA
EXAR'FORDA
REVAL
NIMLÓRIËN OCEAN
N
W
E
LÖTH-ANÁRION
OSTHAVEN ISLES
EMPORIUM SEA
KHAIR TARIN
CALENDRIA
VERDORN
OLD VALINDOR
SKYCREST HOLD
NHILGRAAD EMPIRE

1

BY THE MALLETS OF THE OLD YRTHJÖK

SKÁLDA WOKE a quarter hour before the longboats made landfall. Liv Tamarath had her bundled in blankets at the bulwark, but that was not enough to keep out her feverish shivering. Sweat drenched her ratty robe. Grime smothered her scalp. Her hair was stringy with filth. She cradled her swollen wrist to her breast, silent despite her agony. Against the reflection of Liv's worried eyes, she saw her own, black-ringed with exhaustion. She looked a wild beast the Weremen had towed out of the forests.

As the women rowed closer to the new shoreline, Skálda felt someone staring down at her. This new boat captain was perhaps several solstices older than her. He wore his chestnut hair in long flowing locks, the top tied back in half. His hair was more luxurious than a stallion's mane. She decided to call him Pretty Horse. His eyes were alight with amusement.

"What?" she said darkly.

Pretty Horse just chuckled.

Male thralls in rags moored their longboat. Liv helped Skálda up. Even the slightest movement made the sensation of needles shoot out of her wrist. She hissed in pain.

"Looks like I won't need to tie you." Pretty Horse thumped her upper arm with his axe's haft, pointing to the causeway ahead. He hopped out of the boat, his boots slamming into shallow water.

The passengers from the longboats trudged away from the channel and up into a reddish green tundra. Skálda counted thousands of prisoners, all the survivors of Dellfast. Liv stayed by her side, offering her shoulder for balance and helping her up the hills.

Skálda looked to the royal longboat further down the foreshore. The Draughammr leapt out, followed by Asveig and Lord Jarmon. Pretty Horse, a few paces ahead of her, waved his axe in acknowledgement. Asveig waved back, and the three Vigardians mounted the only horses in sight.

Her eyes would not stop trailing the Draughammr. How had Fjorland's crown prince ever joined the Wereguild? Sorenthor Astoraine. That would be his true name. Did King Leondran know? How could Prince Sorenthor abscond into the traitorous Deep North, when he could have become an Eldari one day, the highest leader in the Republic?

While she retreated into her dark musings, two Wereman yanked Aesir off the royal longboat. He wore a heavy chain around his neck. As they pulled him over the beach, he clutched the iron, struggling to breathe, his face twisted in pain. They handed his fetter to Lord Jarmon. The Vigardian was on the saddle, waiting for him.

"Come along, elf!" He jerked the chain. The force made Aesir crash onto his knees. "I hope you move fast enough, or I will be hauling your elvish carcass to Solhall."

Skálda changed course. Livana hissed at her to stop.

"Draugh!" called Lord Jarmon. "How do you translate this?" He spoke a line in the Svenning.

The Draughammr, ahead on his destrier, called over his shoulder in Elondrian. "Conjure a spell, elf, and we'll kill you!"

The Weremen laughed at Aesir. Skálda made it three more

steps before Liv pulled her back. "No!" the rider whispered fiercely. "If you oppose them, you will only give them more reason to hurt him. And you." The young woman glanced down at her broken wrist. Skálda was freezing and filthy and exhausted, but the fires of Dellfast burned in her.

On the hill now, Pretty Horse called for her. *Dragon girl!*

As the Draughammr and his shield-brothers receded to the front of the train, she locked her gaze on the helmet he wore over his back. It was a familiar one, adorned with tines and black horsehair.

"Who was Fjella Wulfgar?" she said.

Liv followed her trail of sight. "That was the Were Queen."

Skálda turned to stare at her. "I killed his queen?" she whispered.

They scaled the rest of the hill and joined up with Pretty Horse. He was waiting for her patiently, unaffected by the tributaries of thralls and Weremen coursing toward some point in the north.

"Welcome to Vingulmark," he grinned.

The Weremen ordered the hundreds of Dellfast commons to stay on the dirt causeway, which Pretty Horse called the Hammerfest Road. It was the only road Skálda could see out here. There were so many bodies, the Draughammr and his mounted commanders were no longer in sight. To her rear was the dark strait they had sailed across; to her left were towering ridges; and to her right, open country rolled beneath an iron sky. Besides for the stink of bodies around her, the air smelled foul, like mammal carcasses or fetid water left out in the sun. But the worst of it was the eastern horizon's stillness. No beasts of majesty danced over these skies.

As she and Liv trudged on foot, a Dellfast child started tossing stones beyond the causeway. After the third throw, Pretty Horse called, "I wouldn't do that if I were you."

The child ignored him, reaching for another pebble. A strange sucking bubbled out of the mud below the road. Skálda turned her head. A plume of fire burst out of the grasses. The child screamed, and Liv rushed to pull him back. Something long and spiked burst from the earth. It was a bright, poisonous red.

"Oh," said Pretty Horse.

A machine-like screech ground the air. The Dellfast commons shrieked and rampaged into each other. The monster caught a passing snow bunting in midair with its rounds of teeth and sank back into the steaming earth.

Liv released the hysterical child back to his family.

Pretty Horse shouted at the crowds, "Stay on the road, or they will eat you!" He repeated his Svenning in broken Elondrian, but what inadvertently came out was, "The road eats all people!" This made the Dellfasters even more frantic. They attempted to stampede back the way they came.

"What was that thing?" said Skálda.

Pretty Horse was twirling his axe as if fire-belching abominations were the most ordinary thing in the world. In the background, Liv gracefully hollered the correct Elondrian translation, undoing the congestion.

"We are in wyrm country, dragon girl," he said. "The bloodwyrms are hungry. Since Eyrekvald the Great Built in our lands, we are forced further north, into this beautiful paradise..." He extended one arm, gesturing at the tundra that rolled eastward. Skálda stared over her shoulder. That wyrm had been taller than her, and that was with half of it underground.

"As you can see," he drawled, "it's a bit difficult to grow radishes out here."

Liv stepped away from them, warning two fascinated boys in Elondrian not to stray close to the wyrmhole. Pretty Horse glanced over his shoulder. "What's your name, anyway?"

Skálda returned her hard gaze to the road, saying nothing.

"Oh, come. You have a name, don't you? Something better than 'dragon girl'?" He inhaled the sky. "A Republic common who managed to kill Fjella! Cursed yourself, you have. The Draugh won't ever talk when you're mentioned."

"Where is my dragon?"

Pretty Horse laughed good-naturedly. "I am Raldefur Ilfsson," he said, placing a hand on his chest. "Or Rulf, as my shield-brothers call me. If you don't give us your name, the Draughammr will cut it out of you soon enough."

A few hours later, the tundra turned into a grassy mead with a taiga sweeping in from the northeast. More tributaries of commons poured in from that direction. These crowds were laden with wheels, pack animals, and cages. Skálda understood now why the Draughammr had taken the women and children over the water. It was much faster transport than looping in from the wider eastern roads with baggage and male prisoners that required a heavier guard. Liv trained her eyes ahead, though Skálda could tell she was greatly affected by the tides of her people coming in as prisoners. Skálda scoured the crowds merging with theirs for any sign of her friends.

"*Livana*?" someone cried.

They turned their heads. The Wereguild was filing the male prisoners into lines. In one of them stood a red-haired man with bound wrists. The Weremen had stripped him down to his linen tunics and given him the same ratty, patched robe as hers. Grief hollowed his face, and he was paler than a carcass exhumed from the tomb.

"Faelan!" Liv screamed.

He bounded out of the lines and crossed the valley, drawing the shouts from the Were overseers. Skálda walked on with Rulf as they collided into each other's arms. Liv caressed his face, kissed him with urgency, pressing his head to hers.

"I thought they killed you," she whispered.

"I thought the same of you." The rider breathed into her neck in anguish. "Liv... They... the others are dead. Someone from Dragonsteel annulled our city..."

The young woman shut her eyes. Both wept into each other's wools, until suddenly, a Wereman wrested Faelan away.

"Come along, thrall!" he barked, waving his axe. Two more Wereman were waiting off the curbside. They shoved Faelan back toward the queues. Skálda caught his eyes for a fleeting moment.

"Don't hurt him!" Liv screamed. "Please..." She sank to her knees, weeping into her hands. The surrounding Dellfasters shook their heads in pity and stepped around her.

"Liv."

The young woman looked up at the hand Skálda extended to her. Skálda hoisted her up and let Liv lean against her shoulder. Together, they staggered over the final stretch of the Hammerfest Road.

Solhall was a settlement tucked inside mountains, which the myths called the Lupines. This was a city barely comparable to Dellfast. Its curtain walls were barely ten feet, and neither did it have castles or three-story chapels and townhouses. Almost all that populated it were longhouses. Yet there were more longhouses spread over the snow-dusted heights than she ever imagined possible. Tens of thousands of northerners dwelt out here. The sight of Thorgest Vigarda's fief of legends stole her breath. Most Svennish never lived to see more than forty people gathered in one place.

They entered Solhall by way of the Eldruna Valley, a landmark as legendary as the hold awaiting them ahead. It was so green out here, so fertile, the multicolored fields patched like a quilt. Her Realm-Builder mind spun; if only Anders could have Built a post out here. Or better yet, if only she could. Such fecund lands were worth their weight in talents when high-ranking Builders had already claimed the most resourceful free zones in Aranor Elondris. The Draughammr could produce enough food to feed all Fjorland from this valley alone.

She was so deep in her musings that she did not notice the giants until Liv gasped. Between the fields, sharp-eared monoliths crouched over the earth, tapped the scattered trees with their mallets, singing verses in the Old Nhorssn that she did not understand.

"Giants," Liv exclaimed.

"Thomdrim," Rulf corrected.

"They are real?"

"Why wouldn't they be?"

The Thomdrim were descendants of the Old Yrthjök, Giants of twenty feet or more. They were one of the original Nhorssn races that used to inhabit the continent. Like the Vigardians, the Thomdrim had freely walked Old Svenn before the Dragon Wars brought down the empire and all the drim enclaves within.

Skálda widened her eyes, remembering the faces in the tree-root runnel. "It was not a dream..." Like the giants she had seen beneath Dellfast, these wore simple clothes of roughspun flax or linen. Though they had human features, their massive, flat noses and extensive mouths did not quite resemble a man's.

"Earthkeepers," Livana murmured.

As the Thomdrim sang their soulful melody, the trees *moved.* Not the trees—their roots. They emerged from the soil and braided themselves together. The Thomdrim were pruning and mending the earth.

"That is how the Wereguild built their tree-root tunnels," Skálda said.

Liv whispered, "How they built tunnels large enough to collapse Tera Beren..."

Once they were through the stone gates, Rulf gestured at Liv. "Inga will assign your quarters."

A Werewoman was shouting above the crowds, grouping the new thralls and directing them to their longhouses. The districts out here were enclosed with palisades. In Solhall, one was either a thrall or a free Vigardian by the looks of it.

Skálda started to follow Liv, but Rulf held out his arm. "Whoa. You follow me."

Liv gave her an encouraging nod as she joined the chaos of the crowds, though her expression was steeped in worry.

"Come on, dragon girl!" Rulf balanced his axe's haft over his neck and shoulders, hanging his arms over it. "The Draugh wants to see you personally." He chuckled to himself. "Never a good thing when the Draugh calls..."

The pretty Vigardian steered her up the settlement's slopes and into the mountains. Bearded sheep grazed on the windswept hills. It was far less crowded out here, and airier; the cheesy stench of human sweat and unwashed wools no longer pummeled her nose. The skies faded into a dark blue.

As they ascended higher, a bitter musk drifted into the air. She knew that smell. It was one she had not encountered since waking in the Wereguild's hands. Cradling her wrist, she jogged ahead of Rulf, further up the path. He watched her with lazy interest.

Around the bend, inside a gated yard, were *dragons*. Feorya and Nornsir curled against each other over the dirt. The bonded picas wore collars around their necks that picketed them to the ground. Both were sleeping. Several paces from them was Incendra. She rested on all fours, one foreclaw crossed over the other, though her head was erect and she was wide awake. The Weremen had fastened two collars on her neck, accounting for her size, but she was behaving like the others.

Skálda traced her eyes over the square, her heart beating faster. Where was Bale?

Unlike in the slave districts at the bottom of the city, this one had only seven longhouses. Weremen guarded the palisade's entrance. Mat sat on a crate outside the furthest longhouse, his back bent in exhaustion and his hands clasped in thought. He had not noticed her yet. Behind him, through the cottage's open door, Anders lay on a pallet with his eyes closed.

Just as she opened her mouth to call out to Mat, the hills split from a dragon's enraged roar. It came from further up the mountain.

"Bale," she said under her breath.

The sheer noise made Mat lift his head. He saw her and stood up, but Skálda sprinted up the path before he could holler her name. Rulf jogged after her. Every footfall splintered the entire length of her right arm with pain, bringing tears to her eyes, but she refused to slow down.

Skálda followed the uproar of incensed shouts to an enclosed pasture near the mountain's summit. At this hour, Solhall's thralls were lighting firepits along the paths. What she saw made her forget her broken wrist entirely.

Eight Weremen compassed Bale with heavy lances. They were trying to force him into an iron cage at the back of the corral. Three collars clamped his neck, and three Weremen struggled to hold on to his chains, but that was not enough to keep him down. Bale tossed his head, yanking full grown Weremen off the ground. In mid-throw, he smashed them against the corral. Already, four horses lay dead at his feet. It looked like they had given up trying to haul him in mounted. Every time he pulled a chain free, he slammed his horns into the fence in a rage. Wood splintered everywhere. They were fools for trying to restrain a young, virile dragon.

"Bale!" she shouted.

He did not hear her. She tried calling to him through the mind-bond, but he was shut to her, shut to everyone. A Wereman reached for the chain that had flown loose from his collar, but Bale whirled around and snapped down on his hand. The Wereman screamed, pulling away. His right hand was gone, the stump's meat chunks streaming blood down his arm.

The Vigardian in charge shouted at Faelan, whom they had

brought into the pasture. "You, dragon man! Speak to him. Get him in the cage!" He gestured at Bale, his face a bright crimson.

"He is not my dragon—"

"Then I have no use for you!"

Uncrossing his arms, Faelan entered the corral. "Bale!"

The young dragon paid him no need. He was ramming his horns into the fence, at the cage, toward the Weremen, wreaking havoc on the pasture. Skálda could not sprint any faster.

"Bale! Heel!" Faelan tentatively reached for the chains that had fallen onto the grass and tugged. The dragon pulled away from the fence and roared at him. The Primarch fell onto his backside, letting out a short breath. Bale hovered his steaming maw a hand span from his face. Sweat trickled down the rider's neck. Those scorching red eyes saw no recognition in Faelan, or if they did, they cared nothing for him.

Bale roared again, suddenly. A Wereman had stuck his side with a lance. Blood trickled down his obsidian scales. His eyes flashed. He tried to snap at his assailant, but another pierced him on his other flank. Faelan shouted at them to stop, but they kept pricking Bale. He whirled away from them all, cornered, his ember-streaked wings unfurled. They were going to kill him.

Skálda screamed, "Bale!" She caught hold of the corral for balance, nearly falling.

He cocked his head, the rage fading from his eyes. "*Wolf?*"

Rulf caught up to her and pulled her back by the elbow. With her wrist injured, she did not have the strength to fight.

"Let me go to him!" she snarled at the Weremen. "He will obey me—"

Rulf cut her off with a nod. The Weremen resumed cornering him with their glaives and lances. Bale exhaled fury through his nostrils, lowering his horns for another charge.

"Bale, stop!"

Hearing her call again, he turned his head. The scalding brume over their mind-bond was lifting. Breathing hard, she said, *Please, you must stop fighting them.*

"They took away my wolf—"

I am here now. No harm is coming to me, see?

Every eye trained on her. The Weremen looked murderous. She and Bale were standing on ice. If she was not careful, they would follow through with killing him.

"Bale." Tears gathered in her eyes, but she blinked them away. "Settle. Go, into the cage."

He blinked in confusion. *"Into the cage?"*

Do it for me. I will come back for you.

He glanced at the iron bars, his tail flicking uneasily. Yet she felt his immeasurable trust across their mind-bond, and a warm rush like a nuzzle to her face. With that opening, the Weremen mounted him and fastened on more chains around his wings and short fetters on his legs. A fat one beat his head with a spear, forcing him lower for a muzzle.

"Stop striking him!" she shouted. "I'll have all your heads!"

They shoved him into the cage. He quieted, laying his head over his foreclaws. The Weremen finished chaining him down.

"Keep that dragon under guard," Rulf called. "If it escapes, kill it. Draugh's orders."

Skálda stormed into the corral to speak the healing spell over his open wounds, but Rulf wrested her back. Seeing the gesture, Bale growled in his throat.

"Not that way, dragon girl," Rulf said. "*This* way."

Faelan looked like he was struggling for words, but she passed him without a glance. As Rulf marched her back to the path, she wiped away her burning eyes on her sleeve.

At the top of the foothill, an unassuming wooden manse appeared. It had five gables, the fifth stacked on top of the others, all thatched. This had to be Kindruna, the Kindred Hall, the very grounds where Thorgest Vigarda had slept. Rulf took her around the residence and toward the mead hall in the back. Once they made it to the private yard, he shoved her to the ground. It just so happened that she landed on her broken wrist.

Tears of pain beaded in her eyes, but she stayed spitefully silent. Rulf joined his shield-brothers behind a shaded long table ahead of her. Asveig and Lord Jarmon were already there feasting. Rulf and Jarmon clapped arms, and the oldest Vigardian nodded as Rulf took his seat. "Made it in time," said Lord Jarmon, without looking up from the trenchers. "We saved the dregs for you."

The others chuckled and ate. Skálda picked herself up, though she did not dust herself off. Not long passed before the Draughammr himself appeared through the mead hall's doors. He was holding a freckled young girl by the hand. In his other arm was a toddler no older than one solstice. The sight of the children caught her off guard... Then again, why should it surprise her that the Draughammr was a father?

The girl took her place at Rulf's right. Frit was her name, from what Skálda remembered. The child flickered her eyes to her and quickly looked away.

Skálda waited. The Draughammr sat the toddler on his knee and fed him bread Asveig helped break over his plate. When they were not exchanging bawd humor between themselves, the Wereguild's three commanders chuckled, sneered, or frowned at her.

"Are you just going to jeer at me all day?" she said.

"No, dragon girl, did you not hear?" said Lord Jarmon. "We are going to kill you." The braid-bearded Vigardian slurped mead. "We are going to kill you slowly, for killing Fjella. Today. That is why you are here."

"What country maiden can wield an axe so well?" said Rulf, casually reaching for the bread.

"No longer," Asveig said.

They laughed. The Draughammr's face stayed a stone wall as

he fed his wide-eyed son. Few things in this world could unsettle Skálda, but his presence did. Or perhaps it was the helmet hanging over the wall behind him, fixed with the forehorns of a Great Dragon. She imagined him hanging Bale's horns, and thrust the thought back out.

"What is your name?" said the Draughammr.

She did not answer. Lord Jarmon pushed his chair back and freed the axe at his round belly.

"Skálda," she said.

"What sort of name is 'Skálda'?" Jarmon spat her name like it was filth.

"What have you done with my friend?" she said. "The elf."

The Draughammr lifted Aracir from under the table and balanced it by his plate. He kept his eyes on the calligraphy and read aloud the Elvynnöthe, the High Speech, perfectly. As he recited, Skálda's chest clenched, and she recalled what Eyrek had translated to her in the Svenning back in the Skonkauld, when he first gifted her the axe:

"Though distance leaves your bickering forgone,
We shall meet as one blood anon,
To resume your squabbling up on dragonback,
O loving sister, in a most beauteous dawn."

"You are Skálda Branwright." The Draughammr turned the haft so the elvish lines faced her. "You are Eyrekvald Ivarion's sister."

His shield-brothers went agog. Mead spilled over Jarmon's braided beard. Skálda darkened her gaze.

"You think I do not study my foes?" The Draughammr passed Asveig the axe and shelled an almond for the boy. "The Ivarion is my archenemy. I have united many lands in Old Svenn, thirteen Vigardian fiefs in all, to take his head." He slipped an almond between his own lips, chewing, studying her. "That is why the Wereguild has returned."

She recalled the words King Leondran, Aesir, and Liv had spoken separately about Tera Beren, and she pieced everything together. Very quietly, she said, "You destroyed his capital..."

"He is a king no more, albeit in the North, the Vigardians call him the Skitr King."

His brothers laughed with him. Jarmon stood up. "Draugh! His sister! All the more reason to cut her to pieces and send her piecemeal to her lord brother. Why not now?"

"Very well."

Lord Jarmon came around the table with his axe. Rulf swallowed down his last bite, and joined him, reaching for the bow at his back. The girl glanced at Asveig, wide-eyed. With a short sigh, the duck beard warrior stood too, and drew his sword. The three Wereguild commanders closed her into a half-circle of wolves. Skálda took a step back.

"Are you afraid?" said Soren.

The toddler was gnawing on the almond, paying the rest of them no attention. Rulf strung his bow, aiming for her. The other two men were within an arm's reach away now. Lord Jarmon raised his axe for a killing blow, his knee bent for the strike.

"Afraid?" Skálda laughed through her feverishness. "After I break the Order, I will destroy the Wereguild."

"Hold," the Draughammr said.

Lord Jarmon exhaled in annoyance, lowering his axe. These men were chained hounds pulling at the very end of their chokepoint.

Soren said, "You would war against your Order, dragon girl?"

"Not my Order. I am *kvael-akar*."

He raised his dark brows in surprise. The men glanced at him quizzically.

"They are murderers. You saw what Lord Rystendal did to

Dellfast. It was the same with the Skonkauld. My home. I will break them for it."

Jarmon laughed. "With what, your hand?"

"With my dragon." She smiled at the Were King, baring her teeth. "I see you can read Elvynnöthe. So, I trust you know what my dragon is. You would be wise not to kill him. He obeys my command only."

"The Bael are a myth," he said.

She nodded at the Sun he wore over his chest. "Is your Sun God a myth?"

He tucked the metal under his tunic. The Weremen, not following, glanced between each other.

Emboldened, Skálda said, "If any harm should come to my friends..."

Lord Jarmon spat at her feet. "You are not in a position to threaten the Draughammr, dragon wench!" He resumed advancing to her with his axe, but Soren called him back. The Vigardian looked like he might tear out his beard.

The Draughammr appeared thoughtful, ever brooding beneath the shadows. Asveig returned to his seat and whispered in the king's ear. She just managed to catch his words.

"Skáld, Draugh... She is named after the wolves." The older warrior nodded to a set of round shields lining the yard. All four were imprinted with the white skáldhead of the Weres. "It may be an omen."

"Eyrekvald's sister," Soren called to her, "you claim you will destroy Dragonsteel? Do you know that neither the guild, nor any power on the continent, has ever been able to do so?"

"I will kill the Lord Prince."

His commanders roared with laughter. Rulf even cried tears. Skálda stayed expressionless.

The Were King sneered at her. "You're a fool, girl!"

He nodded at Lord Jarmon to press on. The stout Vigardian seized her by the arm.

"I may die today," she said, "but the *Kærdighaeder* is coming for you, Draughammr."

Soren stopped eating. His second quieted. Noticing her father's frozen silence, the girl whispered over the table to Asveig, "What's a *Kærdighaeder*?" But the white-bearded Vigardian shushed her.

Skálda was drifting to the limits of her consciousness. Her face flushed with fever heat and she was keeling over from exhaustion. Yet her gaze on the Draughammr never wavered.

Lord Jarmon finally moved first, shoving her along. In her ear, he hissed, "Have you ever seen a tree stump, Skitr's sister?"

He marched her away from the mead hall toward the manse. Skálda knew she was going to be slaughtered like a swine. Yet she was calm as the glaciers. Soren's shadowed gaze stayed on her.

Not on her. Her pale eyes.

2

THE WERE KING

On the northerly edge of Aranor Elondris, the Divine Republic, one might say the Second Breaking arose from a looming continental conquest devised from elvish shadows; and a blood oath uttered from what would be history's first Baelrider.

In the sweltering darkness of a tree-root tunnel, Skálda Branwright's lips moved faintly with a promise—her promise to break the Dragonsteel Order.

Some fifty feet above, the narrow vista opened into Dellfast City's flaming sky. She blinked, vaguely remembering a fall. A strange, unfamiliar scent soaked the mesh that had caught her. She tried to think, but her mind was a haze. The net was drugged.

Something shuffled in the darkness. The sound of many bodies. Wereguild. They were coming to kill her. Yet she was far too befogged to reach for her belt or even panic.

A circle of faces gazed down upon her. In place of a murderous band of Vigardians were man-like shapes, perhaps twice her height. The closest one had tapered ears, a flat nose, and big hands clasping a wooden mallet. A giant. Surely, she was dreaming. The elderly creature had a kind face, but it looked confused, even afraid of her.

"Bale," Skálda murmured. "Bale..."

She closed her eyes again and drifted away.

THE NEXT TIME Skálda was awake, the shadows of a sheepskin tent enveloped her. Her skáldwolf fur coat no longer warmed her shoulders, but someone had put her in a thin, tatty robe of wool. She pulled her hands in to blow warmth into them, only to find them bound. Neither was Aracir's weight hanging from her waist.

Skálda snapped upright. Her head still ached, but she was suddenly awake. Man-shaped shadows from outside drifted over the tent walls. The freezing air stank of woodsmoke, which meant she was in a campsite. What happened? Where was she?

But she remembered the fires of Dellfast and the giants standing over her in the tree-root tunnel. How much of it had been a dream? She tested the mind-bond, but felt nothing. Was Bale dead?

Hysteria clawed up her throat, but she reminded herself he could not be, or surely, she would feel it.

Evening her breathing, Skálda listened to the voices. Men were barking in the Svenning. Quiet sobs hung like frost in the air. Many people were outside. Many prisoners.

A darker shadow crossed over her tent, and a silhouette burst through the flaps. The day's brooding tones obscured his face.

"Good, you're awake, dragon girl." The Wereman gripped her by the neck and jerked her outside.

Skálda shielded her eyes with her bound hands. Mud soaked through the leather of her boots. The Wereman was dragging her onto a sand shore. The waters beyond were dark and still. Though they did not smell of brine the way the Naüthe did, they stretched as far as she could see through the creeping mists.

She glanced behind her. More tents like hers scattered across the shore. Weremen were putting out the firepits, dragging bound commons toward longboats lined up along the waters. The Álfvindor Alps loomed over them. It was as she feared. They were beyond Republic borders and inside the Deep North.

Her captor shoved her toward the nearest longboat. Skálda studied him with her dark gaze. He was an older man who wore his straight brown hair to his shoulders and his beard braided in two. Creases pinched above his hammer-sized nose. It was all she saw before he shoved her at the bulwark. She stumbled in the calf-high frigid waters, her right knee slamming against the hull. Her gaze darkening even more, she climbed inside, unwieldy with her hands bound.

A dozen more women were already sitting on the benches. Some were unbound and appeared familiar with the proceedings here. But most were roped like Skálda. Several sobbed quietly under their breaths. These had to be the Dellfast survivors who fell through the tree-root tunnels before Rystendal had blown Dellfast to Helgaard. Bound or unbound, one thing was clear. They were now thralls of the Wereguild.

Skálda took her place in the last empty seat near the stern. A ragged young woman, her new rowing mate, glanced at her like a frightened mouse. Behind them, a Wereman cradled an axe to his chest. Bloodthirst was written over his face.

"Row!"

She took it this was the endearing boat captain. Skálda gripped onto her oar. Together with the ragged woman, they propelled their longboat into the watery unknown.

Skálda saw no land through the mists and could not say for how long they would be rowing. She kept testing the mind-bond, calling out to Bale. When he did not answer, she retreated even deeper into her dark mood.

The surrounding women rowed in silence. Anyone who so much as sniffled received a scourging holler from the boat captain.

One common whispered, "I—I must have my coat back..." And he yelled, "I'll throw you over the side, and you'll get your bloody coat!"

Skálda's own hands were turning white as ice. But she kept quiet and studied their surroundings. Dozens of longboats sloshed through water, perhaps a hundred, all moving with a single purpose into the dark, icy mists of morning.

"Where are we going?" she murmured to her rowing mate.

The girl would not look at her. Her stringy hair covered her face. "Solhall."

"Solhall?"

"The Draughammr is King of Vingulmark. Solhall is his capital."

Skálda narrowed her eyes. Solhall was a Svennish myth... like the Vigardians were supposed to be. This was the very settlement where Thorgest Vigarda, the demi-wolf god and forefather of all Vigardians, had built and reigned from eight hundred solstices ago. Vingulmark had to be a Vigardian fief, risen from the ashes of the Old Svenn Empire. Had Thorgest's descendants been amassing beyond the Republic all this time?

"They are transporting prisoners from the battle," the girl whispered. "New thralls to serve in the fields."

She would be no thrall to these Were filth, but she would find Bale. She would leave the Deep North... and find the Lord Prince.

That was when she caught the girl's face at an angle, just as she was swiveling away.

"I know you," Skálda said. "I saw you in the Prannon. You were bound. You are a—"

"Shh," the young woman pressed. In an even smaller whisper, she said, "I am Livana Tamarath. I recall seeing you, too."

It was just as Skálda had thought. She was not only a rider, but this was the missing Dellfast rider Faelan had alluded to several times. Lord Alarek's last surviving child.

"Skálda," she said.

"Well met, Skálda." Liv inclined her head. "It does not do to speak of riders and dragons here. The fate of neither bode well—"

Someone kicked the oar out of Skálda's grip. The boat captain's stinking breath steamed over her cheek. "Not a smile on you, girl, eh?" he grinned. He wrenched her upright by her hair. "No more scheming, you she-demons. Pick up your oar and keep rowing!"

Skálda marked him for death and crawled onto her knees to retrieve it. The captain raised his head and yelled, "Row with more life! All of ya!"

She kept her shoulders bent and turned away from the despicable stink. Through the lank, pale curtain of her hair, a longship thirty paces away caught her eye. This one was far larger than the others, and had eighty oarsmen, at least. The rear half was covered with blue and gilt-threaded awnings. That had to be the royal ship.

She squinted to get a better look at the men sitting behind the wicker walls enclosing the stern. Among them was a fettered man wearing heavy chains on his wrists. Aesir. She was sure of it. Seeing him here, alive, gave her more hope. But there were no signs of her Skoll friends or Bale.

"Where is my dragon?" she murmured.

Liv turned to stare at her. When no one answered, Skálda repeated herself. The captain overheard and gave a raucous laugh.

Skálda said even more quietly, "Where is my axe?"

Several commons gaped at her. Liv's eyes were riven with fear. The captain bellowed a long string of laughter and wrenched Skálda up by the overtunic like she weighed nothing.

"I'll give ya an axe, mouthy wench!"

He swung at her. The women screamed, but Skálda lifted her wrists at the last beat. The blade's momentum cut her bonds loose. She darted under him to the bow, drawing the captain's snarl.

"I'll kill you," he swore, every word puffing a white cloud into the cold air. The women screamed and collided into each other to get out of the way. Skálda kept her dark-eyed stare on the fat Wereman, challenging him with her silence.

He lumbered between the benches and swung again. She leapt aside, fast as a skáldwolf, and swept his legs out from under him. On his way down, she wrenched the axe from him and struck down on his back. The women's screams turned into shrieks.

The captain, on his knees, gazed up at her dumbly. Skálda kneed him in the chest. He plummeted over the side, splashing into the water.

The boat slid to a halt. No one was rowing now. A common whispered, "What have you done?"

Clenching the bloodied axe, Skálda stepped onto a bench to elevate herself.

"Draughammr!" she bellowed at the royal ship. "Where is my dragon?"

Behind the wicker screen, Aesir raised his head. Several of the nearest longboats slid to a stop. Weremen and thralls alike were ogling her in disbelief.

It took several beats before someone marched out from beneath the awning shade. Distance made it difficult for her to see his features, but she recognized him well enough. This was the man with the twixt braided beard who had thrown her out of her tent this morning. He observed her, standing knees bent with a bloodied blade, the captain no longer in sight. The silence that followed made the women on her boat twitch. And then, the Draughammr belted wicked laughter.

"*Dead!*"

That single word penetrated the misty silence, echoing across all the waters.

"Your beast is dead, dragon girl!'

The Vigardians on his ship joined in his laughter.

"If you don't want to die," he said, "I suggest you continue rowing." The Wereman started for his shaded seat again. The infernos of Dellfast were burning slow in a place tucked deep in Skálda's heart.

"Draughammr! You are a coward, the way you fight and kill. Come face me!"

"Hah!" The Vigardian called back, "I will kill you too, dragon girl!"

She stood still as a wraith. Liv hissed at her, "What are you doing?"

"*Come face me*!"

Skálda howled and howled. The Draughammr shot her a look of disgust and glanced back into the shadows beneath the awnings. The boat captains drew their axes, a pack of wolves waiting for the signal to shred her.

The Draughammr and his crew ignored her. Her howls disrupted the channel's eerie quiet. A full minute passed before an irritated shout silenced hers.

"Stop rowing!"

A Wereman she had never seen before emerged from the blue coverings. "This..." He clenched the braid-bearded Vigardian's shoulder. "Is Lord Jarmon." He beat his hand against his own mailed chest. "I am the Draughammr."

Skálda stared at him. Distance made the finer features of his face impossible to see. He bellowed at his men, "Row us closer! Bring me her axe." The Wereman vanished into the coverings again. The Vigardians at the forecastle laughed at her, though none drew their weapons. They all seemed privy to whatever bloody fate awaited her.

As the royal ship lurked closer, not once did Skálda glance away. And the moment came when the looming ship slid in parallel to her dinghy, its deck one hop away. The husky Vigardians across from her grinned. Someone stepped out, blocking her view of them.

The Draughammr held Aracir. He was brushing the haft's polished whitewood, his crusted nails lingering over the lines in

Elvynnöthe. The elvish marks seemed to draw his curiosity. Here was a Svennish weapon wearing rare Anárion steel that only the High Elves carried. His thick lashes obscured what she could see of his eyes; they stayed fixed on the Elvynnöthe. He could not read the calligraphy, that she was certain. No country Svennish would know how to read the High Speech.

He looked up at her. "What is your name?"

She returned his question with her unmoving stare. Behind him, Lord Jarmon tapped the flat of his axe against his palm.

The Draughammr tossed her Aracir. Skálda caught it with her free hand and hurled aside the inferior axe.

Shaking off his heavy hauberk, he leapt into her boat unarmored. The women at his feet shrieked. Liv crashed onto her hands in her attempt to flee him. Two older commons even tossed themselves overboard. The Draughammr drew the axe at his belt.

Skálda stood at the bow; he loomed at the stern. The fog parted between them, revealing more of his features. He was a hulk of muscle and scarred flesh, smelling powerfully of male sweat. This man could not be older than Eyrek's solstices. His black hair was pulled back in a short bun at the crown of his head, the sides braided tight to his skull. This was no uncultured Wereman. The way he stood, his head erect, his rippling thighs at shoulder width, affirmed he was no less than royalty.

The Draughammr extended his arms to full span, as if saying, Well?

Skálda could not stop staring. He had a rough-hewn face with sharp, wide cheekbones. She could not tell if he was upset with her, or nonchalant, or what, for his countenance was like the Álfvindor mountains, an alpine wall. But what struck her most were his brooding eyes. They were too familiar. King Leondran's were olive; his were a deep, glacial blue. Yet they beheld the same regal power that could make a man sober and kneel. The Draughammr appeared a more handsome facsimile to the king.

Skálda narrowed her eyes. "You... you are—"

She never finished. Since she did not attack, he obliged to do so first. He swung his axe at her neck. Skálda lurched back, returning to the present. If she could not read him before, she could now. He was exasperated with her.

Without waiting for a riposte, he thrust again, once at her right, once at her left. They were savage strikes meant to split open the flesh between her ribs. Skálda backed another two steps, raising her axe for an uppercut. The Draughammr was in such a dark mood, he gave no time for even that.

Before she could land her attack, he pivoted around and cracked his haft over her back. She crashed onto her hands. Pain sparked over her vision. Aracir sailed toward the stern. Skálda crawled across deck for it. He crouched down, his warm breath wetting her neck for a beat, just before he seized her by her blade wrist and snapped it.

Skálda screamed.

The surrounding commons sobbed. He fetched her blade from the deck, facing her, crossing both axes over his chest. Her agony was so great, she could hardly see through her tears. Fjella Wulfgar could not even compare with him. The Were King fought like a god.

Her last thought, as both hafts swung toward her head, was that, some twenty solstices ago, the Wereguild must have never murdered Fjorland's crown prince.

3
ONE GREATER THAN YOU IS COMING

One cycle earlier

Sorenthor Draughammr, Axe of Vingulmark, and King of the Weres, marched up the temple steps in a fury.

Chilling winds gusted against the furs on his shoulders. The conifers of the Völundr Reach bowed against the squall rolling over the vale. He glanced at the northern horizon with a sense of foreboding. The world was changing. These ancient lands that had belonged to Vigardians for eight hundred solstices would cease to be free. It would fall under his leadership. The intolerable thought clenched his chest.

He smelled the resinous scent of birchbark incense before he spotted the temple doors. These always stayed open to the blood of Old Svenn. He stormed through.

There she was, sitting on the wooden boards with her back turned to the entrance. All he saw of the shieldmaiden was her tight braids holding her pale hair in a ball to her skull. Flanking her right was the young girl, and in the shieldmaiden's arms the toddler. Seeing them all under this roof incensed him even more.

"Fjella," he called, "how do you step inside Vevolsk?"

She did not turn.

"How do you bring our children here?"

When Fjella would not give him an answer, heat streaked down his neck.

"All of you, leave at once! Frit!"

Flinching, the girl climbed to her feet and shuffled away from the wood pillars at the altar. These symbolized the pagan gods of Old Svenn. The toddler squirmed out of his mother's arms and wobbled toward the entrance. The boy was always happy to see Soren, even when he was in a fury. On his way, the child tripped over his own feet. With a short sigh, Soren scooped up the sniffling toddler and tucked him into his great mantle of wolf furs. With his free hand, he warmed the girl's hand with his.

"Fjella!" he called.

It was not the Were Queen who answered, but the decrepit shape facing her.

"At last, the one whom we have been waiting for is here. Come, join us, Astorheim."

He could not say if it was that hoarse voice, or the sound of his forsaken name in the Svenning, that grated his bones.

Before him was a hjarta. Svennish lore was abundant with them, seers that could read the energies of the northern wilds. Some said they healed and performed small miracles; others swore they cast curses upon those that displeased them.

This hjarta had tangled locks that twisted to the ground. The staff she held onto was topped with animal horns, fur, and shells. He saw nothing behind her tattered hood, but perhaps that was best. These witches were said to have stitched faces with eyes for mouths.

Something in that stare held power over him. He set the toddler down. "Asveig is waiting by the horses," he said to the girl. "Go to him. I will come soon."

Soren kissed their heads. The girl gave his hand an extra squeeze before she skipped out with her brother.

Standing in the doorway, backdropped in the cold white daylight, Soren felt it again. The portent. The sense of great change coming, a continental breaking he was powerless to stop. He was aware of the Sun of Vaeritas hanging openly over his chest, and his heart warred all at once to depart and stay.

In the end, he edged into the temple and lowered himself by Fjella. She took his hand. He turned his gaze back to the shadows behind the hood.

"You wanted to know what future awaits the Deep North," she rasped. "You want to know if you will claim the head of Eyrekvald Ivarion... or if he will claim yours."

Soren closed a fist around his Sun. "I asked to know nothing. God's will be done, not the pagan prophecies of witches."

The hjarta laughed. The noise raked his neck. "Yet here you are, Astorheim. Very well. Then I will not tell you."

Fjella tugged at his sleeve fiercely. The hjarta took a wicker basket of river stones, and upturned it. The clatter was an explosion in the stillness. One by one, she stacked them. Natural law said it should be impossible to pile uneven surfaces like this, but somehow, she did. This was one more thing about the hjartas. The arcane art of stone-stacking was called the Vidarskog. Few men could pull it off, but every hjarta was a master at it.

Nine stones stood like a tower in the air. The hjarta rasped, "Look at them, Astorheim. What do you see?"

He sighed sharply and started to stand, but Fjella caught his hand. "Please," she whispered. "Do this for me. For our children. We cannot afford to lose you, too."

Soren let go of his Sun, and fixed his gaze on the stones. The women quieted as he focused. The firepits in the temple flickered once, then synchronized together.

"What do you see?" the hjarta urged.

"A blade."

Outside, a flock of ravens crawed. A passing cloud darkened the skies above the temple.

"An axe... It has many faces... The Many-Faced Blade, that is its name. And I see..."

A sudden gust blew out all the firepits. It was colder than anything he had felt all solstice. It wrenched him out of his daze, and he found himself shuddering like a babe.

"Soren?" said Fjella.

Though the hjarta never spoke, he heard her bone-dry voice in his mind.

"One greater than you is coming."

The vision she sent turned his blood to ice. "We should have never come here." He stormed out, leaving no chance for an argument.

Once he was back outside, he stopped on the edge of the temple's landing, breathing warmth into his hands. Boots shuffled behind him.

"Vevolsk?" he said, fighting the tremor in his voice. "How could you have come here, Fjel?"

"What did she tell you?" Fjella stopped at his side.

"You told me you would take the Sun, if I claimed you."

"I did take it."

"You say you are Vaeritian, yet you go to Vevolsk Temple to read the tarot stones on our future? How your family would anguish—"

"My family is dead."

Even now, twelve solstices of being bonded with her, her eyes were no less like calving ice.

"The Skitr King murdered them," she said.

"He killed your father. The others are still alive. I vowed to bring them back, even if I must dig all the way to Exar'forda—"

"They are dead, Soren."

A heavier shadow fell over them. Stiffening, he glanced up at the sky, half expecting the Skitr's winged demon. The beginnings of a blizzard passed overhead.

"He is a madman," said Fjella. "He seeks his vengeance and he will have it. You have driven him to insanity."

"Good. Then he knows how I feel." Before Soren could suggest they return home, she took hold of his arm.

"We have done things your way for this long," she whispered, "and where has it gotten us? The dragon men continue to Build, and our people continue to die. Your father has turned his back on us. We face a growing sea of enemies beyond our North. But if a hjarta can warn us of what is to come, at least we can prepare."

Soren exhaled quietly.

"What did she tell you?" Fjella said. He sensed by her tone she would not ask again.

He closed his eyes. The raging winds carried the giggles of his children in the courtyard as Asveig swung them in his arms. Great change was coming. He pulled Fjella closer to him and kneaded her hand. She laid her head against his mantle furs.

"I saw eyes reflected on that blade," he said. "Eyes like pale fire, glowing in the dark. Watching me. These did not belong to any man or elf..."

"Soren?"

"Something is coming for the Wereguild." He opened his eyes, his gaze drifting to his laughing children. The emotion drained from his face. "A *Kærdighaeder*."

4
SILENCE

LEONDRAN ASTORAINE LAY on his back, alone in the darkness. He was vaguely aware of a searing pain in his left calf. A bone had fractured. He shifted his head, but even that took immense effort.

A realm above, the dragon passed in and out of his narrow view of the sky, spewing more flames upon Dellfast City. Leon tried to sit up, but agony speared through his calf and up to his head. He would never make it home.

The grinding steel of hauberks jangled down the tunnel. It was the sound of many bodies in the dark. A stench of body odors and stained furs closed his windpipe. The Wereguild was coming for him.

Leon forced his blurry eyes open. Cold faces gazed down at him. The Vigardians wielded glaives, bearded axes, two-handed halberds; great and terrifying butcher blades that Vaeritas had never meant for man to bear against man.

His lips moved faintly. The bloodthirsty gazes pulled away in surprise. Coarse voices murmured in the Svenning.

"The king..."

"The king, the king..."

"The king is here..."

They had come to kill him.

Someone said, "Leave him."

The menacing circle of Wereguild, afore so ready to slaughter, retreated into the darkness. Delirious, Leon's lips moved with the same word, again and again.

"Soren..."

He was uncertain how long he lay there, how many times he drifted in and out beneath the cadence of beating wings. But when Leon next opened his eyes, he spotted the beast again, soaring through its own flames. The magical ward concealing it cracked. For only a beat, the shimmers parted.

Leon squinted up at the rider, seeing his face. The king's head lulled to the side. He passed out again.

GWYNEVERE AELFWYN, Queen of Fjorland, paced Svennandia's parapet walls in ceaseless circles. It had been a fortnight since news of Dellfast's burning had reached the Council Seat. After she had wept her eyes dry, she persuaded herself, again and again, that Soren would never slay his own father. Any day now, Leon would return. She refused to leave the city gates until he did.

The king had left most of the House Guard in the capital to protect her and Cal, and to barricade anymore visiting riders. Since that time, Brond Maelor, the Lord Captain, never left her side. He was with her on the heights, gazing out into the dells beyond Svennandia with longsuffering. But she felt his members' pity. They all believed Leon dead. The entire Republic did. The Elenntarien, the Republic's Ruling Council, had fallen to chaos.

"My lady..."

She turned at Brond's murmur. A small train on horseback streamed over the thoroughfare. When they reached the bridge over Thercia, the river enclosing the capital, a deep male voice shouted at the traffic to make way. Hooves pounded over wood. The bridge guards took up the shouts and commanded the commons to move to the bulwarks.

Four ashen horsemen pulled up outside the gate. Gwynne pressed her hands to her mouth in disbelief. Every guard with her flocked the edge of the parapet. No one could muster the words to speak.

Halvar Gorm had the king on the saddle. Jory Skard and two more house guards, Orrin and Gendel, were with them. Their faces were ashen. So few of the original retinue had returned.

"Leon!" she screamed.

He was slumped, his eyes closed. Looking up at the wide-eyed crowd above, Halvar shouted, "Your Majesty! Lord Captain. His leg is broken. We need a carriage and a physicker at once."

The moment Gwynne was on ground level again, she sprinted to her husband, the trains of her dress sailing behind her. Halvar stayed patiently in the saddle as she took the king's hand. Leon did not wake. She pressed that hand to her forehead, collapsing into sobs.

The rumors of the king's return spread through Svennandia faster than dragonfire. Once they were in the castle's inner bailey, Prince Calabran emerged from the doors with his attendants, his expression fracturing. A swarm of house guards rushed to barricade the king and queen from unwelcome questions.

Gwynne accompanied the bier that carried Leon up the steps. As she passed Cal, she smiled at her adolescent son through her tears. Emotion warred in his eyes. He did not smile back.

It took two full days for the king to part his eyelids. Gwynne had stayed by his bed in all that time, but the moment he woke, she rushed off her chair to clutch his arms. Vaeritas help her, the tears would not stop streaming.

"Leon," she whispered. "Leon, you are back. You are alive..."

He did not answer.

For an entire fortnight, he spoke to no one, but he remained in his bedchambers. If his splinted leg pained him, it did not show on his haggard face. Always, he stared out the window. He would answer no questions, and seemed to hear no one that spoke to him. The behavior disturbed Gwynne. Within a few days, she wondered if he had truly made it out of Dellfast alive... and if Leondran Astoraine would ever return to the Republic.

Jory kept watch with her by the king's bed. "The Wereguild built the same tunnels as in Tera Beren," the chief advisor whispered. "They attacked during the regionals and withdrew by the late afternoon. We were preparing for home when they collapsed the ground beneath us. The next time I woke, the air above us smelled of fumes. Halvar found me first. It took some time wading through the dark before we found the king. I found no trace of anyone else who had fallen..."

During that fortnight, every Eldari of the Old Faction who heard the news hurried to Svennandia. Gwynne hoped a visit from their Svennish allies, Konrad of Lysmark and Hrafholt of Belfaine, might encourage him to speak. But they came out of his chambers with the same head shakes as everyone else.

Gwynne began to despair. For a cycle, she had held back from speaking to Cal about a coronation. He had not visited his father once, and neither would he attend breakfast with her. How their dining table had grown even emptier! Her heart would break for the day when she must exhort him to forget Dragonsteel and take his father's throne.

Amidst the castle-wide chaos, a last visitor came to see them. Seeing him arrive in the bailey with his Lord Warden and a score of white-uniformed Republic guards, Gwynne almost cried in relief.

"Your Eminence!" She curtsied as the High Eldari strode up to the entrance. Merely his presence weighed an iron authority in the courtyard, everything that Svennandia Castle needed right now.

"Forgive my delay," said Staunnton Berethor. His natural pitch was always a stark shout, but they could expect no less from a former military leader. "Elenntar is in chaos, as you can imagine. Your husband...?"

"Awake, but still in a strange sleep." She stepped aside from the doors, fervent for the Republic's ruler to come through. He was her last hope. "Leon will speak to no one, but perhaps it may be different with you."

"The reports say he broke his leg?"

"That will mend, but I fear the Wereguild might have injured his head. If he won't speak, you can bring an elf from Rhaennöria, can't you? Would the elves not lend a healing spell if you asked?"

Elder Staunnton spoke gravely. "Let me see what I can do first, Gwynevere."

On their way to Leon's chambers, her shoes pattered in a fevered rush against the High Eldari's measured stride. Once they were outside the doors, she knocked once, then stepped through.

"Leon," she called. "His Lord Eminence is here to visit you."

The king kept his back turned and his face to the window. Her eyes swelled again with tears, but she held them back.

"Please," she whispered. "Won't you speak to even him?"

Leon did not answer. Gwynne pulled herself back outside and hugged herself tightly. Elder Staunnton placed a comforting hand on her shoulder and started to step through, but a voice from inside interrupted the stillness.

"Gwynne."

It was hoarse. The sound of it snapped them all to attention. Brond Maelor and the guards of the House near stampeded to the doors.

"Gwynne."

There, it came again, from the king.

She let out a hysterical breath. "Leon! Leon, I am here—"

"Elder!" the High Eldari called, coming inside. "We were all of us prodigiously worried. I have come to—"

"Gwynne. I will speak to Gwynne alone."

They exchanged looks. The High Eldari appeared surprised Leon would not take an audience with him first, but he nodded. As Gwynne stepped through, Brond's guards pulled the doors shut behind her.

Wiping her face, she sat on the bedside. "Leon?"

His hollow eyes stayed fixed on the window. She took his cold wrist and whispered, "Leon, what is it? Please, I am here."

"Soren never massacred Dellfast." He turned to her, his voice deadened.

"Eyrekvald Ivarion did... He burned them all."

5
THE ONE-DAY CAMPAIGN

Lord Jarmon took Skálda to the tree stump behind the Draughammr's mead hall. It had a bloodied hatchet stuck in the wood. Seeing her pale face, he laughed wickedly... and passed it. The wretched Vigardian steered her to the manse and into a spartan bedchamber. "Lie down." He nodded at someone's mattress propped against the wall.

"Sorry, but I don't fancy you at all," she said.

He smiled savagely. "You are lucky the Draugh only broke your wrist." Tucking his axe back to his belt, he stormed out the door. Someone else slipped past him, a woman in a simple chemise. For once, it was not a Vigardian with heavy, stinking mail. She held a wicker basket with folded cheese cloths and poultices.

"If my husband intended to lie with you, *I* would have killed him."

Her eyes glinted with a smile. The woman repeated Lord Jarmon's command, and this time Skálda obeyed. The moment her head hit the wool coverlet, her exhaustion struck her in a wave.

"Bite down on this." The woman handed her a rolled strip of leather.

Skálda eyed her as she pulled up a stool and laid out the basket of goods over the bed. The inevitable was coming, but it was better than death at Jarmon's tree stump. Fitting the leather between her teeth, she braced herself.

The woman took her swollen wrist, and without so much as a merciful pause, snapped the bones back into place. Skálda screamed through the leather, stinging tears rushing down her cheeks.

"You did well." The woman tilted her head and replaced the leather with willow bark to chew on. "This is the part where you close your eyes. You are safe."

The last word made Skálda's lip curl, but she was in too much pain to snark. Now that her head rested on a curled blanket, it struck her how long of a journey it had been since leaving the Skonkauld. She had not slept in a pallet for months, and not properly since Dellfast's slaughter.

While the woman bandaged and splinted her wrist, humming a melancholy Vigardian tune, Skálda fought to keep her drooping lids open. She passed in and out, stubbornly fighting sleep. The last place she was safe in was the Draughammr's residence. In that in between state, she thought she saw him leaning in the doorway, observing her, barely perceptible in the shadows. Perhaps she was dreaming it.

Defeated by exhaustion, Skálda lulled off into a deep slumber.

She did not know how long she slept, but the next time she woke, the skylight colors had changed, and someone was sitting by her mattress.

"Eyrek," she murmured, drifting out of her troubled dreams.

Her vision refocused. A man with a gaze sharper than hers stared down at her. He had a white duck beard, and gray-bronze hair braided at the crown of his head; the rest flowed loose down his strapping shoulders.

"I am no King Skitr," Asveig said scornfully. He was in his

linen tunics, though his sword stayed belted at his waist. It was disorienting not to see him in his heavy mail. Skálda placed her good arm over her eyes, pointedly shutting out the Vigardian. Her wrist still burned like Hel.

"*Eyrek,*" he sang. "You would never fight the Order."

"Give me my dragon, and I will show you."

"Get up, thrall."

"My name is Skálda."

"No, thrall. Here in Solhall, your name is No One. You are a worthless slave. Get up!"

The steel in his voice prompted her to shuffle out of her warm blankets and sit upright. Blood rushed to her head, dizzying her, but she managed to shoot him a dark look.

"You will cook, clean, and weave for the Draugh's household," he said. "You will foremost care for his children. You will protect them and see that they are fed every morrow and evenfall, beginning today."

"I am a hunter. I can hunt."

"You are a thrall."

The way he said it stung.

"I do not know what you were expecting from the Wereguild," he said, "but your life is over. You have no more future." He made to leave, but as if on second thought, he paused at the door.

"The Draugh told me to tell you that if any harm comes to his children, from you or anyone, he will behead your dragon. You will know pain that will make Helgaard seem like a mercy."

He left.

Skálda muttered, "Nice to meet you, too..."

She swung herself off the bed, only to find that sometime in the night, someone had replaced her hunting leathers and linen pants with a roughspun chemise. Her blood boiled. She could be building longhouses, or shepherding, or bloody tilling the fields!

But Soren was punishing her for what she had done. She would kill him for putting her in a dress.

In a small act of defiance, she did not immediately seek the Draugh's children, but left the manse to look for Bale. Several Weremen guarded the pasture he was caged in. She considered calling out to him through the mind-bond, but saw that he was sleeping. He twitched often; it was a troubled slumber.

She decided to let him rest, but before she left, she could not help but murmur the *Lhaer'thri* over him.

The elvish spell revealed the glowing threads of his dragon-script, his soul, oscillating like waves over his body. His were as crimson as the cinderlights streaking his wings. A number impressed himself on her mind. 49.

Her shoulders slumped in disappointment. 49 chapters. It felt like her dragon was advancing so slowly, despite all the danger they had put themselves through. Even after half a solstice, she was not even at Ealdorman rank yet.

She trudged down the slopes in her chemise, her mood fouling. She hated every moment the linen dress chafed against her ankles. Part of her considered tearing it off and running the streets naked to spite the Wereguild. Then again, perhaps that would not spite them at all.

Skálda found her friends in the slave hall in the set of long-houses where she last saw Mat. It was smoky under the roof, dark except for the various pits that burned. Dellfasters she did not recognize murmured quietly around the fires. She called, "Mat!"

Her friend was chattering away with three Dellfast men, but hearing her, he sprang to his feet with his arms spread wide. "Skálda-wolf, come here!"

She ignored the command, but he squeezed her around the middle, anyway. "What a journey, eh?" He sniffed. "Sure beats waiting for Old Rysten to feed us to his dragon."

"Why do you sound happy?"

"I had time to think about everything after the Skonkauld..." He rubbed his neck. "I don't know that I ever wanted to Build."

She narrowed his eyes at him. He dropped his gaze to the rush-strewn floor.

"Anders gave me a better life, a way to support Mum and the family... but I'm no Ivarion. I have Fey with me again. Maybe I can finally find my special girl, start a new life out here."

"And birth a great line of thralls?"

"Better than being executed by Dragonsteel."

"What of Feorya's wings?"

"We decided to let it go, Skáld. I'm just a cottar's son. What can I do about it? Take my revenge on Dragonsteel?"

She shook her head in disgust. None of this should surprise her. No Skoll rider had ever showed an ember of ambition. "Where is Anders?"

"Resting. Old man hasn't done as well on the journey."

Skálda scoured the rest of the hall, hoping to find Aesir. Instead, she spotted a familiar pair sitting quietly in the corner. She nodded to them. "I'll introduce you."

Mat took his bowl of barley porridge and followed her to the smaller fire. "Skálda," said Faelan and Liv in surprise. Evidently, they had not expected her to show up this morning alive.

"This is Mat." Skálda elbowed him. "The arse of Bregan and my brother of sorts."

"They write ballads about her, too," he said. "'The Epic Tales of Skálda, the Almost Adequate.'"

"And you say I'm savage."

Grinning, Mat looped a fond arm around her neck and made a face at the Primarch. "Oh, you. My gaoler."

Faelan set aside his porridge and extended his hand with far more polish. "Faelan Pranathor." He touched his other hand to Liv's arm. "This is Livana Tamarath, my lady wife."

"Just Liv is fine." She smiled politely as Skálda and Mat joined their fire. Faelan dipped his spoon back into his bowl.

"So, the *kvael-akar* survived a wroth Were King."

"I don't know if I have."

"What duty were you assigned?"

Skálda tugged distastefully at her chemise.

Mat said, "I don't think I've ever seen you in a dress." He laughed until Skálda glared at him.

"Whose household?" said Liv.

"Guess."

The young woman's face folded in horror. The men shook their heads in pity.

"What do all of you have?" said Skálda. "Field work?"

"Field work, like Liv," said the older man. "Building work. Whatever requires a strong hand."

"Who wants to trade with me?"

Her companions chuckled. Skálda felt the seedlings of a new circle of friendship. Faelan gestured at the entrance of the hall. "They're giving out porridge over there."

"I'm not hungry. Not after Dellfast."

Her friends sobered. Skálda picked at the thatch. Mat cleared his throat and offered a raunch joke to help with the silence, but no one laughed.

"No one ever told me what happened," Skálda finally said, gesturing between Faelan and Liv. "How you were separated."

"Oh." Liv scooped up the last meager bit of barley in her bowl. "My father received a report that our riders at Fenting had gone missing. Our sister post. I and two others left to scout, but the Wereguild ambushed us. I did not find out until arriving here that we had Built Fenting on a weldin."

"A weldin?"

"Take mine." Faelan passed her the rest of his bowl. She shook her head adamantly, but everyone could see the young woman was all bones. Faelan pressed it into her hands.

Squeezing his wrist, Liv continued, "An earthstead. Where the Thomdrim live. There are so few of them anymore."

"The Wereguild is protecting them," said Skálda.

"If we had known, we would have never Built there." Liv glanced aside. "Fenting was my idea. I surveyed the land, proposed it for a post. I... provoked the guild. They attacked Fenting, and Dellfast, because of me—"

"Liv." Faelan clutched her arms. "You cannot think that way. The Wereguild are demons."

Sensing all eyes on her, Liv cleared her throat and changed the subject. "Skálda tried to rescue me, you know," she told Faelan. "She saw me and Rogar in the Prannon. She risked her life fighting for us."

Faelan raised his brows in surprise and turned back to Skálda. When she said nothing of it, he murmured, "All of us in Dellfast thought Liv was dead. We found the dead scouts. Our physicker attempted to heal Rogar, but the moment he woke, he flew off." He tilted his head to his wife. "To look for her."

"He is out there," Liv whispered. "He must be."

"We will find him." Faelan dipped his head to Skálda with newfound sincerity. "Thank you for all that you've done for us."

"They will not let me see Bale," she said. "Will you protect him for me?"

"As best I can," Faelan promised.

The next silence between them was more comfortable, at least, as much as it could be for all the losses they had suffered. Mat did not attempt to break it this time. They all seemed to have retreated into their own thoughts. After a time, Faelan remembered himself and said, "What about you, Skálda?"

She raised a brow.

"I have had time to think about what happened," he said. "To all of us. To you. I heard reports about what happened to Skoll Post before my own post was destroyed. You've lost a lot too, haven't you?"

All eyes turned to her. She loathed the attention. Her first bent was to shrug it off, but Bale had taught her the importance of opening her heart, just a little.

"I lost my mother," she said.

Mat shook his head. "You don't know that, Skáld. She's probably still out there, roving the Krigs with the rest."

"You know Mum. She'd never survive in the wilderness by herself."

"She wouldn't be by herself. My mum—"

"Without me. She won't survive without me. You know what I mean."

The look she gave made him pull back and nod. Her raving mother had only lived as long as she had because Skálda had brought her breakfast and supper to her sickbed every day. Had Skálda not sacrificed her waking hours to care for her mother, Sigrede Branwright would not have put in the effort to eat. Skálda could not even remember the woman ever washing herself.

"The last thing she told me," she said, "was that she would tell me who my father was the next time we met. She mentioned something about the Arcaenum."

"The Arcaenum?" Mat said loudly, for all the hall to hear. "Your pap's a mage? That would explain—"

At her glare, he shut his mouth. It was not safe speaking of rare human affinities to the open public. Human mages on this continent were hunted, arrested, or murdered. Usually, it was all three. If Skálda had learned one thing about herself this past solstice, it was that she had an inexplicable affinity for magic. One that she was still seeking answers for.

"So..." Faelan asked the question everyone was waiting for. "Who is your father?"

She shrugged. "Jorn Branwright? I don't know. I guess I'll never find out now."

The Primarch opened his mouth to apologize to her, but she shook her head. She did not want pity, least of all now. Seeing her expression, he asked no more questions and his countenance turned solemn again.

While the couple murmured, Skálda glanced over her shoulder. The only Weremen in sight were standing outside, blithely keeping watch over the thralls. None of them imagined unarmed commons would dare mutiny. This was her opportune moment. Skálda lowered her voice to a whisper.

"I am planning an escape."

They blinked at her.

"Once I have Bale and we reach 2,000 chapters, I am going to kill the Lord Prince."

No one spoke. Skálda watched them intently, waiting to see who would join her first.

They burst into laughter.

Their unexpected response dismayed her. This was supposed to be the part where they shared her vengeance. How could they not, after the slaughter they had witnessed in Dellfast? The Lord Prince had also allowed Lord Rystendal to declare the Skonkauld a warzone, or perhaps he ordered it himself. But she would have her reprisal.

Mat laughed out pieces of his breakfast. "Skáld tells better jokes than I do, doesn't she?"

A Wereman pounded a mallet against the doorway. "Ay! Mealtime's over. Get to work, thralls!"

Everyone shuffled to their feet without argument. Mat waved her goodbye. Liv squeezed her wrist. Faelan whispered in passing, "Toiling will keep our minds off what we have lost. My days of Realm-Building are finished." His eyes flickered to the Weremen. "As of late... I question who our real enemies are."

She thought on his words, until she was the last one left in the slave hall.

ON HER WAY back up to the Draugh's manse, Skálda passed the pasture again. She stopped. A thrall had impaled browning meat on a pike and attempted to feed Bale through his bars. He was still chained down, but the Weremen had unbelted his muzzle. As the young man inched toward him, pouring with sweat, Bale growled louder, with more menace.

"He won't eat spoiled meat," she said under her breath. "Let me hunt, and I will take the task of feeding him..."

"Ay!"

She turned her head. Three Weremen around the corral were all looking at her. The one with the shaved head and massive beard warned, "Move along."

Skálda dug her nails into the soft flesh of her palms and continued her march.

Tight-lipped thralls at the manse directed her to the dining hall. When she stepped through the humble room, Skálda gave pause. The children were already seated at the table. Frit, the girl, was serving wheat porridge to her little brother. The moment Frit heard her enter, she whirled around, backing into the corner.

They stared at each other for a moment. Skálda crossed her arms awkwardly. She knew how to raise dragons or any young livestock, but she knew nothing about children. The idea of having babes to wean was as distasteful to her as wearing a chemise.

"Good," Skálda said. "You know how to feed yourselves. Then you don't need me."

She turned on her heels for the door. She would find something else to do in this manse, anything else, besides waiting upon the Draughammr's spawn.

"I will tell Father that *I* fed Evynd," came a voice behind her.

Skálda stopped. The girl puffed out her chest, finding her mettle. "That will make him cross."

"I don't care if he's cross."

"You should. He's not very nice when he's cross." The girl nodded at her broken wrist. "That's when he's being nice."

Skálda clenched her jaw. This was why she did not like children. Spoiled little humans. She marched back to the table and snapped, "Move aside," and wrenched the spoon out of the girl's hand.

"Eat your food!" she ordered the boy.

The toddler blinked up at her.

Skálda tried to stay patient. The boy was not interested in the porridge, but he wriggled off the bench and teetered over to the pot boiling over the fireplace. She lowered the spoon and rushed to him. "What are you doing? You'll burn yourself!"

She dragged the boy back to the bench. He kicked and screamed at her, landing an elbow in her eye. Skálda clamped her mouth shut. The girl took her seat at the other end of the table, lapping at her porridge with a shrug. "Father said he's not allowed to leave until he finishes all his breakfast."

Skálda's mood darkened even more.

An age later, the boy deigned the tall order of eating his porridge on the condition that he could yank at Skálda's hair whenever he pleased. Every time she tried to slip away to evade his torment, he screamed at her and refused to eat anymore.

This was almost worse than being burned alive in Dellfast.

All three of them ate in silence. The girl would not look at her. It was very uncomfortable between these walls. After the girl finished her breakfast, she left the dirty bowl on the table for Skálda to wash and scooted off the bench. "Well?"

"Well, what?" said Skálda.

"Aren't you going to ask our names?"

"I don't care for your names."

"The thralls who don't address us properly get beaten."

She did not flinch at Skálda's stare. The little louse was growing bolder. On the way out, she turned in the doorway. "I'm Fritjolf, but you can just call me Princess Frit. That's Prince Evynd." She pointed at her brother. "Mother had to wash him thrice a day because he won't take off his pants to relieve himself. If you're not sure where to find the well, you can ask Lady Sibbe."

With that, she skipped out, leaving Skálda alone at the mercy of the hair-puller.

Later that afternoon, Asveig found her in the yard outside the servant's quarters, washing the children's laundry. Lady Sibbe, who was also Jarmon's wife, had assigned her a mountain's worth of it. It seemed impossible to Skálda that two children could have so many clothes.

The white-bearded Vigardian stopped in front of her. "Do you always look as if you wish to cut off someone's head?"

"Do you always ask stupid questions?"

"The Draughammr will see you."

Skálda snarled under her breath and tossed the laundry back into the pail's fetid waters.

Asveig took her into a new section of the manse, upstairs from the great hall and into a private council room on the second floor. The Draugh was already at the long table, mulling over a spread of maps. He, too, looked altogether a different man in only his tunics. On the back wall hung a warboard that appeared recently installed and rather modern against the room's ancient furnishings. Waystones, stolen no doubt, reflected the Order's current warboard.

He did not look up as she entered. At Asveig's gesture, Skálda stayed standing as the older warrior took his seat to Soren's right. Someone wriggled in behind them.

"Hello, Skálda!" Frit called, catching her father's arm.

"Princess," she said, careful to address her duly in front of the Draugh. He glanced at the girl with distant surprise.

"What are you doing here, Frit? Are your lessons with Lady Sibbe finished so soon?"

The child nestled herself into the high-backed chair at his left and reached for the fruit bowl.

"How was breakfast?" he said, returning to his maps.

There was more to the question. Skálda caught the girl's eyes. Her neck burned with panic. The moment the spoiled pup opened her mouth, the Draugh would break Skálda's other hand.

"Oh, wonderful," said Frit. "Skálda got Evynd to behave and finish his *whole* bowl of porridge. She told us a story and even stayed to play with Evynd by the fire. Can't wait for supper!"

The Draugh gave a short "hmm" of disinterest. The girl caught eyes with her again, her stare unblinking. Skálda returned a subtle nod. She owed the princess, and the sly pup would make her remember it.

"I am preparing a raid," the Draugh said, by way of address. "The Order has Built again, this time in Eadland, north of us. King Holdvir's lands. In return for his armies, I am bound to protect him." He rubbed off an invisible fleck from his overtunic. "How do I destroy the post?"

He was testing her. It was a dangerous question. Skálda was already hanging onto her life by a wool thread, and every day she drew breath in this manse, she had to convince him she was useful.

Asveig and the girl watched her with anticipation, even curiosity. Skálda raised her splinted wrist. "Not with my axe."

The Draugh smiled maliciously.

"Tell me about the post," she said. "How big is it? Who is the post leader?"

"It would be one of your brother's posts. He has returned to Build." His dark eyes combed her for dismay.

"Yes, obviously." She hardened her voice. "No one else would be stupid enough to Build up here."

Asveig chuckled, reaching for the grapes in the bowl.

"It is a small post." Soren shuffled the maps. "Just an Outpost, by your Order's standards. It has three dragons. Chethems. The riders are green elves. I have no reason to enlist the Thomdrim for tunnels, nor endanger their enclaves needlessly."

"If it is 'just an Outpost,' then why did you call me here?"

"The post leader is what I am concerned about. His name is Garreck Kingsley."

Skálda knew that name all too well. They had met on Bregan Island earlier in the spring. The Draugh noticed her stiffen.

"You know him?"

Eyrek dotes on him, she thought. But Skálda hid her sinking dread and shrugged.

"He hails from the Felraseer Forests, just east of The Borderlands," Soren said.

"He's not a High Elf."

"No."

"Then he only knows his Dragonspells."

"Treacherous all the same. And one of the Ivarion's best riders." Soren inspected the dirt under his nails. "His specialty is the *ciryamor*. The Dragonshield. A fortnight ago, after burning my dragon slayers and decimating my garrison, he advanced past his 1,000 chapters."

Her belly clenched. They were campaigning against a Duke.

"He may be an idol to the Republic," said Soren, "but he is, in truth, a most nefarious elf. The blood of a thousand Thomdrim stain his hands, and lately, hundreds more Svennish villagers. I care nothing for his riders, but it will take strategy to annul him from the boards. I do not have thousands of men to expend for it."

Skálda wished she had not eaten those two sickening bites of porridge earlier. It was one thing to swear vengeance against the

Lord Prince. It was entirely another thing to ravage her brother's dragonpost and annul one of his most beloved riders.

"So?" Soren challenged. "You claimed you would break Dragonsteel. Or was it all the bark of a she-wolf without teeth?"

When Skálda did not answer, he laughed and folded the maps. "Take her out," he told his second. "Give her to Jarmon. I have no further use for the Ivarion's sister."

Asveig swallowed down a last grape and clenched his sword hilt.

"You don't need to expend any of your men," Skálda said. "I will wipe the post with my dragon."

Soren ignored her and took Frit's hand as he rose, his gesture that the meeting was over. Asveig continued his march to her.

"I will advance Bale's chapters," she insisted. Asveig seized her by the elbow. "With bloodwyrms."

Soren gave her a strange look.

"You'll sentence yourself all the same, thrall." Asveig yanked her to the doors.

"If King Holdvir can spare a few weeks—"

"One week," said Soren, moving for the exit. "The Ivarion is amassing forces on the Ískjall Pass to catch us in our attack." He paused, glancing over his shoulder in an extra bout of aloofness. "Oh, and Eadland is one kingdom above Vingulmark."

"How about one day?" Skálda said. "Take me back to wyrm country. When I return, I will annul Lord Garreck. I will need no resources or weapons. It will be a one-day campaign."

"She is mad!" Asveig shouted. "Draugh, she'll never surmount that elf scourge. Why toy with this delicate campaign? Better we deploy our dragon slayers and take our risks. Her dragon is merely—"

"A *Kærdighaeder*," Soren said.

"If I don't come back alive..." Skálda returned his challenge with a villainous smile. "Consider myself beheaded."

6
REPARATIONS

Staunnton Berethor, High Eldari of Aranor Elondris, greatly regretted it as soon as he stepped onto the smoky docks of Brindlemoor Bay's west side.

This district, which the inhabitants called the Slumshores, was just that. As he searched for his destination, various races cursed in tongues he did not understand. One hawked spittle before his polished boots, startling him. He pulled his ragged hood tighter over his face, hating that he could not bring guards. No matter where he turned, the smells were a stinking cauldron of grease from the street stalls, blended with the overwhelming stench of the fish market.

The dock itself was called the Wretched Wharf; whether it was an actual name, he could not say. But the ordure seemed to amuse the locals, which drew his fierce reprobation. It was incredible such squalor existed in Elenntar. One day, when he could take his mind off Enterprise politics, he would flush out the lice and mice from his beloved City-Republic.

"Out of the way, cod!" a sellsword hollered, shoving him back. He crashed into a street vendor selling boiled stinkweed. The noxious orders blasted Staunnton's nose. The tattooed man laughed as he scrambled to get upright.

Patting off his cloak in agitation, he hurried on. Staunnton looked longingly over the bay, where the Castle at Ametista Soleinne, his imperial estate, loomed on private hills. If only these loathsome cutpurses knew he was of the highest royal blood, the eldest born in a line of heroes older than the Republic itself.

On his way to Mirebottom Alley, where his most secret rendezvous would occur, he glanced upward. At this hour of the day, most of the Slumshores wallowed in shadow. But two stone towers, soaring above the rest of the district, were half bathed in twilight.

The Twin Monasteries. This was where the elders of the Church of Elenntar sent the Republic's worst blasphemers, pagans, and adulterers. The sentenced would live between the cracked walls, condemned to a life of religious study and whipped weekly in the public square. The names of every prisoner were displayed prominently on the square's boards, never to be taken down until the offender had passed.

A shadow of portent inched up his neck. He could almost hear the laughter of the crowds, and the entire Republic, as the Towers dragged him barefoot, neck collared, across the entire city. He imagined his family's horror, the indignity of it all, as his Elenntarien saw him off to live with the godless scum of Elondria...

Staunnton shuddered. The she-elf was a ravishing curse and he was powerless to extricate himself from her.

At the fall of night, he made it to Mirebottom. Cloaked men lurked in the shadows. It felt like they were eyeing him, like everyone in the Slumshores was plotting to turn him into the Towers. His paranoia wrangled his windpipe. He ducked through the hanging rag that served as the door to Blightbane Quarter.

If the streets stank, the stench in here was even worse. This tavern had holes for chimneys, barely letting out the odors of unwashed bodies and bodily fluids. Holding his breath, Staunnton looked around the feast hall's packed tables. Another shape as hooded as himself blended in with the corner shadows. On his way over, he almost crashed into the maidservant.

"Could you have not picked another destination?" he hissed under his breath.

"No one would witness us here," said Lhyestrae, Queen of the Elves.

He glanced over his shoulder, certain that he would see someone he knew, but a cold hand rested on his.

"Be at peace, love," she said. "You look as if a mouse's scuttle would impel you to kill a man."

He growled under his breath. Her gleaming eyes were the only part of her face visible behind her hood.

"Well?" she said. "What did you urgently need to council about?"

Staunnton took a deep breath. "Leondran met with me privately."

Her face shadowed even more.

"You must have heard what happened in Fjorland," he said. "It was a Dragonsteel city. Dellfast."

"The Wereguild burned it."

He shook his head. "That is the story your son and Lord Eyrekvald pleaded to. The truth is—"

"A drink, sirs?"

Swiveling to his right, Staunnton dropped his hand to his sword. The young maidservant he had knocked into earlier held two tankards of ale.

"What?" he said wildly.

The elvish queen spoke to the girl with utmost grace. "No, thank you."

Even after the girl left, his thick neck poured sweat. "Leondran told me your Second Rider burned the city on dragonback. It was only by slim fortune that he escaped through a Wereguild tunnel."

Lhyra pondered this. "What reason would my son have to send Eyrekvald on such a massacre?"

"Leondran also told me..." He lowered his voice even more, and explained how the Second Rider and his followers had knowingly campaigned against brothers and sisters of the faith. He told her how the Second Rider had threatened Leondran, an *Eldari*, to keep the truth from the Elenntarien or die.

In the background, a round copperbit clattered to the floor. Staunnton jumped. Lhyestrae mulled everything over. He could not read her mood.

"I still have the Ivarion's damned wildfire to put out," Staunnton went on. "The elvish mages of your empire haven't been enough to keep the fires from spreading into northern Fjorland. You have given me every reason to lend Leondran my iron fist."

Still no answer. Frustrated, Staunnton picked at a splinter in the wood. He came at it at the wrong angle, and it tore open the flesh under his nail. He bared his teeth.

"The Elder appealed to me for justice," he said. "He wants Eyrekvald arrested and sentenced. He wants the same for your son. Above all, he wants the Order abolished—"

The high queen laughed.

His stomach twisted with sickness. In a moment of clarity, he realized he should have never disclosed their private council, not even with her. Breaching Leondran's trust in confidentiality was as profane as sharing a church confession. It was wrong, entirely wrong.

When had he become like this? Staunnton Berethor, Hero-King of Ebrennia, devout benefactor of the Church, the champion of rectitude. This was not him. He was not a profaner. He was not an adulterer.

All over again, he saw a future in the Towers.

"I care nothing for what Leondran wants," said Lhyra.

He slammed a fist over the table. "Put aside your personal feelings about him! The fact is, an Eldari has brought before me charges worthy of terminating your Enterprise—"

"Ours, Staunn."

"I want nothing to do with either, if this is your manner of operation! Do you understand the gravity of this? Do you not know how precarious the peace between the factions is? If my Elenntarien finds out, this will break Aranor Elondris into war!"

"Staunn." Her voice was gentle, very comforting. "Who else knows about this?"

"He told only me, for now. I asked him to keep it in confidence."

"Of course I will do something about this." She sat back. "We will give Elder Leondran his reparations."

"Good. I will tell him the Elenntarien will convene for two trials. You and I will plead with him not to permit his faction to declare war. If he demands an end to Realm-Building—"

"No."

He laughed roughly. "No?"

"If you take my son's Second Rider, he will war against *you*. He will burn all Aranor Elondris, beginning with your family."

Staunnton swallowed. "Eyrekvald Ivarion once served me well, but ever since Tera Beren's fall, he has corrupted his sanity. And your son?" He swatted his bleeding finger against his cloak. "They are demons both, Lhyra. They feed off each other like bloodwyrms. But I will not let them off without my sword of justice. I will not let the Order's interests destroy—"

"My sweet High Eldari." The she-elf left the opposite bench and came to sit by him. The touch of her fair, warm thigh against his drew a shiver out of him. "You are hurting." She took his hand, the one with the bleeding finger, and slipped it under the table.

"*Anora'thil.*"

His broken flesh weaved itself together. The potent magic of the High Elves never ceased to dumbfound him.

"The only reason I brook my debased spittoon of a son," Lhyestrae said, "is because he can run Dragonsteel better than anyone alive."

Staunnton sneered. "It is his Second Rider that runs it, not him—"

"No, Staunn. He may appear to waste away his existence, but he is still a conniving varlet. Even now, he is scheming, though I cannot yet say what."

He sighed.

"The Order needs a virulent hand," she said. "It does not need Eyrekvald Branwright."

"But you said..." He rubbed his balding hairline begrudgingly. "We cannot take Eyrekvald away from him."

"I said that *you* cannot take him away. But do you not know me by now?" She kissed his forehead, and whispered, "I would never allow another war to come to this continent."

He grunted.

"I will absolve this." She released his hand. He examined his finger. Blood still crusted his nail, but the sting was gone. In fact, it felt even better than before.

Staunnton pulled away. "I must give my answer to Leondran."

"Tell him," said Lhyra, "that Eyrekvald will die. Until then, Fjorland must be kept silent."

She rose, the sudden recession of her warmth as destabilizing as a stool with two legs. "Rhaennöria requires me. Do not forget your first promise, love."

The she-elf left a lingering kiss on his lips. It rendered him breathless and lewd in want. He burned to keep his promise and rid himself of Jeinna right then. He had to have this woman, even if it cost him his soul!

And she was out the door. Vaeritas almighty, Lhyestrae Morghûl moved like a ghoul through the Republic. He turned away from the blazing hearths, sweating harder.

Briefly, he considered going behind her back and setting a trial, anyway. It would resolve the inferno of a conundrum at his bedside. Yet the she-elf terrified him as much as she enamored him.

"Lord of Light," he whispered. "Help me..."

What great mesh had he entangled himself in?

Once he bundled up his nerves enough to make the long trek home on foot, he accidentally caught gazes with the maidservant across the hall. Staunnton froze. The red-haired girl would not stop staring at him. Her eyes were like Vaeritas's swords twisting their righteous fires into his wicked heart.

Staunnton abruptly turned away and hurried out the door. The humidity behind his hood drenched his pate.

He had seen one of Vharyn's birds. He was certain of it. He was certain the Lord Prince had just learned what he was hiding with the Queen of Elves.

7

THE FIRST BAELRIDER SPEAKS, ÉAD'HEL!

THE NEXT MORNING, the Were King set out southward with a mounted Vigardian contingent. Skálda followed him on foot, cradling her broken wrist to her chest. They were back on the Hammerfest Road, retracing the path she had taken to Solhall. They passed the Hammerfest Dike, two gated stone walls enclosing a manmade, or rather, Thomdrim-made river the giants were tending to. When they reached the other side, Soren pulled up on the causeway.

Beyond them was an open mead that stretched into rolling hills in the east. Wildflowers swayed in the summer winds. It was silent and tranquil. Skálda recalled seeing it on their way to Solhall.

Soren snatched a pebble off the ground and tossed it over the curb. His Weremen watched in anticipation.

Suddenly, a brown bole burst out of the earth, surging toward the sky with a livid shriek. Skálda widened her eyes. Its many mandibles ground together, searching for food. A stench fouled the air, like a thousand fish putrefying under her nose. Finding no prey, it let out a gravelly noise and slunk back under the wildflowers. Skálda held her nose.

"Welcome to wyrm country," said Soren.

She edged closer to the curb and looked over the side.

"*Careful*, dragon girl," Rulf drawled from Soren's right.

"It looked different from the other one." Skálda glanced back. "The one Rulf and I saw."

"Firewyrm," the younger Vigardian clarified.

The Draugh pointed at the mead. "This used to be one of Vingulmark's most fertile valleys. Thurs Runja. Three solstices ago, the Red Spore crossed over the eastern hills and a new bed infested the entire land. Within weeks, the wyrms killed all the villagers." He pointed further west. "Thurs Village was there."

Skálda narrowed her eyes. She could just make out the ruins of several longhouses.

"I entreated the Thomdrim to build that canal, but the loss in production was irreparable. Every solstice that passes, the Spore spreads more eggs across the Deep North. They infest what farmlands we have left. My people have no choice but to retreat further north, into the tundras and glaciers where the wyrms cannot survive, and little food can grow."

"How many wyrms are here?" she said.

"Hundreds." Rulf shrugged. "Thousands by now."

"How far are we from Lord Garreck's post?"

Rulf rubbed a hand over his head, tugging at the thin braid that fell to his shoulders. "Eight days on foot, Draugh?"

"Are there more wyrmfields between here and there?" she said.

"Maybe we'll get lucky and one will eat your brother."

Rulf's blithe comment drew laughter. Skálda pulled away from the edge. "Bale should be big enough to ride, but I haven't tried. I will need to cut him a saddle and counsel with Aesir—"

"The elf stays chained," Soren interrupted. "He will never leave his cell and divulge our location to his whore queen."

"Keep him chained, then. But I still must speak with him."

The mead rumbled. Skálda glanced at the dirt beneath her

boots. The little pebbles were trembling. A few breaths later, the ground was still again.

"What was that?"

"The Big One," said Rulf.

"How big?"

"*Big*, dragon girl."

"How do I draw it out?"

The Weremen laughed.

"You have one day," Soren reminded her. "One day to advance your dragonling to 1,000 chapters, or whatever foolish rank you dream of. I am departing at dawn."

"One day is all I need."

The Vigardians taunted her with singsongs about wyrm fodder, but Skálda trudged back to Solhall, ignoring them all.

They made quick time back to the settlement. While Rulf and Jarmon left to retrieve Aesir, the rest of the Vigardians escorted her to the pasture. "Bring the dragon slayers here," the Draugh murmured to Asveig. The moment the cage came into sight again, Skálda sprinted over the grass and into the corral.

"Bale!"

He lifted his horned head, his chains rattling. *"My wolf."*

She reached through the bars and cupped her hand around his tail, gently sliding down the thick musculature until she reached the tip. He extended his nose as far as it would go through the bars, but they kept him from nuzzling her.

Have they fed you?

"Only spoiled meat." He bared his teeth. *"I won't eat it."*

Right, you only eat the spiced moose Aesir cooks for you.

"When the wolf lets me free, I will eat them all."

Yes, Bale, just not yet.

He turned his head at the growing crowd. The Draughammr was watching everything from the saddle. *"Wolf is letting me out today?"*

She felt his uneasiness through his low rumble. The last time the Weremen had gathered like this, they prodded him with lances and threatened to kill him.

"Bale..." Skálda rubbed his scaled nose. "We are on dangerous ground. I promise you will go free, but first, I need your help." She told him about their immediate predicament and her campaign plans. When she finished, she said, *What do you think?*

He eyed her in curiosity. *"You want to ride a Bael?"*

The question troubled her. Lord Jarmon shouted from the road. He and Rulf dismounted, hauling Aesir across the pasture by his neck chain. His wrists were fettered, and his face was swollen from new bruises. For some odd reason, they had removed his rings. Above all, she was stunned to see a dark beard tangling his mouth and chin. Elves could not grow beards. It made him look so much like a man. He, too, seemed too conscious of it, the way he kept darting his eyes as if waiting for someone's judgment. Aesir must have done painstaking work keeping himself clean-shaven across the Prannon.

"Spoiled meat!" Bale roared with fondness, drawing nervous glances from the Weremen. Skálda did not fail to notice the three dragon slayers the Draugh's men wheeled into the pasture.

Aesir inclined his head, smiling darkly. "Baelaeryx."

"They chained him too," Bale spat. *"But I will break his irons and we will feast on their bad flesh!"*

Skálda loped over to Aesir. His smile turned sardonic as he looked her up and down, seeing no chain on her. Skálda hated that they could not speak in privacy, and doubly that the Draugh and his shield-brothers were staring down their shoulders.

"They put me in a dress." Skálda tugged at the chemise.

Aesir returned her no humor.

"I need your help," she said. "Can you craft Bale a saddle and guide me on flying him?"

"Why?"

"I agreed to campaign for them—"

"Against Dragonsteel? What of our agreement?"

He made no effort to lower his voice. Skálda lurched closer and hissed, "Yes, against Dragonsteel. You saw what they did to Dellfast!"

"Why should it surprise you? Do you not know who Vharyn Morghûl is?"

His tone grated on her. None of this was going as expected.

"I need to earn their trust," she whispered, "if you want us to have any chance of freedom."

"You think they will ever let me free?" He laughed in disbelief. "Don't you know who I serve?"

"You need not be a thrall any longer—"

"You assume I do not serve the Highmark out of my own accord?"

His relentless questioning astonished her. "It is as you said, Aesir. The Morghûls would massacre an entire human city without a second thought. And you would defend—"

"Lhyestrae Morghûl is the only one keeping us from another continental war. The Morghûls may be cruel, but they do what is necessary for Elondria. What no one else has the mettle for." He nodded to the Weremen. "Which one of them bled for Elondria during the War of Treason? You think an army of them can compare to even one Morghûl? If you are trying to convince me to turn against the Dragons..." He spoke for all the courtyard to hear. "Then I choose death!"

"Hmm," the Draugh said.

She seized him by the elbow, irate that he would take the Morghûls' side. "I am not asking you to turn against Rhaennöria! I am asking you to help me with a saddle so I can fly Bale."

The Imperial Ranger sighed sharply, staring at the ground between them. It looked like he wanted to say more. He was furious with her. But she could not address it with the Draughammr standing over them.

"Never trust elves," Lord Jarmon muttered.

"We elves trust a Vigardian stench about as much," Aesir snapped back. "Bring me a horse's saddle! I will mark Bale's breadth."

Skálda glanced up at Soren, towering over her on his destrier. "I need to unchain my dragon."

"You see those?" Soren gestured at the super ballistae. "Rulf is the best marksman in all the North. He shot down the riders of Tera Beren."

"Oh, Draugh," said Rulf, overhearing. "You flatter me!" The young Vigardian offered a coy smile. "Dragon girl, our Draughammr is a better marksman than all of us. Sometimes, we miss. But he did not miss the great Leofraen Amanoor."

Soren said, "Is my meaning clear?"

"Perfectly," said Skálda.

"Then let him out."

Rulf dismounted and unbuckled the saddle on his own mare. Soren called to his men, "Ready the slayers!"

While Rulf tossed Aesir the saddle, Skálda returned to the cage. Some thirty eyes were on her. She hated the attention. Rulf, Jarmon, and Asveig moved the ballistae to the front, aiming the Anárion steel bolts at Bale. The tension in her shoulders grew unbearable.

Bale, she said, stopping in front of the bars. *I am going to let you out, but you must not attack anyone. Do you understand?*

He gazed down at her with his bright red eyes. By the ravens, this was a hatchling no more. Even on his haunches, he was as tall as her.

Bale, understand?

The dragon said nothing. Skálda prayed to whatever Svennish god would listen that he obeyed. She climbed inside and started with his leg fetters, pulling the iron pins out. It was agonizing, with only one good hand to work with. Her damp chemise clung to her back. Bale watched her labor with attentiveness. Every moment of it, she felt the dragon slayers aimed at them.

His collars were the last to come off. When the last one clanged onto the cage bed, Skálda backed a step, waiting. The young Bael stared down at her without a word. Skálda began to doubt herself.

Come, Bale. She waved.

He gouged the wood with his talons and charged. Skálda failed to move away in time. He rushed at her with such a fury, he barely missed trampling her. The moment his claws touched grass, he spread his wings and took to the skies in a roar.

She hurried out of the cage, fixing her worried gaze on him. The Draugh held up a fist, his signal for his marksmen to prepare to fire. He trailed Bale with his eyes. Her dragon was one signal away from death.

Bale soared high over Solhall, stretching out his neck and expanding his wings to full breadth. His elation rushed over their mind-bond. He had not stopped growing since Dellfast, and this was the first time since his capture that he was flying at heights he could not before.

Soren did not seem to understand the emotion behind Bale's roaring. His fingers twitched.

"Don't shoot," Skálda begged.

He regarded her coldly.

"Please."

"Call him down."

Bale circled over the Lupine Ridge, drawing screams all over the city. Soren was observing how much control she really had. She could not afford to let the Draughammr think for a moment that her Bael would not obey her. She remembered one of Aesir's first lessons and pressed their mind-bond.

Baelaeryx, come down at once!

The strong command in her voice surprised him. He finished his loop and dove, stretching out his neck and tucking in his legs with such speed that even the nearby Weremen shouted. He pulled up over the pasture, beating his wings thrice as he landed on his claws. The young Bael extended his head protectively over her shoulder, snarling softly at the Vigardians.

"I have come, Wolf."

Soren's men watched her with newfound awe and fear, which greatly pleased her. She brushed the length of Bale's nose ridge. Even Soren appeared surprised. At his nod, his commanders released the ballistae.

"The saddle," Skálda called.

As Aesir approached with it, Bale shook his head and retreated several steps. His tail snapped like he was being cornered again.

"Come, Bale!" Aesir said.

He snarled through his parted teeth. The Ranger marched closer, undaunted. Bale roared.

"Hold on," she said, extending her arm between them. *What is it?*

"I am no dragon of the Order to be saddled like a dumb beast," he spat. *"They are slaves, but we Bael are never ridden! We crush all who try."*

Would you crush me?

Bale loomed his parted maw over her. Aesir murmured her name, a warning for her to step back. But she trusted her instincts and met his glowing eyes with a still calm, something she had learned to do with the skáldwolves.

"How much does the wolf hope of calling herself my rider one day?" he said.

Skálda glanced away in embarrassment, but he rumbled, touching his muzzle to her cheek. Love warmed their mind-bond, and all the tension crumbled from her. She clasped his nose with both hands.

Maybe a little, she admitted.

"Maybe very much." He nuzzled her.

She stroked the ridges of his eye hollows, then kneaded him under the throat. His rumbling deepened in pleasure. Her own love swelled for him, and she blurted, *You belong to no one. You have no rider.*

"But the wolf will always be mine." He let go of her and craned his neck around, pointing his snout at his back. *"Very well. Do you dare?"*

It was an invitation without a saddle.

High feelings rushed through her, like she was swallowing the wind. A ride on dragonback. The High Elves of the Imperial Dragonguard had ridden on dragonback. But this was an impossible dream she had long since crushed as an impoverished human child on Skuller's Row.

Yet this was different. It was as Bale said. One thousand years ago, during the Breaking of the Realms, the greatest elves had tried to mount the Bael. All had perished.

But their unlikely bond ran deeper than friendship. If she rode him, she would overturn all Nhorssn history.

Everyone was watching. Soren's face stayed expressionless, but Aesir's hatred of the Wereguild was forgotten to wonder. Even the Were commanders were fidgeting. Asveig clenched his fists in hope, and Rulf even smiled. They were not delighting in her, but drinking in the impossibility of a Svennish common mounting a Bael's back.

Before he could change his mind, Skálda climbed onto his extended foreleg. Big as he had gotten, he was still small; at least, small compared to mature flights like Crixalas and Tythandrell. Even with one good hand, it was easy enough getting onto his back and fitting herself into the nook between neck and shoulders.

Skálda clenched one of his spikes and wrapped her right arm around his neck. She was on a dragon. She was on a *Bael.*

And she did what she had longed to do so desperately as a child, just like in all the elvish legends. She recollected the Elvynnöthe command Eyrek had once called to Tythandrell.

"*Éad'hel!*"

Bale bared his teeth and stampeded forth into a new charge. Aesir, Soren, and the Weremen in their path rushed out of the way. Beating his wings, he bounded off the pasture.

With her unaccustomed weight on his back, they just managed to clear the dragon slayers. The guards cried out and ducked. Bale beat his wings harder, obliging her urgent yearning to fly, and took them into the freedom of the skies.

8
THE BIG WYRM

FOUR CENTURIES AGO, Vhylaeras Morghûl had named the First Flight the *Lúndalorin.* There was no end to the ballads every High Elvish rider since had written about the *Lúndalorin*, for it was one of nine greatest wonders of life.

Skálda understood it now, even felt a kinship with those elvish lords, for a thrill she never felt before surged her. No majestic vista of the Krigsgaald, no climb to Hrafenfjall's summit, could compare with this. She had not truly *lived* until today.

Dragon scales chafed between her legs, with no ground beneath her. The intensity of the winds blasted pale strands from her face. As the hems of her chemise soared behind her, Skálda let herself imagine, like a child, that it was a great mantle, and she was an elvish prince. The muscles in Bale's shoulders rippled, and he pounded his wings harder, ascending even higher above Solhall.

Vingulmark's brooding landscape tilted at an angle. At this height, she took comfort in the rhythmic beat of his fire-streaked wings. Up here, in these cold skies, it felt like no power on the continent could hurt her.

She knew she ought to be terrified. Every Builder rode his

dragon with stirrups, a belt around the waist, and a pommel on the saddle. Anders would have berated her for doing none of these things. He had told her most human riders who took the *Lúndalorin* vomited their insides. More than half never went on to become Builders of rank because they could never get over their fear of flying.

But she was not afraid. As Bale vaned his wingtips, settling into a glide, Skálda let go of his neck and spread her arms. Winds rushed over and under her. The northwoods looked like toys from this height.

Feeling her euphoria across their mind-bond, Bale roared with her. It was a dragoncall of pure joy. Their high emotions merged, fusing like cooled gold, and a new rapture fired into Skálda's spirit. Their heartbeats were synchronizing. The blazing colors of their emotions overlaid each other, becoming one, scintillating into a collage of new lusters. Bale's dragonsoul thrummed in her own body, as he felt her soul beating in his.

The myths about the Bael were wrong, she gasped. *We have a Binding. Do you feel it?*

He rumbled, pleased with her childlike thrill.

Bale... you would choose to Bind with me?

"Not a Binding, Wolf. I don't dare make the full Bind. You are a Fourth-Realmer; I am a child of Atallgaard. When I'm older, a Bind with my script would break you. But I am giving you what I can."

It feels like a Binding.

He snorted. *"Because I'm twice any dragon."*

Four times.

A tide of pleasure washed over her. It felt entirely like her own.

"Are you afraid to fly, Wolf?"

"*Éad'hel!*" she shouted back.

Bale roared, accelerating their flight. He streaked them further north, where not even the touch of summer was enough to melt the snows. They skimmed the top of a cliff, and then he tucked in his wings.

They were falling over the side. Skálda widened her eyes. They surged over a steep white slope. The wind sting gnawed at the tips of her ears, but it was nothing compared to the way her intestines were springing up into her chest. Skálda opened her mouth for a scream, but nothing came out.

Just before they could splatter at the bottom of the rift, Bale abruptly banked. He skimmed his wings and tail over a lake, spraying frigid waters behind them. Before she could process where they were now, he twisted sharply to the right. Skálda clenched a neck spike. Her intestines were in her throat now. Bale thundered in laughter. Beating his wings, he spiraled them up and over the steep aretes. One moment, the earth was on top, the sky beneath; the next, she was a grab away from the tips of pines. The deafening turbulence blinded her. Now she understood why Dragonsteel required riders to wear windhelms during all flights.

Bale ended their spiraling with a straight flight into the heavy mists of the northerly alpines. Skálda's heart rammed against her chest. She swore her ribs must have all rearranged themselves.

Let's go again, she gasped.

"Enough for one day, Wolf. You almost lost your bladder."

Then we'll go again tomorrow.

"Tomorrow we annul the elf."

Then the tomorrow after that!

"You are kind of good. Rode with only one good hand. No one rides a Bael with one hand."

Because I am twice any Dragonsteel rider.

He laughed through his teeth. She overheard his contentment rumbling through their Binding. *"My wolf rider."* He tested those words to himself possessively. *"My wolf human. My wolf, my wolf..."*

BALE LANDED them on a small ridge overlooking the Deep North's unknown mountains east of Solhall. Once she was grounded, he rested his spiked head over her lap. Mist cloaked them. The skies remained a dark slate. Their eyes were closed, their hearts still singing from their Binding's new heights.

"I dream of falling," said Bale.

"I dream of falling..."

Behind the dark curtain of her closed eyes, she saw again the Naüthe's glaciers, and the chilling expanse of the *faolrún* rushing closer. The winds burned her. The powerless terror of her descent consumed her.

Skálda opened her eyes. "In the days before you fell, I dreamt of it," she said. "Why did you call out to me?"

"You were the only one who would listen."

Looking down at him, she brushed his deep eye hollows, the iron scales of his headplate, the ever-growing curve of his four horns. Bale sighed sleepily through his nostrils.

He is so beautiful, she thought, caressing the terrible pitch of his fang-shaped scales. His tail curled around her.

I am going to kill the Lord Prince, she said. *Will you help me?*

This greatly troubled him. She sensed it as a portentous cloud through their Binding. As a higher being, he felt the echo of Vharyn Morghûl's power through the scripts of all the Midgaard dragons.

"You are a strong affinite," said Bale, *"but he is very, very powerful. Too many chapters to name."*

You don't want me to face him, even after all he has done.

Bale flicked his tail in worry, avoiding her gaze.

"I... can't ask that of you," she said. I promised to take you to Traust."

"No!"

His abruptness startled her.

We talked about this. We agreed—

"No." Bale pulled away from her lap and shuffled to the edge of the cliff. *"Can't go back."*

"Bale?"

His hysterical fear hit her in a blast. This was the same full-fledged terror as when he had fallen through Midgaard's veiling. It threw her onto all fours.

"Bale," she hissed, "let go!"

"Can't go back... Can't go back..."

Suppressed memories raced over her vision, too swift for her to make sense of. But she felt a ponderous dread he could not put to words. Bale was remembering. Something horrendous would happen if he returned to Atallgaard.

He released his terror from the Binding.

Skálda wobbled to her feet. She placed a hand on his side. He was tremoring.

"You came here for a reason," she said. "You were searching for someone to help you."

Can't go back, Wolf. Please.

"Bale... what was chasing you?"

A bright vision cut through her mind, the memory of the colossal *faolrún* spanning the Naüthe's glaciers. Ebbs of hysteria throbbed against the Binding again. Skálda stroked him. "Shh, alright. Let it go. We won't think on it."

His muscles shivered under her touch. *"I will stay here with my wolf. Never go back. We will hunt and fly."*

He was pleading with her. She and Aesir had sealed their decision in the Skonkauld, yet here she was, questioning it all over again.

"We can't stay here forever," she said. "We must go back."

"No!"

"We will go back to Solhall—"

"No more chains!"

"If we don't, they will kill Aesir. They will kill our friends. We came out here to—"

"Advance the chapters. Always with the wolf, it's advancing chapters."

Sensing his testiness, she delivered him a throat rub. "I told you our plan, and you agreed to it." He lashed his tail. "I need your help with the wyrms... Remember what I said about being lazy?"

"Lazy?" He sounded offended.

"Then why will you not go?"

"Tired."

"So, you're afraid."

"Afraid?"

"The mighty Bael, afraid of wyrms—"

"Afraid!" he spat. He extended his foreleg. *"Hurry up, Wolf. Afraid!"*

Skálda smiled and climbed on.

THE FIRST RAYS peeked over the hills on their return flight to Thurs Runja. Both of them were jittery. As before, the vast mead was deceptively tranquil. The wildflowers swayed in the low winds.

Ready to kill some wyrms?

"I am afraid of no wyrms!"

At her prompting, he descended toward the Hammerfest causeway. A small warband camped on the hills west of the mead. Skálda squinted. Asveig, Jarmon, and Rulf were picnicking over roasting meat skewers. Here to entertain themselves with her demise, no doubt. Catching sight of Bale over the eastern forests, Rulf nudged them and pointed.

Bale landed before their firepit. Lord Jarmon sneered, "Here to die?"

"I need some hauberks."

The paunchy Vigardian's laughter turned uproarious. "And Vaeritas's shield and sword, too?"

As she waited in wolfish silence, Bale kneaded his talons over the grass, growling low. His hostility unnerved them enough to wipe the grins from their faces. Rulf shrugged and called out to his men to bring her what she needed. A minute later, a thrall edged toward Bale with three suits of mail. Bale parted his jagged jaws. The young man gulped and tossed the hauberks, dashing away.

Bale clamped onto them with his teeth and gently handed them to her. She draped them over her incapacitated arm. The Were commanders stopped eating. They were watching her suspiciously, wondering what she was up to this time.

Without a word, she turned Bale around and they took off.

Fly lower, she said. *Not too low. Be prepared.*

He descended to twenty feet. His warped shadow streamed over the flowers. Skálda kept her eyes on the grasses, searching. Waiting. Even at Bale's proximity, nothing emerged out of the earth.

Odd... Rulf said there were thousands of them here.

"Maybe they're tired."

I doubt it.

She considered the way Soren had thrown a pebble over the curbside, how it triggered a wyrm. She remembered a Dellfast child doing the same on the road to Solhall, only to awaken a different fiery predator.

They're not drawn by movement...

"Then what?"

Perhaps... sound vibration.

At her bidding, he flew even lower, to fifteen feet. The grasses stayed quiet. They were very tense. Skálda had seen how one wyrm could shoot out of the earth at twelve feet, without warning, and shred through flesh.

"They can shred through dragonhide?" said Bale.

We're going to find out.

They scoured the grasses. Bale risked flying three feet lower. With his steady wingbeats, the wildflowers swayed. A low shush rustled across the valley, following Bale's soft flight trail.

A distant grinding noise hummed under the earth.

"Bale, they come!" she shouted.

Something putrid and green, wet with mucous, burst into the air. Bale sharply turned, evading. More popped out like heinous radish sprouts, grinding their mandibles together and shrilling.

"Small," Bale snorted.

Catching nothing, the wyrms hurried to sink back under the earth. Skálda narrowed her eyes.

"They hate the light," Bale observed.

A cloud passed over the sun. Rays of light passed in and out over the vale. Even when he flew low, triggering the grasses with his wingbeats, they would not emerge where the sun touched.

You're right... There seems to be a pattern of how they come out. They never just burst out immediately. It's like they know we are a moving target. They wait and plan on where we will *be.*

"Should I try again?"

Skálda nodded. Bale zigzagged through the patches of sunlight, provoking the wyrms with stronger wingbeats. She counted the time. It was about eight beats when the next wyrm sprang at them. Bale tucked his legs and twirled up and out of reach.

Twelve feet range, it looks like. And an eight count delay.

They stimulated the wyrms a few more times before Skálda confirmed this was how they attacked.

"This is kind of fun," Bale tittered.

Within the hour, they awakened numerous beds, wyrms of all shades and builds. They yauped and puled, writhing over each other like maggots. It was a revolting sight that would have made any Skonkauld islander back at home faint. Skálda dropped a hauberk into the maws of the little wyrms, which appeared to be most of what inhabited Thurs Runja.

They squawked in hunger. Five dangling finger-like wyrms rushed back down to the earth and tore at the mail. Skálda squinted. Several beats later, the sun forced them under. They left the hauberk over the grass like indigestible gristle. This worried Skálda.

Soren said Garrek's specialty is the Dragonshield. How strong would it be?

"The rider's spell is only as strong as the dragon. His shield is as hard as his dragon's scales."

"1,000 chapters," she murmured aloud. "It will certainly be tougher than a Wereman's hauberk."

Bale took it upon himself to swerve around the wyrmholes and lure them back out. They shrilled piteously as he sunk his teeth into their foul hide, tore off their eyeless heads. Alarmed, Skálda called, *What are you doing?*

"Advancing the chapters."

He tilted his head back with a dragonish grin. Despite herself, Skálda offered one of her own.

Bale was tearing through his twelfth wyrm when a booming shriek overpowered the little wyrm's keen. Fire belched at them so unexpectedly, Bale lost his balance and jerked in mid air. A far larger wyrm, fifteen feet tall at least, snapped at them, leaping over the blind heads of the little ones. It was coming straight for Skálda.

"Wolf!"

She ducked. They watched in horror as its shadow sailed over Bale, forming an ominous arc in the sky. The stench of fish carcasses smothered her. By the ravens, its breadth was dreadful. It was almost ten counts before its eight beady eyes crashed back under the earth.

They shivered together. It had been a narrow death.

Was that the Big One?

Bale rumbled nervously. *"No more playing with the wyrms."*

I wonder what brings out the bigger ones. Skálda goaded the reluctant young Bael to circle back around to the hole where the firewyrm had disappeared. She thought on what happened. Only when the little wyrms were crying had the bigger one emerged.

Sound... More sound draws them out. That firewyrm didn't seem as troubled by the sunlight as the others.

"Nasty, nasty wyrms. They don't taste good."

Skálda drew a deep breath and gave her bloodiest scream. In the distance, the Weremen snapped to their feet. Skálda thought bitterly to herself, Look how they liven when they think I'm dying.

Eight beats later, flames plumed out of the earth, blackening all the wildflowers within range. The firewyrm soared out to strike at them again, screeching in rage. Bale roared back, diving under its armored head. But this monster was more limber than the little wyrms. It turned with him, burrowing its bloodsucking mouth into his left thigh.

Bale roared louder. Skálda shouted for him, craning around. The wyrm's rows of little saws were lodged in his scales, and its weight was pulling him down. He flapped his wings in flurried panic, but he was dropping in altitude. The noise aroused larger wyrms. Six husky trunks burst out of the earth.

Skálda suffocated under the panic blasting across their Binding. Bale beat his tail against the firewyrm's head, but it would not let go. They were less than ten feet from the ground. If Bale's claws touched it, it would be over. The other wyrms would enmesh them and drag them under the mead.

His roars cracked into desperate cries. He snapped at the firewyrm, but nothing would daunt it to release him. Skálda clenched her broken fist. If only she had her axe... but she still had her affinity.

"Hethrîth in'loeg mírael!" she shouted.

It was a familiar spell, one of the few she had learned from Aesir during her journey with him on the road. At another time and place, she had used it to save Bale from a much larger predator.

Cool magic coursed through her blood. The firewyrm shrieked as it levitated in the air. Bale pumped his wings and tore himself free of its grip. It gave him enough time to swerve away from the other six wyrms. His flank was awash in crimson.

"We must turn back," Skálda said breathlessly. "I have put you in danger."

To her surprise, she felt not fear, but a hot anger sweltering into her mind. He did not reply to her, but dove around to the firewyrm. The adult monster was heavy and the spell's exertion rapidly drained her, but she held on with all her might. It saw them coming and snapped at them, wroth that it was trapped in the air. Bale ducked and clamped down on its throat, beneath its head armor. It dragged out a doleful caterwaul, its mandibles crackling together. Bale snapped down harder.

A wyrmhead tumbled to the ground. Skálda let go of the spell, and the rest of its body followed. At the angle Bale flew, the hauberks slid down her arm. She tried to catch them, but one plummeted after the firewyrm's carcass. Its bigger cousins snatched the hauberk up greedily. When they realized it was not flesh, they shrank back under the earth, leaving it behind. But the metal was shredded through.

"Bale?" she said tentatively.

He was furious, but not at her. *"Spoiled nasty wyrms. I'll eat them all!"*

Thurs Runja tremored. Skálda lifted her head, feeling a deep foreboding. All the rumpus was drawing out another wyrm, a bigger one... The smaller and large wyrms wailed and scuttled out of the way, their burrows breaking the earth's surface. The valley was caving from a sinkhole. Bale suspended himself high in the air in a steady glide.

What Skálda saw wrenched the breath out of her. A mouth the size of Bregan Island appeared below them. Flowers, gravel, even the wretched bodies of firewyrms sank into the grinding abyss. Hot, fetid air blasted over them. The last hauberk slid off her arm and vanished into the maw.

"Oh," she said. "The Big One."

The infinite rows of teeth appeared for only a beat before the titan sank back under the earth. Where it had risen, an entirely new rift formed. It was almost a full minute before either of them could remember to speak.

"Alright, afraid," Bale admitted.

The sun lowered over the western slopes of the Lupines. The Weremen were still watching. Brushing sweat off her forehead, she patted Bale's neck. *You did well. Let's go back?*

"One day," he said, gliding gently to the causeway, *"we should kill all these wyrms. Help the villagers. Let them live free again. Help, help."*

The passion in his suggestion surprised her. He seemed far more avid about this good deed than fighting the Lord Prince, or engaging in any human skirmish she had urged him into.

It was... odd, for a Bael. And it made her strangely defensive.

They almost made it back to the Hammerfest Road when the brown bloodwyrm she saw earlier in the day burst out of the earth. Bale slapped his wings together, startled. The Weremen directly below gaped at the shadowed column falling over them. It wrapped itself around Bale, forcing his wings against himself. He bellowed. Skálda screamed. Before she could shout the levitation spell, the wyrm dragged them under the mud.

Asveig, Jarmon, and Rulf jogged down from the hill, joining the Weremen on the causeway. They stared over the side. The valley had gone silent.

"Skit," said Rulf. "They almost made it."

Lord Jarmon burst into laughter. "See? The Draugh said it would happen. She executed herself!"

"Good," Asveig said.

Shaking off their adrenaline, the Vigardians chuckled amongst themselves and pulled back to Solhall. The last of the sun sank over the horizon.

THAT EVENFALL, the lords of Solhall feasted with the Draughammr at the mead hall as they prepared for their looming campaign. Weremen roared with drunken laughter and caroused in the private yard.

It was the smell everyone noticed first, like a thousand rotten fish. Some laughter died away, though most warriors were too drunk to notice anything amiss—until a wyrmhead crashed into the yard.

The Vigardians screamed and dispersed into the hall. Skálda dismounted from Bale's back, drenched in steaming brown ichor. She dragged the decapitated head down the hall and tossed it over the long table at the front. Wet brains upturned the mead cups spilling over the trenchers.

The Wereguild's commanders gawked at her, but it was Soren, seated in the center, his great skáldwolf furs freshly pressed, that appeared the most dumbstruck.

Wiping her face, Skálda said, "I need to wash. What hour did you say we're leaving?"

9

WORTH A THOUSAND WERE SAVAGES

Eyrekvald Ivarion, Second Rider of the Order, greatest of all Dragonlords, waited in the cold. His enhanced eyes traced the eastern gap between Mt. Kóri and the Nifvinter Mountains. Even with a dragon's soul coursing through his, he could not see as well as an elf. But the enhancement still gave him thrice his normal range of vision.

The rest of his ground forces were drawing closer from the east. He felt it in the trembling air, gusts that skirted and fled him. Presently, his commanders would be exiting the Vigardian kingdom of Isgardia. Any day now, they would enter Dussex's southern border, appearing below, in the narrow Ískjall Pass that emptied into more uncharted pine forests. A plethora of dark zones surrounded him, waiting to be turned into Dragonsteel warzones. As the Lord Prince's Second Rider, all he had to do was stamp the warboards with his seal. He spitefully considered whether to mark them as a Level 8 or 9 warzone...

His post seconds awaited on the rock ledge several steps behind him, keeping silent. Everyone was tense. Somewhere in the unknown forests below, a raven called ominously. Thane's colossal shadow passed in and over them, patrolling the foothills and wealds. If any Wereguild were hiding nearby, they would not dare attack. Eyrek almost wished they would. It was all he needed to turn this pristine landscape into red tiles on the Order's boards—tiles marking open war.

Summer though it was, the befogged skies grew darker in the early hour. The Northern cold penetrated his thick Ebrennian furs. With every beat that he waited, his hatred of the land deepened in his heart. These were his ancestral lands; as a Svennish and descendant of Vigardians, he felt the Deep North running through his blood. Yet it had betrayed him.

He would destroy it. He would Build on it. He would make Isgardia Kingdom's recent obliteration seem like nothing to the Were King.

The obsession of it resurged him with thrill. Leondran Astoraine, his greatest political enemy in the Republic, was dead. He was liberated. There was no one left to stand in his way; no one in the Elenntarien to stop him from burning all the Deep North for taking his crown.

At last, the sound of boots crunching over a needle carpet made them shift out of their private musings. A silver-blond head appeared over the slope.

"Finally," Detherys called. "Sloth."

Eyrek offered a gloved hand, pulling Garreck onto the ledge. "Brother," he greeted, and they clasped arms.

"My Lord." The young elf panted and nodded at Torsten and Detherys behind him. "Forgive the delay."

"You have everything you need?" said Eyrek.

"My riders finished scouting. The lands for the post are cleared. I submitted our tiles to the Order for officiation." The elf nodded over the ledge, to the village that lay atop a bluff overlooking shallow streams. Already, his engineers and stoneworkers were a third of the way through building a curtain wall.

"A strategic location, isn't it? We are surrounded by smaller hills. We can develop those into watch towers. The rivers are abundant and the forests are few, but close enough for timber. It would make a Wereguild surprise attack difficult." Garreck rubbed his riding gloves together for warmth. "I have decided to name her Tera Vera."

Eyrek smiled, and switched from Elondrian to Garreck's mother tongue. "*Thir'anara taurenn.*" A good name. Sensing their need for privacy, Torsten and Detherys pulled away from the ledge.

"So, your first post." Eyrek nodded at the silver dragon ring on his thumb. It was a recent reward from Exar'forda, the High Post. "Why did it take you so long to start one?"

Garreck joined his side, and together, they gazed out over the unforgiving forests.

"Do you remember how we met?" the elf said, replying in the elvish speech.

A raven called again. It was so silent out there, in the unknown north.

"Mayhap not," said Garreck. "You have recruited so many to your cause. But I could never forget."

They listened to the comforting beat of Tythandrell's wings.

"Six weeks before you arrived at Felraseer, my father sold me as a slave to Carrion Watch. I was the youngest of six, bearing human ancestry... As you know, it rendered my worth naught to the Empire." Their gazes flickered awkwardly for a moment. "The captain treated me worse than a ha'elf. I was striped and starved like a beast. When I caught ill, he did not have the silvermarks or care to send me to a physicker... And then, you arrived."

Eyrek kept his eyes on the dark wilderness.

"You were searching Rildion's outskirts for new riders. But you found none worthy. Of course not." Garreck laughed softly. "We were scum, all of us, hopeless, immoral little rantipoles that tried to thieve from your wagons. Before you left, you noticed an elf-child tossed out in the garrison's cesspit. The child was so ill, he did not stir. You were the only one in all the Empire who would climb waist-high into the feculence and lend a hand. You pulled me out. You looked into my eyes, and you said, 'Follow me.'"

"I remember."

"I have not Built a post until now," said Garreck, "because I found more passion in following you."

Emotion weighed on Eyrek. When they first met, Eyrek had not even been a Duke himself. Yet this elf had followed him for almost as long as Torsten. He was a direct recruit, one of Eyrek's family.

"Garreck," he murmured, "you know the risks of what I am asking. But it is an ask, not a command. Are you certain you would Build here?"

"If this is our best chance of luring the Were King, then yes. I will follow you, my Lord."

Eyrek turned then, clenching his shoulders. "Do not engage in any attacks until our land forces arrive. I must have them positioned below that pass and ready to ambush the Wereguild. If they attack before we are ready, you will abandon the post and pull your riders back to the mountain. Swear it."

"Count it done, Lordship."

It was so difficult to let go. Perhaps because when he looked at Garreck, he saw his Dragonlords' severed heads. He saw all of Tera Beren burning. But he forced himself to smile roughly.

"Well, Duke, you are now one of my post seconds. You know my standards. I fully expect you to hasten to Dragonlord rank."

Garreck called in Elondrian over his shoulder, "Hear that, Ulvrik? Hasten to Dragonlord rank, novice man!"

The Baron muttered in the Svenning. Garreck returned a smile to Eyrek. "Tribulation is strength, my Lord."

"Tribulation is strength. Stay alert, brother."

His new Duke bowed low and left to make the climb back to Tera Vera Post. When Eyrek stayed on the ledge, staring after the spot where Garreck had been, Detherys came to stand by him.

"I am sending him to the wolves," said Eyrek.

"He's Garreck. Garreck is worth one thousand Were savages. He'll take care of himself."

Leofraen Amanoor was worth one thousand Were savages, he almost said. And so were Rowenna, and Damorlin, and all their riders. Yet they had fallen in one night. He could not shake the haunt that he was reliving that last night in Tera Beren, saying goodbye to a family member he would never see again.

"My Lord!"

The new shout stole him out of his troubles. Rhysaeran Velandrion leapt onto the ridge with two imperial guards. Detherys and Torsten immediately did obeisance, clearing a path for him and Eyrek.

"Your Grace," they murmured.

"Prince," Eyrek acknowledged.

"Our cavalry is moving faster than expected," said Rhysaeran. "I have an early arrival standing by at the pass. Two cohorts. An emergency force."

"Send them to Garreck at once."

The High Elf retreated to relay his orders, his face unreadable with shadow. Eyrek clenched his sword hilt and glanced at his awaiting seconds. "Our purpose today is done. Go, and Build your respective posts. The Were King will come to attack one of them... We will find out which soon."

They saluted him and swiftly called for their dragons. Eyrek glanced back at Tera Vera, his last post to deploy. If his land forces reached the pass in time, his host would be positioned and ready to capture the Were King.

10

GARRECK KINGSLEY

AT THE DAWN of their march against Tera Vera, Lord Jarmon brought Skálda out to the train, keeping her under guard. It would be a heavy march, with most Vigardians travelling by foot like her, along with three massive dragon slayers on wheels and a cage for Bale.

At this hour, everyone was present. Soren appeared on his destrier last, cantering to the front. Seeing the Draugh, Asveig bellowed a forward march. One thousand Vigardians with shields and axes moved toward the gate.

Skálda was the only one who stayed. Now that the day was here, she found the prospect of raising steel against her older brother paralyzing. She could not do it, not against the man she loved most in the world.

Her friends watched the activity from the longhouse Liv had been assigned. A few ogling thralls dared speculate where the Vigardian army was headed, but most kept their heads down and shuffled along. It was time for the thralls to begin fieldwork.

Faelan and Liv came to her first. Liv slipped her bread she had pilfered from the slave hall, while Faelan whistled. "Garreck Kingsley. I haven't met him, but I've heard of him plenty. One of the most brilliant Builders in the Order."

"You don't think I can win a campaign against him."

"How many chapters does Bale have now?"

Skálda almost refused to answer. "54."

Faelan clenched her arm. "That is good. He was under 30 when we first met, remember?"

Kind words, but they did nothing to mollify her growing distress. Shouldering his way through, Mat said, "She doesn't like to be touched, dragon man." Then he squeezed her around the torso. "It'll be just like ritefest, yeah? You'll have to use your wits—assuming you still have any."

"I'm flattered."

"Just remember, this time, you're not competing against skitfishes, but one of your brother's Primarchs. I mean, Duke now. Try not to die."

"Try not to eat skit," she snapped, and jogged to join the departing train. The guards were waiting for her, among them Rulf. Her friends waved, though Mat closed his eyes and muttered, "Well, there goes my best friend."

A league into their march, they passed the tree line of what Rulf called the Völundr Reach, the northwoods east of Solhall. The chanting of many Svennish haunted the air. Behind the trees, a log temple appeared on a knoll. As Soren passed, he and his commanders bowed their heads. A great lamentation hung over Vingulmark's lands.

"What is it?" Skálda said.

Rulf kept his eyes at the dull bronze Sun on the back wall. In the shadows behind the temple's doors, it flickered weakly. "They are still in mourning."

"Mourning?"

"The Battle of Dromvoll Church."

"What of it?"

"It was a battle in Isgardia, dragon girl. Isgardia was a Vigardian kingdom. When the Wulfgars lost, all the lands and people burned. King Inaric was a close friend, the Draugh's Vigardian father. He is the reason why the Draugh ever wore Solhall's fallen crown, when none in the Wereguild were worthy to claim it. Inaric stood up for us and kept the dragon men out of Vingulmark. He did it by luring them to his own lands, to protect us."

Skálda narrowed her eyes. Rulf went on, "The elves captured his family, and Little Inaric was forced to turn against him. No one will say it, but the Wulfgars are dead. Even the children. Your dragon prince doesn't keep prisoners for long."

"Hold on," Skálda said, in disbelief. "An entire people burned?" Like Dellfast. But Rulf was speaking of an entire *kingdom*. "The Lord Prince did this?"

The marksman frowned at her. "Your brother. Who else?"

"Eyrek would never..."

"King Skitr is the most murderous man in all Elondria," said Rulf. "He has always been cruel to us."

"I know him. He has saved thousands of lives, gave them a better life under the Enterprise—"

"Oh, you *don't* know him, dragon girl."

Skálda tried to make sense of this. Eyrek was not a man to kill innocents. He rescued the wretched and the poor, hopeless commons like herself. It was what made him the most beloved rider on Elondria. She had witnessed it in the Skonkauld.

She glanced at Bale through the bars. He rested on his claws, listening to everything. Soren was not far ahead. Though his back was turned, she was certain he had overheard everything.

"Tera Beren." She pieced everything together. "You attacked Tera Beren. You stole his crown, everything he spent his life Building. How can you fault him for wanting to burn you to the ground?"

Soren laughed. Lord Jarmon, on the saddle beside him, glanced over his shoulder. "Careful, thrall. If you do not mind your tongue, I will cut it out."

"Are you sure you will annul the elf?" Rulf cocked a lazy brow at her. "When you're defending Skitr?"

"Stop speaking of him in the Draugh's presence," Asveig called. "This is enough."

Worry pressed on her. She had given her oath to Soren to annul Lord Garreck. If she turned on him now, he would kill her and Bale... What if she encountered Eyrek at Tera Vera?

"You told me your brother is a good man," Bale offered. *"Is he?"*

She shared with him her recent memories of Eyrek in the Skonkauld. *He is more than that. He's... everything to me.*

"He's good meat, yes. You must tell him what happened at Dellfast. Once he finds out, he'll turn against the Dragon Chainer. Don't you think?"

You're right.

Eyrek would take an audience with her. Perhaps she could even get the two men to ally with each other against their true enemy. It was the only choice she had. Soren would have to cut off her hand before she ever struck her brother.

On the second day of their march, they entered deeper into the Völundr forests. All signs of human life vanished. Though it was midsummer, the air dropped in temperature. It was so dark in here, not a ray of the lustrous, golden strata above touched the forest floor. It smelled of dew and fog; raven calls and the shuffle of boots on detritus were the only noises. Yet it was strangely comforting to her, this untamed darkness. Out here, the Order's reign seemed so far away.

It was near midday when the rush of water vitalized the cool air. From the front, Soren pulled the reins and dismounted. Slipping off his boots, he ventured barefoot over the lush mosses.

"Halt!" Asveig shouted.

Chainmail jangled as the Vigardian army rolled to a stop.

Skálda glanced at Bale, her brows raised. Everyone waited in the forest's silent tranquility. No one asked questions.

The spongy mosses yielded to Soren's bare soles. He stopped where the soaring northpines ended and knelt before a river bank. A mountain fall cascaded over the rocks. The waters tossed, letting out wild roars. The Draugh cupped both hands into the untamed river and raised dirt and dripping water to his face. He kneaded the black earth with his fingers. Some great emotion overcame him, and he shut his eyes.

Not a single Vigardian interrupted, but a sacred reverence kept them in silence. Skálda hiked to Asveig's mounted stature. "What is he doing?"

"He loves this land." The wistful sheen in the warrior's eyes reflected the king. "A long time ago, he came to it in chains. Old Svenn obeys him now. It *is* him. No one greater has come before him to lead us, and no one ever will."

As Soren beheld water and earth, his commanders withdrew into a strange emotion. Skálda interpreted it as grief, nostalgia, and always, that reverberant love that, for some reason, felt familiar.

"We will camp here," Asveig called.

The warbands broke into cohorts and chopped wood. The Draughammr and his shield-brothers shared a private fire. As Rulf spitted a salted boar they had brought for the road, Asveig noticed her wandering alone and waved at her. "Thrall! Come share our fire."

Skálda stopped before the Draughammr. "I'm not hungry," she told him. He was sharing a log with Asveig and passing around crackled skewers.

"Can I have my axe back?"

Soren flicked his gaze up at her. His commanders glanced at her splinted wrist. Their expressions showed puzzlement, even distrust, but Soren nodded at Asveig, who nodded at the other two.

Lord Jarmon scowled. Rulf, being the youngest, got up and slipped into their tent. "Catch, dragon girl!"

The marksman tossed, and Aracir spiraled through the air. One miss could mean steel in her breast.

Skálda raised her right hand and caught it by the haft.

The men quieted, impressed. Catching a flying axe like that was an old Vigardian skill. What they did not know was the immense pain shooting down her arm as she stalked away.

Lord Jarmon chuckled. "Perhaps you need to break it again, Draugh."

Behind her, Soren murmured to Asveig, "She is nothing but bones. When has she last eaten?"

"I cannot say," Asveig admitted.

While the hordes of men caroused and laughed at their fires, Skálda skulked along the camp's perimeters, watching the forest floor for moving shadows. Squirrels darted about the trees. Her belly pulled with intense hunger, but she ignored the mouthwatering smells of meat and tried to focus. Seeing the next squirrel, she tossed Aracir with her left hand.

Her aim was off. It missed the entire tree.

Clenching her jaw, she left camp to retrieve her axe deeper between the conifers. At first, the Vigardians ignored her. But for the next hour, she tossed—and missed every single time. The men could not help but notice. Soren's attention flickered to her more than anyone else.

Skálda missed squirrels, ravens, even a pheasant. It drew more and more of her frustration. She was never this poor of a shot in the Skonkauld, and throwing with her left hand felt like learning the axe all over again.

One hour later, most of the Weremen had left their firepits and, on Asveig's order, packed up. Skálda kept hunting, despite her exhaustion. The next time the pheasant reappeared between the shrubs, she glanced down at her splinted hand. Transferring

Aracir from her left to right, she counted the throbbing pulses under her sweating temple. On the third count, she threw with all her might.

It was like barbed arrows shooting down her wrist to her elbow, searing the flesh. Skálda screamed. Hot tears spilled out of her eyes. The pain had set Aracir entirely off course. The pheasant saw the axe sailing overhead and pattered away into the underbrush, vanishing for good.

Skálda sank onto her heels, grinding her teeth against tears of agony. The Wereguild commanders were the few still sitting around a fire. Soren said, "What is she doing?"

Asveig murmured back, "Her dragon. She is hunting for fresh quarry. It won't eat what we feed it."

"Because you feed it skit."

"It's all we can spare."

Wiping her tears, Skálda willed herself to stand and fetch Aracir again. Her wrist was aflame and swollen again. Several nearby Vigardians taunted her. She gazed about the trees for another squirrel.

"Dragon girl!"

Soren gestured to the roasted pig. Shoulders hunching in exhaustion, Skálda lowered her axe and trudged to his fire.

"But Draugh," Jarmon protested, "that's enough meat to fill us for another—"

"You may take it all," said Soren.

Bowing her head, Skálda murmured, "Thank you, Draugh." She skulked past him and attempted to lift the spit, but it was unwieldy with one hand. Skálda closed her eyes and reached with her right to augment the weight.

"Rulf, help her." Soren guzzled water from his freshly filled skin. "We are departing," he told her. "I don't have time for you to picnic with your dragon. Toss it through, and if you cannot keep up, we will cut you loose."

He marched past her and shouted orders. Skálda avoided his eyes. He had meant, they would cut her throat.

As she fed Bale through the bars, he nuzzled her in ever deepening affection.

On the morning they would arrive at Tera Vera, the forests grew sparser. Through the openings of the cedars, Skálda gazed out into the western distance. Steel clouds hung over the land. On this summer day, even the jewel of the skies would not show itself.

"The land hurts," Bale observed from his cage.

Wintry gusts scraped her face. The palpable enmity between Eyrek and Soren burdened the air. It sank deep beneath the earth's roots; the river surface below the dark slopes rippled like grass blades shivering in the mistrals. Their hatred was poisoning all the Deep North. Above all, it was gall to her soul.

"A continental war is already here," she murmured to Bale. "And we are caught in the middle of it."

"They'll break this earth," he said uneasily. *"But we'll share rashers with your brother, make him our friend. Maybe he likes wyrmheads?"*

Skálda was suddenly uncertain she could turn the two kings into friends.

"Halt!" Soren shouted.

She and Bale looked at each other. *It's time,* she said. A thousand bloodwyrms were writhing in her belly. She prayed to Finngólfa, and all the Svennish gods, she would not meet Eyrek today.

"Thrall!"

Skálda pulled away from Bale. Everyone stayed put as the Draughammr and his commanders spurred their mounts off the road. She jogged to catch up to Soren. He did not glance at her. "Is it enough?"

"Enough for what?"

His lower lip was edging into a sneer. He was mocking her.

"No, it isn't enough," she snapped. "Bale's 54 chapters against Lord Garreck's 1,000—"

"1,014."

"Finngolfa's ravens!" she swore under her breath. How was everyone in Aranor Elondris advancing so fast while she trundled along with her Bael?

"When your dragon comes against his..." Rulf tsked. "He'll turn you to vapor."

Soren dismounted. Skálda followed him and squatted by the tree line, where the Völundr Reach ended in a sharp drop. This was a valley abundant with small ponds and lakes, all dull beneath the oppressive clouds. The dragonpost roosted itself on the highest of the foothills. An eight-foot stone wall with round turrets already fortified it. Ravens, she thought, the Duke moved fast. Eyrek's colors, a gilt crowned sun against crimson, flapped from the crenellations.

She studied the landscape. Of all the zones Garreck could have claimed in the North, he had selected his with ingenious strategy. Out here, he had plenty of resources like water and timber, yet he would also spot an ambush from several leagues. It was the perfect spot for a dragonpost, though not everyone would have noticed it; she certainly would not have, not on her own. Before them was an advanced Builder.

Skálda doubted herself all over again. She could not bring herself to assault a rider Eyrek loved. Of course, this was all assuming that, with her amateur amount of chapters, she would not be cleaved apart.

The commanders finalized their plans in murmurs. Sobs in the wind caught her attention. The post's gates parted a slit. Six horsemen hauled a family of commons along by rope. Among them were two children Frit's age. The woman pleaded with them, but the soldiers ignored them and tugged them inside. The gates shut again.

"What are they doing?" Skálda said.

Soren pointed. Across the rocky, taupe shore, a pile of bodies smoked at the edge of the river. "The remains of Rekya Village."

"They killed the commons?" Skálda hissed. "Why?"

"The Elessir prefers not to have a human stain to manage. Easier to cleanse the zones and bring in more elves. Civilized work force. Better population out here for the Order than free human savages, no?"

At Skálda's disgusted look, Asveig said, "Do not say your brother would never do such a thing."

"He is human!"

"He is a thrall," said Jarmon. "An elvish weapon of war. Why do you suppose the Lord Prince dotes on him, a human? Are you a fool?"

"Those commons escaped," Soren said, "and they will be purged like the rest on Lord Elessir's orders. Does that answer your question?"

Skálda clenched her axe. They could not be twisting the truth. She remembered the way Lord Rystendal had treated the human riders of Skoll Post; the way Kirylith and her Rangers beat Aesir in Wyre Village. And Dellfast—that she would never forget. Power in Elondria lay with the elves; it always had. To the Lord Prince, human riders were expendable, perhaps no more than a political necessity to fabricate unity between men and elves. It was all only to please the Elenntarien. And suddenly, her anger returned in low flames.

"Good." Skálda stood. "This will be suitable practice for Bale and me when we go to face the Lord Prince."

The commanders glanced at her with surprise. As she marched back through the trees, Soren ordered, "Stop."

"I told you I would annul Garreck Kingsley. I said it would be a one-day campaign, but I think I will not even need the full day. Neither do I need any of your men getting in my way."

Soren laughed. "You really thought I would give this campaign to you?"

"You brought me here, didn't you?" She spread her arms. "And what do you suppose will happen when you lay siege on the Duke? You think he won't flee to my brother? What will you have left but pickings of his ground forces?" She curled her lip in a taunt. "All you will do is advance him to Dragonlord. The elf will Build on your bones."

The Weremen glanced at Soren.

"Stay in the trees, Draugh." She flexed her shoulders. "Do not deploy your dragon slayers. Do not show yourself, or you *will* lose the campaign." She tossed him Aracir. "Here!" He caught it only by reflex. "Keep it for me." His shield-brothers gaped at her.

Skálda returned to the awaiting contingent. "Bale!" she said. He was quiet on his foreclaws, but at her call, he raised his head attentively. She freed the latch to his cage and hopped in, drawing roars from the Weremen. Skálda climbed onto Bale's back just as Soren and his shield-brothers reemerged through the conifers.

They glanced at their king, their hands readied on their axes. But Soren gave no orders to stop her.

"*Éad'hel,*" she murmured.

Bale wriggled out of the cage, his ominous frame taking no account for the Weremen in his way. They dove to escape his maw. In several beats, Bale cleared the treetops, and they were streaming above the river valley, straight for the post.

It only took three breaths for the Elevere, the horn of the Order, to ring over the hills. "*Dah-laa'h!*" it bayed ominously, in elvish high notes. The post watch had spotted them. Skálda tightened her grip on Bale's spike, breathing quietly to steady the galloping in her chest. This was just like ritefest, Mat had said... except they were not racing to Hrafjenfall.

Bale alighted on the parapet above the gate, sinking his talons into the stone. The human guards on duty rushed out of the way, gasping at the sight of her young dragon.

"Garreck Kingsley!" she shouted.

A score of uniformed guards rushed into the yard. Tera Vera was little more than a stone wall built over a captured hamlet. She traced her eyes over the longhouses. The elvish ruling lord had left no human common alive, not even to till for him. In their place, his wide-eyed riders looked up from cabbage patches. It was a ridiculous sight, and flaunted the depth of hate for her kind.

An older elf marched out of a tower still under construction, accompanied by more guards. Skálda murmured the *Lhaer'thri* over him and read 102 chapters. *Not him,* she told Bale.

"The post second. Looks stringy."

The Ealdorman stopped below the gate, shouting, "Archers!"

Where are the dragons?

Bale turned his neck. *"The barns. No eyrie built yet."*

As the guards on the parapet trained dozens of bows on her, she traced her eyes over the hamlet. He was right. Young chethems were poking their heads through a barn door near the tower. Catching scent of the males, Bale tossed his horns belligerently.

"You are surrounded!" the second hollered.

"Where is your leader?"

They spoke to each other in Elondrian. The Ealdorman glared up at her. His riders rushed to back him. They were all young Fair Elves by the looks of their short tapers. No High Elvish mages she needed to fear here.

When none would speak, Skálda shouted at the skies, "Garreck!"

A last elf emerged from the tower. He wore his long, silver-gold hair over his shoulders, tucked behind his sharp ears. A flowing robe, laid over a glistening white vest, brushed his tall boots as he marched. Resting his hand on his elvish longsword, he raised his dark eyes at her. Her belly clenched, but only for a moment. Would he recognize her from their brief meet earlier last spring?

"Who calls?" he said.

Skálda indulged him with a smile.

"Speak quickly," said Lord Garreck. "Post and rank."

Perhaps he did not remember her. After all, they met briefly under the cover of night, and Bregan Island had been disorderly with the crowds.

Everyone was tense. It was a most unsettling occurrence for a post to encounter an unannounced rider. She remembered the effect Eyrek's arrival had on the Skonkauld not so long ago. Yet the post leader was pointedly twirling his silver ring around his thumb. He was too smug in his rank to fear her.

Skálda sneered down at him. "Look at where we are, Garreck. You think I have a rank?"

The younger elves gasped. The post second roared, "You will address the Lord Duke properly!"

"My name is Kvael-Akar, Duke of scum, and you Build on my lands!"

Astonishment silenced the post. Yet Garreck kept his eyes on her, his wiry frame more self-possessed than when they first had met.

The Ealdorman leaned over and whispered, "It's possible, my Lord. Did the Order not mention Lord Rystendal is hunting a *kvael-akar?*"

Garreck kept twirling his ring.

"Need to gnaw his bones some more," Bale suggested.

"You have stolen and killed my subjects, *Elessir*," she mocked. Out in the Republic's fringes, it was a human's deferential form of address for an elf. "Do you suppose you will have my mercy?"

"What if it is a Wereguild trap?" the second whispered.

"Unlikely," Garreck murmured. "Their *mahlenn* king abides no riders." He shouted back at her, "*Kvael-akar,* you are an idiot for coming here. Your dragon has 54 chapters. Do you even know whom you are speaking to?"

"You think I fear you? Rystendal Vacerys is a foe to be regarded, yet I bespelled his dragon and evaded him time and again. What are you compared to him?" She laughed. "I will feed your silly pointed ears to my beast!"

Bale shook his head. *"Don't like elf gristle."*

"An affinite," the post second whispered in surprise.

"Or she is bluffing."

"Come face me like a grown rider, elf-child!"

"I'll give the order to shoot," said his second.

"Stand down!" Lord Garreck commanded his post. The archers lowered their bows. "Do you take me for a fool?" he said to her. "I have the Order's warnings about you. But rest assured, I will transmit your presence here to Exar'forda. His Lordship has sealed you for death."

"I take you for a coward," she jeered. He dismissed his goggling riders and marched back to his tower. Skálda barked, "Flee from me, little elf! But mark me, your invasion of my holdings will not go unpunished. I will return. I will send your bloody ring back to Exar'forda. I will tell them they gave it to the wrong Duke."

Bale snarled and sprang back into the skies. As they soared away from the post, Skálda waited. The mild winds kept them suspended in a glide.

He's not coming, she said in dismay.

"You didn't gnaw on him enough."

You think gelding him on Rysten's name in front of all his riders wasn't enough? If that wasn't enough to—

A dragon's roar thundered over the hills.

"Skit," she said. "He's coming. Go, Bale!"

He pounded his wings faster, surging them into an acceleration. As they streaked over the Völundr Stretch, she felt Soren and his Vigardians gazing up at them from the shadows.

What had taken their heavy train eight days to traverse blurred by on dragonback. A second, larger shadow rushed over the trees. Skálda glanced over her shoulder.

Lord Garreck rode a silvery jade eldragon larger than Asulf, the late Lord Alarek's eld. The bestiaries had taught her that elds were one of the swiftest dragons in Elondria. Skálda screamed above the winds for Bale to fly faster, but even with a five-minute lead time, the adult eld was rapidly closing the distance.

They made it to the end of the Völundr's endless reach when the eld dove for Bale. It snapped its jaws at his head. Bale spiraled away. The eld whirled deftly with him, sinking its hind talons into Bale's flank. Bale bellowed, beating his tail against the eld. It pinioned him, forcing him into a rapid drop toward the rolling mead below.

Skálda was aghast. Bale was hardly strong enough to throw off the larger male dragon. Within the minute, Garreck would crush them against the ground at full speed. They were going to die.

Lord Garreck loomed over her from his saddle, his eyes bright with bloodthirst. "See?" his lips said. "I knew you were nothing, *kvael-akar*."

The Thurs Runja valley rushed ever closer. Bale strained to fight against the eld. Garreck's dragon sank its teeth into his right wing membrane. Bale roared. Skálda screamed with him, feeling his pain through the Binding.

Fifteen feet from their crash, a firewyrm burst out of the earth. The eld shrieked, caught by surprise, and veered away. While the wyrm bathed the eld's side in fire, Bale, now freed, beat his wings just in time to slow himself from a crash. But his hind legs touched the mead, then his foreclaws. He deaccelerated in a gallop. Skálda screamed, "Get off the ground! Get off the ground!"

It was only the eight-count that saved them. He launched himself back up just as a mass of wyrms split the earth.

"Skit," she gasped. Bale's landing had awakened so many, a bed of at least twenty. Their shared adrenaline scored their chests.

They had no time to plan their next move, for Garreck was already locked in a sharp dive. His eld stayed fearless in the path of the wyrms. The Duke called, "*Ciryamor!*"

A translucent green shield alighted in front of him, demolishing the wyrms in his way. It split the heads off the smaller wyrms, but even the large ones whimpered and retreated under the earth.

Skálda's head spun. She suddenly loathed herself for putting them through this campaign. What had she been thinking? The most difficult endeavor on the continent was advancing a dragon, and Garreck had advanced to the Order's second highest rank. She would never overpower him.

"Not overpower," Bale panted, as he maneuvered around bursts of wyrms. He recalled her ritefest victory through their Binding's mind-share. *"Outsmart."*

The clouds parted, and sunlight spilled over the fields. At its touch, all the wyrms mewled and fled back into the earth.

"No!" She clenched her fist.

Lord Garreck let go of the Dragonshield. His flight extended its claws to grab Bale, but her dragon folded his wings, forced to crash into the mead. Skálda shut her eyes, clinging to his neck spike as they rolled several times. The eld's outstretched talons shattered the earth behind them. Bale hastened to spring back into flight. Lord Garreck summoned the Dragonshield back just as six angry wyrms wriggled out to snap at him.

The sunlight faded in and out, keeping the wyrms underground. Bale fought to ascend. The eldragon circled around for them. Skálda's first instinct was to panic. It was as Rulf had said. Bale's chapters were nothing compared to this Duke's eld. They were losing the fight. But she recalled how, during her ritefest earlier that spring, she had fallen over the Third Flight. She had kept calm. She had found a way to victory.

This was her fall over the Third Flight, but she was going to pull herself and Bale back up again.

We need to awaken the Big One, she said. *Garreck's shield will repel all the other wyrms.*

Bale squandered no time and drew deep within his belly, roaring as if unleashing dragonfire to lure the titan out.

"*Ruthra'ruín!*" Garreck shouted, drawing his longsword.

Dragonstrength. A new spell unlocked at Duke rank. It would give him the equivalent strength of his dragon, and he would have over 1,000 chapters to burn through before the eld exhausted. One stick of that sword into Bale, and her dragon's innards would spill open in a red cascade.

Bale's roaring was not enough to draw out the Big One. Skálda closed her eyes. The Third Flight, she reminded herself. Against the raging winds, she sensed Garreck streaming closer.

She lost herself in the Binding, and rushed Bale with heartfelt warmth and courage. Feeling her surge of emotion, he responded back, reciprocating her. Their Binding reverberated with hot energy. With their minds fused, Skálda roared with him across the mead.

The sound that came out was neither human nor dragon, but exponentially greater. Skálda sent Bale an image in her mind to fly close to the ground again. Garreck watched them stream back to the mead for a moment, then followed voraciously.

Bale flew parallel to the grass. In her head, Skálda counted the beats. Garreck was gaining.

On the sixth count, Skálda screamed through their Binding, *Pull up!*

Bale obeyed. A gargantuan chitinous head sundered the earth. The valley roared and quaked. Its maw compassed them, soaking them in shadow. Skálda glanced below her in dread. It would have swallowed her and Bale whole, if not for the eld beneath them. The Big Wyrm closed its jagged, dagger-length saws over the larger dragon, catching both its hind legs. The eld shrieked, beating its wings with all its strength, but the larger predator dragged it back to the earth.

Lord Garreck tumbled off the saddle, landing on his hands. "Aeyrinth!" he bellowed.

As Bale took them higher, she glanced at the mead far below. It was appalling, seeing a dragon eaten by another lifeform. Aeyrinth resisted the pull by spreading his wings, like elbows pinning the earth. But the wyrm kept tugging. The eld groaned, and his head vanished beneath the wildflowers.

Bale looped over the silent field.

Lord Garreck was still on all fours. His eyes were frozen wide. In only a few beats, he had lost his dragon. As reality startled to settle in, he tore his hair and howled at the sky.

He bayed, and bayed.

A cloud passed over the sun, and the skies darkened again. The elf keened louder. Hundreds of burrows broke the earth's surface. They were slithering to him.

Dozens of eyeless wyrms poked their heads out of the ground. Gravel sprinkled the grasses. These wyrms came in all sizes and grotesque shades. Even from up here, Skálda caught wind of their rancid fish stench. The elf quieted, and looked up.

They tittered, clicking their many mandibles together. Garreck's eyes stretched wider.

For a few beats, it was eerily silent.

They lunged. Garreck attempted to run, but they caught him by each of his limbs. The wyrms held him down, and sucked him up. Garreck wrestled, cursed them all, wept. Skálda and Bale watched quietly as a last wyrm kissed him, silencing his screams.

11

I FEAR IT IS A BEGINNING

Soren was furious with her.

"You lured him straight to Solhall!" he bellowed. Behind him, his men hauled open the gates of the captured post. All the riders had fled, but the ground forces were trapped inside.

Skálda ignored him, scouring the hamlet for the Svennish commons the guards had hauled in earlier. He jerked her around by the arm. "Do you hear?"

"Why does it matter?" she said, irritated. "He's dead."

"And if you failed?"

"But I didn't fail." She tugged herself free and jogged away.

"I will have your head, thrall!"

Skálda pulled to a halt. "*Sorenthor Astoraine.*"

All the nearby Vigardians hissed at her use of his Republic name. She glanced over her shoulder.

"When I campaign," she said, "I do not lose."

Activity rushed into the background. At any moment, the Weremen would begin their slaughter. Skálda hurried to untie the commons and whispered, "Stay by my dragon. He will keep you safe."

They wept and pressed their foreheads against her good hand. The children rushed to hug Bale's monster talons. He rumbled with pleasure, curling his tail around them. Skálda climbed onto his back just as the Weremen were drawing their axes.

"Dragonpost of Tera Vera!"

At her bellow in Elondrian, Vigardians and Ebrennians alike stopped to peer up at her.

"Who is the commander here?"

After a pause, a chained Ebrennian wrestled himself out of a Wereman's grip. "I am," he spat.

"What is your name?"

"Renvar Trevin."

"I am Skálda Branwright," she said, "of no rank, and no post. You will kneel—"

"I never kneel to *kvael-akar*!" he snarled. "Lord Eyrekvald tolerates no traitors—"

"This is my dragon, Baelaeryx." She patted his sleek black neck. "You fear Lord Eyrekvald? He would behead you. But if you do not kneel in the dust, Renvar Trevin, and swear your sword to King Sorenthor, my dragon will decide, depending on his mood, whether to eat you or reunite you with your wretched Elessir."

Soren glanced at her in surprise, the anger in his brows levelling.

"I won't repeat myself," said Skálda.

"A-alright." Swallowing, the petty officer dropped to his knees. "I swear my sword to—"

"Not to me." Skálda pointed at Soren. "To him."

The commander hurried to do her bidding. When she presented the same offer to the rest of the Ebrennians, they clambered over themselves to follow their leader's example.

Skálda climbed down from Bale and joined Soren's side. "Fortunate we don't have a Vigardian bloodfest on our hands," she said, surveying the post. "And you have two hundred more thralls with no men lost today, as promised. Brilliant strategy, Draugh."

He regarded her without expression. Or thanks. Stubborn mule.

She looked up him and down. "So? Where's my axe?"

WHEN SOLHALL CAME into sight again, eight days later, the gates were already open. The Svennish people stood outside the walls, cheering for the Vigardian train. Their return meant victory. And they were doubly uproarious to see their none of their Vigardian family members had been lost.

"*Draughammr! Draughammr! Draughammr!*"

Skálda kept pace by Bale's cage, staying silent, but Soren glanced back at her. Rulf reined his mare around to loop a familiar arm around her. "*Draughammr, Draughammr,*" he drawled into her ear, to annoy her. Skálda elbowed him aside, though she could not help her smile. Lord Jarmon kept scowling. Asveig looked troubled.

She found her friends outside the private slave district where the riders quartered, their faces and arms blackened from dirt. They were feeding the dragons, but hearing the approaching contingent, they turned to the road. Seeing her, Faelan and Liv waved with vigor. Incendra and the picas roared her a greeting. It turned more heads around them.

"Ravens, she's alive!" Mat sprinted across the dirt. Paying no heed to the Vigardians guarding her, hulks armed to the teeth, he shouldered through them and hugged her, pretending a sob. "I can't believe it... Feorya and I even prepared your funeral rites and everything."

"Thoughtful, Mat."

"You really did it?" He let go of her. "You annulled the elf? A Duke?"

"It was just like ritefest, as you said."

He shook his head in disbelief. "And you're keeping her a thrall?" he cried to the Vigardians.

His sentimentalism made her fidget, especially since Soren had stopped to listen in. She cleared her throat loudly, but Mat did not pick up on the cue.

"Anders is awake," he said, as Faelan trotted over to join them. "You should go see him."

Feeling Soren's stare, she said, "I have to see to the children first."

Faelan was far less oblivious than Mat. As he approached her, he felt the loom of the Wereguild's supreme leaders. To her consternation, he even dared to look at Soren with open venom.

"Faelan," she hissed, pulling him into an embarrassed handshake. "Enough." The last thing she needed was to watch Lord Jarmon eviscerate her Dellfast friend.

"You and Liv are alright?" she whispered.

This pulled his attention back to her. He laughed. "I should ask the same of you. How did you do it?"

"Necessity."

"Necessity never kept Incendra and me from bleeding during a campaign."

She leaned in closer. "You and the other riders are alive because he still sees use in me. So, I had no choice but to win."

Humbling his deportment, Faelan murmured, "Never liked elves. It is too bad you can't Realm-Build, Skálda. You would make a dread post leader."

His words caught her by surprise. He clapped her back like a man and returned to Liv. Skálda's mouth formed a wistful line as she watched her friends resume feeding their dragons. Soren leaned into Asveig's ear, whispering something, then started his destrier forward again to the manse.

The white-bearded Vigardian pulled up beside her. "The Draugh says you may feed your dragon yourself."

Skálda raised her brows. Asveig nodded at Bale's cage, which stayed at a halt on the road. "He may come out of his bars, but he will stay collared. If he maims a single Svennish, the Draugh will see through executing him."

"Of course." Skálda bowed her head, waiting for him to pass before she looked up to catch Bale's eye. He returned her a dragonish grin.

After Skálda scrubbed Soren's butt-naked children clean with her bare hands, and washed and returned the children's dirty bowls to their proper places, she hurried back to the pasture. Frit poked her head out of the manse's entrance.

"Where're you going, Skálda?"

Skálda exhaled in annoyance and kept her rapid pace. "I need to feed my dragon."

"I want to feed him!"

Frit bounded to her and caught her good hand. Someone screamed behind them, "I feed! I feed!"

Evynd hobbled onto the road, vexing her even more. He tripped over his own feet and crashed onto his knees. A beat later, he erupted into screams, like she was trying to bloody murder him. With all her annoyance vanishing, Skálda rushed to scoop him up.

"Shh!" she hissed, looking wildly around for Soren. "Evynd, stop crying!" Amending her voice, she cooed, "You want to pet the dragon? I'll let you pet him, alright?"

Instantly, he perked up. "No, I want FEED HIM!"

"Yes! Alright. You can feed him, you sweet little princeling..."

He screamed in joy, his tears forgotten. To her relief, the Draughammr never appeared in the doorway with his axe.

Bale found her trundling down the hill with a toddler to her chest and an arm looped around the princess. He gushed in amusement. *"Sweet wolf. They share my mother."*

Don't ever call me that, she snapped. *I'm not your mother!*

Skálda set the toddler onto the grass and hopped into the cage with a dragon collar. Frit widened her eyes. The princess whispered to her brother that he was the "Mean Dragon," the one that killed four horses, maimed twelve Weremen, and snapped off Invar's hand.

"He won't bite you to death?" Frit whispered.

Skálda looked up at him. "I don't know. Will you, Bale?"

He snorted. *"I don't eat my mothers."*

She hefted the neck collar. *Lower your fat head. I can't reach you.*

Bale snapped his insidious teeth at her face. The children jumped back.

"He gonna eat her!" Evynd cried.

May you lower your head so I can let you out? Skálda bowed to him. *Kindly please, Bael, Your Great Mightiness?*

"Better, thrall." Growling, he extended his neck for her. *"But only this time."*

"My thanks, Your Majesty," she muttered.

A minute later, Skálda led Bale out of the cage on his iron chain. The collar Soren required of him was pricking his temper. If it were anyone else but her leashing him, he would have gorged them down. To let the continent know of his peevishness, he shook his horns and kneaded his front talons into the grass.

"So," said Skálda, "who wants to feed him first?"

Neither child raised a hand.

She stayed in the pasture that afternoon, showing Frit and Evynd how to flatten their palms when they offered the meat. That way, she explained, Bale would not accidentally decapitate their hands. Evynd resorted to hurling him pieces of mutton at a distance, his eyes wide. Dozens of Weremen gathered outside the corral, curious that the horned beast was tame with Skálda.

Once Bale put some weight into his belly, his bellicosity softened. He slumped into his foreclaws for a nap. After healing his wounds, she took the cloth and beeswax she had fetched from the manse and labored on her knees to polish his scales.

Frit said, "How aren't you afraid of him?"

"This lazy beast?"

Bale pulled back his lip to show his teeth. Skálda bent down lower to clean his stained claws. "Dirty beast, I mean." As she massaged, his growl softened into a purr.

"What a monster," Frit whispered. "Look at those talons."

"Monster," Evynd cooed.

"But I know it's all just pretend." Frit skipped to his neck and hugged him. Bale flicked open a slitted red eye, looking up at her. "You're actually just as nice as Skálda, aren't you?"

Bale grumbled. As if conceding, he wrapped his tail around her to return the hug. All the Weremen watching laughed.

Caught in a rare smile, Skálda turned her head. She accidentally met eyes with someone sitting at the edge of the pasture on a blanket. This was someone she had not spoken to for cycles. Her smile fading, she left Bale and the children and climbed over the corral to join the Fjorlander.

"Anders," she said.

"Skálda. Well met."

Together, they gazed out at the children leapfrogging around Bale. Frit and Evynd laughed as he tried to catch them in nuzzles.

"I had a feeling," he said finally.

Skálda glanced at him. It was impossible to read the emotion in those words. She stared at her hands.

"I am sorry," she said. "What happened to Skoll Post..."

"Look at you." He nodded at Bale. "Remember when we tried so hard to get the picas to hatch for you? Those days feel so long ago, don't they?"

She shared his smile.

"I can see why no other dragon Binded with you," said Anders. "You were meant to find each other. He is something special, like you."

This was Anders, always encouraging her when he should have been infuriated with her betrayal.

"I heard about the Duke." The Ealdorman took something from around his neck and pressed it into her hands. Skálda looked down. It was a necklace with a metal Sun glinting from the daylight.

It was a long moment before she could find words. "I had a feeling."

"I never wanted my personal faith to get in the way of reaching my people," he said. "So, I kept it hidden."

She felt the intensity of his discomfort. Anders was never one to speak of religious creeds or the Elenntarien's political factions. In some regions of the Republic, both topics could arouse people to murder. Yet for all his courage with her, she could not keep the disappointment from her voice.

"You hosted ritefest for us. I didn't want to think you bought into the idol of Sunblinded politicians."

"In the beginning, I joined the Enterprise only to Build," he said. "But as time went on, it became more of a means to give the orphans a better life."

"You always cared about the little dogs." She shrugged. "It's what made you a great post leader."

Emotion rarely beset her, but the truth was, Anders had raised her, and Mat, and Egil. It was Anders who taught her the axe, and how to survive a lonely world without Eyrek protecting her from the hunger and cold. He never expected anything in return. It was who he was.

He rubbed his neck self-consciously. "The truth is, Realm-Building became a way for me to turn children to Vaeritas."

She offered the Sun back. "I don't want it."

"Skálda, just consider—"

"The holy leaders of the Republic worship their Sun, yet they suck the blood out of their people. Which of them ever cared about the Skonkauld? We starved, and they still taxed us. And what have they done about Dellfast—"

"I taxed you."

"No, Anders. You gave from your own coffers to cover our portion."

He pushed the Sun back to her. "There are many evil men and elves who call themselves Vaeritians. The Suncreed is the Republic's instrument for uniting all the realms and races, no? But most politicians are not Vaeritas's true followers. His followers extend a hand to the broken, for that is the true Creed of the Sun. I have seen God's Light change stone hearts—"

"Anders, what's your point?"

"I fear, Skálda. I fear Garreck was not the end, but a beginning."

"He was an evil elf!"

"Your dragon is not evil. Neither are you."

"This is why you never made it past your 119 chapters," she hissed. "You would never strike leeches for bleeding you to death." Dropping the Sun on his lap, she marched out of the pasture. Her face was blistering. Bale felt her fury and trailed her with his glowing eyes.

"We should go," Frit whispered to her brother. "Bye, Bale!" They hurried to catch up with her, fighting each other to clasp her good hand.

Anders was lecturing her on becoming Sunblinded so she would turn too Sun-benevolent to annul more murderous elves?

She almost spat at the ground. What would he do if she told him she was going to annul his Vaeritian Lord Prince?

Yet perhaps she was not angry, but afraid. In attacking a Dragonsteel post and killing a rider, she had become not Builder, but Breaker. Tera Vera's fall was her doing, not Bale's. She was training him to Break, when what he wanted was to kill wyrms to help villagers.

For the first time, she wondered who the true Realm-Breaker was.

IN THE EVENING, while Skálda toiled in the scullery, Asveig passed along the Draughammr's summons. She wiped her soiled hands on her chemise and followed him out to the council room on the manse's second floor.

The other Wereguild leaders were already inside, seated at the tables and murmuring to each other. Soren was the only one standing by the warboard. He wore a linen tunic with a humble V neckline. At her entrance, he turned around a little quicker than usual.

Skálda wiped the sweat from her brow. "Yes, Draugh?"

"How is it doing?" He gestured to her wrist.

The question surprised her. Warily, she said, "The one you broke? Fine."

It was not fine. All the jostling on Bale's back had returned the swelling. Soren picked up on her pithiness and retreated behind an even stronger wall of apathy. "Sit, thrall."

"I'll stay standing."

"Your brother's remaining seconds have Built. Both posts thieve the lands and resources of my allies." He lifted his axe and tapped the warboard behind them. "The nearest, Ruadhán, is overseen by a Torsten Ulvrik."

Torsten. Her chest sank. She had also met Torsten at her ritefest.

"He is Svennish. Like us. Baron, a low rank. But he is the Ivarion's oldest rider and his closest friend." Soren studied her for a reaction. When he found none, he said, "Will you help me annul him?"

Skálda glanced between his commanders. None were sneering at her anymore. Her gaze flitted back to Soren, and to the filigreed Sun hanging over his molded chest. What did it mean to be Vaeritian? To be like Soren? Like Eyrek? Like Anders? They all thought themselves true sons of the Prince of Light.

Anders's appeal was gnawing at her.

"If I say no?" Skálda said. "Will you kill my dragon?"

Soren gave no reply.

"So you would not?" she challenged.

Quietly, he nodded at Asveig. The Vigardian stood to take her out, but Skálda waved at him to stay himself. She pulled back a chair, sat down, and planted her elbows on the table. Her deliberately pensive silence made them squirm.

"I will help you." She flicked her gaze up to Soren. "On one condition, Draugh."

He raised his brow.

"Never put me in another flaming dress." She slapped the table with her good hand and rose again. "I'll see myself out," she told Asveig. Just before she reached the doorway, Soren called to her.

"Skálda."

She turned. He lowered his axe awkwardly.

"Leave the work and get some rest," he said. "We head out in the morning."

12

A VISITOR ARRIVES IN KAR'THUUL-DÛR

JACCORIAS VIKARIE, Illuminator Exarch, and present Warden of Kar'thuul-dur Keep, examined his array of torture instruments. It was seldom these days when he had the time to "temper the inmates," as his brethren called it. But this was a prisoner that needed his personal attention from time to time.

After some deliberation, he settled on a bonebreaker, an easy little warmup, and padded over to his guest. The uneven stones were slick with blood that the drains had not sucked away yet.

He stopped a groat away from the prisoner's face. It irked Jaccorias that even with his emaciated arms wrenched over his slumped head, the young man still loomed over him. But to his triumph, the prisoner was as still as a raptor with broken wings. There was a time when this one had given such a fierce fight that it had taken six brothers just to tie him down.

His overpowering stink of festering skin, urine, and sonnifera did not bother Jaccorias. Quite on the contrary, he had grown to love the smell. All the prisoners of Kar'thuul-dur smelled this way, and they were kept naked. This was his policy, though it made cleaning the feculence more difficult. There was a pleasure to seeing their animal bareness break them over the days. Most of all, he loved to witness their bladders lose control during a particularly fruitful Illumination.

"It's me again," Jaccorias said, breathing his cheer onto the prisoner's face.

Of course, the prisoner could not see him well. Jaccorias's prentice had fitted a rusting iron mask over the inmate's face, shaped like a swine with a crown. He adored seeing this prisoner hang so defeated. Vaeritas knew getting to this point had taken a lot of hard work.

"Oh, come now," Jaccorias droned. "Not a single spit at me today?"

The chains rattled as the faceless prisoner swung quietly from his wrists.

"How are you healing, sha'daath?" The warden reached up to examine the knuckles on the prisoner's right hand. "It has been some time since your last Illumination. I thought you might be granted a longer respite before we gave it another go. Rest well? We'll start easy..."

The prisoner moaned something under his breath.

Jaccorias leaned in. "What was that, sha'daath?" He tsked. "You aren't healing as well as I hoped. No matter." He tossed the instrument back onto the table. "We can skip straight to the Illumination."

"Please," the prisoner muttered.

"Hah!" Jaccorias grinned. "Please, what?"

"Please, Agonmai..."

"Look at how polite you've become. We will only do ten minutes today, hmm? How about that?"

The walls of these chambers would be thick enough to blot out his screams. The prisoner wept. Jaccorias opened his mouth to speak the session into life, at the same time the cell door swung open.

"What in Vaeritas's Light!" he yelped.

Zarek, the block's gaoler, glanced away in fear. He knew Jaccorias was about to give him an earful. Before he could bellow in anger, two slender Rhaennörian guards in silver-gold mantles sallied to the front.

Jaccorias backed away in terror, his spine colliding against the wall. Elves. What was this? Was he under arrest?

A third elf sauntered through. The visitor was obscured by a flowing cloak of the purest white. It nearly blinded Jaccorias for all his days of lurking underground. The visitor stopped profile to him and pulled back his hood. All at once, Jaccorias saw a stunningly fair face, and the viciously sharp ears of a High Elf.

"You may leave," said the elf.

The Rhaennörian guards surged Zarek back out and shut the door. The elf turned his face portrait, bringing to light the hideous scar on the right side of his face.

"My name is Vharyn Morghûl, and I take it you are Jak."

Terror slammed into the warden. What by the Holy Sun was the Lord of Dragonsteel doing all the way out here? Was he not supposed to be wasting away in Exar'forda's towers?

"Are you here to kill me?" Jaccorias hated the squeal in his voice.

"I do not annul Illuminators." The Lord Prince drifted past him, barely more than a shadow. "Until you give me a reason to. I am here to talk."

"T-talk?"

"I have been in negotiations through the Seeing-Stones. Surely you received instructions from your master. I am here to ascertain your progress. He said any further word for him should be spoken to you."

Jaccorias cleared his throat. So he would not die by a Morghûl today. The Morghûls were said to have affinities ten times that of a human mage, which would make sense, since they were closer to gods than elves. Supposedly, the only reason why the Dragonsteel Order existed—why dragons would even allow elves and men to saddle them—was because their ancestors had learned to fear the elvish ruling family. He could not imagine being Illuminated by one of *them*.

The warden carefully bowed. "Your Imperial Grace."

Prince Vharyn glanced at the weeping, pig-masked prisoner. "Anyone I know?"

"Oh, certainly." Jaccorias coughed again, making his voice more amicable. "The worst of the *kvael-akar*."

The Lord Prince's smile made the Illuminator wriggle. "There is presently one worst *kvael-akar*."

"We can go to my office if it pleases—"

"This is suitable enough."

"A-as—as you will, Your Grace."

"What advancements with my prisoners?"

"Which are your...?"

"The Vigardians. The Wulfgars."

"Ah. None but the boy spoke, but then again, we started with him." Jaccorias glanced uneasily at his sha'daath. It was bad practice to speak of underground business in front of anyone, even a corpse with a life sentence. He moved in closer to the elf and whispered all his findings.

"If this were to leak to the Republic..." Jaccorias chuckled nervously. "It could ruin a certain Eldari."

The Lord Prince's expression was a dark pall, though Jaccorias was sure he was listening. His mere presence, and the heavy stench of wine on his breath, drew the Illuminator's hackles.

"Thank you," said the elf, when he finished. The prince folded his hands together and paced in slow circles.

His silence unnerved Jaccorias all the more. When it became too unbearable, he cried, "Your Grace, is there anything else—"

"Do you keep Kru'ul?"

"What?"

Prince Vharyn stopped pacing.

"Yes—yes we do." He pounded his chest. His throat had gone hoarse. "Did our leader tell you about...? N-no matter. Follow me, please."

Jaccorias all but zipped out of the chamber. He ignored two gaping Lightcloaks, his fellow brethren, as they caught sight of Vharyn Morghûl trailing behind him like an ill shadow.

After several more twists and winds deeper into the Keep, they stopped outside a barred door shaped in a half-circle. He pointed. "We keep one or two if a prisoner must be put out quickly, though with excruciating pain..."

At the sound of Jaccorias's voice, a monster stirred in the darkness. He fought his foul habit of biting his nails. A beat later, a bestial shriek shattered the silence. He lurched back by impulse, but the Lord Prince stayed his ground.

A deformed elf creature clattered the bars with all its strength. It was half and one the breadth of a Fair Elf, though the resemblances ended there. Its skin was a scaled gray, plagued by crosshatches of varicose veins; in the darkness, they looked like grotesque lash marks. That decaying hide was stretched too thin over bloated muscles that looked powerful enough to crush human necks with just a little squeeze. It had no eyes, but sensed through its oversized, sharp ears and slitted nostrils. Every ragged grunt it let out smelled of a good vegetable patch gone rancid. Jaccorias choked and pinched his nose, despising the creature.

"So, they are real," the Lord Prince said in wonder.

"My leader breeds them in the most remote regions of Fel Tirion," said Jaccorias, and immediately regretted it. Perhaps he had said too much.

"Is it true, that they are elves of old fallen through ruptures in the Mordgaard veiling?"

"I... could not say, Your Grace. Perhaps that is a question for the head of my order."

Prince Vharyn turned his back to the Kru'ul as if it were no more than a pup snarling behind him. "Your master has promised me an army. I must deploy it no later than in the next cycle. Thanks to you, Jak, I have my destination. In return, when my purpose is fulfilled, he will have his realm."

"A *realm*?"

"And a place in the Elenntarien."

Jaccorias dropped his jaw. "Which realm?"

The Lord Prince calmly marked his face. "Your master told me I could convey everything to you."

Closing his mouth, he nodded quickly, terrified by the scrutiny. "Your message is safe with me."

"I would also have sonnifera. Three lumens."

Jaccorias almost sank to his knees then. "Your Grace," he croaked. "It is legally for the sha'daaths only. An Illuminator, even such as myself, could be executed for selling..."

"Who says you are not administering to a sha'daath?"

"...But I am sure I can find a stash somewhere..." Jaccorias glanced around, his neck soaked in sweat. "In fact, I will give you *five* lumens free of charge."

"Send it to my attendant." The Lord Prince swept past him before he could ask how exactly he was supposed to avoid Republic customs between here and Exar'forda.

He fought to hold in his disgust for the elf. The rumors were not all false, then. What did the Lord Prince do these days besides hide in the shadows to drown himself in wine and the numbing herb?

...And devise continental chaos with his leader?

"Your Grace!" he called after the elf. Footsteps receded into the darkness. "What of your prisoners?"

No answer came. He rushed to the landing and shouted up the

stairwell. "Would you like them returned? We can ship them free of charge to Exar'forda, now that you have everything you need. All but the little ones are dead, sorry."

In the following silence, Jaccorias cursed it and crunched down on his nails. But a return call came, quieter than the torches.

"Give them to the Kru'ul."

It was the last he heard from that elf. He bit down so hard onto his nail, his flesh smarted, and he tasted blood. Jaccorias cursed and pulled his pointer away. Already, with the Lord Prince gone, the foul energies in Kar'thuul-dur felt much lighter.

He prayed to Vaeritas he would never meet Vharyn Morghûl in person again. Rumors were abundant among the Illuminators of what he could even do to dragons—what he had done to *his* dragon. Mercy on anyone who crossed him.

13

THE GREATEST WELDIN IN THE NORTH

"Bale wants you to transport him on wheels," Skálda told Soren at dawn of their departure.

Activity rushed about before the settlement's gates. In the background, Asveig shouted at the Vigardians to hasten their bloody arses into formation. Most were still recovering from their tankards the night before. They laughed and exchanged Skitr jokes, animated by their new campaign. The last one had gone exceptionally. Everyone's spirits were soaring high.

Skálda caught the Draugh at the front of the train, just as he was stepping into the stirrups.

"He wants us to bring him into a cage?" said Soren.

She glanced back at Bale. Two Weremen tentatively led him by the neck chain down the slopes. The picas were cute, and Incendra was imposing, but the sight of a black adolescent with glowing red eyes and four malignant horns sent the thralls amok. The Vigardians thumbed their hafts nervously. The "Mean Dragon" was coming. Skálda shrugged at Bale's guards. They had insisted on escorting him.

"He thinks you move too slow to keep up with him in flight," she said. "He would have you cart him."

"It will slow us down."

"Perhaps."

"He can walk."

"He doesn't like to."

"Very well," Soren said flatly.

"He says he would prefer a carriage, not a cage, and one padded with velvet blankets."

Soren shot her a blistering look and rode past her.

In the end, they put Bale in a cage, and her on a horse. As they marched deeper into the forests, Bale yawned and dozed on his claws.

"Careful, Bael," she warned, riding alongside him. "You are getting used to bars like a captive songbird."

He ignored her and covered his eyes with his wing.

"You *are* lazy," she said.

As they traversed through the dramatic wilderness of the Deep North, Skálda soon found herself caught in the land. The Völundr forests were such a verdant black, untouched by the Republic. She breathed in the evergreen scents of freedom. Hooves crunched over snow that refused to melt to summer. It was such a fierce land; the heart of Old Svenn beat so mightily in the earth. Her ancestral lands were calling out to her, washing all her fears away with a healing peace. And Skálda understood who the Wereguild were, why they were fighting so ferociously to defend these wilds.

On the third day, the Völundr Reach opened to Isolund, the legendary Lakesea, to her right. That great body of mystery reflected the dark crystal of the skies. Like all Svennish children, she had heard of its vastness from the stories. Out here, she was *living* Vigardian lore.

Skálda lingered by the shores, listening to the backwash of the waters against a pebble shore. Seeing her linger, Soren pulled away from the main train to ride beside her.

"You feel it as well," he said.

She steeped herself in the chilly breezes that rustled against her cloak, breathing deeply.

"When I first came to this land," said Soren, "it brought me to my knees. Fjorland, Belfaine, and Lysmark are shards of Old Svenn, yet those realms are not Vigardian. Not like this."

"The Skonkauld never felt like this," she agreed. "Even out there, on the fringes of the Republic, we had forgotten who we were... The Vigardians were no more than a whisper of what we used to be. Just a faded dream." She brushed Aracir's sheathed axe head. "But I always sensed a greater power beating in the trees of the Krigsgaald, in the skáldwolves running free. Anders held rite-fest every five solstices, but..."

"Ritefest in the Republic Svennish realms is a jest. You felt your Vigardian lineage. I know, because I felt the same echo a long time ago."

Skálda took in his great mantled frame. It struck her suddenly how little she knew about the fallen Crown Prince of Fjorland.

"The Republic churns, the Republic Builds," he said. "Always, it wars to claim the stories in our scripts, to replace it with its own. But my people see it for what it is." He drifted his gaze to his fellow Weremen. "A war machine."

Skálda pulled on the reins. "I cannot go back."

Soren raised his dark brow.

"When I fled the Skonkauld with Bale," she said, "I heard a call from the Joa Fjord. The ice was singing to me a longing I could never put to words... But now I understand what it was." She looked at him squarely. "I want to be what you are. I want to be Vigardian."

"You already are." The corner of his lip tilted. "The blood of Thorgest Vigarda, and Old Svenn, beats inside you." He pointed toward the Álfvindor Alps. "When you crossed that border, your soul found your inheritance again. Now, you are awakened."

Passing Weremen glanced their way from the forest path. Rulf and Jarmon stared at them from over their shoulders, murmuring curiously to each other. Soren started his destrier forward again. Skálda followed at his side and ventured to ask the question that had been itching at her since her capture.

"Does your father know you live?"

Soren lapsed into a silence. As always, his dark, brooding expression was unreadable.

"Leondran is a good king," she said. "I met him in Dellfast. He offered a kindness that—"

"He is nothing to me."

The rancor in those words caught her by surprise.

"The Republic has declared war on the Vigardian kingdoms," he said. "Old Svenn may have fallen, but Vigardian blood still lives. We rekindled it when the dragon men invaded our lands."

He turned to her then, his thick lashes hooding his eyes.

"I am no longer Sorenthor Astoraine of Fjorland, but I am the Draughammr that will kill your brother."

Soren spurred his destrier, galloping ahead of her. She trailed his frame with her eyes, his braided black bun, the heavy fur mantle that pounded against the stallion's flank. He took his place at the front. Skálda glanced back over the Lakesea. For all the crucibles that lay ahead, the Vigardian land settled an unprecedented peace in her.

On the seventh day of their march into the eastern Nifvinter Mountains, a Were scout yelled from elevation. It was impossible to decipher his words from this distance. Soren's host slowed.

Skálda, riding by Bale's cage, turned back the way they came.

They had just exited the sprawling Völundr Reach and were part of the way up a mountain. At this height, she saw nothing out-of-place over the infinite dell of trees below.

The Wereman yelled incoherent words again, some urgent message. The breezes out here were too mild to carry it. Soren narrowed his eyes and glanced upward, to the tight clump of rock mountains that lay ahead of them. Most of the snows out here were melted; the sparse slopes were harsh and littered with scree.

The Vigardians brushed their axes, poised to draw against an enemy they could not see. Bale growled low. *"Look to the skies, not the earth."*

Skálda lifted her gaze to the open canvass of dark daylight. The winds were rising. Skims brushed the edges of her boots, the wool fibers draping her shoulders. Suddenly, she understood the Were scout's pressing call. *Take cover!*

"Rider!" she shouted to Soren.

The scout screamed in the distance, the sound of a tortured man in the throes of death.

"Back to the trees!" Soren bellowed. "Leave everything!" The aspens and firs below were some two hundred paces away. The Vigardians, all on foot besides Soren and his commanders, pounded back down the slope.

Skálda was the only one that stayed behind, rushing to undo the latch on Bale's cage. Sweat drenched her back. Soren, who had started a gallop, saw her linger and pulled up sharply. "Skálda!" The last Weremen thundered past them, shaking the mountain into frenetic chaos.

The moment the cage door swung open, Bale leapt out and expanded his wings, diving ahead of the Were host. *"Wolf!"* he called. *"Hurry!"*

"The cage," she hissed at Soren. "They'll see it."

"Leave it!"

They galloped down the rest of the slope together, their mounts tripping over the falling scree. Skálda dared a glance over her shoulder, but it was impossible to see anything behind the mountainous horizon. The trees ahead swayed now from the might of dragon wings. All the birds quieted like the hand of death had fallen over the dell.

A beat after they made it beneath the firs, a colossal shadow streamed over the slopes. This dragon was no pica, or even a grown eld. The Vigardians around her crouched between the brush, holding their breaths. Bale snarled, the muscles in his neck tremoring.

The dragon was flying low. Crystal patches of its belly armor flashed over the dark canopy.

"The Ivarion's beast," Lord Jarmon hissed. The flesh between his brows creased with disgusted fear.

"No," said Skálda.

The icescourge circled around them, releasing a hair-raising screech.

"*AOOOOWR-ii! AOWR-iiiiiii!*"

The Vigardians groaned, clamping their hands over their ears. A few crashed onto their knees. It was so loud, so terribly pitched. The boles of the very trees seemed to split.

"Rystendal Vacerys," said Skálda. "He is a Judge. He knows we are here."

Crixalas circled and roared at them. He flew low enough that the mace of icicles on his tail dragged over the trees, splintering them to pieces. The Weremen exclaimed and flattened themselves against the needles.

"If he knows we are here," Jarmon snarled, shielding his head with his arms, "then why does his beast not blast us with flames?"

"He wants me alive," she said.

The Wereguild commanders glanced at her. Amidst the splintering destruction and uproar, many Vigardians clenched their axes.

"Let the dragon scum come!" a bald one said. "We are one thousand strong."

"No," said Soren. "He is a High Elf, a rider of the Old Dragonguard. This is a foe beyond any of you."

The Judge tormented them with his icescourge. Crixalas seemed exultant to terrorize them as he circled overhead, breaking the trees, drowning them with his mammoth shadow. Every several beats, a sinister yellow eye glowed above the trees.

"If he is merely here for Skitr's sister," Lord Jarmon shouted, "then toss her over to him, Draugh!"

"Shut your mouth, Danheim," Asveig snapped.

The Judge pulled away from the forests. Crixalas stopped shrieking. She wondered if they were retreating.

Skálda glanced past the tree line, to the empty cage, and three dragon slayers that remained on the slopes. No Wereman was breathing now. Bale's terror quaked the Binding, unbalancing her. He remembered how that icescourge had chased him as a hatchling over the Derefter Wall.

Just when the Vigardians were picking themselves up, torrential heat blasted over the trees. The Weremen screamed. Skálda shut her eyes. Völundr's forest grounds quaked and roared.

Crixalas flapped his wings, suspending himself in the air, as he burned the dragon slayers with his astringent breath. The cage nearby caught fire. It sickened Skálda, watching the iron bars smelt in the merciless swelter.

When it was done, and their war machines were left in charred cinders, Crixalas clapped his giant wings together and soared back over the mountaintop. Elvish magic amplified the Judge's shout over the wilderness.

Kvael-akar!

It echoed ominously several times. A minute passed before anyone would rise again. Everyone's eyes were stretched wide. One Vigardian even leaned over and dry vomited.

"We are alive." The bald Wereman exhaled. "He left us alive?"

"It was a warning." Soren gathered himself and sat erect in the saddle again. Even his pallor was white as bones.

"Well..." Rulf tugged at his half ponytail. "Our dragon slayers are gone."

"We have Skálda," Asveig said.

Jarmon laughed.

Skálda glanced back at Bale. He looked suddenly small compared to that malignant monster. *Are you alright?*

He was too shaken to answer.

Soren trained his eyes on the mountainous horizon, their path to Ruadhán Post. Everyone was looking to him for direction.

"That elf will be watching the east," he finally said. "We have no choice but to stay here until he passes."

NO ONE STARTED any fires that night, but they ate sheep jerky and bread in the darkness. Skálda skipped dinner and laid her head against Bale's belly, joining no fire and speaking to no one. He kept his wing partially folded over her like a protective awning. Though he was too young to breathe fire, his body was like a hearth in the Northern cold.

After the Draugh had his fill, he left his circle and marched to her. Seeing him approach, Bale flexed his talons.

"You are troubled," he said.

"I led Lord Rystendal to us," she said. "Garreck must have transmitted my presence here to the Order."

"That is not what troubles you."

"How can you know what troubles me?" she said scornfully.

"I have watched you," he said. "You speak little. You take a great interest in the land, but I think it is a distraction. Tell me, dragon girl, tell me the truth. When we arrive at Ruadhán, will you be prepared to annul Ulvrik?" When she said nothing, he said, "Can the Draughammr trust you?"

She bore her eyes up at him. "Are you waiting for me to get on my knees and beg you to?"

"But this is not about Ulvrik. If your brother makes an appearance, you would not fight against him. I am inclined to believe you might even turn against me and join him."

"Believe whatever you will, Draugh."

"I cannot take those chances. So, you will come with me."

He mounted his destrier and rode into the trees without waiting for an answer. As he passed his commanders, they glanced at him and resumed their low murmurs. Soren was taking no guards.

Bale folded his wing tighter over her. *"I won't let him take you to a tree stump!"*

Maybe he'll throw me to the wyrms.

Her dragon found no humor in it.

"Don't keep the Draugh waiting, dragon girl!" Asveig called. The Vigardian did not look up from his firepit. "He has something he wants to show you."

Something in his voice piqued her curiosity. *I think it'll be alright,* she told Bale.

"How do you know?"

She climbed to her feet. *They're not calling me thrall, for one.*

"Must I stay with the bad wolves?"

I will call to you if there is any danger. She rubbed him between the horns. *If any bad wolves want to pet you, try to be a good dragon.*

He snorted. *"I'm no good dragon. I eat wyrms and scourges!"*

"Can you eat Rysten for me?" Skálda swung herself onto her charger. Just as she was catching the reins, Asveig said, "Better bring a waterskin." He tossed her a purse. "And food. It will be a long ride."

She narrowed her eyes, but none of Soren's shield-brothers

would betray anything. They were in a strange mood. Skálda nodded a goodbye to Bale and followed Soren's path deep into the Völundr.

Skálda soon caught up with the Draugh. Their ride through the forests spanned one day, then three, and many more. They did not talk during most of it. That suited her well enough. She lost herself in her own silence and in the roar of the wilds.

On a day when she was certain Soren was not looking, she traced her gaze over his black side braids, his short, high bun. She found herself entranced by the way the North's winds caressed him, swaying his skáldwolf furs like white knives. Everything about the Draughammr was supremely savage. She inhaled the unwashed scents of calfskin and male sweat. They were smells that made her feel powerful, Vigardian, like him.

Soren must have sensed this, for he glanced back at her. Skálda casually looked away at the trees, her neck warming. He smirked, but his eyes gleamed.

It was not long before the Álfvindor Alps reappeared in the south. Seeing them made her belly unexpectedly clench. He was taking her back toward Aranor Elondris. It did not occur to her until now how much she loathed going back to the old world she knew. But their silence had been a game between them. She would not be the first to break it with questions.

On the second week of their trek, Soren bade her to dismount. They climbed up a granite scarp together, emerging into a new forested elevation. "Quiet," he said. As she followed him on foot, a new, sacred silence soaked the grounds. The northpines here were more ancient than anything she had seen yet in the Deep North. Silver moss draped their branches; they soared into the dark blue dawn, telling of great age past.

"We are here," Soren said.

The trees opened into a clearing tucked deep into the Álfvindors. Skálda shuffled past him in wonder.

If the trees were giants, they were nothing compared to the nine monoliths of stone that reached for the heavens. Skálda weaved between them, laying her hands on the lichen. Symbols incised the stone—Nhorssn runes, the language of the First Peoples. They whispered stories she could not understand, yet her heart heard them in the soul tranquility of the pines.

"What is this place?" she said.

Soren joined her at the monolith. "The Standing Stones. They were built by the Yrthjök. The Nhorssn ancestors of the Thomdrim."

He followed her as she trailed along the landmarks, studying each of them. All had different sets of runes that told the various stories of the earth's scripts. She could not fathom how any creature could have built such colossal stones.

"The runes you see recount the Breaking of Realms, the divine war between Vaeritas and the Golaths." Soren tucked his hands behind him. "It is said that when Emperor Baelaeryx fell, the impact formed the Álfvindor Alps. All life within a hundred leagues blackened and perished. But the Yrthjök that had descended from the Sixth Realm ventured into this land. They were the only race that knew how to mend the earth. They sang to the trees, brought green back to northern Elondria."

They stopped before the largest of the monoliths.

"The Thomdrim are the balancers of nature, fundamental to the continent. The Red Spore continues to spread beds of bloodwyrms. Where the blight has infested us, the Thomdrim cleanse the land."

He pointed. On the Standing Stone before them, a Thomdrim had more recently carved glyphs like twisting wyrms and scenes of revitalized trees conquering old beds.

"In the valleys with smaller beds, where we have been able to catch the eggs in time, the Thomdrim saved the Vigardians from a full outbreak."

"Outbreaks like Thurs Runja," she murmured.

"Yes. Without the Thomdrim, most of the Deep North would have been infested already."

"The old Svennish stories are known in the Skonkauld," she said. "They live in great sanctuaries of forests. Is this one of them?"

Soren paced away from the stones. An emotion she could not read shadowed his face. "This is no weldin, but I have brought you here to show you the greatest of them." He pointed beyond the mountains. "This journey must be taken by foot."

The prospect of seeing a mythical weldin enthralled her. What Thomdrim landmark could be greater than even the Standing Stones?

"Lead the way," she said.

The trek through the mountains took about another week. She was glad to leave behind the Álfvindors for the western unknown. The familiarity of those alpines was unsettling. It was strange to remember that, in another season, she had lived on the other side of these mountains, entirely oblivious to the Vigardian world.

At the end of the week, when the ghyll next opened, twilight's last dregs sank over the horizon. Darkness washed over the land beyond. Soren withdrew further into himself. For some odd reason, his hand was shaking, and he almost seemed reluctant to go any further. But Skálda thrummed with anticipation. It was not every day a Svennish of the Republic saw a weldin of lore.

Soren knelt behind a span of boulders and pointed. "There, the greatest of them all."

Skálda turned her gaze, and it was like Soren had thrust an axe into her belly.

The ruins of a city littered the vale. Dozens of abandoned burrows snaked under its outworks. These were the same manner of tree-root tunnels that had fractured Dellfast. The curtain walls were caved; it looked as if the city had collapsed into itself.

"That... is Tera Beren."

"Vérinngen was once Isgardia's lifeblood," said Soren. "Fjella's family relied on the Thomdrim to keep the vale fertile. It fed not only their people, but Vingulmark's. Mine. And thousands more Vigardians. For generations, we lived in harmony with the giants."

The shadows only deepened.

"Five solstices ago," said Soren, "your brother came to this land with Leofraen Amanoor. They ripped the trees from their roots, scorched the land with their dragons to clear a way for their post. When they found the Thomdrim... the Ivarion declared it a private warzone."

Skálda slowly shook her head. Soren looked into the southern horizon without seeming to see. "Have you ever heard a dying Thomdrim?"

A frigid breeze soughed over them.

"It haunts a man for the rest of his life." Soren quieted even more. "Now, imagine ten thousand slaughtered in one night."

"*Ten thousand?*"

"Your brother invited only his most elite riders into the zone. Before dawn, he had advanced 1,000 chapters. He and Leofraen spared none."

Skálda was certain he was speaking of another Ivarion. This was not her brother. It could not be.

"The next day," said Soren, "their songs ceased. The lands between the Beorthas Mountains all the way to the Mourning Moors, in Isgardia's far north, fell silent. When I woke that dawn in Solhall, beside Fjella..." His gaze grew distant. "We could feel it. Something terrible had happened. The Deep North had lost something we could never get back."

"Draugh..."

"Your brother and the Amanoors kept the Thomdrim a jealously guarded secret. The size and the breadth of their souls meant a supercharge for a dragon's advancement, you understand. The ease of killing them made them a Builder's trove. Your brother hunted the Thomdrim near to extinction. I had no choice but to take them under Wereguild protection; I hid them in the caverns beneath Solhall, away from their weldins. The earth suffered for it. So did they, living in the darkness away from their trees." Soren shook his head. "The Red Spore strengthens. Every solstice, the bloodwyrms take more land. I fear now, with most of the Thomdrim gone, that we are beyond saving."

"The Battle of Dromvoll Church," she said. "When he could not hold Vérinngen, he burned all Isgardia."

"I did not kill his riders merely for vengeance," said Soren. "I killed them to protect the free races of Old Svenn. That was my charge when I accepted Solhall and the Were Crown. Their dragonfires would have spread and destroyed all the Deep North."

"You are afraid for your children."

He gave pause, then admitted, "Yes. I cannot allow Fritjolf and Evynd to grow up on a continent where the Ivarion lives." Soren turned his back to the city. "The Republic believes I slaughtered his commons, but that is not my way. I took them as my thralls and I will defend them. One day, when their descendants choose to live in harmony with the Vigardians, they may go free."

"I don't understand," she said. "No one ever found out what Eyrek did here?"

"Do you suppose the Lord Prince cared?"

She clenched her axe.

"The Republic need not know," he said. "But do not think the Elenntarien has no notion of what occurs in the warzones. Dragonsteel tells them they will Build, and the Elenntarien looks away so long as the Republic strengthens. They Build and Build for a false invasion."

Skálda tilted her head, stunned. "You think the Betrayer is not invading?"

Soren looked her straight in the eye. "If the Betrayer wished to invade us, he would have long ago."

No words would touch her tongue. Skálda walked back the way they had come, but Soren caught her arm.

"You already knew the truth," he said. "Your brother's script was always one of villainy, though he deceived you like the rest of the continent." He gave pause, seeing how his words were affecting her. "Only a Great Dragon could have expunged a post like Dellfast."

She closed her eyes.

"Two Great Dragons fly on this continent. It was not Lumaerrax. She is aging. The Lord Prince is fading away. In time, he will be merely a memory. Your brother is head of the Enterprise, and in many ways, Lord of Dragonsteel. He is Elondria's true enemy."

She yanked her arm free. Aracir tumbled from her clammy grip.

"You say you want to break the Order," he said. "If that is true..." Soren picked up her axe. "Help me break the Realm-Building Enterprise." He held it out to her. "Help me kill him."

She kept her back turned.

"Skálda?"

Wresting Aracir from him, she broke into a run. Soren called after her. She raced off the mountain path, twisting through the Cauldwood's northpines and squeezing herself under the deep foliage. Soren tried to pursue her, but he could not keep up with her swift wolf paws. The Were King's shout echoed over the mountains. *Skálda!*

14
TORSTEN ULVRIK

"Eyrek!" Skálda bellowed.

Her grip on Bale's neck spike was slipping. The heavy rains made his onyx hide slick. Thunder clapped in the pitch-darkness. He beat his wings hard, fighting to navigate through the late summer hurricane.

She did not know where exactly Ruadhán Post was, but the memories of Dellfast were overtaking her. She would find it. She would find him.

On the other side of the Nifvinter Mountains, a woodland she could not name rolled beneath her. They were flying high, at least two thousand feet from the evergreens. They swayed violently in the gusts. It was impossible to see through the deluge. She was relying entirely on Bale, on his enhanced dragon sight, to fly through the dark. His distress pulled their Binding taut, but all she could feel was her own fury; she could not stop it from rushing back over the Binding and overwhelming her dragon.

"Eyrek!"

Bale roared with her.

In the next lightning flash, she saw them. Dragon silhouettes.

Dozens upon dozens in the dark. These were Eyrek's surviving riders. Bale pulled up sharply, keeping her suspended in the raging heavens. They were everywhere, flitting past them in the air, impossible to track. Their shouts in Elondrian echoed like distant thunder through the rains.

We'll kill you, kvael-akar*!*

The elves were vengeful over Garreck's death. Six of them charged at her from every direction.

"Fly, Bale!" she shouted.

He was exhausted. They had flown above the Nifvinter Mountains as soon as she had returned to camp nearly two cycles after her initial departure. For four hours, they had not rested. He kept them suspended, even as the dragons rushed at them. Skálda bellowed his name. At the last beat, he tucked in his wings.

They dropped sharply. The elvish riders crashed into each other. As winds blasted her face, she heard their startled cries far above her. The violent impact sent some chethems dropping into the unknown timberland.

Skálda tightened her grip on Bale's spike with her good hand, and looped her other arm around his neck. They were diving so steeply, her belly crashed like tidal waves on rocks. It was only her rage that kept her from screaming in terror.

The winds strengthened. They were flying deeper into the storm. More elves surged at them in the dark. These were swifter than the chethems riders, Builders with chapters in the hundreds. Bale strained to pound his wings faster. He twisted around them, looped them upside down to lose them in their pursuit. Skálda was forced to squeeze her knees around his shoulders with all her might. When they were right-side up again, Bale panted, *"Tiring, wolf..."*

Her dragon was faltering. They were flying blind, with no bearings on where Torsten's post was.

A voice of reason told her she had brought herself and Bale

needlessly to their deaths, yet for every breath that passed, the fires of fury only swelled. She would find Eyrek, or the storm would bring them down.

"Kvael-akar!"

A Dragonshielded flight slammed into Bale. The impact spiraled them through the air. Skálda clenched his neck, her grip on his rain-stained spike slipping. For a beat, Bale's surge of distress swallowed up her rage. As he fought to regain control in the air, Skálda glanced over his glistening neck. Lightning illuminated the distant clouds, revealing the elvish silhouette that had struck them. The rider drew his sword. He was circling back for them.

"Take us back around." If they could not outrun him, she would need to slay him.

All the jostling was shooting pins up her right arm, but she paid it no heed and drew Aracir with her left hand. Bale's short breaths puffed out white vapor in the dark. The adolescent was too overwhelmed to resist her rage, and in a few more beats, her emotions overpowered him again. He roared and lugged himself around for a straight charge at the elf.

The two dragons bolted toward each other. The elf's flight was still Dragonshielded. A swift *Lhaer'thri* revealed his 557 chapters. Skálda realized that when they made impact, it would slam Bale out of the sky with an impact that would kill them both.

But her rage was too great, and there was nowhere else to run. She and Bale had made it this far. Eyrek had not come out for her.

Before the Dragonshield could crush their bones, another dragon swooped up from beneath. The Primarch pulled up sharply, just in time. He lapsed his shield. He would no longer attack her, but she felt his hateful gaze through the rains.

As she was trying to make sense of this, a call in the Svenning echoed from above.

Skálda!

"Torsten," she said.

The elf would not attack, for his post second was bidding her to come. Her faithful Bael drew his last reserves of strength and beat his wings, taking them back into elevation.

The Baron's dragon hovered even higher than she and Bale had flown before. The northwoods rapidly shrank. It seemed that for every one hundred feet they ascended, the rains pounded even harder. Lightning flashed. No riders attacked now. Skálda tightened her grip on Aracir, preparing for the killing throw.

It felt like an eternity before Bale was level with the Baron's she-dragon. All of the wilds bordering the Nifvinter Mountains exposed themselves at this sheer height. The next time lightning clapped, she saw Torsten's bearded face. Handsome was the last thing this man was. Yet, unlike any of Eyrek's other riders, the eyes beneath his scowling brows were windows of compassion, steeped in deep worry.

"Where is he?" she bellowed.

"Skálda, please, stop."

Thunder tremored the air like a second heartbeat. She adjusted her grip on Aracir to prepare for the throw.

"You are on a path of hate, and it will destroy you," said Torsten. "Your brother knows now you are the *kvael-akar*. He knows you killed Garreck. Yet after what you have done to us, he still loves you."

Her grip faltered.

"Come home," he said. "You have a place in Aranor Elondris. You always will."

"No, Torsten. I am Vigardian now."

The Baron let out a breath of despair. "Your brother is suffering from heartbreak. I beg you, Skálda. I have known Eyrekvald for many solstices. Nothing can take down that man, but these dark days past, he has lost too much. Your enmity will be the final thing—"

"You say you know him," she said, "but do you know what he did to Dellfast? How he Built Tera Beren?"

"The Wereguild has twisted your mind. But they are not your blood. You know your brother's heart. You saw him in the Skonkauld. You saw all that he gave for you."

"He never told you the truth," she whispered.

The high winds beat against them. Their dragons struggled to stay aloft in the storm.

"Eyrekvald sent me to bring you home," said Torsten. "He knew we could not stay Dragon's Helm's ire, but I hastened to personally protect you from my riders. I assure you a safe passage—"

"Tell him to leave his walls and meet me himself."

"I swear on Vaeritas, your brother and I only want you returned. If it means we must bear arms to defend you against the Judges, even the Lord Prince himself, so be it... Please."

She stared at the Baron's extended hand. The rage slowly ebbed in her. Nothing rose to fill it. She felt only that hollowness that had begun with Skoll Post's brutal annulling.

"Skálda," Torsten whispered. "Will you come?"

"I—"

She never finished. A radiant blaze manifolded from the heavens. She looked overhead. So ponderous it was, so blinding, she wondered for a beat, in the emptiness of her emotion, if it was the Sun God himself.

Bale veered away from the bolt in time. His sharp bank sent them in another upside-down loop. It was only by sheer fortune she did not plummet off his back. But Torsten's dragon never moved away fast enough. Lightning struck his she-dragon.

Skálda froze in shock. The stench of scorched flesh overpowered the air. Torsten plunged down into the darkness of the heavy rains.

15
TRIBULATION IS STRENGTH

Eyrek paced about the grounds of Ruadhán Post, watching the skies. He had stood out in these thrashing rains for nearly a day, though he long stopped feeling them. All the other riders besides Detherys had retreated beneath longhouse roofs.

Torsten should have returned with Skálda by now. Instead, an unexpected hurricane had swept over these unknown wilds. He would not have even flown Tythandrell in such weather, yet his friend was still out there.

He clutched his Sun tight, praying to Vaeritas that he had not made the wrong decision sending Torsten to Skálda. Garreck's murder had already brought him to his knees. But he would never abide Torsten's death.

His elvish riders were outraged that he would defend Skálda and send their post second to offer her redemption and a place in the Order. What they did not know was that the Wereguild had coerced her into luring out Garreck. The Were King had killed him, not her. Eyrek was certain. Torsten would return with his little sister, and she would corroborate him. He would never again abandon her to wolves and the cold, as he had done twelve solstices ago. Any minute now, they would both appear over the mountains.

Detherys stayed by his side, watching the mountains with him. The rains soaked them to the bones. Eyrek could not shake the feeling that the Were King was picking off his post seconds one by one. Leofraen and Garreck were gone. It would only be a matter of time before he murdered Torsten and Detherys in like. The Were King had even abducted his little sister and weaponized her against him. That malevolent man had not just stolen his crown, but what mattered most to him in this world. His closest family.

But Torsten would return with Skálda. He would not allow his faith to falter.

"Eyrek..." Detherys narrowed her elf eyes at the horizon.

"What do you see?" he said.

"Not anything I see. I hear him..."

He summoned the Dragonsight. A gilt sheen glossed over the darkness, and the rain glistened like falling gold. But nothing appeared through the churning clouds.

"He's shouting for help," Detherys said.

Eyrek turned to his riders. "Prepare for battle!" The elves immediately called their dragons. Fear and uncertainty drowned the air.

Detherys suddenly clenched his arm. He followed her gaze. A silhouette was breaking out of the clouds. He recognized the mood dragon's slim build. It was Elda. Nearly the entirety of her left wing was gone. She was beating her other wing desperately to bring Torsten safely to land.

They were falling.

"Eyrek, they'll never make it..."

He pulled away from Detherys. "Thane!" He could not breathe. "Where are you?"

The chaos of emotions kept him from calling his dragon through the Binding. Every beat that passed, he was suffocating.

Eyrek kept glancing back at Torsten's shape. They were descending toward the Nifvinter peaks.

A leviathan shadow swept out of the sky and landed by him. Detherys mounted her own she-dragon. Before Eyrek had fully strapped himself into the saddle, he shouted in Elvynnöthe, "Fly, Thane!"

In four mighty wingbeats, they were rising above the post. Eyrek pressed their Binding, willing his flight to move faster. Tythandrell thundered a cry. Eyrek's anguish was distressing the Great Dragon. Detherys's dragon soared close behind them, laboring to keep up in the hurricane.

Torsten and Elda plummeted toward the peaks at a sharp, rapid angle. Within several minutes of flying into these rains, they were less than twenty paces from Eyrek. They would make it.

He extended a hand to Torsten. Exhaustion weakened Elda. Her left wing arm barely beat now. Tythandrell pounded his own tremendous pinions with all his might, exerting himself to reach them. At this distance, Eyrek could see his friend's features without the Dragonsight. He let go of it.

Fear tightened the creases on Torsten's face. His dragon's desperation burdened the air. Eyrek felt it like a weight crushing his bones. Elda was trying to protect her rider from a fatal fall, but she was helpless with her broken wing.

"Torsten!" Eyrek unstrapped himself in the saddle and dug his right heel into the stirrup. He reached out even further. It was only his advanced flight experience that kept him from slipping off Thane's back at these wind speeds. One sudden jerk and he would tumble to his death.

"Thane! You must fly faster!" he bellowed. At his desperate plea, his dragon rumbled in anguish. They were in a ninety-degree descent now, struggling to keep up with Elda's fall.

"Torsten." He did not recognize his voice. It sounded too strangled to be his own. "Skit on everything! *Reach*!"

The Svennish man looked into his eyes. The rains, or perhaps tears, dampened them into a sheen. Reflected in the intensity of that gaze, Eyrek saw all their days of Building together. He saw the day they had met in Gristle Town, two awkward boys with no home but Fjorland's stinking gutters. He saw himself extending a hand, and stuttering, "You ever, um, heard of the Realm-Building Enterprise?" Torsten had been the first to take that hand, trusting him with his life and future, though Eyrek had nothing but the rags on his back.

The Baron kept his hand extended for a little more, then smiled.

"Tribulation is strength, my king."

He pulled back, embracing Elda around the neck. Torsten closed his eyes. Elda stopped beating her wings. In the next breath, the darkness swallowed them.

"Torsten, no!"

Eyrek's bellow pealed above the storm.

Tythandrell kept them suspended in the air. Every beat of his wings was thunder to Eyrek's heightened senses. His vision was mottling. Something kept him from invoking the Dragonsight to see what was below.

Detherys caught up to him. They stayed in the air. All the surviving riders of his Ebrennian posts formed a half circle with them. The rains were ebbing. No one spoke, though the Dragon's Helm flights would not stop roaring for their post seconds.

The lightning flashed, one final time that night. Shards of the approaching dawn spangled Elda's broken body below. She was crumpled over the summit. Blood blackened the earth. Torsten lay close to her, his arm still clasped around her neck.

His eyes stayed fixed upward, on the weeping heavens.

16
THE TALE OF ELARMIR THE EVENHEART

When Skálda landed at camp with Bale, a tide of Vigardians rushed at her. Soren pushed to the front.

"Torsten is dead," she said.

The Were commanders glanced at each other in astonishment. She was drenched to the scalp, though the rains from last night were fading with the dawn.

"You killed him?" someone called.

She barely heard. What she saw was not hundreds of Were faces, but Torsten falling in the dark. All she smelled was burning dragonflesh.

Someone clenched her shoulders. "You killed him?" Soren pressed.

She looked up at him. Something in her rain-stained eyes made him sober and let go.

"They will think I did," she said.

She marched away into the woods with Bale. The Vigardians gazed after her, feeling the intensity of her silence and the need to be alone. No one cheered. Soren did not stop her.

Skálda gazed over the headland overlooking Vingulmark's breathtaking infinity of verts and soulful blue-greens. Last night, the hurricane had transmogrified these forests into a hellish realm. Yet the dawn following the lightning rains backlit all the foreground trees in a molten copper. The dew was so tasteful and clean on her tongue. A menagerie of warbles and trills vitalized the forests. It was as if Torsten had never perished.

"I am not a murderer," she said.

Bale rested quietly on his claws, his wings folded. They gazed out over the misted treetops.

"And I am," she said. "I run it over and over in my mind. If I had moved, I could have saved him... But I wonder if I had stayed because I wanted to see Eyrek suffer."

"You did not kill the red-beard."

"There was a time when I dreamed of Realm-Building." The sun rose higher, yet where she sat, it would not touch her. "I wish... none of this had ever happened. I wish I was back in the Skonkauld, helping Anders and Mat prepare for ritefest." She listened to the forest's euphonous ballad of dawn. "I wish I'd had the courage to tell Kael I loved him. If he had stayed, he would have kept me from walking this path."

"Do you wish I had never fallen?"

His question brought her to the present. Skálda slipped off the boulder and caught him by his horns, knuckling his head with rubs. He playfully tried to wrest himself away and nipped her hand. She rubbed down his deep eye hollows next, then maneuvered around his chin spikes and rubbed under his throat, his favorite spot of all. He all but melted into her, rumbling with joy.

"I love you, Bale," she said.

He surged their Binding with warmth. *"My wolf. She is good, very good."*

"We should keep moving." She gave him a last thump on the neck. "Soren will be looking for me, and I'd rather drink gall than take more of his questioning."

They climbed higher onto elevation. Though the morning waxed, the canopy kept them in the shadows.

"What are we going to do now?" said Bale.

"Eyrek will come for me." She panted as they hiked between the trees. "Nothing else has changed. We will gather strength and kill the Lord Prince. I will face Eyrek if I must."

Bale sighed. The youngling was blaming himself for everything, for being a Bael.

Skálda stroked his neck scales, and whispered the *Lhaer'thri* over him. Once more, she sank in disappointment. His dragonscript bore only 61 chapters, which seemed impossible for all the campaigning she had put him through since the morning of Tera Vera.

She troubled greatly over her low rank, and kept 2,000 chapters at the forefront of her mind. At that rank, she would not be Dragonlord, but *Bael Lord*. She wondered what it would be like for her Realm-Breaker to breathe fire...

For the rest of that morning, they hunted in the Völundr together. Bale, ever concerned for her hurting wrist, took the lead on finding quarry. In the end, he captured for her a family of coneys, pinning them all under his claws. Skálda found no appetite in her and let him have them all.

"I'll cook them for you," she offered. Bale preferred his meat cooked, and to flames with Aesir calling him spoiled. He had flown well last night.

He barely heard her. He was far too famished to wait and dug right in.

Skálda rested against a tree and observed him from a distance.

Her dragon ravaged those helpless critters with fangs sharper than whetted Wereguild axes. The infants gave soft cries he silenced at once. When the last remained, a ball of fur smaller than her palm, he tossed it between his claws. It tried to escape in its terror, but he would not let it. He was playing.

As she watched him, a faded memory surfaced over their Binding. Resting in his place was the spectral projection of a far, far bigger Bael. He was bouncing between his claws captive elves, dwarves, and dragons. They were motes compared to his titanic breadth. Every time they tried to escape, he punctured them with his talons. Their cries of pain made him roar in delight. Both in the memories and in the present realm, the black-scaled Golath swung his tail.

"Bale," she suddenly said.

His soul-memory faded, and with it, the other Bael. Her dragon looked up at her expectantly. He was not aware of what she had seen.

Sensing Bale's shifted focus, the baby coney sprang over his claw and bounded back into the forest. Bale roared with animation, merely pouncing to catch it in his jaws. He crushed it with a single snap.

Skálda casually started a walk back to Soren's camp. He immediately noticed. The adolescent would not let her anywhere without him. Gulping down his meal, Bale sprang toward her, shaking the earth beneath his bulky claws. Skálda forced herself not to worry.

"*Wolf!*" He ducked under her arm and caught her hand between his four horns, playfully lifting it up. The young Bael sensed the way Torsten's death was still weighing on her and meant to keep her mind off it. He is such a good beast, she thought to herself.

"Clean my claws later, Good Wolf? I was a good dragon last night, I flew and flew without tiring at all."

"You *were* a good dragon. I'll massage you once we're back at camp." She went on her toes to knead his jaws. He closed his eyes, rumbling in pleasure.

"You didn't have to play with those coneys like that," she said. "You could've just eaten them quickly."

"They were good, good, good! Like my wolf!"

Skálda decided not to let the implications trouble her. Dragons, after all, ate flesh...

He jerked himself away, suddenly. His roar of terror prompted her to heft her axe from her belt. But no enemy she could see or hear was present. Her hunter's ears would have picked up on an intruder.

"What is it? Are Soren's men near?"

"Here they are again. They come!"

He unfurled his wings and tried to sail through the trees, but their trunks were too narrow for flight. Whatever harried him made him half-glide, half-gallop away from her. Skálda broke into a sprint, calling after him.

She exited through the tree line. Bale was perched on the edge of a sheer crag, his neck bent, looking down. His fear blasted through their Binding. They were coming from his falling terrors, what she called the trepidation plaguing his soul since his fall into Midgaard. The turbulence of his emotions crushed her ability to think. She bared her teeth, fighting to speak, to tell him to let go of their mind share, but his terror overpowered her like wroth gusts.

A thousand feet below, otherworldly glyphs incised an alpine tundra. These were the same gargantuan horrors she had seen atop Hrafenfjall, the highest mountain back at home.

"*Faolrún*," she whispered.

His scales quivered. He looked too nervous to know whether to stay put or fly.

"These glyphs are following us," she said. "What are they?"

He sent another blast through their Binding. She was plummeting again. Elondria's boundless plane was aslant at these heights. A fiery shield surged over her hatchling body, to protect her from breaking through the repellent energies of Midgaard's veiling. All she knew was terror, the terror of falling, and the terror of what was chasing her. She was desperate to escape.

"Stop," she hissed. "Bale—"

Uncontrollable terror burned out the memory. She saw herself from Bale's eyes, emerging from the pines and finding him in the Krigsgaald. The ice-haired hunter's pale eyes glowed in the darkness. She cradled a hatchling Bale into her arms and spoke in a distorted tongue she did not recognize.

I will not take you to Traust. I promise, Baelaeryx.

The sentiment was a whisper at first, but then it crept to all corners of her mind. It soothed her. It overwhelmed her. It was the only thing she could think of, her greatest desire. Yes, she would keep Bale in Midgaard. She would see to it with her life.

In a shard of clarity, Skálda realized he was controlling her mind.

"Bale!" she bellowed. "Let go of me!"

But he plunged her under his control, and her terror petered back into a mesmerizing desire to stay in Midgaard. Stay here. She would stay here in these forests with Bale, forever. She was his human. She would love him with her entire heart. She would serve and protect him.

Fading deeper into the cage of his mind, she saw his soulscript then, for the first time, in its *entirety*—and that was when her suppressed terror threatened to shatter her. For she saw an inferno spanning the Nine Realms, lighting up the universe. She was caught in the storm of a thousand unworldly roars, made of an ether that could Break anything in existence, living or inanimate. An all-consuming smolder blasted the hair from her eyes. The black ashes of wastelands and lost worlds fouled her lungs. Only the bleak void knew how to survive out here.

This inferno was the merging of all fallen Bael souls, now contained in Baelaeryx, the last Realm-Breaker.

Skálda screamed, suddenly seeing everything that he was. But this malignant plane muted her voice. His soulscript was an entire Realm in itself. In the real plane, she felt a faraway part of her begging anyone who would listen for help. Bale's hold on her was growing stronger. She sensed if he kept her under any longer, her mind would stay trapped here for an eternity.

Her screams drew a band of Vigardians out of the trees. The world without was shimmering like a river surface. The Draughammr had come. His bellows at Bale sounded like an echo of thunder from the other side of the continent.

Release her! Soren drew his axe. His Weremen strung a dozen bows at Bale. *Release her, I said. Monster!*

Bale's emotions churned her numbness with torrents of confusion and helplessness. Monster. She was not a monster. It was not until Soren took a running leap that panic made Bale let go. The roaring brilliance vanished, and the air suddenly turned cool.

Skálda rebounded backwards, collapsing onto her back. Her mind was her own again. Bale leapt off the cliff, evading the arrows with a sharp dive. He slammed his wings against the air and fled behind the mountain bend.

"Skálda."

Someone hoisted her up. She blinked. A haze obscured her ability to think, and her mind ached. The excruciating agony brought a flood of tears to her eyes. Bale had crushed her so thoroughly, and released her to the surface too soon.

It took minutes of someone's ceaseless shaking for her to realize it was Soren. Grooves deepened the flesh between his brows.

She mumbled, "I want to stay in the forests forever... I will never take us to Traust... I only live to serve..."

"Asveig! Bring me a waterskin!"

Skálda closed her eyes. Soft leather touched her lips. She

drank, the frigid river water clearing more of her mind. The next time she opened her eyes, they spilled tears.

"Soren?"

He did not reply. The Draugh had narrowly saved her from a mind-death.

Her belly clenched. A retch of hysteria surged up unbidden. She collapsed into his furs, and sobbed.

LATER THAT EVENING, they camped on the forested overlook. Skálda paced along the cliff, her eyes crusted. Her head felt like it had been trampled under horses. She kept looking out into the mottled woodlands for Bale, but of course, he would not return. He had shut off their mind-bond completely.

Is this it? she wondered. Is this how everything ends?

All Aesir's warnings about him were beginning to make sense. To think, as an adolescent, such mind-control was only a seed of Bale's power. When he grew to be an adult Bael, she wondered if he would do to Elondria what his ancestors had done to the upper Realms. How could he not, when she had seen Baelaeryx, the Great Scourge, living in his soul?

Soren sat with his commanders by the firepit. His elbow was propped on his knee and his hand rested on his forehead. The Draugh had not spoken for hours since the incident. His shield-brothers were basting two spits of squirrels, murmuring between each other.

"Why can't we keep him alive?" one whispered. "He seemed a good dragon. Perhaps he needs more taming."

"No, Rulf. You saw what he did. You know what he is."

"He *looks* like a dragon."

Asveig turned to Soren. "Draugh, I warned you from the beginning—"

Soren raised his fist, a gesture to be silent.

"The meat is ready," Lord Jarmon offered.

No one moved.

Jarmon got up. "I will bring some mead from—"

"He is a *demon.*" Soren's words, the first he had spoken since Bale's escape, silenced them all. Skálda kept watching the skies. Bale would return, as he always did. She was certain of it. Her stubborn hope seemed to vex the Draugh even more.

"You knew what he was," he said. "Yet you pampered him like a little chethem."

When she did not respond, Asveig called, "Come, eat, Skálda. We will discuss the Bael tomorrow—"

"Rulf," Soren interrupted, "take a contingent of men. Bring a dragon slayer if you must. See that the demon is put down immediately."

"No." Skálda whirled around. "If you kill him, I will kill you."

"Was it not enough that he tried to kill you?" Soren leapt into an incredulous shout. "He is a *Kærdighaeder*. A Destroyer of Worlds, if you cannot understand!"

She ignored him and kept her gaze on the skies.

"Have you not read Nhorssn history? Or am I the only one here who knows what the Bael are?" He extended his arms to full length as he shouted. "You are a fool, a *fool* to ever think you could be his rider, when there has never been such a thing as a Baelrider! You—"

She could take it no more. Skálda marched over and seized him by the furs. "Will you *shut your mouth*? I don't care for any more of your royal arrogance. I've had enough of it shoved into my throat and forced down my arse!"

Rulf whistled low, glancing away at Asveig. Jarmon cleared his throat awkwardly. Few in Elondria could talk to Soren that way without getting eviscerated.

"Hands off the king, thrall," he said quietly.

Skálda let go, returning to her ledge. This time, she did not pace, but stared off into the distance. Ever since the night at Tera Beren, it felt like everything around her was breaking. She could not have lost Bale, not like this. Not this soon. He would return to her... yet the instinctual part of her hoped, in her lingering terror, that he never would.

She placed a hand over her face. For a long time, she stood there, her back facing the Vigardians. Lord Jarmon cleared his throat again, and muttered to Soren, "All yours, Draugh."

The three commanders zipped away through the trees, leaving Soren alone with her. After a long moment, he gave a sharp sigh and came to her, speaking roughly.

"Stop crying."

"Go away."

"Crying like a child will not resolve—"

"If you do not go away, Sorenthor Astoraine of Fjorland, I will throw you off this cliff."

He buried his face in his hands, and exhaled deeply.

"Skálda," he finally said. He took her wrist and lowered it with gentleness. "I need to splint that again for you."

"It's healing. I could throw axes at arrogant Draughammrs and not miss."

With her face uncovered, he saw the fullness of her disheveled tears and grimaced. She sent him her most seething glower.

"Don't look at me like that," he said. "I am not Skitr."

The tears streamed harder, though she stayed silent.

Soren took her other wrist. "You are Vigardian, remember? Or have you forgotten?"

She closed her eyes. The trees swayed from a sudden mild wind.

"What did you see of his script?" he said.

She did not answer. In truth, she was afraid that if she did, she would break down from terror again.

Soren allowed silence for a little more, before he pressed on. "In truth, I am wroth with myself. I kept you alive because I knew what your dragon was. I had thought I could bring him to bear under the Skáld banners, but this was an unholy desire."

"Go away, Draugh—"

"After I returned to Solhall," Soren said, "I searched the annals. I found tomes on the old Golaths. The elves of Mholnigaard had done as I have. Illusions of power tempted them to ride the greatest of the Breakers, but all failed. None could control them, and the Bael knew it. They reveled in it."

"Bale is not like that."

"The temptation besotted too many elves. They degenerated into slaves of chaos, serving Baelaeryx and ravaging the lands until his Baels grew bored with them. When that happened, they shattered elven minds like they were but vermin beneath the boot. Have you not heard the tale of Elarmir the Evenheart?"

Skálda ignored him. The last thing she wanted was a regaling of history.

"He was the most noble of the High Elves." He curled his lip. "At a time when elves were still *noble*. They called him the Champion of Illyndor, the elven empire that reigned from Quendra." He raised his brows at her, as if to see if she was understanding a word he said.

Skálda's neck warmed, and she could not help but snap, "I may be a common, but I am no fool."

"Quendra was the greatest of the continents spanning Mholnigaard, home world of the elves." Skálda wanted to axe him. "When the Bael came, Elarmir exhorted the elves to parley. He was convinced the Golaths must have good in them, if even paltry good. He offered himself as Illyndor's envoy. Baelaeryx agreed to council with the elf. And when the champion stood before the Emperor of Breakers, a monster with a wingspan of eight hundred paces across..."

Eight hundred paces! she wanted to cry. Tythandrell could not be more than half and two hundred, which made him the largest dragon in Midgaard. Skálda loathed that he was putting her through this.

"The Great Scourge seized his mind in one breath." Soren crushed his fist. "For eight nights, he stayed in the elf's head and tortured him. By day, he made Elarmir his thrall and forced him to bear sword against his allies. On the eighth dawn, before the Scourge let go, he made Elarmir slay his own family. When Elarmir was himself again, all he could hear, on his knees, was the Scourge's laughter. It rumbled over all the skies, bled them crimson as the Breaking of Mholnigaard began. In the end, the continent burned in Baelfire. The Champion of Illyndor plunged his sword to heart. There was no happy ending for the Saga of Elves. Baelaeryx saw to that."

Skálda could not muster herself to look at him.

"Every ancient scribe wrote of Baelaeryx alike. He was cruel, a delighter in spite and suffering. That is why no dragon would call a Bael 'dragon.'"

My Bale is not like that, she wanted to insist. But the words died on her tongue. She was doubting—and that doubt alone, of Bale's true nature, scored her.

Soren softened his voice. "When I saw your beast, I had a vision of the power I would wield in my hand. I swore to myself I would not share Elarmir's fate, nor that of any Mholnigaard elf. In my..." He smiled wryly at her. "In my arrogance, I thought I would be different. I was more learned of mind. I would use a Bael for good. The uncontested power I would gain over Elondria would mean the end of the Order and all wars against Old Svenn."

Skálda closed her eyes.

"I was wrong," he said. "I put you in danger, because I hungered only to see Skitr dead. I opened a path for that Bael to kill you."

"He did not mean it."

"You *still* defend him?" His voice was hard. "You were his closest friend, yet he tried to Break you!"

Birdsong faded across the forest.

"This is my fault," he said suddenly. "Killing Skitr consumed my mind, yet I see now I have a higher, more important duty. Vaeritas placed the Bael in my hands for a reason. I do not pretend to understand the strangeness of fate, but after what I have seen, I know what I must do."

"No, Soren."

"You call your beast Baelaeryx, do you not?"

She pulled away from him.

"That your Bael chose this name should have been an omen to us. One day, when he matures, he will stop obeying you. He will have a will of his own. You will not be his rider, but you will be his living-dead thrall. That is the nature of the Bael. To destroy minds and worlds whole. It has already begun."

She circled around him to retreat into the forest, but he caught her arm. "Do you truly not see it?"

It took everything for her to look up at him. "I have sacrificed everything for him."

"I understand—"

"No, you do not. I am here—" Skálda extended her arms. "I am *here* because of him. I chose this path. And I have to know it was not for nothing."

He must have heard the quiet desperation in her voice, for he bowed his head.

"I understand," he said, more sincerely. "Five solstices ago, when I made the decision to build the tree-root tunnels under Tera Beren, I knew I could not turn back. Later, Isgardia burned for my actions. I questioned everything. Even now, Frit and Evynd are on my mind. Fjella is on my mind. They are always on my mind. I must know it was not for nothing."

The trees were swaying harder. Another storm was coming.

"I am sorry about Fjella," she said.

"Today, we will not talk about Fjella." Even as he said this, she sensed his deep pain. "The most important decisions we make are never simple. Making the moral choice oft brings great consequences we must be prepared to pay, for that is the price of virtue in a broken world. You acted out of compassion. Though we must hunt the Bael now, that did not mean you made the wrong decision to save him from the Order."

"The Order can never find out what he is."

"No," he agreed. "Neither can the Republic. It would plunge Elondria, perhaps all Midgaard, into war."

Winds battered their faces. Skálda stayed in place. She needed a trusted friend right now. She needed the Draughammr's confidence when she was spiraling into chaos.

"I will make it quick," Soren said. "He will not suffer."

She could not disagree, or agree. All she could see was a baby hatchling wrestling with her mother for milk; chasing dragonflies through the Prannon; nuzzling her with unreserved love when the world would give the eccentric skáld hunter no affection. He was *everything*, an inseparable part of her.

"Skitr can wait," he said. "Promise you will help me with this before it is too late."

It was in that moment that Skálda noticed every bird had gone silent. She glanced up at the whipping tops of the pines. She yanked herself out of his grip.

A deafening cadence of wings drowned the air. They backed away from the cliff. A crystal dragon hovered before the overlook, its single yellow eye glowing with hunger.

17
BLOODFEST

"Hello, *mahlenn*."

The unexpected female voice made Skálda swivel around. Opposite Lord Rystendal, a she-elf emerged out of the trees. It was Xandria Kirylith, head of the Rangers. More mounted elves fanned out beside her. Serrated swords, nets, and bludgeons were readied over their laps. These were the same Rangers that had destroyed her home; the same Rangers that had chased her across the continent, intending to find and kill her dragon.

Skálda looked into Soren's eyes.

"Go!" he bellowed.

He drew his axe and turned around to face the elves, at the same time Crixalas's giant claws lunged for her. Skálda ducked, rolling beneath his scaled belly. The next time she was upright, her breaths came up short.

She never had time to glance back at Soren. Drawing Aracir, she rushed beneath Crixalas's tail and skipped down the forested slope. In her haste, her boots became a blur beneath her.

Lord Rystendal called, "Great *kvael-akar*, slayer of riders and dragons! Why do you flee Dragonsteel?" His laughter boomed into the distance.

I do not flee, she thought, but today, I will annul you like the rest.

Her boots slammed against earth, and she made it to ground level. Skálda resumed her sprint. Crixalas swooped after her, staying above the dark canopy. The sounds of clashing steel faded behind her. Her mind raced to formulate a plan. She could almost hear Mat's voice. This was just another ritefest. She was racing a High Elf... to where?

Skáldwolves sprinted with her through the backdrop of trees, fleeing the colossal predator above them. Squirrels darted out of her way. She sorted through all her memories of the landscapes she had seen from Bale's back. The spears of conifers offered her little shelter. If Rystendal tore through them and landed, it would be over. She would never be able to repel his mage spells.

Her pulse thundered in her ears. The first seeds of her plan came to her. She had to keep him in flight. She had to find a way to kill him and Crixalas while they were in the air... albeit the Judge had destroyed all the dragon slayers they had brought from Solhall.

Think, she told herself. Where was she racing him to?

Shouts rose from the trees ahead. Bands of Weremen, hearing the clamor, discharged past the trees. Asveig and Lord Jarmon ran ahead of the wave, toward her, their blades unsheathed.

"Where is the Draugh?" Asveig shouted.

"Out of my way!" she screamed, shoving past them. The Weremen appeared torn on whether to pursue her. Lord Jarmon looked like he might throw his axe at her heels, but a roar of dragonfire hurled them all onto their sides. Fear bled over their eyes. Crixalas circled above them, exhaling a raging pillar of destruction at the sky. The sheer power of his prolonged flame quaked this section of the Völundr.

"Vaeritas help us," Asveig murmured.

Crixalas stopped long enough only to catch his breath, then started the whims of his flame-throwing all over again. None of the Weremen dared lift themselves off their hands. Lord Rystendal merged the chord of Crixalas's cacophony with his laughter.

They waited for the Judge to give the order to burn the forest.

But he never did. Skálda narrowed her eyes. Something Aesir once said came back to her. Lord Rystendal barely had the icescourge on a leash. A well-trained dragon only breathed flame upon his rider's *m'ethil* command, yet Crixalas was terrorizing them as he pleased. That would explain why the Judge would not land to capture her himself with his spells. He was pandering to his dragon. That vengeful beast remembered what she had done to him at the Derefter Wall back in the spring, and he wanted to be the one to hunt her.

She could use this to her advantage. Suddenly, she knew where she must go.

"Rangers," she told Asveig, helping him up. "Twelve. Xandria Kirylith is with them. Be careful."

Skálda resumed sprinting. The Were commanders' stares trailed her. Now that she was moving again, so did Crixalas. Every beat of his wings bowed the evergreens. Occasionally, he unleashed a fiery column above the canopy to terrify her. Stupid dragon. She did not stop running.

Seeing how his flames would not daunt her, Crixalas resorted to screaming at her.

"AWORRR! AWOOOOOR! AWOR-iiiii!"

Aesir would be so upset to learn he had not been invited to hunt his favorite dragon.

The pines and aspens blurred past. White daylight glowed ahead of her. She was nearly at the tree line. When she emerged, if she failed to make it to her destination in time, Crixalas would seize her with his talons and this bloodfest would be over.

Skálda burst out of the Völundr Reach and into the lake valley she and Bale had soared over during their First Flight. The glaciers were a hundred paces away. It took Crixalas a moment to notice she had exited the forest. He looped around for her, his maw parting in a grin.

Her thighs were burning, but she willed herself to maintain her sprint. The glaciers in the mountainside had melted enough to form an opening. It looked like the entrance to a natural passageway in the ice. Haunting memories of the Isendal River Valley and the Derefter Wall rushed over her eyes. She could not say how deep it was, or how stable. But this was her only hope.

Crixalas descended, soaring parallel to the lake. As she vaulted over scree and half-melted ice, he opened his jaws wider. Skálda felt the flames even at a distance. They cut across the lake, shattering the water into soaring sprays. The valley roared. The sweltering column was rushing toward her. Perhaps she had miscalculated everything. The Judge was here to incinerate her after all.

Lord Rystendal bellowed in Elvynnöthe. The icescourge begrudgingly let go of his flames a few beats before it could touch her.

Skálda was breathless now. She darted through the cave's dripping entrance. It was large enough to fit Crixalas at full wingspan. Once she was inside, she had a far better view of the cave's depth. The vaults near the opening were the highest, but the ice formed a tunnel that narrowed at about every five hundred feet. Even a thousand paces in, it would still allow Crixalas to pass through.

The icescourge's silhouette coalesced behind the cave mouth. He dove at full speed, his wings folded in. The walls tremored at the force of his entry. Icicles broke loose, crashing all around them. Some were bigger than even her. As she ran, Crixalas's blurry form grew larger, larger. The cave was narrowing. A dragon head snapped down at her. It was like a great drill slamming into the snow. Skálda pivoted to her right, her back colliding against the cave wall. Ice crystals flew into her eyes. Crixalas shrilled. His mere panting melted more ice. Cracks rushed over the ceiling. It took her several breaths to realize the High Elf was shouting at Crixalas to pull out.

The icescourge did not.

Skálda resumed her race. The cave ahead narrowed enough to force Crixalas to fold his wings. He chased her on foot now, snapping, tearing up the snow with his talons. A berserk hatred blistered through his good eye. But as a wyvern on two feet, he was cumbersome on the ground, even slow compared to her.

Skálda made it to the end of her race and clambered to the safety of a narrower cavern. Catching her breath, she glanced behind her. The icescourge was still in a gallop, but only until a massive stalactite cracked off the ceiling and shattered over his headplate.

Crixalas pulled up short and thrashed his head like a hysterical child. His writhing threw Lord Rystendal off the saddle. More stalactites deluged around them. The icescourge was taking down the outer cave. Skálda presumed he would retreat, especially when several ice spears nearly impaled Rystendal. But Crixalas went on crying.

The Judge climbed to his feet. "Enough! Take us out!"

In the wake of the torrential ice-rain, Lord Rystendal invoked the Dragonshield and raced back to the cave mouth on foot. The smaller spears crashed over Crixalas's back, but his scales armored him from injury. In his selfishness of mourning his own pain, he ignored the true danger his rider was in.

Stupid dragon.

Skálda drew Aracir from her belt and climbed out of her warren. The corner of his eye caught her small shape approaching him. Immediately, he quieted and turned his enormous head. The rapaciousness in that glowing eye returned, and Crixalas forgot his pain. The monster slowly parted his jaw. Steaming saliva dribbled down his teeth.

He came off his haunches. Lord Rystendal, now at the cave mouth, stopped to glance behind him. He widened his eyes. He saw what Skálda did. If his dragon stayed any longer, the outer cave would collapse over him.

"Crixalas! Pull out, I said!"

The icescourge, still unable to fly, resumed his clumsy gallop. He was so hungry for her, every slam of his claws shook the cave harder. The great razors in his maw snapped. Skálda saw two fates before her—the one she longed for, and the one where Crixalas shredded her to pieces. Yet she, too, fell in a run, as light and swift as skáldwolf paws on snow.

"Crix," the Judge yelled. "Stop!"

They closed the gap between them. The icescourge loomed over her. Skálda wondered how Rystendal had ever Binded with this monster from icy Hel. With his jaws fully parted, good eye flaming with fury, Crixalas plunged headfirst at her.

Skálda inhaled deeply, keeping her eye on her target. The surrounding air heated from the dragon's breath. Crixalas was upon her. As the shadows of his maw closed over her, she tossed with all her might. Her wrist screamed. She was not sure it would hit her target.

Aracir flipped in six circles and landed—off course from exactly where she intended, but still deep in the icescourge's throat.

The maw encompassing her stopped. Crixalas widened his eye. He never gave a last shriek or so much as a wail. The icescourge pulled away from her, teetering. Lord Rystendal watched everything from the entrance. The dragon's neck slackened.

The Judge crumpled onto his hands. "*NO!*"

Crixalas's mammoth body crashed over the snow. His eye stayed open, though the glow was fading. The High Elf's face paled into shock. He might have stayed there for eternity, but the outer cave was collapsing, forcing him to flee.

"Rystendal!"

He glanced over his shoulder. Skálda climbed out whole from Crixalas's maw, raising Aracir over her head. Dragon blood drenched the Anárion elvish steel.

"My regards to your Lord Prince."

And the cave collapsed, blocking anymore of his view of her.

18
A SONG FOR CRIXALAS

It took over a week for Eyrek to return to Exar'forda from the ruins of the Deep North. When Tythandrell made landfall in Dragon's Landing, no one came out to cheer. But one rider who had seen him from the skies emerged from the stronghold's towers to meet him, then another, until a swarm gathered around him and Thane.

Eyrek dismounted without a word. He carried Torsten's blood-stained body in his arms, training his steeled eyes ahead. As he passed through the crowds, the elvish murmurs fell silent.

He made straight for the Cárielorn, the ceremonial courtyard at the heart of the High Post. A week ago, when he arrived at the Dragonsteel embassy in Normarch, the capital of Belfaine, Detherys had taken it upon herself to assume his controls as Second Rider. She transmitted to all the Dragonlords on Aranor Elondris what had occurred in the North.

Yet as Eyrek passed the Cárielorn's soaring white arches, it was far more than Dragonlords crowding the courtyard. Amassing under the clouds were Ealdormans, Barons, and every rank of rider under the Order. Many had even brought their families to grieve alongside him.

The skies were dark, bruised from the rains soaking Eyrek's stained mantle. No one smiled. Few spoke. This normally stunning venue celebrated new ranks with banquets, fetes, and rewards. Today, however, the tapered twin towers behind the High Terrace's fountained waterfalls felt portentous.

He continued his silent march past the packed long tables. Seeing the Second Rider, Builders nudged each other and hushed. Among them were the young elves of Haverley. As Tythandrell alighted between the soaring towers, the dragons quieted before their Day King.

Eyrek had climbed the carpeted staircase to the High Terrace for speeches many times, but it was a momentous task with Torsten in his arms. When he made it to the top, standing in front of the gilt-domed towers, he laid Torsten on the terrace's concave balustrade. No pall covered him. Seeing the Baron displayed in this crass way drew wails from the crowds. It did not move Eyrek. He wanted them all to look upon Torsten's face.

The rains blurred the tears he had not stopped shedding since his friend's death. The Second Rider overlooked the courtyard with a callousness that the Dragonsteel riders had never seen from him before.

They had come for another galvanizing speech. He saw it in their glistening eyes. These Realm-Builders were desperate for him to say anything that would undo his iron spirit.

"Brothers and Sisters of the Order—"

The double doors at the Cárielorn's rear entrance opened, stopping any more of his words. A silhouette drifted down the steps. Heads turned to follow Eyrek's gaze. Upon seeing the Lord Prince, everyone gasped. Most had never looked upon their supreme leader before, but most had heard rumors about his hideous scar. They could guess who this High Elf was.

He was having difficulty walking straight. Rage burned Eyrek's chest.

Two vast side staircases led to the High Terrace, and both had four sets of stairs and landings. The prince teetered his way up. It was a dreadfully embarrassing eternity before he made it to the terrace, bumping up beside Eyrek. His breath stank of a saccharine herb.

Eyrek did not acknowledge him. Vharyn staggered to the front, forcing Eyrek to move aside. Instead of speaking, he removed his nor'harp from its case and began to play.

It started as a mellifluous song, but with every passing breath, it only became more haunting. Every note fraught Eyrek, making the hairs on his arms stand straight as daggers. After the third chorus, an eld stretched her neck and mourned at the sky. Dozens of dragons followed suit, until even Tythandrell joined his Lord Prince's lament.

At the song's finish, Vharyn kept his eyes closed. His fingers lingered on the strings. Thunder rumbled beneath the clouds. Not even a child dared whisper.

"Forgive my tardiness, brethren," the elf said. "I was composing a melody. It was entitled, *The Song for Crixalas.*"

His voice was slurred, more than Eyrek knew was usual for him. No one laughed. Everyone was aghast or too stunned.

"Oh. But you have all come here to be inspired." The Lord Prince opened his eyes and sneered. "Here, your speech! The rumors you grovel for are true. The *kvael-akar* who slew your brother riders is the *kvael-akar* who caused a *saer'ammath.*" A Severed Binding.

He leaned over the balustrade, the hideous half of his face on full display. It drew more horrified breaths.

"*I* issue *saer'ammaths. I* speak the *Níthrael'yr. I* execute you and your dragons. You would do well to remember. Now, return to your posts and Build something worthwhile for your Lord Prince."

Vharyn swayed back down the stair. Cup-shot as he was, everyone he neared straightened their backs. Only the Lords of the Old Dragonguard grinned, High Elves delighted by their sovereign. He passed the front tables, and the tables after that, until he came to one at the courtyard's rear. It was vacant, but for a single, withered elf.

Sensing a shadow, Rystendal Vacerys slowly turned. With the Lord Prince all but looming over him, he sprang to his knees. "Your Grace. My—my thanks. It was beautiful."

The courtyard was breathless. Vharyn placed a hand on his shoulder.

"Take the time you need to mourn, my brother. The Order shall grieve alongside you and our Second Rider." Vharyn narrowed his gaze at Torsten's displayed corpse. "This was a..." He circled his wrist, struggling for words. "*Terrible* tragedy."

Rystendal could contain himself no more. That sulking elf of few words howled into sobs.

The Lord Prince ghosted back through the doors. The crowd's shock reverberated through the courtyard. All but the High Elves were rapaciously pleased by it all.

Eyrek bore little love for the former Imperial Dragonguard, riders that answered to Vharyn alone; the prince's performance incensed him. In this dark hour, this was the last thing the younger riders needed. Eyrek remembered once more why Vharyn had made him the face of the Enterprise. Even the elvish prince knew he was a little kinder.

The Haverley elves glanced hopefully at him. Surely, he had a more comforting speech to follow this? Was anything to be done about the Were King and his *kvael-akar*?

Keeping Torsten on the balustrade, Eyrek stormed down the steps and swept for the double doors.

Eyrek burst through the Lord Prince's office. For once, it was occupied, but that did nothing to assuage his fury.

"Vharyn!"

The High Elf sat at the council table, facing the warboard. It was powered on. A chalice was in his hand. His nor'harp sprawled over the table.

"I helped Rysten raise him," Vharyn said bitterly. "I fed him as a hatchling, named him, since he spoke to me even before Rysten."

Eyrek marched the length of the chamber.

"Rysten said he would not obey his command to pull out." Perhaps Vharyn was speaking to the warboard. "But he always obeyed me. Rysten could never control him. This is his fault. If I had been there—"

Eyrek yanked him around. He almost dared suggest that precious Crix was a demon in dragon skin, and they were all the better with him dead.

The prince looked up. His eyes were swollen, but seeing Eyrek's expression, he laughed. "I understand. You are upset because I only composed a song for Crix—"

"*Why didn't you tell me?*" Eyrek bellowed.

"That your *mahlenn* sister Severed a Judge's Binding and murdered my dragon?"

He slammed his fist against the table. Hair-sized cracks appeared over the finished whitewood. "You knew she was the *kvael-akar* this entire time! You withheld the truth from me. You allowed it progress this far—"

"Sit, and we shall discuss your sister's fate—"

"You deserve to be thrown over Exar'forda's towers!"

Vharyn laughed. "Many on Elondria would agree." He pulled

up a chair. "I did not tell you because Tera Beren was ravaging you."

"She is my sister! You sent a Judge after her!"

"Did you follow my speech with a fairer one, Ivarion? How fared telling our riders that your beloved sister murdered Garreck and the Baron? That she aids the enemy that brought down your realm?" At his silence, Vharyn said, "Oh. You did not."

Eyrek tore at his hair. He could not think. Even now, he could not face all that Skálda had done to him. Tera Beren was one thing, but this—this went beyond betrayal.

"Elder Leondran is alive," said Vharyn.

The unexpected words thunderstruck him. Eyrek turned around, squinting. "What... did you say?"

"He knows what we did to Dellfast. It appears he has not yet told the Elenntarien or you and I would be halfway to Kar'thuul-dur Keep. But when he speaks, it *will* bring down the Order."

"No, that..." Eyrek shook his head. "Vharyn, that is impossible. I cleansed the entire city. I would never fail you in this."

The look the elf gave him drained the marrow from his knees. The Lord Prince stood, pacing airily around him.

"I learned everything I needed from the Isgardian spoils you brought me. The Were King is Leondran's son, the long-dead Prince Sorenthor." He laughed. "Who would have surmised?"

Eyrek's hands were shaking. "I... I promised the boy they would not be harmed..."

"He is dead now, worry not. They all are. The child told me where Solhall is. I have deployed a Kru'ul army."

"Vaeritas, what—Kru'ul?"

"Wasteland Elves, they are called. They have been breeding under Fel Tiron for centuries. The Lord of True Light has many more under his command."

Eyrek struggled for words. "Vharyn... I don't understand... You would negotiate with rogue fanatics... Does the Elenntarien know?"

"Their warlords answer to me alone," he said. "When Elder Leondran discovers my war plans, and he certainly shall, I predict he will leave Svennandia's walls to save his beloved boy. That will leave us with Calabran Astoraine, but I already have the child in the palm of my hand." Vharyn smiled. "Since you have not been able to rid us of the Elder, I will. I will reach out my hand, and pluck Fjorland for my own."

He stared at the Lord Prince.

"That surprises you." Vharyn poured himself wine. "It should not. The Astoraines have been a thorn in my side for too long. But I planned the end of that *mahlenn* bloodline long ago..." He flicked his gaze to Eyrek. "Sometimes, the royal families seem to forget how miniscule they are to the House of Morghûl."

A shard of clarity gouged Eyrek's shock. All this time, everyone had stopped paying attention to Lhyestrae's youngest child. He was a fallen legend, they thought. But while the Elenntarien had bickered and politicked over their Conclaves, Vharyn had plotted an entire *realm's* demise from the shadows. By the Light, and for how long? His carousing had merely been a deception.

Had he ever really known the Lord Prince?

"The only thing I cannot make sense of..." The elf brushed a thumb down his scar. "Why would your sister declare war on me over one hatchling? Was it truly her desperation to become a rider?"

Eyrek's forehead tightened.

"No matter." The Lord Prince nodded at the warboard. Old Svenn and Fjorland were blistering red. Now, Solhall appeared on the map for all posts to see. Vharyn had declared it a Level 10 warzone. It meant Aranor Elondris was now at war.

"The truth is, your sister defected to the wrong side. You humans do not seem to understand that Elondria has only one side.

Mine." Vharyn reached for his nor'harp. "I am taking matters into my own hands, Second. By the laws of the Order, my laws, she will die. My trusted leaders will see to it."

Eyrek closed his eyes. The prince laid a hand on his shoulder.

"I do not imagine you could pull through with it, nor do I expect you to. I have watched the enemy ravage you enough, Ivarion."

Ivarion. His elvish name burned his ears. It was all the Order knew him by.

"But I hope you will forgive me for not moving sooner on your behalf."

The prince's countenance darkened to something Eyrek had never seen before; the true face of Vharyn Morghûl, in all his elvish cruelty.

He swept through the doors, leaving Eyrek alone with the Order's inflamed warboard. Outside in the hallway, the dulcet notes of a nor'harp started again.

Eyrek avoided the crowds, answering no questions, and left straight for the High Eyrie. Two elvish guards stood at the entrance. More were posted on the surrounding turrets. This was a landmark very few, besides the Lord Prince, were permitted to enter.

With his rank, no guards were required to accompany him. He ascended the tower, a stone spire of seventy-five levels. It was one of the oldest structures in the Morghûl Empire, built by dwarves and High Elven magic centuries ago. His enhanced Dragonlord body kept him from panting at the top.

"Thane!"

His shout desecrated the silence. He stormed over the fresh bed of rush the ha'elf handlers had left. The low torches were enough to keep him from invoking the Dragonsight.

"Thane, where are you?"

A quiet rumble replied. He found his Great tucked away behind an olden pillar. If it were even possible, a dragon larger than Tythandrell sprawled over the rush. Her scales were a pure white, but solstices of neglect in the Eyrie's shadows had accumulated layers of grime on her. Thane kept his neck resting over hers, watching over her in sleep.

"Rise," Eyrek said. "We must return to the North."

His rough command sent a low whine in Tythandrell's throat. They had just arrived, and he was unwilling to leave his mate so soon. The continent's only other Great kept her eyes closed.

"Come, I said!"

The whine grew louder, more wounded. Tythandrell was torn between obeying him and entangling himself over Lumaerrax.

Someone stepped out from between them. Eyrek halted in his tracks. "Vhenna," he said.

"Stop this madness." The princess's furious eyes were even more swollen than his. She rested a hand on her late father's dragon. "Ever since Tera Beren, I have seen vengeance drive you to insanity. This is not the Eyrek I know, nor the man I fell in love with."

He marched past her and wrenched Thane up by the great forehorn. "Rise. I won't tell you again!"

This time, Tythandrell obeyed, lifting himself onto his claws. Anguish rushed through their Binding. Lumaerrax kept her eyes closed. Vhalentae blocked his path and seized his wrist.

"Eyrek!" she hissed. "Let the Enterprise go. Live for the life we have in Rhaennöria, not for the life you had in Teralynn!"

"I cannot," he said. "I failed the Order. I failed the Lord Prince. He is involving himself because I was too weak to stop this, but no more. I am going to kill her. I am going to kill them all."

He tried to climb onto Tythandrell's outstretched wing, but her grip on him tightened even more.

"Eyrek," she whispered. "I am carrying your child."

Those words thundered into his chest. He looked down at her. She was fighting tears.

"For how long?" he said.

"I-I do not know. A cycle perhaps. I would have told you sooner, but I could not reach you."

He placed a hand on her belly, and said softly, "Then I have even more reason to go."

"No—"

"Our child will grow up on a continent that is safe," he said. "The only way I can ensure this is to purge the Wereguild, and all Vigardians."

With his greater Dragonlord strength, he wrenched himself free and climbed onto Tythandrell. Vhalentae collapsed onto her hands.

"I am begging you, Eyrek." Hearing a Morghûl's anguish made the Great Dragons shift in distress. "Vengeance is a wildfire that leaves no victors. This obsession will destroy you."

"The Light has appointed me this duty," he said. "I see it now. The Were King's death is my charge. I alone can see it through. On Vaeritas's name, I will save our continent."

His betrothed shut her eyes.

"*Éad'hel!*"

On his command, Tythandrell charged over the rush. In several leaps and reverberating wingbeats, they were airborne, streaming toward a colossal outer dragon arch. The crown princess wept into her hands.

19
VERDORN'S FAILURE WAKES FROM THE EAST

"SIRE, a transmission—you must come to the council room at once!"

Jory galloped across the hills of the Edholt, Leon's private hunting grounds. He and Gwynne turned in their saddles. Lately, since the events of Dellfast, Leon had spent most of his time here, with her, away from any elvish birds that might overhear anything they said.

King Leon, normally effusive in public, had declined to make any appearances even before his political faction. His allies were restless. They sensed he was soul-shaken, that something beyond the official reports had happened in Dellfast. But though his tongue burned to scourge the Order before the public, he honored his oath to Elder Staunnton to stay silent. He only hoped that the High Eldari would transmit to him soon, and affirm the Ivarion and Lord Prince's life sentences.

It was the only thing cleaving him to sanity.

Breathless, Jory pulled the reins before the king's destrier. "A live transmission, for your ears alone, sire." He bowed his head to Gwynne. "My Lady Queen."

"Elder Staunnton?" said Leon.

Jory appeared strangled. "Not His Eminence... It bears the crest of Exar'forda. The verse says the Lord Prince wishes to speak with you."

Leon sucked in a sharp breath. Gwynne looked like she was about to plummet off her saddle.

"*Vharyn Morghûl* wishes to speak with me?" he hissed.

"That is the only verse we received, sire..."

Their worried gazes fell on him. "Impossible," Leon said. The Lord Prince had not transmitted to anyone outside the Order in four solstices, much less shown himself to the Republic.

"You are sure?" said Leon.

"Come see for yourself, sire."

Gwynne whispered, "What could he possibly want with you?"

Leon leaned in to kiss her. "We will know soon." He heeled his destrier into a canter back to his castle proper.

Eleven weeks had passed since Dellfast's burning and he could walk again, albeit a wrong angle still shot his calf with pain. He nodded at the guards posted outside the council room. They bowed low and parted the doors for him. Leon took his seat at the head, in front of the cobalt banner of Fjorland.

Jory had spoken true. The Order's white dragon crest blazed against his face. His hand wavered. Did the elvish prince know what he had disclosed to the High Eldari? That he was pushing for a Kar'thuul-dur life sentence, even an end to the Order?

With a sense of foreboding, Leon touched the lodestone, accepting the transmission.

At once, the white dragon flickered out of the waystones. In its place was a hologram of the Lord of Dragonsteel. No amount of preparation could have prepared Leon for such an audience. Vharyn Morghûl, like all elves, had a far glossier sheen to his eyes and flesh. As a High Elf, that beauty was even more pronounced in the refined symmetry of his face, the cascade of hair that was not black so much as a lustrous sable.

Yet he was as grotesque as he was resplendent. The rumors were not false. His alabaster face, all sharp angles, might have been stunning if not for the mutilation running down the entire right side, from forehead to jaw. The raised scar tissue was horribly perforated, the thickness of almost three fingers put together. It sickened the king to look upon it.

"Elder Leondran," he said, in the official tongue.

He had met the Lord Prince once; actually, just before Vharyn left for what was supposed to be Elondria's greatest campaign in history. Beneath the monoliths of the Basilica, the prince had appealed to the Holy Elenntarien for approval to campaign in the southern continent. He meant to retake the islands of Old Valindor, which now belonged to the growing Nhilgraad Empire. Above all, ambition convinced him he would be the one to annul the Betrayer.

So self-assured he was back then, albeit in hindsight, they had all been fools to believe in him. The lords of Elondria had bought into his glorious vision, donating immeasurable soldiers, resources, and coin. The continent had hailed him off as a hero. Only a fortnight later, the Betrayer's generals had returned their champion in a boat, unconscious, chained, and mutilated with a spell that could never be undone. The word "DOG" had been written on Vharyn's forehead in blood. The horizon boomed with Nhilgraadian laughter, a harrowing noise Leon would never forget—nor, he presumed, Vharyn.

Afterward, the masses had shown the elf no pity; but they had excoriated him for the one hundred thousand Elondrians slaughtered under his command. The campaign had been an utter debacle. Even with dragons, Vharyn had not made it further than the shores of Verdorn, the largest of Old Valindor's islands.

"Prince Vharyn," he said carefully. "Well met."

"Is it well, Elder?"

"Is there... something Fjorland can do for you?"

The Lord Prince was standing over his council table, pouring wine into a chalice. "This is your formal notice that in a few weeks, my host will cross into your borders."

Leon chuckled incredulously. "I am not certain I heard you correctly."

"We are merely passing through, do not worry. My warlords shall leave Fjorland as they found it."

The king snorted. "What do you speak of, Prince Vharyn? You are leading another army?"

"The Elenntarien has already granted approval."

"The Elenntarien—" Leon snapped forward. "They approved of *what*?"

"I am only contacting you now, as you all but shut off your transmitter to the Republic." He paced his office, sipping wine. "In fact, consider this a courtesy. It was His Eminence that bade me to transmit to you in his place, since he believes brothers of the faith should try to get along." The prince turned his back. "He is a royal naïf, isn't he?"

What was Prince Vharyn even saying? Leon could no longer feel his face.

"But we should try for him, nonetheless." As the Lord Prince leisurely paced, he waved his chalice. "I know you will give me no resistance, as we are indeed brothers caught in a most delicate situation."

"What situation?"

The Lord Prince stopped to look at him oddly. "You have not heard, Elder? The Order secured Solhall's location. On behalf of the Republic, I am marching to annul the Wereguild, and all Vigardians, from our continent." He lapped at wine black as ichor. "Perhaps this is a military campaign I can win, no?"

Leon's mouth dropped open, though he was not entirely aware of it. "His Eminence... granted this?"

Prince Vharyn pulled back his chair. "Why such a port of surprise, Elder? Is Sorenthor Astoraine not also your enemy?"

Hearing his own son's name on this transmission plunged a sword into Leon's soul. The prince's eyes beheld a vengeful glint. There was no doubt now that the elf knew everything he had disclosed to the High Eldari. And yet, for all the bloodshed the Order had committed... His Eminence chose to take Vharyn's side?

This was a complete betrayal. More than that—it was treachery of the highest order. Yet Leon was not angry. He was frightened. All his career, he had campaigned against the Morghûls, defended mankind from the shameless hegemony of the elves. He thought he had elevated the Old Faction to the seat of Elondria's true power. But power lay not with Lhyestrae and her supporters, or even the High Eldari...

It dawned on Leon that his family was no longer safe. The Elenntarien had abandoned him to face the wrath of the Order on his own.

"I take your silence as agreement," said the Lord Prince. "On behalf of the Republic of Aranor Elondris, I thank you, Elder."

The hologram flickered out. It took Leon a boundless amount of time to realize he was staring at a blank board. He could not think. War on Elondria again. War against his bloodline at the hands of Vharyn Morghûl. That was impossible... and a war he could not win.

The Lord Prince was marching to obliterate Soren.

"Gwynne!" he bellowed, staggering out of his seat. "Jory! Where are you?"

It was not long before the king's wife and closest friend joined him at the council table. Leon shut the doors tightly behind them.

"Verdorn's failure wakes from the east," he said. "This time, he marches upon us."

Jory folded his hands into his face in despair.

"I must go to Soren," Leon said.

"This is the end of us," the chief advisor muttered. "His Eminence has abandoned Fjorland..."

The queen's eyes were swollen, but she said firmly, "Leon, you cannot go. There is no hope for Vingulmark. You heard what the Order did to Isgardia."

"He is my son."

"He is our son, but Fjorland will not profit from your death. If you go, they will kill you."

"You can't know that."

Gwynne seized his wrists. "We both know it, Leon! Did it not strike you that the prince was using that transmission to provoke you into leaving Republic borders? Out there in the Deep North, there are no laws! The Order can do whatever it will!"

Leon shook his head. The shock of what was happening, the abrupt inversion of power, still had not settled in. What blind fools he and Lhyestrae had been to keep their eyes fixed on each other, when their true enemy had plotted behind their backs!

"If no one will stand against the Order," said Leon, "then our freedom is already lost. It is not merely a war for the Vigardians, don't you understand?"

Jory began, "Sire—"

"It is for the freedom of mankind's sovereignty against elves! Against the Morghûls. If no one will stop them now, then what is to stop them from turning all Aranor Elondris into their empire?" He glared at his cobalt banner. "We all know that is what they have always wanted. And the day that were ever to happen, woe upon mankind..."

"Please." Gwynne fell onto her knees. "Leon, you are the *King of Fjorland.* You cannot go."

"There will always be another king. This is far bigger than that."

"Soren made his decision long ago not to return. He is a grown man; he knew the consequences of taking a Vigardian crown—and by the Light, attacking the Ivarion! Did he think no one would eventually find him out? Did we not plead with him many times to come home?"

"Gwynne," he said gently.

"But Cal and I, the realm—the Republic, we need you."

Leon saw suddenly the family oil painting hanging in his hallway, the faces of two boys he had lost. Perciven was dead, and for many solstices, he had thought the same of Soren. He still remembered like yesterday the day he received a transmission from his long fallen son, revealing that he had been alive all along, and newly coronated over the greatest Vigardian fiefdom.

How Soren had taken Thorgest Vigarda's seat, or aroused war against the elves, Leon did not know. It was unfathomable. All he knew were the memories of Soren as a child, the way Soren used to hug him tight every night before bed, and whisper, "I love you, Da. Don't forget."

Leon met his wife's eyes. "My boy needs me."

Gwynne shook her head in despair.

"For all his life," said Leon, "I was King of Fjorland. I professed to love him, but when the time came to prove it, I turned my back on him for the Republic." He clenched his fist. "But he is alive, and it may not be for much longer if I stay here and do nothing. Vaeritas is granting me a second chance."

The queen pressed a hand to her head and wept. Jory looked like he was making every effort not to shed a tear.

Leon stood. "I will take few guards with me, for no one must know of my absence. Do not tell Cal about this. The Order will come for us, but you must protect him above all. Do I have your oaths?"

They nodded unwillingly.

"I will return soon." The king strode to the door. "I am going to bring my son home."

Jory called, "But sire, how will you find him?"

The question made Leon pause at the door. He glanced over his shoulder. "I won't need to. The Draughammr will find me."

20
PICKLE, PICKLE, CRINKLE THE WINKLE

SOREN's main camp fell into a maelstrom of chaos. On his orders, his Weremen combed the wealds for Skálda, but most were still riding off their relief to see their Draughammr back and alive. His shield-brothers barraged him with questions. Elf blood drenched his face and arms. His battle axe was still in his hand.

But Soren's attention stayed between the evergreens. He could no longer hear the ice monster, and his fears were rising. The Judge must have captured her.

As he steeped in these thoughts, a small, wiry shape appeared in the corner of his eye. Noticing his sudden silence, his shield-brothers turned with him.

There she was, marching toward camp in all her dusky quietude. As always, the burning opals in her eyes glowered at the world. The lank, ashen strands of her hair clung to her neck. Her face was as bloody as her elvish axe. Skálda Branwright looked like a savage Vigardian if there ever was one.

Seeing him, she shouted, "Soren!" Skálda broke into a sprint. Just before her blade could axe him, she dropped it and embraced him around the neck. The emotion in her skinny limbs startled him.

Letting go, she went on her toes and caressed his bearded jaw. "You're alive."

It felt marvelous to be touched like that by a woman again. "As you," he said. "I had thought—"

Soren immediately stopped, feeling his shield-brothers' stares. He and Skálda backed away from each other in embarrassment. She pulled him aside and lowered her voice. "How aren't you dead?"

He snorted. "Were you hoping for me to return dead?"

"I don't believe you killed Xandria Kirylith."

"Not her. Just eight others. The rest fled."

Skálda looked at him like he was insane.

"You killed eight Rangers?" she said. "Eight *elves*?"

"Am I not the Draughammr?" he said wryly. Before she could ask anything he would not be inclined to answer, he continued, "And I assume you lost the Judge?"

"I killed his dragon."

Soren laughed. "What?"

She bore her unsettling eyes on him. His smile faded. It was his turn to look at her like she was insane.

"You killed a High Elf's dragon," he repeated flatly.

"Like you killed eight elves, Draughammr."

The corner of his lip twitched with a little smile he could not control. Skálda truly intrigued him.

Rulf butted between them. "Dragon girl, you're a jester. What did you kill that beast with, your bare hands?"

She shrugged. "We shouldn't let his hide go to waste." Pointing her axe in the direction she came, she said, "Should we skin him now, or after supper?"

His shield-brothers gawked at her.

On the way to their mounts, Skálda leaned into Soren's furs. After some careful thought, he wrapped an arm around her, merely to keep her warm. Perhaps that was his mistake. He heard too late the *Lhaer'thri* she invoked over him, under her breath.

DURING THE WEEK it took to return to Solhall, Skálda did not stop searching the skies from the saddle. Soren seemed to notice. Though he said nothing of it to her, his mouth formed a tight line.

When they were back at the manse, Soren went first to see his children. They sprinted out to meet him before he had even dismounted. While he caught them in his arms, Skálda took it to mean she would not be feeding them and went to wash herself. Bale's absence, and that ever pressing need to see him, ached her. Her heart was already hollow enough.

She was helping Lady Sibbe wash laundry when Asveig abruptly stepped out into the central yard.

"Where is the Draugh?" he said.

His urgency was unusual. Skálda gave him a bare stare that said, How should I know?

Frit and Evynd's laughter echoed over the rooftops. Asveig marched past them and shouted, "Draugh!"

Some time later, Soren reemerged with the white-bearded Vigardian, holding his children by the hands. Asveig's news had turned the Draugh back into Vingulmark's thundercloud. Skálda pointedly tried to catch his eye, until he relented with a call. "Come, dragon girl!"

At his invite, Skálda abandoned the laundry and slunk after him. Lady Sibbe shook her head in disapproval.

They filed into the council room on the second floor. Asveig took his seat at a wing table and nodded at her to do the same with the children. Soren assumed his place at the center table and reached for the lodestone that would power on his transmitter.

"You are certain?" he asked his second.

Asveig nodded. "Let your own eyes see it, Draugh. The cipher was Fjorland's coat-of-arms."

Skálda raised her brows. That could only mean an incoming message from one man in Elondria. Soren's shadowed gaze stayed on his board. He was anguishing over whether to take the transmission. His look alone told her he had not spoken with his father for many solstices; perhaps not since becoming King of the Weres.

Everyone was watching him, waiting to see what he would do.

Soren awakened the waystone screen. It was the length of the back wall and thrice Anders's board in breadth. At the center hovered a holographic royal crest, two eagles rearing on a shield emblazoned with the Sun. It was crowned with the scales of justice.

His thumb twitched. "Keep silent," Soren told them. He touched the lodestone to accept the message.

Fjorland's crest faded out. Leondran Astoraine appeared on the other end, seated before a magnificent cobalt tapestry with his family heraldry. He looked far more haggard than Skálda remembered, when they last met in Dellfast. For one, he was unshaved, and his short waves had grown out to his shoulders. Most prominent of all were the bags beneath his eyes, like he had gotten no sleep since Dellfast's burning.

"Vaeritas..." The king sounded astonished to see his son, even though he had initiated the transmission. Emotion tightened the creases on his face. "Soren..."

"Why have you contacted me?"

The Draugh's voice was even colder than when she first met him on the longboats. Leondran's eyes glistened. This transmission was straining them both. Skálda could not help but think of her mother and their last days together in the Skonkauld.

Leondran fortified his voice, assuming the polished carriage of an Eldari. "I come with a warning."

"Generous of Fjorland." Soren sneered. "I already know your Skitr King is coming for me."

"That is not—"

"Perhaps you should have warned me that you would turn your back on my family when they begged you for aid. Not that it should have confounded Inaric. This is what you do for the Republic."

"Soren, please listen—"

"Do not call me that. You know who I am to you."

"You must—"

"Don't contact me again."

He reached for the lodestone. Sitting here listening to them felt like getting pulled apart slowly on a torture rack. She considered leaving the room.

"Vharyn Morghûl has deployed a Kru'ul army against you," said Leon.

Soren stopped cold. Hearing mention of the Lord Prince, Skálda sat taller in her seat. The Draugh narrowed his eyes. "Kru'ul?"

"Wasteland Elves. Part elf, part ghoul. They were born halfway between Midgaard and Mordgaard, and now, I have reason to believe—"

"Kru'ul?" Soren laughed. "There have not been hordes of Kru'ul for a thousand solstices. Do you speak Vollmark's lore to me now?" The king's gaze stayed shadowed. "I don't believe for a moment the Elenntarien would allow that disgraced elvish skit to lead anything, much less—"

"Vharyn himself transmitted to me not an hour ago."

The room fell into a stunned silence. Skálda retreated into herself. Elondria had not seen bloodshed since the War of Treason. Though she was not alive then to witness it, she knew how much the mere memory still affected the older folk. Kael's grandmother said the war had blackened the entire earth, wiped entire realms and bloodlines off the map. Six in every ten Elondrians perished in the field. All Skálda knew about Republic politics was that the silver-robed Elders would never allow another continental war.

She still felt their defeat to the Betrayer as an echo haunting the earth.

"The Elenntarien allowed this?" Soren said, dumbstruck by the impossibility of it. "They allow a host to march freely across the land? A host of *Kru'ul*, led by *Vharyn*?"

"I can't say if they are really Kru'ul, for I haven't seen his troops. But a host is coming. The High Eldari sealed it on his executive order."

"How many?"

"Twenty thousand strong, according to what I learned. I verified it with the Elenntarien."

"Light have mercy." Asveig rose from his seat, turning his back to the board.

"And dragons?" said Soren.

"No dragons. Vharyn appears unwilling to spare anymore of his riders to the guild. He thinks the Kru'ul will be sufficient."

"The Ivarion will come of his own accord," Asveig murmured across the room. "We still have his tomb to dig."

"The Lord Prince's forces have crossed north out of the Sundered Mountains," King Leondran said. "That was two fortnights ago. They will be in Lysmark soon. There is little time left."

"Lysmark is Old Faction." The Draugh's face shadowed even more. "Your ally. You have betrayed me again."

"You know what the Wereguild is to the Republic, son. You know a private army of Vharyn's is indisputably neutral to all factions. Much as I despise the High Eldari for what he has done, I know he could not argue against it. You think even he has the power to stop twenty thousand Kru'ul, or the Illuminators that allied with Vharyn?"

"Those fanatics are also involved? You speak madness!"

"What are Illuminators?" Skálda murmured. Frit warned her to hush.

"Who else could supply such a host?" said Leon. "Who else

could be breeding armies of Kru'ul? It would take magic not even the Morghûls have a taste for."

"Fjorland granted them access." Soren said this reproachfully.

"They will come whether or not I grant it."

"Did you tell him about Solhall?"

"I don't know who revealed Solhall's location," Leondran said, "or that you are the Were King. But you must understand this army is larger than all the armies of the Svennish realms combined. The Old Faction cannot stop this."

"So? What is your purpose here?"

"Vingulmark is lost. Every Vigardian kingdom is lost. The Order will ravage anything it can find. This is not the Ivarion you are facing, Soren. The Lord Prince means to do to the Deep North what he failed to do to Calendria."

Soren glanced at his lodestone in disgust. "If that is all the counsel you have, Elder, then you never should have contacted me."

"I contacted you because the Vigardians are beyond saving. But I can protect you. Allow me this, Soren. Let me amend this unnecessary rift between us. Bring your family and whomever you will; the Republic will not find out." His next words came in a whisper. "Come home."

"If that is all the counsel you have..." Soren leaned forward in his seat. "Then you never should have contacted me."

He shut off the transmitter.

Asveig was too flummoxed to speak. Frit leaned over to Skálda and whispered, "That sounded terrible. Are we at war?" When Skálda had no response, she called, "Father, are we at war? Skálda wants to know who the Illuminators are."

Soren pressed his hands to his face, slumping over the table. In his father's absence, his exhaustion and despair finally showed. But Skálda stayed still in thought. The Draugh had been wrong about the Lord Prince. Vharyn Morghûl was far from fallen. Her nemesis was making his move—and it was time for her to make hers.

"You must release Aesir," she said.

Soren shifted to look at her.

"Let me speak to him. He'll know what to do." Skálda left the room without waiting for his answer.

"Aesir." Skálda pulled open the door to the decrepit shed that was his prison.

The elf-man slowly raised his head. He slouched on a bench in the dark, wrists shackled to the clay floor. It looked like the Vigardians had drilled them in place just for him, fortifying them with double the nails to account for his superior elvish strength. There was little else inside but the straw.

As he looked up at her, she stopped. Tangles of his beard clumped beneath his chin. The right side of his face was freshly bruised, and his right eye was swollen shut. He looked at her as if she had done this to him.

"Finngólfa," she said. "I didn't know."

His caustic stare discomforted her.

"I came to free you—"

He laughed, cutting her short. Skálda knelt by him, clenching his chains.

"Soren!" she bellowed. "Let Jarmon beat him again, and I will string him by his bollocks and cut off his head!"

There came no answer. Skálda shouted in frustration and turned back to Aesir. "I need your help."

"You remembered me again."

She ignored his off-putting tone and recounted the transmission from King Leondran. In the fires of her anger, she almost blurted what had happened with Bale as well, but instinct stopped her in time. What would the Imperial Ranger do if she admitted her Bael had developed his mind-control powers, or that she had seen the inconceivable power dormant in his script?

"The reason I haven't come to you sooner," she said, "is because I have been little more than a thrall myself. In the time I've campaigned, I gained the Draugh's trust. He will let you go if I show him that you, too, can help Solhall."

Aesir leaned his head back against the wall. "You are a fool, she-wolf."

Skálda exhaled in impatience.

The elf said, "You think I care for the fall of Vigardians?"

"This is going to be the start of a continental war, don't you see?" she snapped. "Didn't you say your queen lives for peace? No one in Aranor Elondris can stop Vharyn, but the Deep North can."

"Leave me be, she-wolf."

"If Vharyn wins this war, he will burn everything. The Order will kill you with the rest!"

He looked her straight in the eye. "You made a promise to me in the Prannon. But you went behind that promise to fight Dragonsteel. Worse, you slew riders."

"I did not kill Torsten, and Garreck was—"

"My greatest error," he interrupted, "was defending you against the Order. I see now you never intended to bring that Bael to Traust."

Her voice turned cold. "That's all you ever think about. Bale loves you, but you have always hated him. Should I hate you for being an elf?"

"Oh, your Vigardian friends already do—"

"What I don't understand is how you are blind to Bale's terrors. Something in Atallgaard caused him to fall into our Realm—"

"I told you nothing lives in Atallgaard."

"He implored me to protect him. If you even felt a thread of his fear—"

"Ah!" Aesir snapped forward, wrestling with his chains. "With you, it is always one more day. One more quest you need the Bael for. Your coddling never ends. You heed none of my warnings that one day, he *will* Break you and all Elondria. You ride him like a dragon. You would use him to war against *the Order*—"

"You saw what the Lord Prince did to Dellfast! What he did to my home!"

"So, you are going to annul the Lord Prince now?"

When she did not answer, he laughed. "Look at you, Skálda. Look at what you've become."

She turned her burning gaze to the ground. "How do you, of all *men*, not see what the Morghûls are?"

"They are what Elondria needs—"

"Dellfast? The slaughter of mankind is what Elondria needs?" Her shout brought activity outside the shed. Weremen were gathering outside with axes drawn.

"You think I am evil," she hissed, "when you serve the elvish family that massacres humans without consequence! Human villages and cities are nothing to them. Commons are nothing. You are human, you see what they do to our kind. They heap chains on you, their Rangers beat you, and you still grovel at the elves—"

"I serve the power that would keep this continent at peace!" he roared, pulling at his chains. "If the Lord Prince has risen from the grave, it is because you have provoked him. You killed his Builders. The end to *forty solstices* of peacetime is your doing!"

His words scalded her.

"You have undone *everything* Lhyestrae and I sacrificed to protect." He slammed his chains against the bench. "You betrayed my trust, Skálda. I had hoped to find something better than Realm-Building in you, but all I have seen is that you are more of a Breaker than that Bael."

A knife was slowly twisting into her gut. This was the last thing she ever expected to hear from her elvish friend.

"Break realms all you wish," said Aesir, "but I am no traitor. If you have any decency left, tell your friends to be done with their play and kill the elf. Leave me, now."

A Wereman's stare burned her back. Soren was looming in the doorway, listening to everything. She flushed, wondering how much he had overheard.

Lowering her voice, she said, "You once told me you would grant me a *calar'calai*." She was invoking the sacred elvish boon he had offered her in the Prannon forests. As she understood it, once it was given, an elf was bound by it.

Aesir widened his eyes in alarm, then narrowed them in resentment.

"Leave Vingulmark," she said. "Go back to your queen. Disclose nothing of the Wereguild or anything you have seen in the North." She stood. "Neither do I wish to see you again."

Astonishment broke over Aesir's face, but she swept away before he could say anymore. Soren would not move aside, so she glowered up at him. The shock of her fury kept her from thinking straight.

"Move!" she snarled.

His arms were crossed, but he obliged. Over her shoulder, she called, "I take it the Draugh who reads Elvynnöthe knows what a *calar'calai* is."

It was not a question. Skálda whirled around as she marched backwards, paying no heed to the spectating Weremen. "He will be of no harm to you. Or keep him here, and I will cut off Jarmon's wrist by morning tomorrow."

"And string you up by the bollocks," Rulf whispered to his side. "You should leave Solhall tonight."

Jarmon snorted. Aesir called behind her, "I will die, or I will go free with my rings!"

"Give him his belongings," Skálda said.

Soren looked at her for a long time. "I will have Jarmon escort him to the border, if that is your wish."

She glanced over her shoulder. Aesir's eyes were dappled with pain. They had come so far, defended each other from Rangers, raised Bale together.

"Farewell, Elessir," she whispered, and left the yard.

AESIR WAS CONVINCED the Draughammr had ordered his men to make his journey to the border Hel. That most loathsome Vigardian, the one with two beard braids, dragged him along on foot from horseback. Aesir was leaving the Deep North the way he came in, but his wrists were chained in front of him, at least. He had to keep it that way—and find a private moment alone.

Since Two Beard shot him foul looks, Aesir said in the Svenning, "If we are truthful with each other, I hate Vharyn Mhorgûl like a Vigardian axe stuck up your buttocks."

The band of ten ignored him as they trudged through the mountains.

"Even then, I hope he destroys you, buttocks withal."

A Wereman on foot, his guard, struck Aesir's jaw with the vicious sharp of his knuckles. Aesir crashed onto his knees.

"Shut up, elf," the Wereman said.

Two Beard glanced back from the saddle. "An elf man that speaks the Svenning. I don't know of any more abominable creation in Elondria." He yanked the chain, jerking Aesir's wrists painfully. "Vaeritas must have a sense of humor, eh, skit!"

Two more cruel tugs forced Aesir back onto his feet. He stumbled and spat blood.

"Abominable," he said in the Svenning, "or vexing?"

"Shut up, I said!" his guard warned.

"But what must be truly vexing," Aesir trilled, "is having to carry two pigtails everywhere one goes. *I* think they are cute, to be clear. Now the village where I am from, the little girls all braided their hair that way."

Two Beard halted his horse. Drawing the axe at his belt, he leapt off his saddle. His heavy boots slammed against the dirt. Aesir started another quip, but never finished. The Vigardian struck him with all the boiling wrath of the North.

The next time Aesir woke, chains secured him to an alpine tree. The Vigardians gathered around a fire, sharing supper and ribald elf jokes beneath the curtain of night. Not to his surprise, he was not invited.

Vaeritas was good.

His head throbbed from the impact of Two Beard's blow, and his vision was still blurred from fatigue, but he focused on his new surroundings. He was hugging a tree with his hands tied in front. Very good. Aesir reached for the waystone ring he had twisted back on in Solhall.

He tapped the stone seven times, then spoke the elvish translation for "pickle, pickle, crinkle the winkle, fickle-diddle a great mickle jiggle." Then he murmured a most grave greeting.

"Your Sovereignty?"

It was cycles since he sent his last transmission to the ruling Morghûl, the one whom he most loved and hated. He prayed both that a response would come quickly and none would come at all.

Just when the wait became unbearable, the waystone talked back to him.

"Speak."

It was never a good thing when the waystone was furious.

Aesir stared at the ants crawling on the trunk. He knew what he must say, but the words lodged in his heart. For a season, he had anguished over this very moment. Making the moral decision kept him from sleep. The girl was like his own blood... the child he always wanted, and almost had, with Tessyn.

Yet something about her drew his hackles. His gut feeling in the Skonkauld was that power never ought to fall to this pale-eyed common. And he was right. The more power she acquired through the Bael, the more of Elondria she was breaking. He would keep himself bound to his *calar'calai* and say nothing of the Vigardians. But he would tell the truth.

"I found the *faolrún* as you commanded..." Aesir forced himself on. "I found what fell, Lhyra."

21
THE IVARION'S OATH UPON THE ELLDHÈLEN

Over the following two cycles, Vingulmark's allies camped in the Eldruna Valley to prepare for war. Heeding Soren's call to arms were the Duke Einnar Valda of Dussex and Earl Solfreid Wulfgar of East Wexar, among other chieftains. But most unexpected of all was the belly-deep horn that blew at the end of the second cycle.

It raised every head in the manse. Skálda came out onto the path with Soren to look. Frit dropped her mouth.

Marching up the slopes of Solhall were *giants*. But these were not like the Thomdrim Skálda had seen during her early days of capture. They wore hauberks and leather gambesons like Vigardians in battle, and held axes larger than her face. The nostrils of their big, flat noses seemed to flare with every step.

Every Vigardian present went agog. Surely such a sight had been pulled out of a storybook from the days of Old Svenn. The Thomdrim, a cousin race of the Vjolgaard dwarves, had not fought side-by-side with men since the days of the Dragon Wars.

A hulking Thomdrim with quills for hair stopped several paces ahead of the warband. The ends of his cascading eyebrows were braided. He clenched his axe like he was going to cut through them all.

Frit leaned over to Skálda and whispered, "Wow, Thomdrim with axes... They're kind of cute, aren't they?"

"*Cute?*"

The brow-braided giant turned to her, overhearing. "Did you just call me *cute*, little girl?"

Frit leapt into the air like a cat with its back arched in pure terror. Soren marched past them. "Roagrim!"

"Draughammr," the giant roared back.

They clasped arms, grinning at each other. While the Weremen went on gawking in the background, Soren said, "This is unexpected. I had thought the fighting drim enclaves had long departed to the Freeholds."

"The Leafweavers are the last to remain. Something about these wealds keeps our hearts rooted in the trees."

"Old Svenn is your home," said Soren.

"Ours, friend. I have brought my Leafweavers—" Roagrim gestured with his axe at the rest of his Thomdrim. "We heard that most vile elf sent Kru'ul against our friends. Kru'ul!"

"It is madness, yes—but so is this strange age."

The giant gave a solemn nod. "Since we cannot bear to leave our lands, we have decided to stay. We will die here. We will lend our axes to the Draughammr and resurrect the old alliance between Thomdrim and Thorgest Vigarda's children." Roagrim lowered his axe. "Though it has been many hundreds of solstices, we see Vigarda's heirs in you, Sorenthor."

The grizzly giant knelt. All the Thomdrim followed their leader. Frit's eyes glistened in awe.

"That's my father!" she told everyone with pride.

Knowing it was time for an explanation, Soren turned to face his people. "Roagrim is an old friend. Long ago, when I was taken into the North as a thrall, he saved my life too many times to count."

Skálda sensed these unexpected words were meant for her. These days, Soren's attention was oft on her.

"And I shall do it again"—Roagrim rose to his looming height—"for all that you have done for the Thomdrim. We will shield the Wolves as many times as we must to drive the elves and their dragon thralls off our lands!"

This prompted the Leafweavers to raise their giant axes and roar. The Vigardians joined them in a jubilant cry.

All in all, by the end of the second cycle, Soren had gathered ten thousand of Old Svenn's axes. But Skálda knew it was still not enough. Nothing would be enough against twenty thousand ghoul elves of another age... if even such an army could exist.

Skálda insisted on leaving Solhall many times to look for her Bael. She could not accept that Rulf and his dragon slayers were still scouring the forests for him. When she vaguely told Soren she would ride out to try her hand, he clasped her wrist.

"It's healed," he said. "Which means we must remind it how to wield an axe again."

"Soren—"

"But you are Vigardian now. I will show you how to fight like a proper one."

His eyes were glinting. When he looked at her like that, Skálda found herself unable to resist him.

"Very well, Thorgest Vigarda." She rolled her eyes. "Show me how *you* wield an axe."

Soren's training sessions were a welcome distraction from the growing hollow of Bale's absence. He seemed to sense this, and spent any free time he had with her, showing her advanced axe combinations she had never seen before. Soren's excellent bladesmanship never ceased to awe her. It came as little wonder the Vigardians of Thorgest's old lands had chosen him for their leader.

Every day, before the early dawn and after midnight, they trained tirelessly in the privacy behind the manse. They trained until Skálda could throw with her right hand better than ever before.

When she was not dueling Soren, or serving on his war councils as an advisor, she labored with the Vigardians to prepare for war. On the Draugh's orders, they dug potholes into the Hammerfest Road on the other side of the dike. She got down on her knees in the dirt beside Soren, excavating holes two paces wide, and fit in steel-tipped stakes. The Vigardians then concealed these holes with meshes of branches and dirt.

During this time, the Leafweaver Enclave joined the non-fighting Thomdrim refugees to conduct work under the Eldruna Valley. When Skálda asked Soren about this, he would not give an answer.

Under Soren's oversight, they forged as many weapons as they could. Fourteen tremendous dragon slayers, with all their complicated contraptions and engineer work, turned into twenty-eight. Roagrim's Leafweavers helped forge them, working into the night. The Vigardians handed all spare axes and small shields to the free commons. Where they could not forge enough axes and pikes, Soren equipped all other peasants with bows. By the time all was said and done, every spare common in Vingulmark was turned into a foot archer. The Thomdrim kept engineering, and the Vigardians kept digging, but they were as prepared as they could be for Vharyn's host.

With the bulk of the preparations finished, Skálda left to find her oldest friend. Anders was in the guarded rider courtyard, on his knees, examining Nornsir's claws.

"Curvature looks good," he mused. He gently thumped the foreleg's knee joint with a mallet. "Very good... bones remain strong..."

The dark gray pica rumbled with pleasure as Anders wrestled out loose stones caught in the skin folds between his talons. Right after, Anders rubbed them with beeswax. Feorya trotted around the rider impatiently, butting at his backside with her stubby head.

"Alright, alright," said Anders, "you'll have your turn soon, Feorya!"

A heavier chain rattled, and a third shadow fell over the picas and their post leader. Feorya plunked onto her haunches, her eyes widening. Incendra lowered her bigger head and butted Anders on the rear end, too.

The Ealdorman burst into laughter. "Yes, and you, beauty." He stroked the scarlet eld down the length of her nose ridge. Incendra nuzzled him, drawing out an even fonder smile from Anders.

Skálda stopped behind him. "Still haven't lost your touch with dragons, I see."

"Did Bale join our queue, too?" Anders wiped the sweat off his brow.

She glanced away. "I still haven't found him."

"I am sorry, Skálda. With wild dragons, it is different..."

"Can you talk?" she said.

Skoll's post leader gestured at an ash tree across the yard. All three dragons padded after him like eager pups waiting for a treat. Anders glanced over his shoulder and chuckled.

They picked their spots under the shade. Before Skálda could even sit, Feorya rudely wedged herself between them, pressing her body up against Anders and laying her head on his lap.

"Greedy," Skálda said. "You can't just have Anders all to yourself."

The she-pica snorted at her and tightened her tail around his ankles. Anders smiled, stroking her between the short ears. The other two bedded down beside him. Dragons were wary creatures. They only closed their eyes when they felt completely certain they were safe, yet these three dozed right off.

"I never asked how you doctor dragons so well," said Skálda, "but perhaps I should have asked you for advice on how to become Ealdorman. Bale's script advances so slowly."

"Ah." He waved his hand. "When you find him, you'll surpass my rank in no time."

"The Lord Prince's forces are coming, Anders," she said. "Soren's commanders handed out weapons, but Rulf told me you would not take any."

Anders stroked Feorya's head, avoiding her gaze. "I'm no fighter, Skálda."

"You are an Ealdorman, no matter what the Order says."

"Do you know how Norn and I advanced to 119 chapters?"

Skálda shrugged. "You killed foes?"

"We killed northerners," he said. "In the warzones. We killed their wives and children. Unarmed commons. That was twenty solstices ago, yet even after all this time, the campaigns I fought still plague me..." His forehead creased. "Some days, I still question if Vaeritas would accept me in Aethragaard."

She went silent. She had never known this side of Anders before, the side that had killed commons.

He shook his head in sorrow. "For many seasons, I kept campaigning. The guilt came from Norn. He pleaded with me to stop. When the agony of his emotions became too great to bear, I could do it no longer." Anders stared at the lines on his palms. "So, I came to the Skonkauld and decided to use what provision I was given to protect and serve where Fjorland needed it most."

"The Kru'ul aren't the wives and children of northerners, Anders."

"I am beyond the age of having any business wielding a sword."

"Asveig is older than you, and he's a savage."

"Skálda." He looked at her with intent. "Have you given any thought to what we last spoke of?"

She inched toward leaving their spot. She did not want to

revisit this conversation. Anders sensed this and gently took her wrist.

"Your brother is not Vaeritian. The Were King is not Vaeritian. Neither is the Lord Prince, nor most of those who rule our Republic, though they would all call themselves Sun worshippers."

"Then what makes a Vaeritian?" she said sardonically. "You?"

"You already know."

She knew nothing and did not care to be Sunblinded. As he stroked, Feorya purred into him, slipping into sweet dreams.

"It took me murdering innocent lives to learn how to love," said Anders. "But I pray you do not follow my path. It will be a chain you carry for the rest of your life."

Skálda sighed impatiently. She loathed this. She loathed getting lectured about the Suncreed, especially when it was coming from her post leader. "I need to go." She tried to rise, but Anders held onto her.

"I attended university in Elenntar a long time ago," he said. "I am well read in my histories. Here in Solhall, I have had the time to think on everything. I know what your dragon is, Skálda."

She stopped, her shoulders stiffening. It would have been so easy to march away, and every inclination in her wanted to do it. But this was Anders. A small conviction made her stay and face him.

"I am a *kvael-akar*," Skálda said. "I have fought against riders, Rangers, and Judges. My decision to protect Bale cost you your dreams. I am no Vaeritian, Anders."

"In truth... I was afraid that night you returned from the Krigsgaald with him."

She let her wrist drop to her side. Once more, she saw a flash of Bale's soulscript—and it terrified her no less now than two cycles ago. It was a burden having to keep it to herself, from Anders even.

"You were the rider I always dreamed of having."

His words surprised her. This was not what she had been

expecting. "When I saw it before me, Skálda, within my grasp, after all my solstices of searching, I was petrified. I saw you would rise far beyond Skoll Post, beyond what I could ever give you—a caliber of legend like Aeogorath the Great, or Eyrekvald the Unbroken. I do not wonder why the Bael chose you."

She found herself speechless. Here she was, speaking the *Lhaer'thri* relentlessly over Bale, troubling over her poor, lowly rank—and he saw a Dragonlord in her?

"You have a great power in you," he said. "Both of you. If you cannot use what I taught you to Realm-Build, then promise you will use it for good. Help those who cannot help themselves. This is what it means to be Vaeritian. The weak need it."

"You know that I—"

"Skáld." The falling sunlight was like a curtain closing over his eyes. She shivered. "The Wereguild is finished, and so are all the thralls. But you have a future. You don't need to stay and fight here."

"I would not abandon Soren's people."

"Be not *kvael-akar* and Bael, nor rider and dragon, but stun the world, Skálda. Show them something they have no name for."

His words sent a shiver up her spine. This had been her very vision during her last moments in Dellfast.

As Skálda was mustering a reply, three Vigardians marched across the yard. The way they moved curtly, with singular purpose, made Skálda and Anders sit straighter. Thralls scrambled out of the way, though it was obvious who they were here for.

Asveig stopped before the ash tree with his guards. He did not seem affected in the slightest by the lovable scene of dragons curled all around Anders. "Come with me now," he said, turning to her.

"Why?" she said.

"We have an incoming transmission with the Ivarion's crest. The written verse states he would speak with you alone."

She could not read anymore in Asveig's stark expression.

Anders's brows curved into worry. Her own belly was sinking, but she rose to follow the Wereguild second.

"Skálda," Anders called.

While Asveig and his men strode back the way they came, she glanced over her shoulder.

"To have seen the makings of a legend in one of my own... that is worth dying for."

The smile on Anders's face was so abounding with love, it overwhelmed her. In every manner, she and Anders were opposites. She was reticent, cold, unpredictable, just like the Draughammr. Yet he always carried a patient gentleness that drew the entire world to him. How had she ever built a friendship with this man?

Skálda picked up her pace to catch up with Asveig.

CONTRARY TO WHAT SHE EXPECTED, the council room was not empty. The moment she stepped through the door, Soren looked up from the center. Asveig and Lord Jarmon were not present, which was unusual, until she considered they were taking Aesir to the border. Lord Einnar and Lord Solfreid were sitting on the opposite side, with Roagrim standing. All other warband leaders were present except Rulf. Seeing her notice this, Soren abruptly came to meet her.

"I take it I won't be speaking with Eyrek 'alone,'" she said.

"He knows you won't be alone. And he won't be either. But we will grant each other the formality."

She glanced at the transmission. A holograph of the Ivarion crest, a crowned Sun, awaited her. It was one thing to fight Eyrek's riders. It was entirely another to have to sit down and talk to him.

"Are you ready?" said Soren.

Skálda nodded.

He left the center and joined his shield-brothers in the shadows. Skálda took the Draughammr's seat, the grand chair draped in wolf furs. Her chest felt like it would implode, but no one would have known by her resting glower.

Every eye was on her. Skálda's shaking hand reached for the lodestone to accept the message.

The crest vanished. The other end of the screen was blank. Tension blazed in the room as they waited. She did not know how she would react the moment she saw her older brother again. Their last, sweet memory together in the Skonkauld was a garrote around her neck.

A face appeared on the board. "Hello, murderer of my friends."

It was not Eyrek. A she-elf smiled at her. Her copper hair was glossier than any human's, and she was slim as a crane. That smile of hers was more vicious than anything Skálda had ever seen from Garrek or any of Eyrek's other riders.

"My name is Detherys Lorathari, post second of Skygate, rank of Dragonlord."

"My name is Kvael-Akar, and I don't care for your post and rank," said Skálda. "Although you left out your new post. Emberglade, I believe? We have it as a warzone on our board."

The Vigardians snickered. Detherys lost her smile.

"The Wereguild keeps boards too, Elessa." Skálda picked at a splinter on the table. "Don't worry, I am coming to annul you in due time."

"Yes, that is exactly what I am here to talk to you about."

"So, you *are* afraid of me." Skálda leaned back in the king's seat. "Alright. I will consider whether I will give you mercy, elf. What are we parleying over?"

Detherys sneered. "Garreck's riders told me the filth threats you issued before you murdered him. But you are nothing to me, *mahlenn*. It is one thing to murder Barons and Dukes, but it is an entirely a different matter to face a Dragonlord. Can you even fathom it?"

"I can't fathom how you have time to blather during wartime."

Detherys's eyes flashed. "Here is my proposal, *mahlenn.* His Lordship has agreed that we cannot afford to lose any more riders, as I am certain you cannot lose more of your Vigardians."

"Which Vigardians have we lost?"

The men chuckled from the shadows. The she-elf's face darkened.

"Come to my post," said Detherys. "We will duel one to one. You may have any handheld weapon and spell at your disposal, as will I. If I have the victory, I will kill you slowly. After a time, I will take your head to be displayed on Exar'forda's towers—"

"Spare me the speech, elf," she said. "Why would I ever trust you to fight one to one?"

Detherys lifted something from her desk. "Do you know what this is, human?" It appeared to be a golden scroll engraved with calligraphy. "Anyone who swears upon an *elldhèlen*, a Rhún-infused artifact, is bound forever by that oath. I will swear to honor the terms of a one-to-one duel. None but the duelers will be present in Emberglade."

When Skálda did not answer, the she-elf spoke the oath and set it back down. Her dagger smile returned. "Satisfied, Kvael-Akar?"

"And if I win?"

"His Lordship will pull out. He and his riders will cease to Build on Vigardian lands—"

"That is not enough." Skálda leaned forward again. "The Draughammr has laid his claim on your lord. We must be assured that the Ivarion will never return. If I win, you will turn him over to the Wereguild."

A strange look clouded Detherys's face. Skálda could not see Soren in the dark, but she felt the intense concentration of his gaze.

"A pity he ever loved you," said the she-elf.

Skálda showed no emotion. This was how it must be, if the Vigardians were to remain free. Eyrek had already shown enough of his true heart in these lands. Detherys said, "Very well. If you are the victor, His Lordship will submit himself to your *mahlenn* king."

She could hear no one breathing anymore. Skálda almost glanced at Soren to make sure he was still there.

"Swear it over the *elldhèlen*," said Skálda.

The she-elf did.

"As you know where our post is," said the Dragonlord, "we know where yours is, thanks to His Grace. You have a fortnight to come alone. If you do not, my king will fly to Solhall and destroy you, just as we destroyed Isgardia." She smiled. "Die well, *mahlenn*."

The transmission flickered out.

Everyone let out an audible breath. Skálda stayed in her seat. Soren glanced at her. Her expression betrayed nothing, but her chest felt crushed. She did not entirely notice when Soren came to sit by her on the table's edge.

"You are one of us," he said.

She looked up.

"Vigardian." He placed a hand on her shoulder, his eyes abounding with pride. "We will depart for Isolund tonight."

Skálda exhaled the breath she had been holding in. "You heard her. I must go alone."

"She swore on the Rhún. You did not. You are not bound by her terms."

"The Lord Prince's forces are going to arrive any day now. The Wereguild needs you here to lead them."

"This transmission was authored by Skitr. He yearns for me to come. He was listening in the entire time—you know that, don't you?"

The idea of Eyrek listening to everything she said, especially the part about turning him over to the guild…

"If you come," said Skálda, "who will protect Solhall when he flies here with Tythandrell?"

"I will deploy dragon slayers around my capital, and he will see if the Wereguild does not shoot him down like the lords of Tera Beren."

"You saw what he did to Dellfast. Tythandrell is a Great Dragon. You can't take those chances."

"And you cannot fight one on one with an elf," he insisted. "You are human. She already has the advantage."

"I'll think of something."

Soren looked like he was going to say more, but she said, "Trust me. It will be a one-day campaign, Draugh."

Something flickered in his eyes, an emotion she could not read. She felt his shield-brothers watching. This time, instead of pulling away, he took her healed hand. He was on the verge of doing something reckless—something only Kael should do. It terrified Skálda.

At the very last moment, he said, "Go, then." The Draughammr's hulking frame swept out of the room without a farewell.

22
SURROUNDED

It confounded King Leon, as he crossed into the Álfvindor mountain pass, that the season had changed. The land wore the colors of fall, a baronial quilt of deep evergreens mottled with fiery reds and oranges. The ridgetops were awash in the ambers of twilight.

The memories of Tera Beren's fall seemed like only yesterday. Who would have ever thought that it would set into motion nightmares even half a solstice later, into fall, with no foreseeable end.

A mistral blew harder over the pass. Leon wrapped himself tighter in his furs. Halvar Gorm, Orrin Ragmar, Gendel Dagfinn, and three more of his most trusted house guards rode close beside him. Out here, beyond the borders of the Republic, no roads existed between these mountains. Knowing that his own son ruled the silence of this mighty, untamed wilderness unsettled him.

For four days past, they had encountered no other traveler in these Vigardian lands. Truthfully, Leon did not entirely know if he was going the right way. He was trusting the holographic waystone maps now plastered all over the Republic with Solhall's location.

Thus, he was caught entirely by surprise when, on the evening of the fifth day, a hooded stranger appeared in the ghyll. Halvar called a halt and drew his broadsword. Orrin, Gendel, and the others followed, enclosing Leon into a box.

"Who goes there?" Halvar yelled.

The shape kept shuffling toward them without an answer. He was armed with at least a quiver and bow. Leon shielded his eyes against the rising mistrals. When the stranger was ten paces from them, Halvar bellowed, "Halt, and show yourself, or Fjorland will take your head from your shoulders!"

The murky stranger slowly pulled back his hood, revealing his disheveled face. Leon widened his eyes. His shorn hair gusted in the winds, revealing softly tapered ears. His wrists and neck were blue from many days of wearing shackles.

"An elf," Halvar hissed under his breath.

Not any. Elves did not grow beards, and this one had dark, oily strands hanging down his chin. Leon raised a hand for his guards to stay themselves.

"Imperial Ranger!"

He had seen the high queen's closest advisor plenty of times in the Basilica's halls. But what was the elf-man doing all the way out in this wilderness? Had he been the Wereguild's prisoner?

The Ranger must have seen the astonishment in his eyes. Aesir, too, would know who he was. But he seemed to have no fire left in him to quip or question why the King of Fjorland was out here as well.

Pulling the hood back over his face, the Ranger continued his trek, paying no heed to the Fjorlander eyes that trailed him. Halvar glanced at Leon in bewilderment, but Leon nodded for them to let him go and continue. These were baffling times they were living in. Little should surprise him anymore.

They had ridden a bit further when Halvar pulled the reins again. His guards tensed. Leon glanced to his right. "Hal?"

"We aren't alone, Your Majesty," the big man growled.

Leon first saw a shadow from the corner of his eyes, then another, and another, until about a dozen Vigardians had them surrounded in the narrow ghyll. Their glaives and axes were drawn. The king was not entirely certain anymore that the Wereguild would spare his life simply because he was the Were King's father.

But Leon could not abide seeing his faithful friends slaughtered for his inane mission. The king urged his destrier past the barricade. Wisdom warned him not to shout to them in Elondrian, but in their shared mother tongue.

"I am Leondran Astoraine, King of Fjorland! I seek an audience with your Draughammr."

None lowered their weapons. Halvar and the guards tightened their grip on theirs. Leon's chest pounded harder. He had entirely miscalculated everything. The Wereguild would never bring him as far as Solhall.

A rider emerged out of the gusts. A set of heavy chains and a collar rested over his saddle. This Vigardian had chestnut hair billowing furiously against his hauberk and a beard braided in two.

"We know, Elder."

His eyes were far from kind.

Leon backed away. His guards quickened their breaths, each one coming out in short vaporous puffs. If it came to a fight against Vigardians, the Vigardians would slaughter them.

"King of Fjorland!"

This shout was spoken in Svenning far less heavy than the Wereman with beard braids. A last rider galloped out into the ghyll to meet them. Leon's narrowed eyes suddenly stretched wide. The white-bearded Vigardian pulled up beside his paunchy shield-brother.

"*Asveig Torfiner*?" Leon exclaimed.

This was once his brilliant chief advisor, a longtime friend even closer than Jory. After the hunt that had supposedly killed Soren in the North, twenty solstices ago, Asveig had vanished from Svennandia.

His old advisor, who appeared to be in charge, gestured at the Weremen to standdown. To repay his goodwill, Leon nodded at the guards to do the same, albeit he hid from his face his amazement. Once a groomed Republic courtier, Asveig now carried himself like a savage. A hauberk and thick brown gambeson armored his broad shoulders. He wore his long hair partially braided back. A sword and axe were tucked at his belt. Asveig had never worn weapons in Svennandia's halls.

"I am here to see my son," said the king.

His former advisor answered with a starkness that was foreign to Leon.

"We know, Elder."

The Vigardians closed in on Leon's small retinue. It was not just the braid-bearded Wereman grinning now.

23
DETHERYS LORATHARI

The night of Detherys's transmission, Skálda stayed in Solhall to get what rest she could. Before leaving for bed, she found Mat in his longhouse in the rider courtyard. He was sharing it with Anders and Faelan. Seeing her through the window, he left his pallet and padded outside.

"You're leaving again, aren't you?" he said.

"This might be the last time we see each other."

Mat laughed. "Skit, I can never tell when you're being serious or a plain savage."

When she said nothing, the humor left his face. "Oh. You aren't joking." He rubbed the back of his neck. Instead of leaving, Skálda sat on the chest outside the door and gazed up at the spray of stars. Out here, in the Deep North's feral wilderness, they were far more brilliant than in the Republic. Mat came to join her.

"It'd be New Lea at this time," he said. "Back at home."

The songs of crickets and rustling leaves swathed the night, yet she felt little peace. Mat was right. She had not even considered the turn of the season. They ought to be celebrating the coming harvest, welcoming the Juh Rholari clans, the only people in all

Elondria that cared to bring their wagons and trade with the Skonkaulders. The brown-skinned migrants would offer fresh dirt for planting, rock trinkets, even spicy herbs that could not be grown in the glaciers. Sometimes, Kael would buy her new brushes and paints to keep her mind off hunting. And of course, Mat would find every excuse to drag her to the mead hall and get her drunk.

"Instead of preparing for harvest..." He picked at a frayed thread on his sleeve. "Here we are preparing for war."

Skálda found herself unable to even speak of New Lea, or the terrible reminder of Kael's absence. If he were alive, they must all be wondering if the Juh Rholari would come this solstice, not knowing the Skonkauld had been destroyed.

"I wanted to redefine myself." She pushed the festival out of her mind, swallowing down her dryness. "All of us."

He glanced at her.

"It was an oath I made in Dellfast, just before we fell. But I'm further from an answer now than I was then."

Mat rubbed his hands together. "Well, you're not Skálda the Skáld Hunter anymore... but Skálda the Vigardian?" She did not smile. "We'll find you something good, something with a legendary ring. Skálda the Savage? Or, how about..." He studied her closely. "Skálda the Starstruck?"

He burst into laughter. She wondered how he always found so much humor in anything.

"Oh, come on, Skáld." He looped an arm around her. "Forget New Lea. You're upset because you haven't zinged to Dragonlord rank yet. Am I right?"

She kept searching the stars.

"Don't think I don't see the way you're always whispering the *Lhaer'thri* over your poor dragon." He was trying to force humor in his voice. "Maybe it's why he flew off, eh?"

"He's not coming back."

"Of course he's coming back. That's like saying Feorya doesn't want breakfast, lunch, luncheon, lunchlings, lunchlore—oh, and supper. You think she'd get all that in the wild?"

"Even if he did return... even if I had another dragon..." Speaking those words crushed her. "My rank is low. Bale was never advancing fast enough. It isn't good enough." She exhaled. "I am not enough."

He observed her for a long time. "Well, if you—"

"Mat... *don't*." She pulled away from him. She was not in the mood for a fest of the wits when she was hurting so much. As she made to stand, he rose with her.

"Hear me out," he said. "I know ranks are everything with the Order. Hel, rank is everything in Elondria. But it really doesn't matter."

She stared at him incredulously.

"I mean, you're *kvael-akar*. We both are. You think Exar'forda's going to send you a ring even *if* you make it to Dragonlord?"

"It's not about that!" At her unexpected outburst, the picas and Incendra raised their heads from across the courtyard. Mat lurched away, taken aback. "How can you think this is about a *ring*?"

"Shush, Skáld, you're waking the dragons—"

"I don't care about Vharyn's rewards!" she said. "I need my dragon to make it to 2,000 chapters so I know he's strong enough to face the Order. For us to stop this Second Breaking that's coming to Elondria!"

Unbidden emotions surged out of her, wresting a sheen out of her eyes. Skálda blinked back her burning tears. Mat awkwardly glanced back at his longhouse. It was unlike her to succumb to her feelings, and she doubly hated losing control.

After a moment, Mat came in and took her shoulders again. "Hey, Skáld. It... it's going to be alright." But he sounded doubtful.

She wiped her eyes. "I've tried to make sense of it all," she said. "All this chaos and *breaking* on Elondria. It's my fault. I've tried to redefine myself as anything other than *kvael-akar*. But all I know are the Order's terms. I don't see anything better than what they've established—and if that's true, Mat..." She clenched her fist. "I can't accept being at Rider rank, not when it's my responsibility to stop this Breaking."

"Breaking," Mat repeated.

"I think another Breaking is here—but it's not coming from above this time, but from within." She pressed a hand over her face. "Aesir tried to warn me. It's all happening because I've been sheltering a Bael. I know what this is all going to lead to."

He took her arm and led her back to the crate, sitting her down. He moved in so they were side-by-side. "Rank really doesn't matter."

"Then what matters?" she snapped.

He spoke his next words very gently. "I know you think I'm a lazy pile of dragon skit, and I am. But what I mean is, it doesn't matter to Feorya. My dragon loves me for who I am. She always did. She hatched for a common, Skáld. I was nothing then. I guess you could say I'm even less now—"

"You're not," she said, as ferocious as before.

"I mean, by the Order's standards. They define me as *kvael-akar*. The skit of skits. But Feorya has another name for me." He shrugged. "Mat. Just Mat."

Skálda burrowed her glare into him, still not comprehending. Her friend had more fire in him when he first became a rider of Skoll Post. Like most new Builders, he had burned to become Dragonlord; swore it, even. But then, as the days passed, and the grueling work of advancing a dragon settled into reality, he had lost that fire. Just like all the other Skoll riders. Just like most riders in Elondria. But this could not be her answer. She would keep searching, keep fighting to redefine herself and her Bael—all their lives depended on it.

Seeing her expression, Mat sensed it was time to let the topic go. "You never said. Where are you going?"

She brushed her face again. "A last campaign. I'm going to annul Detherys Lorathari."

Mat understood everything that was implied. By the time she returned, if she returned, they would all be dead. But he stayed on the crate with her, staying strong for her sake; as he always had on Bregan Island.

"I've seen you handle everything from skáldwolves to Kjetil Asger to Judges and their dragons," he said. "If the continent's breaking, at least we have your brains. That kind of makes a difference?"

"Mat..."

"Plus, if this Breaking is 'from within,' maybe it's just fate's tavern deciding to rearrange the tankards. We'll make sure the keg doesn't knock over Anders, eh?"

She looked up at him, her Skoll Post big brother. It dawned on her that he had no idea what a Breaking was, or even what a Bael was... and that was alright. Perhaps it was better that way. Skálda smiled.

"Oh, c'mere." He tried to clasp arms with her like brothers, but she came in and embraced him tightly.

"Take care of the others for me," she said. "Especially Anders. I worry about him these days."

"When you go to this last campaign, don't forget. It'll be just like ritefest, yeah?"

Skálda nodded. "Just like ritefest." She forced herself to let go and not look back.

WHEN SKÁLDA LEFT the manse the following morning, the dawn she emerged into was the most beautiful she had ever seen yet. Golden daylight poured through the dappled trees. The heights smelled wild, like damp, fecund earth. She tasted dew hanging over the Lupines.

She found Soren at the terrace on the third floor. He looked out over the mighty view of Solhall. Beyond it was the Eldruna Valley in all its bountiful glory, and the boundless, soul-blue Völundr Reach rolling to the east and north.

"I wonder what the Lord Prince promised the Illuminators," he said, without taking his eyes off his majestic realm.

"I suppose we'll find out soon enough."

"I would rather not."

"I came to say goodbye."

"What time of day do you favor most?" he said suddenly.

"I don't indulge in sentimental questions, Draugh."

"Mine is in the early morning," he said, keeping his elbows on the wooden parapet, "when the world still sleeps but the birds are filled with song. Listen."

For several breaths, it was silent between them. Yet the wilds beheld a deep peace she had encountered nowhere in Aranor Elondris.

"They have many notes to sing," said Soren. "Their calls are different every morning..."

"I should go," she suggested. "It's getting late."

"Yet man sings no song," the Draugh continued. "His lyres are broken; the cups of his soul have long run dry. His head is upturned to heaven. Our race has no more songs."

"This won't be forever," she said. "We will bring the Enterprise to an end."

Soren pulled his gaze away from his lands. "I have reflected again and again on the war that comes to Solhall. Was I a fool to bring my people into this fight? Have I sentenced us all to this elvish war against men?"

"You can never win it, Draugh."

"No," he said, "because a new age is coming. I feel it. The elves have lived alongside us for one thousand solstices, but it is time they have always wanted. It is time they take the Middle Realm."

"And they will one day, under the current rules of Elondria."

Soren glanced at her.

"But I am going to break the Realm-Building Enterprise," she said.

"You're going to kill Vharyn Morghûl." Soren laughed. He still did not believe her. Of course not. No one in the Wereguild did.

Seeing the seriousness in her stare, Soren withdrew from the parapet and touched her back fondly. "Come with me, Kvael-Akar. There is another matter I have reflected deeply on... but I believe I have made my decision."

They took a different section down to ground level, in the wing where Soren's private quarters were. He vanished through the door. Skálda stayed outside in the yard. The next time he emerged, he was holding a helmet. A mane of black horsehair washed down the metal, with two pairs of tines fixed to the head. He held it out to her. This was once Fjella Wulfgar's helmet.

The gesture stunned her. "Draugh?"

"Will you take it?"

"Of course I cannot..."

"A cycle before she fell," Soren said, "a hjarta showed me a vision. Through the Vidarskog Stones, I thought I would see the Ivarion... but I saw you." His voice quieted even more. "I must know. Is it your purpose to break the guild?"

"I thought the Sunblinded don't listen to hjartas." She kept her tone buoyant to bring levity to her terror, for she knew what it would mean to accept this helmet. His expression did not lift, which strangled her even more.

An apology was on Skálda's lips, but she knew he did not want an apology right now. Not to fill the silence. He wanted her to partner with him. He wanted her to help him take the Wereguild to new heights, perhaps heights far greater than Fjella's reign.

Skálda of the Skonkauld, standing here before the highest Vigardian royalty. How had rescuing one Bael ever led to this?

If she took this helmet, he would claim her in the darkness behind that door. When it was done, no man in his clan would ever touch her again. This was the Vigardian way.

The tips of her fingers wavered. She was Kvael-Akar. Could she ever submit to any power? Could she submit to him, not out of love, but necessity for them both?

She would become a queen... and a little voice in her said this had always been her destiny. One day, she would become greater than the Morghûls.

"I am here to break only one." Skálda reached for the helmet.

"My Lord!"

They turned. Horsemen rushed into the yard. Skálda pulled back from the Draugh, though Soren made no attempt to hide what he had just offered her. Asveig and Lord Jarmon were at the front. Their eyes flickered to the helmet. The former showed no reaction, but Jarmon's face twisted in agony. Soren calmly embraced Fjella's helmet to his chest, just before the Vigardians parted to reveal their prisoners—several riders in foreign raiment.

"We found them at the border when we freed the elf," Asveig called.

The last to appear at the front was King Leondran.

"Soren," he said.

The Draugh froze. That name alone was spoken with so much emotion. The king dismounted, coming before his taller son. The way they looked at each other, unable to speak, told Skálda they had not seen each other in person for a lifetime. She backed away to give them space. Seeing her example, the Vigardians did the same, and the circle slowly opened.

Soren exhaled into his hands. "What are you doing here?"

"I came to bring you home."

"You are a fool!"

"I commend your honor and bravery, but this is not your home, Soren. It never was."

The Vigardians tightened their grips on their axes. Leondran glanced past Soren's shoulder, into the darkness of his quarters, as if waiting for someone to come out.

"Think about Fjella. And your children. They are Astoraines. Their place is in Fjorland—"

"Get out," Soren said quietly. "And do not come back."

"I welcomed you to bring whatever family you will," the king said. "If that means all of you..." He gazed about the Weremen. "Then so be it. All of you are under Fjorland's protection."

The Vigardians glanced at each other in surprise. The Draugh sneered. "You would bring hordes of Vigardians and Thomdrim into your borders?"

"The Republic has declared war on my family, so, it has declared war on Fjorland."

"It's too late for that. We will not abandon the lands of our forebears."

"Then I will give you my sword."

Everyone gasped, even the king's guards. The big one shouted at him in protest. The king's eyes were glistening, though he kept himself stark and erect. Emotions between father and son were running high.

Soren stepped closer. "You should not have come here," he murmured. "You are an *Eldari*, not a Vigardian. You are abandoning your high seat for treason and madness."

"Out here, I am no one but your father—"

"That is *not* who you are."

"If it is your decision to stay... then I will die with you, as I should have many solstices ago—"

"I don't want your sword," the Draugh bellowed. "Neither do I need it. I will never again need it!"

He blustered away into his quarters, taking Fjella's helmet with him. Skálda dared inch her head to look at the king. The moment he closed his eyes, the thick tears fell. Right then, not even his royal visage could keep his shoulders from shaking. His guards dismounted and led Leondran away.

The late hour harried Skálda, but she could take this no more. She stormed through the door, shutting it behind her. Soren would let no light into his quarters except what managed to filter through the windows. His back stayed turned to her. Fjella's helmet was still pressed to his heart.

"He's your father," she hissed. "Can't you have been any kinder?"

To her astonishment, he held his free hand over his face. In the darkness, he wept.

"Soren," she said. "Go to him."

Beyond the window, Asveig jostled through the royal guards and took the king's shoulder, murmuring low words.

"Your anger is ravaging him," said Skálda. "He came here for you."

"I needed him in Isgardia, not now..." He slammed the wall with his fist. "I needed him twenty solstices ago, not now!" He set the helmet on his bed, making no effort to hide his grief. "He is half the Elenntarien. Half the Republic. I won't be responsible for his death."

Skálda crossed her arms, refusing to leave.

"Twenty solstices ago, he betrayed me, Skálda. He betrayed Fjorland. The Morghûls tried to murder me when I was a boy—"

"The Morghûls?" she said. "Why?"

"Never mind why." He waved his hand. "I had no choice but to escape North. Neither could I return home, for the Wereguild captured me in the Álfvindors. They fitted a collar round my neck, and in all that time I served Vigardian lords on my bare knees. The Republic assumed I was dead. It was not until after I became the

Were King that I transmitted again to my father... and found out the truth."

She waited in the silence. Soren gave a short sigh.

"He did something terrible, Skálda. My best man was with me the day the Morghûls attempted their hand. He told my father the truth of what happened, but my father gave false witness in the high courts. He blamed my man for causing my supposed death, not the Morghûls. Under the Elenntarien's ruling, he sent my friend to Kar'thuul-dur to serve a life sentence... and the Morghûls were never even questioned."

As she stood there, staring at his back, it occurred to her how little she knew about Soren, even after a season of lending him her axe. She had questions, too many questions, but she sensed they would only bleed his wounds. Like her, the Draughammr was not one to dwell on the past. He was one only to wear a hauberk of the most tempered steel.

Soren shook his head. "I cannot forgive him."

A horn sounded in the distance. They turned to the window. Soren wiped his eyes with his sleeve and strode to the door. As he passed, his hand brushed her wrist. The unexpected gesture of kindness reminded her of his open offer.

"The Lord Prince's host is within ten leagues!" Soren shouted at the yard. His Weremen rushed about in a frenzy. "Kvael-Akar!" He glanced over his shoulder. "Fight well." Then he marched past everyone to prepare for battle.

So that was their goodbye, Skálda thought. But that was the Draughammr to his core. A Vigardian warrior. Skálda gently closed the door behind her. The strands of fate were strange. Fate would not let her have Fjella's helmet if this battle was not won... and she was determined to win it.

She circled around Asveig and dipped her head at King Leondran. "Your Majesty."

"Skálda," he said in surprise. He recognized her from their encounter in Dellfast.

"The Draugh is very touched you have come and gives you his most tender thanks."

The king raised his head, confounded and hopeful. Soren would garrote her if he found out. She raised Aracir into the air as she marched to the stables. "I leave now!"

Asveig and the remaining Wereman turned their stares on her. Several murmured between themselves. Her departure on the eve of battle unsettled them. They needed her, wanted her, in Solhall.

"I am going to annul Detherys Lorathari," she said.

THE JOURNEY to Emberglade and back would be a long one on foot. According to the maps Soren had guided Skálda through, the dragonpost would overlook Isolund, the Great Lakesea, west of the Ískjall Pass, and due north above the Lupines. Eyrek's post seconds had Built around Mt. Kóri, the greatest peak touching Isolund. It was the final point that formed a triangle between the former Tera Vera and Ruadhán Posts.

Skálda galloped through the dense Völundr, stopping little for rest.

It was outlandish, the eerie peace beneath the hazels, yews, and rowans. The Battle for Solhall would have begun by now. She could not shake the haunt that she *was* abandoning them, going in the opposite direction from where her king needed her. But she pressed on. Planning her campaign strategy became her singular purpose.

Three days later, the Lakesea of Old Svenn's greatest ballads appeared to her left. Even then, her mind weaved no solutions on how she would annul a Dragonlord... none but one.

Bale, she called with her mind.

He did not answer her. He never did, even when her calls turned into shouts, then pleas. Without the ruckus of Vigardian activity in Solhall to distract her, she felt his absence even more in the forests. The full dawning that he would never return felt like the weight of Elondria crushing her.

Please, Bale. Please, come back to me... I can't bear the days without you.

But he would not. He was protecting her from himself.

On the fourth day of her voyage, she pulled the reins. Beyond Völundr's tree line, the Emberglade Crag twisted high above her like a gnarled oaken staff scraping the heavens. She took this to be Mt. Kóri itself. The only road to the summit was an unhewn path twisting around the outer rock face. No barricades would keep a traveler from plunging over the side. It would fit one man abreast. An elite rider could reach the top on dragonback in minutes, but it would be a grueling climb for a common.

It was time.

She drew in a deep breath, and slipped off the saddle. Skálda slapped the gelding's rump and did not look back. A horse would not have enough room on that path, and whatever happened today, she would not be coming down that same road.

Skálda took her first step out of the trees, then another, and steadily began her trek.

An hour later, the heights allowed her a better vista of Isolund's herculean plane. At this falling golden hour, the waters were alight against the blinding heavens. The Dragon Wars seemed to come to life in its crystal mirror. Even a Svennish common would know all the songs and poems. Over four hundred solstices ago, a child of Old Svenn stole a Great Dragon's egg during a royal hunt. It ignited a full war between dragons and men that not even the last emperor of Svenn could stop. For fifty solstices, flights of dragons torched the Svenn Empire with fire. On the Lakesea's waters, she saw harrowing scenes of Emperor Eveillan marching into battle against the dragons with Vigardians, Thomdrim, and even dwarves at his side. She saw Vigardians clashing against the wild flights that would eventually desolate the entire northern half of Elondria. In those days, not even the Morghûls knew how to ride dragons.

Skálda thought it strange that, four hundred solstices later, Old Svenn would become a battleground for men, giants, and elves to kill each other over the same thing that had brought down Svenn—dragons. Only now, the dragons were saddled. They had a new name: the Enterprise.

A vermilion sun, livid with fire, sank over the horizon. Skálda narrowed her eyes at the burgeoning glare. Vaeritas blazed over the blood-streaked land, silent and distant, as his children battled, warred, and murdered in his name. How could any of them wear him over his chest?

One day, after she killed the Lord Prince, she would find a way to battle that god with her blade.

It was not much farther to the top. She called to Bale with every step, fusing her pleas with forgiveness and love. *Bale, please, Bale...*

She could not campaign without him. Her soul threads were moving toward an end.

At the end of the evening, Skálda made it to the apex. She was so high in the sky, she could reach up with her hand and almost touch the clouds. It was impossible to entirely see ahead. Shielding her eyes from the twilight glare, Skálda padded away to the crag's sheer edge to survey her battleground.

What happened next occurred in less than a beat—the sun's dregs flashed, and on the Lakesea's reflection, she saw not the Dragon Wars, but the *faolrún*. Their howling scrollwork spanned the horizon, clawing at her soul. Skálda let out a breath and jerked away from the edge, but they vanished as soon as they appeared.

The last of the sun sank into its nightly tomb. Skálda shuddered. It was as if the *faolrún* were following her... Something about them was more terrifying than the prospect of facing Detherys alone.

Turning her back to Isolund, she reminded herself of her looming enemy and willed herself to calm. Skálda edged into the alpine fog swathing the crag, a little at a time, until the outlines ahead coalesced. She was standing before a crude redoubt. The wooden gate in the palisade was open. Torches lit either side of it. She heard no voices, nor even the growls or snorts of dragons. The she-elf had kept her word.

The fog was even thicker inside the post. Skálda drew Aracir.

"Elf!" she shouted.

Skálda waited. All she heard were the winds passing over the palisade points. Nothing behind those gates stirred. She had no plan now but to fight the Dragonlord with her bare hands. In the back of her mind, she kept pleading, pleading Bale to come. She swore all of Old Svenn could hear the roaring in her chest.

A new noise picked up in the breezes. The sound of boots. Someone was coming. Skálda's palm was so clammy, she readjusted her grip on the axe.

In a few more breaths, a silhouette appeared ahead of her. She squinted, but the fog made it hard to see. The she-elf was approaching at a measured pace. Every fall of her boots was a dragon's roar in these heights.

Skálda bent her knees, willing her heart to calm as she held her breath, focusing on nothing but her enemy.

The silhouette drifted nearer. The approaching boot falls drowned out the thunder in Skálda's chest. Detherys was holding a massive sword, perhaps even a greatsword, which few on the continent owned. They were too heavy for most humans to carry into battle. Her frame seemed rather large for a she-elf.

It was not Detherys who emerged out of the gate, but an entirely different Dragonlord.

Her breath snagged in her throat. This was not anyone she

knew. Grief and madness ravaged his eyes. His once neat elvish forebraids were undone, shuttering his unshaven face like overgrown briars. All the rumors about him were true. Skálda jerked away from him.

"Eyrek—"

He kept marching, clenching his man-reaver tighter. Platinum hair, the same shade as hers, whipped against his neck. She tripped over her heels. Her mind whorled. This was *Eyrek*. Now that the moment had come, she could not bring herself to strike him. She could not think. She kept backing to the ledge.

Leathery wings pounded the air. Something was ascending to Emberglade's summit. Skálda exhaled sharply. Bale was coming for her. Bale was here.

Eyrek tossed aside his giant sword and steepled his fingers together. An airborne shadow loomed over her. She swiveled around.

"Skálda!"

Anders reached for her from Nornsir's saddle. She broke into a sprint away from the Dragonlord, her fingers outstretched to his.

The skies shuddered from an almighty bellow.

"*M'ethil!*"

From the corner of her eye, sweltering light engulfed the Second Rider. Skálda turned, and that was her mistake. It was like looking straight into the glowing jaws of a Great Dragon. The firestorm that rushed at her was the equivalent of Tythandrell's breath, thrice anything Crixalas had ever unleashed. Once more, she saw Dellfast burning before her eyes.

Flames her height rushed at her. Their heat was so potent, the earth where the light touched instantly blackened. Even at this distance, the tips of her hair singed.

So, this is what it means to be Dragonlord, she thought. She had nowhere to run. Skálda closed her eyes, and waited.

Nornsir crashed into her. On Anders's order, the pica swept his tail against her, forcing her off the ledge.

A beat later, dragonfire smote flight and rider. Nornsir's body blocked the initial scorch from touching her. Against the strength of Eyrek's 6,554 chapters, Anders' and Nornsir's silhouettes vanished like sand grains into the light.

Skálda fell screaming over the side.

24
THE WHITE TERROR

Vharyn Morghûl ascended the forlorn steps of the High Eyrie, its olden shadows drenching him.

This tower was one of the most ancient structures in Rhaennöria. His forefather Aeogorath Morghûl I had built it to curry favor with the dragons at a time when the continents of Elondria and Calendria were one, and the Nhorssn aboriginals of Midgaard had walked freely across the land. While most visitors would have huffed by now, the unceasing twist into the dark heavens did not cow the elf. He brushed the cracked, dusted walls with focused reverence. The stones were whispering to him alone, ancestral memories of his lineage echoing in his blood. The Morghûls would continue to ascend as masters of the world, because dragons were their thralls.

He reminded himself of this, as he left the last step and arrived at his dread destination.

In this silence, crunching over fresh beds of rush sounded like a fired trebuchet. Vharyn glanced upward. The vaults were another twenty stories, great arches that would allow Exar'forda's high queen to pass through at will. A stone balustrade marked every story, a shelf for the thousands of eggs that belonged to the Order. Some were as old as even his bloodline. The matron thought she owned those eggs, but they were his, all his.

He reminded himself of this.

The Eyrie itself was an abandoned dragon city of steps, firepits, landings, and lofty townhouses. Few things ever disturbed Vharyn, but the silence of the Imperial Eyrie did. On his quest to find the matron, he passed small skeletons of ha'elves and the occasional human slave. The handlers. He chuckled, as delighted by her as he was afraid.

Lumaerrax first appeared as an enormous white tail hanging over a staircase. Vharyn almost stopped then. Most days the leviathan of Elondria slept, and the Second Rider could pass in and out freely in this section to beckon Tythandrell. But this day, after many solstices, Vharyn was not here to pass through.

He was here to awaken.

More skeletons moaned up at him as he entered between two drake-shaped monoliths. She was such a behemoth, he could not find her head at first. Easily she was two elves tall. It grieved him that her scales, once a pure white, were now ashen and dimmed from so many solstices away from the sun. Most assumed she was a Great Dragon, albeit more accurately, she was an Auralith. A Sundragon of the light. She was never meant to lay and breed here like this, but to fly... and destroy.

After an eternity, he found her head resting on the thrush. Its breadth was his entire height. Of course, her eyes were closed like she was made of stone. The rush next to her was flattened; her mate must have rested by her not long ago. She was sluggish, gravid with Tythandrell's clutch. The eggs would come any day now. A she-dragon should never be flown in this state.

"Oh, Luma..."

He fell onto his knees, brushing the stained scales along her neck. Stirring, she let out a heavy breath through her nostrils, a groan. He saw also in her age, great age, and the sight of it almost brought tears to his eyes.

"Oh, my poor Luma..."

An unexpected tide of emotion overcame him. Though all the dragons were his, he belonged only to her. That magnifying conviction, which he was certain was not entirely his own, countered his earlier oath to himself that he was master; that he was the greater of the two minds.

"My Luma... what have you become?"

A colossal eye to his left burst open. That infernal purple ember, the entire size of his head, glowed in the dark. The inner membrane blinked, and then the slitted pupil rolled down to him.

Only one dragon in the world could take him by terror.

Vharyn backed away.

The Auralith arched her neck, raising her spiny head until she was looming over him. Now, two insidious eyes burned in the dark. These showed no recognition of him, but they belonged to a beast too ancient for even a High Elf's mastery.

He dropped his gaze in time. Legends had it that when Lumaerrax made eye contact, she would kill the one she looked upon. And those legends were true. No elf or man alive on the continent had ever survived to tell the tale. Even during the sparse times he had ridden her in the past, he had never, under any circumstances, met her eyes.

From the peripheries of his vision, her giant lip pulled back. Rows of teeth glistened against the firepits. A hot reek stinking of carcasses blew over his unbraided snags.

Vharyn carefully bowed his head. Lumaerrax was beyond him. He saw that now. And he was no longer assured his fate would not follow the ha'elves. It was imbecility for anyone to think she was tame simply because she had once flown for his mother—that was, before he had Severed their Binding. Perhaps it was all Lumaerrax remembered of him now.

Then again, as he used to oft remind Luma, her former rider had chosen the crown over her. He had only been following orders...

The Auralith's feral stare scorched him. When she did not move, he took a tiffany cloth from his sleeve, very slowly, so she would not be provoked by his movement. He spoke aloud in the High Elven.

"A child once visited the Freeholds with his father and overheard a brood of mages exchanging tales of dragons..."

Keeping his head in obeisance, he inched around the rippling muscles of her breastplate. He saw from his peripheries her villainous embers trailing him.

"The boy asked them who the most powerful dragon in Midgaard was. A hush fell over the men."

Under his breath, he murmured the spell for water, and doused the tiffany. He touched it to her blackened scales. A foul discord rose in her throat, rattling his bones. But he kept his countenance measured. This was how it must be with Lumaerrax; the moment one showed fear, she would sense it and spring.

"When they could next utter, they spoke of one dragon that took flight during the War of Treason. A solstice before, the Betrayer had ravaged all Elondria. Every realm and bloodline fell to his human hand..."

On his knees, Vharyn washed the great monster with the same deep love he bore for his nor'harp.

"But when his host rushed at the gates of Löth-Anárion, the last free stronghold, she soared into the heavens. She scourged all their superior swordsmen, even the Juh Rholari horse archers. She scourged so ponderously, the Great Betrayer himself could not abide her."

As he regaled, he began to hum.

"When the Betrayer fled, she scourged all the seven cities he had captured and made his own. She left them as scorched earth, entire little civilizations built over centuries and destroyed over three days. She did not tire, not like the paltry beasts of today's Enterprise. Where all other races on the continent had knelt to the enemy, she went on scourging, and scourging, with a vengeance. For she would bow to no one."

The scales beneath his hands emerged out of their grime, scintillating again in the fires.

"It was but for her alone that the Betrayer conceded. If not for her, they said, he would have taken Elondria. Rhaennöria, and all the ruling seats, would have become his slaves; the House of Morghûl would have been put to sword. So shaken the Betrayer was, he vowed never to return. Against the light of his burning cities, he took his ships and sailed away..."

As Vharyn continued with his story, deep into the night, the Eyrie fell silent again but for the trance of his voice.

"When the war was finished, all Elondria feared her. So terrible she was, the seat of Rhaennöria decided she would be set aside only for breeding. Her purpose was shelved. Yet the child never forgot the tale from the Freeholds. He resolved to one day meet her."

His painstaking labor was finished, a full circle round the giant completed. Vharyn returned to his place before her.

"And that child did. The world soon forgot her to peace, but every time he looked upon her in the shadows, he saw only majesty, grace, and a power above all races. He visited her every day. He saw again the White Terror... and one day, as a grown elf, he found the mettle to accept her challenge to Bind."

She was still watching him, none of her draconic attention lost.

Vharyn knelt.

"Where you conquered the Betrayer, I fell to him." He brushed his forefingers down his revolting scar. "I allowed my insecurities, my defeat, to grow us apart."

The Auralith snapped her tail like a wroth chain, caving the stones around him.

"But I appeal to you, Sovereignty, to exhume our Binding. Allow me to renew my oaths of loyalty to you, High Queen of all dragons. Let us never be separated, as your last rider separated from you."

He raised his head, and calmly did what no mortal ever could—he met the eyes of Lumaerrax.

"Will you deign a *Lúndalorin* with Vharyn Morghûl?"

25
DEFEND THE HAMMERFEST DIKE

Skálda emerged out of the Isolund's waters, her hands pressed to her forehead in hysteria. She was not entirely aware of when she had staggered back onto land. All she could see was Anders and Nornsir vaporizing in dragonfire. She saw her brother's pale hair whipping against his bloodshot face as he watched her without pity.

Her boot snagged on a root. She seized the wet leather off her foot and hurled it aside.

Anders was gone. He could not be gone. Eyrek had murdered him. Was that what she had just seen?

She turned toward the crag, looking into the distance, waiting to see Anders soaring over the Lakesea on Nornsir's back. Her post leader would return to her, assure her with his foolish, longsuffering warmth that everything would be alright.

He never did.

The fullness of what happened settled into her bones. She clenched her teeth and collapsed onto her knees.

"You *fool*. You *fool*, you *fool*! Anders, I *hate* you—"

She screamed through her sobs. Her body rocked, and she pressed her head to the mud. Only one man could bring her down like this. One man who, a long time ago, had extended his hand to a hungry child; the only man in Elondria that had enough surplus love in his heart to also love the cold-hearted skáld hunter of Bregan.

When she could scream no more, into the earth, she wept.

It was only the thunder of wings that gave her enough strength to pull herself onto her hands.

A Great Dragon's silhouette ascended above Emberglade Post. Even one league away, she felt the power of those wings displacing the airspace over Isolund. It was the same impossible power she had seen in Dellfast, before the city's total desolation.

Roaring a war call, the Day King soared eastward, toward Solhall.

Her eyes continued to stream, but she fell silent as Old Svenn's wolves. Something in her soul hardened. Losing her post leader was a piece of herself she would never get back.

Staking Aracir's haft into the ground, she hauled herself back to her feet. Her eyes were so blurred, she had to douse them with her sleeve, though more came soon enough to replace them. Even now, she loathed Anders. She loathed that he had the power to do this to her.

Skálda gazed in the direction where the golden dragon had flown. Soren's shield brothers were right. The Second Rider was no hero, but the villain of the continent. So many masks he had worn, even to her. But Jofreid Anders would be the last Elondrian to die by him and the Enterprise. This, she swore.

She started the long journey home on foot.

Four days before, the Were King's scouts continued to blow horns over Solhall. At the rate that the Kru'ul were moving, they would be upon Solhall in three days.

Leon Astoraine remained in the manse's courtyard with Halvar and his guards, refusing to leave his son. Soren made it a point to ignore him, but his irritation only grew when Leon followed him through the citadel, never keeping him out of sight. The war commanders seemed to be waiting for Soren's orders to deploy, but he would not issue any, not yet.

A scout arrived not a day after the first horns started. The young Vigardian galloped up the slopes of Solhall, drawing anxious glances. Passing the manse's gates, he rapidly dismounted and knelt before his king.

"Rulf." Soren helped him up. "What news?"

The Wereman lowered his voice. "I failed you, Draugh. I could not find the Bael."

Soren placed a hand on his shoulder. "We will focus on the matter at hand."

"The Kru'ul are moving quickly," Rulf continued, "but they travel heavy. It's their plate armor. Most wield cleavers, clubs, and any manner of crude battle axes. They move fast and don't appear to tire."

"Have they archers?" said Leon.

The two men glanced back at the king, standing a short distance away. He was listening to everything intently. Rulf widened his eyes. "Our great... Is that..." He must have pieced together who Leon was by his resemblance to his son. "Ah—Draugh, what's the proper way to address a Republic king?"

Soren scowled for his answer.

Rulf settled with "Kjoster," the Svennish word for "king." Crouching back on one knee, he said, "They have few archers. Warlords in white command them, all mages of a sort. I could not make out how many. They are quite the unformed mess."

"Illuminators," Leon said in Elondrian, nodding.

"Thank you, Kjoster. It appears these warlords are depending on their numbers to crush us."

Leon mused, "Cavalry..."

More Vigardians were gathering in the yard to listen in.

"What is your name, son?" said the king.

Rulf fell lower to the ground, which seemed to annoy Soren. "Raldefur, Elder Kjoster."

"Raldefur, you say they are heavily armored, yet move quickly. They have loose formation. How large are they?"

"Large, Kjoster. Bigger than a man, all bulk."

Leon rubbed his chin. "This seems to me closer to cavalry than heavy infantry." He turned to his house guards. "Hal? What do you think?"

"I heartily agree, sire," his bulky friend said.

Soren called, "Stay out of my affairs, Elder!"

"Let him speak, Draugh." Asveig rubbed his big duck beard in interest. "Don't forget that His Majesty commanded hosts during the War of Treason. He was half your age."

Soren snarled. Leon nodded at his old advisor in thanks and turned to the rest. "You fear their numbers, yet those numbers will not matter if we deploy strategically. I have seen the land beyond the Hammerfest Dike. It is a muddy mead plagued with bloodwyrms. They will be forced to stay on the narrow causeway." Leon paced, circling his hand in the air. "Let us play them for horses caparisoned in armor. If that were the case, they would be encumbered by a front line of pikemen and archers stationed ahead. Pikemen must be our central strategy in this."

Lord Jarmon laughed. "Don't deprive Vigardians of their axes, Kjoster."

"My friend, I do not care for your Vigardian esteem. If you wish to win this battle, and you have half the numbers, you will need to rally behind pikes. When they flee, we will pursue them.

We will pursue them hard, so that they do not have any chance of reforming in the south."

"You are out of your mind," Jarmon cried. "You would have peasant pikemen win the day, not Vigardians?"

"You can pick up a pike, can't you?" Leon placed a hand on his beefy shoulder. "Don't worry, you will have plenty of opportunity to axe Kru'ul."

The coarse man frowned as Leon stopped by Soren's side. "I have heard your battle plan with your council," he said. "It is a good plan. But someone needs to command Solhall's walls to defend against dragons, and you are the Wereguild's finest marksman."

Soren turned to him in surprise. None of them knew how closely Leon had listened in to everything.

"It would be a waste of talent to have you at the front lines," Leon said, "when I can command them."

The Were King raised his brows higher, and then flattened them sharply. "Do you take me for a coward? You think I will send my men beyond the walls while I stay behind them?"

"I don't think anyone here considers you a coward, Soren."

The spectating Vigardians murmured in agreement.

Soren ground his teeth, fighting back the words Leon sensed he had wanted to speak all along. "You are a Light-cursed *Eldari*. I will not send you to the front lines!"

He was afraid to lose his father. Seeing his son like this heartened Leon.

"I am a son of Svenn, like you." The King of Fjorland gazed about the faces, projecting in his rich Basilica tenor. "I may have been born south of the Álfvindor Alps, but my ancestors once ruled a Vigardian empire. Is the battlefield not in my blood?"

"By the ravens," Jarmon muttered in Asveig's ear. "An Elder King fighting as Wereguild?"

Asveig's lips twitched with a smile, but the hardy man kept a stark face and raised his fist.

"Hail the Astoraine!"

At his call, the rest of the Vigardians took up his war shout in the Svenning. *Astorheim! Astorheim!* Soren looked uncomfortable as his war leaders chanted his family name. Leon tried to catch his eye, hoping their alliance might release the rancor between them. But his eldest marched away without looking at him.

By the fifth hour of the next day, Leon was rested and fully armored in his battle plates. His royal blue mantle washed behind him as he mounted his giant white destrier. Halvar and his guards enclosed him in a tight shield.

Soren marched out of his manse not long after, heavily armored in a hauberk and thick gambeson patterned like dragon scales. His helmet, adorned with the hollowed horns of Xyransul the Great, was fitted on his head. The sight of it was dreadful and drew the stares of all he passed.

From the citadel, in the darkness of the predawn hours, he issued his orders. Asveig repeated them in shouts. Leon observed his son from a distance. With pride and sadness, he wondered when the child he used to dandle on his knee had grown into such a self-assured king.

"All marksmen assigned to the dragon slayers will remain on the city walls!" the Draughammr called. "Skitr's dragons will come. The Skitr King *will* come, and it falls on you to ensure his demon never penetrates Solhall's airspace. If you should fail, Vingulmark shall fall forever."

The squadron of marksmen stood before him solemnly. Rulf was among them at the front.

"Jarmon!"

The braid-bearded Vigardian came forward to kneel.

"I am giving you command of the city. The hauberker teams, halberdiers, and dragon slayers are yours. Protect Solhall and her people."

The stout man bowed his head, then drew his axe and beat the flat against his mailed chest. "Draughammr!" he shouted, raising his blade into the air. The rest of the warbands took up his call.

"Draughammr! Draughammr! Draughammr!"

While they roared in the background, Leon pulled his horse parallel to Soren's. "I insist you stay behind the walls, son," he said. "When Lord Eyrekvald comes, they will need you behind—"

"A dragon slayer is ready for me on the field."

"Open battle is not your strength. Yours is special operations. Let me handle the field—"

"I can command well enough without you."

"No one can stop airborne riders better than you. Are you going to abandon your men simply for—"

The Were King jabbed a finger into his breastplate. "You are reckless," he hissed. "You are half the Elenntarien. Half the *Republic*, and the only hope the continent has against the Morghûls. You know what the Realm-Building Enterprise is. You know they are turning all Elondria into their empire. You are the only one in the south with the mettle to defend free men. You dare speak to me about staying safe behind walls, yet you go out there to throw yourself to the Kru'ul!"

"Out here, I am only your father."

"Flames on you, if you remind me again!" Soren heeled his mount and galloped down Solhall's slopes. Asveig and his train of elite shield-brothers thundered behind him. Leon could not help but smile as he nudged his destrier after the younger Astoraine.

At the gate, Soren stopped to pull Asveig aside. The rest of his Vigardians continued on, their chargers booming through the gate and onto the field. Leon briefly pulled the reins. He heard their piecemeal murmurs.

"...stay by him," Soren was saying. "Protect him at all costs. Asveig, I cannot have any Kru'ul blade falling on him..."

A heaviness stirred in Leon's heart. "None of that," he told himself, and spurred on his horse. Adults though they were now, Soren was his boy. Soren would always be his beloved boy.

Leon streamed across the Eldruna Valley, the drum-like hoofbeats of his guards following behind him. Seeing him, the greatness of his mantle surging over his destrier's flank, the Weremen on the field raised their heads in curiosity. Once he was at the front, Leon pulled to a halt. It was not long before another set of hoofbeats pounded toward him, joining his entourage of guards.

Asveig dipped his head. "I am to stay with you, the Draugh says."

"Torfiner at my side again, just like the old days."

He gave pause. "I left you in Svennandia—"

"To protect Soren."

"The boy needed guidance."

"He needed guidance and a father. You did what I could never have asked." Leon placed a hand on his old friend's shoulder. "Today, we will not think of the past, but we will kill Kru'ul."

"Aye, sire." Asveig's eyes glistened.

Leon raised his gloved fist at the field. "Deploy, all of you!" he shouted. "We are at the eve of war, and you lounge about like besotted gallants in a mead hall? Make haste, you sons of vagabonds, or Fjorland shall set the Kru'ul upon you! Double time!"

The armed commons, startled by his tone, shuffled off their backsides.

"Aye, that's the Draugh's father," Asveig murmured to Roagrim, who had come to watch.

The Were King and his retinue cantered across the field, bound for the Hammerfest Dike. Seeing the way Leon roared at his men, a smile creased the corners of his eyes.

"Roagrim!" Soren gestured southward with his axe. The Thomdrim leader boomed at his enclave to fall in, and the giants broke into an effortless jog after the Were King's gallop.

"Remember the horn!" Soren hollered, raising his axe into the air as he receded into the distance. The Vigardian warbands on the field brandished their axes in like, a salute to their supreme leader.

I will see you soon, Leon thought wistfully. He returned his attention to the Eldruna Valley. While Soren's retinue thundered southward, the peasant fighters and even the Vigardian units continued to mill about.

Leon shook his head in disbelief and turned to Asveig. "Why aren't they deploying?"

"Forgive me, sire. They do not understand you."

"I spoke in the Svenning, not elvish tongue."

"Allow me." Asveig pealed in a heavy country drawl that was entirely another tongue to Leon.

"*You heard the Elder Kjoster, maggot-pated sots! Pikemen at the front, packed tight! Archers! First cohort, at the front! Second and third cohorts, take your place at the flanks! Vigardians, make for the rear! Remain in your warbands and keep yourselves behind the pike-men. Protect the rear. If you allow the enemy to touch our rear, you Svennish sores of the eyes,* SO HELP YOUR HIDES!"

At his roar, the host straightened in terror. "Yes, Kjoster!" they cried at Leon. "At once, Kjoster..." The war leaders repeated the commands in an even heavier twang. All the various centuries rushed to pack into formation.

"Better, no?" said Asveig.

"The Light, Torfiner, what strange speech was that?"

"I assure you, it was the Svenning." The broad Vigardian clapped his shoulder. "You are too Republic, my Lord."

While the Vigardian equivalent of two legions deployed, Leon turned his worried gaze in the dike's direction. He knew it was only a matter of time before that barrier fell. The Kru'ul would have arrived by now, and Soren was riding straight into them.

JUST BEFORE SOREN made it to the dike with Roagrim and his personal guard, he heard the howls of Kru'ul from the other side. It was a noise that made his hairs stand up. Once more, he was whisked to the night he had heard ten thousand dying Thomdrim; but these shrieks were far harsher, and grating to his skin. He tugged on the reins.

"Draugh?" said Roagrim, slowing his jog.

"Go on. I will join you."

The chieftain noticed the consternation in his shoulders. He gave a short nod to his Leafweavers to halt. "This is a good distance for us to deploy."

The presence of so many men and Thomdrim harried Soren, but it could not be helped. They were on the battlefield. There was no place to hide and do this. He ignored the little voice inside him to keep his dangerous secret, and raised his fist.

"*Arendùr ilenion!*"

The elvish power behind the words amplified their strength. An invisible ripple of Rhún energy blasted over the forests and mountains of Vingulmark. None of the men noticed, but the Thomdrim, ancient beings of magic, certainly did.

Roagrim and his one hundred followers turned to Soren. He pretended not to notice their wary stares, nor feel the weight of them. He heeled his destrier back into a gallop to the dike. As he closed the gap, he glanced up at the brightening skies. For all his outward disposition of confidence, he was afraid, greatly afraid. It was impossible they could win this battle.

Nothing appeared in the skies.

This agitated him even more, but he kept it from his countenance and pulled up to the contingent of men behind the twelve-foot-high dike. The moment his boots touched ground, he felt the earth vibrating from the many thundering of Kru'ul feet.

"My Lord," his men greeted him. They beat their axes against their mailed chests in salute. He clasped arms with Lord Solfreid Wulfgar at the front.

"Uncle."

"Draugh." The earl inclined his head. They climbed up a narrow flight of stairs to the top of the outer gate. What Soren saw made him suck in his breath. A tide of monsters surged down the Hammerfest causeway. It was as Rulf said. They were heavily armored brutes, wearing all manner of blackened metal. Some had spiked pauldrons and vambraces, while others had visors shaped like maws. Some were potbellied. Others were gangling sinews. None had eyes, and all moved at the pace of a horse in canter. They keened ghoulish notes that made the Vigardian chargers toss in disquiet.

"Light help us," Soren murmured. "How could such foulness walk our continent..."

"They did not know about the wyrms at first," Lord Sol told him. "The fools fanned off the causeway into Thurs Runja. They must have lost a few hundred, perhaps a thousand, if we are lucky."

"Still not enough."

"See over there?" The earl pointed. Holding back from the tide was a rider draped in white robes. A white headdress concealed his face. He wielded what appeared to be an ivory scepter enclosing a large, foreign gemstone. Something about his facelessness was more frightening than even the Kru'ul.

"One of the warlords," said Soren.

"An Illuminator."

He clenched his jaw. "We have not the resources to fight against twenty thousand Kru'ul *and* fanatic mages!"

"My scouts tell me they appear to control the beasts entirely."

Soren had no time to adjust his war strategy. The Kru'ul were less than twenty paces away now. "Brace the dike," he bellowed. "Archers!"

The light bowman on the parapet strung their arrows, their breaths falling heavy. Soren felt their terror in the tremoring air. Before the charge could slam against their earth wall, a Kru'ul roared. It had plunged into a pothole. The steel-tipped stake beneath impaled the monster through the breastplate. The Kru'ul around it similarly fell. Shrieks crushed the air. The charge slowed, then came to a full stop.

The archers cheered in victory. Lord Solfreid recounted the sightings to the anxious men and Thomdrim awaiting below. The potholes would not be enough to stop the waves, but they stopped a charge that would have brought down the dike upon impact.

"Let them come!" Roagrim raised his axe. "Let those pretty elves kiss my steel!"

The bestial screeching became more distraught. The Kru'ul would not charge forth anymore, knowing more potholes concealed themselves between there and the dike. Neither could they turn back, for the Kru'ul host blockaded them from behind. Notwithstanding, the mountainside was to their left, and wyrms were to their right. They had nowhere to go.

His plans were working.

The nearby Illuminator seemed to sense Soren's smirk, for he slowly turned and picked him out above the gate. Soren lost his smile. Even with the warlord's face hidden behind a headdress, Soren felt the mage's hair-raising gaze fixing on him.

A grating, pitchless energy rumbled into the air. As if entranced, the Kru'ul fell quiet. Soren understood none of what was happening, besides that the gemstone was channeling a creeping power. It tingled his flesh. This was no elvish magic he had ever encountered.

The Kru'ul, utterly mesmerized, shuffled forward, their limbs and heads hanging unnaturally. More fell into the potholes. They groaned as the spears skewered them. But the tide kept coming, slow as their pace was. Eventually, so many of the Kru'ul were dying, layers of carcasses formed a thick bridge between the rest of the host and the dike's outer gate.

The Seregal warlord raised his scepter and warbled a new command in his eccentric tongue. With this, the Kru'ul's pace picked up, and they broke into a fresh charge. None seemed affected by their forced galloping over their dead brethren. Lord Sol's smile was short-lived.

"Fire at will!" Soren shouted.

The archers released. But the parapet on this outer wall was narrow, hardly enough to hold over fifty men. Its entire purpose was only to keep out the bloodwyrms. The Kru'ul on the front lines crashed to the ground, arrows quilling their limbs and faces, but more Kru'ul kept coming.

"*Brace the dike!*"

The slam came, shaking Soren off balance. He caught the bulwark to keep from falling over. It was not as devastating a blow as he had anticipated, thanks to the potholes. The men below felt the impact and shouted war cries, leaning their shoulders against the iron fortified gate. The Thomdrim beat their axes against their chests, hungering for Kru'ul blood.

The gray-scaled ghouls kept slamming their armored chests and bellies against the gate. They were dumb brutes, moaning and hissing at the earthworks like they were half aware that they were even alive. The archers kept firing. Several Kru'ul collapsed off the causeway. At the mere thud of their bodies against the earth, wyrms burst out and hooked their mandibles into them, wrestling to drag them underground. Gravelly shrieks manifolded with the Kru'ul roars and the slamming at the dike's gate.

"What a flaming mess," Lord Sol muttered.

Soon, the piles of Kru'ul carcasses formed natural barriers on either side of the causeway. The archers stopped firing. The earl glanced at Soren with worry. "We're out of missiles."

Soren drew his axe. They all knew it would come to this moment. He skipped down the parapet and onto ground level, joining his men and Thomdrim on the causeway over the canal. Following King Leondran's strategy, they kept pikemen at the front, their polearms lowered and readied for a cavalry charge. Behind them were the earl's Vigardians and Roagrim's Leafweavers. Seeing Soren dismounted and joining them on the ground, his allies raised their shoulders with greater morale.

"If they break through your ranks," Soren murmured to Roagrim, "you will call a retreat to Eldruna. Do you understand?"

The giant muttered something. His battle axe was poised. He was all but ready to eat Kru'ul.

Lord Solfreid joined Soren's side, drawing his longsword. The gate ahead of them pounded. Now the archers had retreated to the rear of his fighting cohorts. Soren flicked his gaze again to the skies, but they remained empty of dragons. The direction of his glances did not pass Roagrim's notice.

"My Lord," the earl murmured, "should we not take this time to retreat to the valley?"

"I will staunch them here. If they cannot pass through us, they cannot deploy and make their charge to our allies in Eldruna. They will be at their weakest right here." Soren tightened his grip on the haft as the gate splintered. "I will not squander this opportunity."

Roagrim shouted in assent, but creases appeared on Solfreid's forehead.

Soren bellowed, "*We are...*"

The gate split open. The first of the Kru'ul clawed to get through. Soren bent his knees. Together, his men shouted the final roar to the old chorus.

"VIGARDIANS!"

A wave of Kru'ul slammed into the pikemen, impaling themselves as they did in the potholes. But so many of them spurted forth, thrusting the line of pikemen into the rear ranks of Vigardian axe men. As many battles as Soren had fought lately, he could never get used to the clangorous vibrations of striking steel, the hateful roars, the screams of dying men. The Kru'ul kept pushing. It was not long before they penetrated the front ranks and made it to the Vigardian warband.

Drawing his heel back for momentum, Soren catapulted himself forward and hacked through a Kru'ul's throat. Beside him, Roagrim slammed his battle axe down on a wailing Kru'ul's armored shoulder, slicing all the way down to its knee. Foul ichor spattered Soren's face.

And then he was caught in the thick of it. Kru'ul rushed past. Fetid gray bodies quashed the pikemen. The sound of swinging steel was everywhere at once, at all angles. A platoon of Kru'ul swarmed up a Thomdrim's body, taking the giant down. Sweat poured down Soren's neck as he thrust and swung. He had underestimated how strong these Wasteland Elves were. They had been penetrated so soon.

Any moment now, the Kru'ul masses would compass them. If the Kru'ul reached Soren's rear in this narrow pass and closed them in before they could retreat, it would be over. He could not let that happen.

Clenching his jaw, he raised a fist and pleaded, "*Arendùr ilenion!*"

Soren searched the skies. So many silhouettes were rushing past his peripheries. Nothing appeared above. His dragon-enhanced body would strengthen his endurance, but endurance meant little when too many Kru'ul to stop were flitting past him. Soon, their numbers swelled so much, he was trapped inside the turbulence of their stinking armor, unable to fight. If he would not die by their blades, he would be trampled in the mud.

Soren lost sight of Roagrim's retreating ranks.

26
VIÐ ERUM... VIGARDIANS!

THE WORST OF Leon's fears came true as he pulled up before the Hammerfest Dike. The Kru'ul were rushing through, demolishing the Svennish archers and Vigardians they passed. Soren vanished into the surge.

Somewhere behind Leon, Asveig shouted at him to stop. The Were commander drew his sword and pursed his mouth tight as he cut down Kru'ul from the saddle. Leon dismounted and pressed on into the tossing storm. Kru'ul snarled and swung at him. Parrying, he charged against the tide, staying close to the canal's edge. Most of the Kru'ul paid him no heed, hungering instead to pursue the contingent of five hundred that were withdrawing back to Eldruna.

From the corner of his eye, Leon spotted too late a heavyset Kru'ul with fangs swinging at him. He raised his longsword and pivoted to the right, as much as he could in this stampede. But the Kru'ul, with its greater strength, cut its serrated blade deep through Leon's left upper arm.

The sting of pain burst across Leon's senses. He grunted quietly, pulling away, and wrested Soren upright from the ground. They shuffled into the shallow canal waters, out of the stampede.

Pressing a hand to his wound, Leon panted, "I almost thought I lost—"

"*What are you doing here?*" Soren's roar overpowered even the clangor. By the Light, he was enraged. Grasses clung to his mud-blackened face. "I told you to stay away from the front lines!"

"If I had not stepped in, they would have overcome you—"

"And they almost overcame *you*!" Soren would not take his eyes off Leon's bleeding arm. "You'll kill me, Father!"

Oh, Leon thought. His son was not livid, but hysterical. Leon was not sure which wrangled him more—the plea twisting Soren's voice, or that, after twenty solstices, Soren had just called him "father."

"You knew better than to ride out here, son," Leon chided above the din. "You knew they would overcome the dike. Of course I had to come back for you."

Soren sighed with impatience, but Leon could see he was shaken. "I did not expect they would be so strong," the Draugh admitted. "I thought we could cripple them for a little longer and have time for a retreat."

Someone was shouting from the other side of the canal. Asveig waved at them. Leon had never seen the man look so frantic. Lord Solfreid and the bulk of his vanguard had withdrawn safely through the ghyll, but Roagrim and twelve of his giants remained. They formed a wall and were covering the retreat, blocking anymore of the Kru'ul from advancing. It was only a matter of time before Leon and Soren were completely surrounded, and beyond an escape.

Soren said under his breath, "If I see you do anything this reckless again..." He yanked Leon along by the good arm, giving no thanks for his rescue.

Leon chucked. *I* was reckless? he thought. But the king had the wisdom to keep his mouth closed.

Together, they fought side by side, breaking through the Kru'ul ranks to reach the safety behind the Thomdrim line. Despite the sting of his arm, Leon felt exhilarated doing battle alongside his now adult son. Forty solstices it had been since he battled like this.

"I still remember when you were practicing wooden swords with Torfiner in the yard," Leon shouted. He grunted as steaming Kru'ul blood spattered his helmet. "You barely knew how to parry then!" Ducking, he slashed his blade across the unarmored throat of a gangling Kru'ul. "Your mother would be so proud, albeit she would faint if she saw you fighting with a Vigardian axe. Not very Fjorlander of you."

"The Light. Save your maypole dancing for another time!" Soren used both hands to yank his blade out of a Kru'ul's spilling potbelly. He would not stray more than a few steps from Leon. That boy was focused on protecting him instead of covering his own flanks. Leon wanted so much to clout him, but the best he could do was pull Soren out of this dike before another bout of stupidity killed him for good.

Once they were behind Roagrim's Leafweavers, Leon at last clobbered him hard. Soren lurched back in surprise, holding his offended cheek.

"Are you trying to throw away your life?" Leon demanded.

"You strike a king—"

"I strike my half-baked son. I am not so senescent that you should defend me in place of yourself."

Soren gestured with his axe at Leon's arm. "Then what is that?"

"Next time, I'll lose the whole if I have to salvage you again!"

"I was well without you—"

"You think being stampeded by Kru'ul was 'well'?"

"I am the Draughammr!" Soren spat. "I have fought plenty of battles. I don't need to be lectured at like a child—"

"For the Light of Vaeritas." Asveig pulled his steed between them. "*Mount your horses before I strike you both myself!*"

They looked up at him, quieting.

"Please, Your Majesties," he added politely, coughing.

Once they were back in the saddles, Leon's house guards closed him in again. Halvar looked paler than Soren had been, though tact kept him from blustering in his own hysteria.

"I'll try not to do it again," Leon said, sparing him the speech.

Soren glanced back from his saddle. "Roagrim!"

The Thomdrim leader turned slightly, though he did not slow any of his blows against the Kru'ul.

"Roagrim!" Soren bellowed again. "Withdraw!"

After several more strikes, the Thomdrim shouted back, "No, Draugh. Go, we will hold them at bay for as long as we can."

Soren receded behind an expressionless wall. The enclave leader meant to sacrifice himself so that they could escape. At the speed the Kru'ul were moving, they would never return to the Eldruna Valley with enough time to make it safely behind the lines of their archers.

"Draugh," Asveig said quietly.

When the Wereman would not move, Leon rode closer and clutched his arm. "Come, son," he said. "We have little time."

A shadow fell over Soren's face. He pulled away from Leon and spurred his destrier into a gallop without a further word to his Thomdrim friend. Leon, Asveig, and the house guards thundered after him along the causeway.

Before they reached the bend, some two thousand paces away, the ghyll tossed with a groan. It was a noise of such suffering that, by impulse, Leon glanced over his shoulder. The Kru'ul had penetrated the Thomdrim line. But instead of rushing past them to chase the Astoraines, the odious creatures swarmed up the giants like insects. Already, all but four had fallen. The Kru'ul pulled them to the ground like great felled oaks. They leapt onto them while they were trapped on their backs, hacking at the helpless giants.

Soren pulled to a halt, though the rest of them galloped on.

Roagrim kept fighting until a white-robed warlord appeared through the chaos and gestured with his scepter at the Thomdrim leader. The Kru'ul glanced away from the Thomdrim they had pinned. Like hungry beasts, the tide turned and charged at the greatest of the giants. The nearest ones crawled up his mighty limbs. So many there were, his savage axe swings could not stop them all. Soon, they clambered over even his head and face. The Kru'ul hacked away. Roagrim roared. In the distance, the giant crumpled and vanished under the writhing swarm.

No emotion penetrated Soren's face, though a sheen thickened in his eyes, reflecting the destruction climaxing at the Hammerfest Dike. After a few breaths more, he reined back around and resumed his gallop behind Leon and the rest.

It was the fifteenth hour when King Leondran was back at the front ranks of the Wereguild's legions. All cohorts were in formation, stationed exactly where he had commanded. In the backdrop were the mighty slopes of the Lupines, and all twenty-four dragon slayers on Solhall's parapets pointed at the bright skies. It would have been quite the epic for a tapestry or castle painting, Leon thought. Perhaps a few hundred solstices from now, the continent would commemorate not Old Svenn, but the men and Thomdrim who fought in this battle for the Deep North.

The ground thundered. The Kru'ul were swarming through the ghyll. Any moment, they would appear through the darkness of the Eldruna Pass and into the valley.

Leon glanced at Soren, who was on the saddle to his right. This was the prime moment for a battle speech. It was either now or never. Brave as these men and women were, they needed a mighty lift in morale.

As if coming to a final decision, the younger Astoraine pulled his horse behind Leon, and bowed his head.

Asveig and the war commanders at the front shifted their eyes to Fjorland's king. Drums hammered behind Leon's breastplate. If there was one thing he knew better than orating at crowds, it was this. The battlefield. After forty solstices, the battlefield was his once more.

King Leon sat higher and heeled his caparisoned destrier past the tremendous front line. In the distance, the first of the Kru'ul poured out of the pass. It drew sharp hisses from the archers. The elf-ghouls appeared as blackened vermin, so many of them that would keep pouring in like a broken dam.

Leon turned his horse to face the legions. At this angle, the prodigious numbers of Soren's men were a terrific sight. Yes, he thought, this would make for a great Elondrian saga. He was proud, as these northerners must be, that he was living in such a heroic age, even if it would end in their deaths. This was the age, finally, when the race of man would rise and prove the beating strength and unbreakable courage of his heart.

King Leon reached deep into his belly and thundered in his Eldari voice.

"Look upon the field! The enemy comes! The Morghûls have sent a host we can never match in numbers or strength. The days ahead of us will be red days. Will you surrender now to fear?"

Even from the saddle, Leon felt the growing rumble of the earth. He looked at the faces before him, faces of commons, warriors, shieldmaidens, and giants. Indeed, he found terror. Few believed this battle could be won.

"I am Leondran Astoraine! On the other side of those mountains, you know me as the King of Fjorland. You know me as an Eldari. You know me as the Republic! But out here, on the living lands of Old Svenn, none of those things matter."

Unsheathing his greatsword, an ancestral blade that had once belonged to Svenn's emperors, he raised it at the sky.

"Out here, today, I bear none of those titles. On this soil, I am neither Republic nor Wereguild. I am not Svennish nor Vigardian. I am your brother Elondrian, and I have come to fight for you—for we are not fighting for the Republic or Vingulmark. We are not fighting for Solhall."

In the pause that followed, the rumble of approaching Kru'ul made the Wereguild host held their breaths.

"Brothers and sisters of the Deep North, we are here today to fight against the elves for the freedom of Elondria—and we *will* have the victory!"

Sundry warbands raised their axes.

"All who stand against us will know the wrath of our blades. They will know the ice of the North. No elf or dragon has ever been able to surmount you, and the Kru'ul will not now. For you are Wereguild, the keepers of Old Svenn! You are the descendants of Thorgest Vigarda! You are the Elondrians that rose out of the ashes of the Dragon Wars with your axes still in hand. You are the defenders of the free races!"

The war shouts that followed could have brought down the skies. Leon felt the heart of Old Svenn overpowering the very beat of his own. No longer did he see fear in the men ahead of him, but the wrath of resolve.

With the speech now finished, Soren took his place beside Leon. The cheers manifolded as the northerners saw their Draughammr at last reunited with Fjorland, his old heritage. Soren beat his axe against his chest, then raised it again at his armies.

"Remember the horn!"

"*Remember the horn!*" all chorused back.

"Where our axes feed..."

"*Our enemies will bleed!*"

"Where our axes strike thunder..."

"Our enemies greatly suffer!"

"We are the wolves of war..."

"We are the wolves of war!"

Two war horns from scouts blared over the battlefield, though this was not the final horn signal. The Kru'ul had just passed into firing range.

Leon shouted, "Archers, draw!"

Asveig and the war commanders repeated his orders across the field. Soren raised his axe and bellowed the final chorus. All the northerners in the Eldruna Valley joined him.

"We are... VIGARDIANS!"

With that, Leon dismounted, and Orrin led his horse away. Soren followed his example, taking the left flank with Duke Einnar. Seeing both kings grounded like the rest of them drew the battle roars into a greater furor of morale.

"Well done, sire," Asveig said, as Leon returned to his place behind the cohorts of archers. "I am convinced now that you are Vigardian."

"Oh, I would not take it *that* far." Leon made to cover his ears. "Eldari at the peak of their quarrels aren't this loud."

"A Vigardian trait," Asveig said proudly.

"They turned even you savage, Torfiner." Leon tsked and shouted at the top of his lungs, "*Loose!*"

On his orders, one thousand foot archers released. A swarm of quarrels blackened the air. It did not last long, but the dreadful proportion of it mesmerized Leon. For several beats, not even the daylight shone through. The memories of his younger days during the War of Treason suddenly rushed back, turning his calves to water. *This* was what the Elenntarien had fought so hard to stop, yet here it was again. War. No matter how epic the sagas might paint it later, war would always be war.

Leon never had the time to ponder how things had ever come to this—for the arrows struck. Animal shrieks tore across the valley, claws raking down his back. The missiles decimated the foe's front lines. Yet the black combers kept coming, more and more pouring out of the pass. It heartened Leon to see that they had no formation whatsoever. That meant his field strategy was still sound.

He ordered two more volleys before commanding the archers to retreat to the flanks. The pound of Kru'ul tremored the grass beneath his feet. He was close enough now to see the stinking puffs coming out from the darkness behind their visors.

"It is time," Asveig murmured.

"Yes." Leon bent his knees. "Time for them to die." The Kru'ul were now one cohort away from the lancers at the front. Behind Leon, Vigardians in their thick gambesons and mail dug their massive, heavy shields into the mud.

"They cannot penetrate us," he said under his breath. "That is all that matters. We cannot let them penetrate us..."

The wave of Kru'ul slammed against their frontier. Even at this distance, the might of its power alarmed Leon. It was not enough pikemen. Even a thousand pikemen ahead of the heavily armed Vigardian warbands and giants would not be enough.

"So the War for Elondria begins," Leon said, suddenly doubting everything.

27

ALL GORE, NO GLORY

Eight days after her departure from Solhall, Skálda pulled up at the edge of the Völundr Reach.

"What in Finngolfa's ravens..."

The entire Eldruna Valley had turned into a pandemonium of divine proportions. Even from here, under the cool shade of the Völundr's pines, the fury of war trembled the heavens. Gray, wax-fleshed ghouls with tapered ears entangled themselves in Soren's host. She was not sure what she had been expecting, but the scene of chaos in the distance was beyond what she had ever imagined possible on the continent. And to think, ritefests had once been the most important event in her peasant life.

Fresh reserves of Wereguild awaited on opposite sides of the battlefield. Then again, perhaps not fresh. The cohorts hung their heads with exhaustion, which suggested the field commander had swapped them out to the flanks to give them respite. Both sides must have been fighting for days, which she supposed made sense. In the epics, battles seemed to climax over one day; but in real life, when both sides had tens of thousands in number, even the commanders would need rest. No one could battle straight for twenty-four hours, after all. She tried to imagine falling asleep on a battlefield shared with deformed elves and felt a tinge of cold.

Solhall was not besieged yet, at least. The Kru'ul had not penetrated the Wereguild host.

She tightened her grip on her axe, tracing the field with a twist of excitement and unease. If only Bale were here. This would be a paradise of chapter advancements—assuming the northerners would still be alive by the end of the night. Where was Soren?

A vortex of chaos in the south caught her attention. A gap was opening around a single rider in a sweeping black mantle. His gloved hand swayed through the air in a strange pattern of oscillations and swift, severing-like motions. Every time the elf's fingers made a cutting motion, a human screamed. A pikeman soared overhead, slamming headfirst into another Vigardian. Another had his spear pulled out of his hands. The weapon sailed away from him, spun around mid-way through the air, and plunged back into his chest. The surrounding Svennish crashed to their knees or howled suddenly from a decapitated limb. But the spellcaster never left his saddle.

Elvish magic. Whatever those spells, they were wreaking havoc on Soren's forces.

"Rystendal," she murmured. Even from this distance, she felt the burn of his madness. That elf must have come of his own accord; his *saer'ammath*, the Severed Binding, was succumbing him to insanity, perhaps the same way losing Tera Beren had succumbed Eyrek.

The elf's skill mesmerized her. The spells were so potent, a power that could ravage upon merely a few spoken words. Rystendal's dragon might be dead, and his source to the Dragonspells gone, but he was still a High Elf. He had an affinity for the Magia. The death around him was only spiraling larger.

Skálda tightened her grip on her axe. Eyrek was nowhere in the skies, but that was no matter. She had her target. It was long overdue that Crix be reunited with his precious rider. Above all... she needed to hear and learn what words Rystendal was using for his spells. Her hunger to know her affinity kindled again in her.

She broke into a jog down the slopes. Once she was on ground level, she took a running charge, entering the first ranks of Kru'ul in a leap. Finngólfa almighty, the ghouls' sweat smelled like burning iron. At the same time she started her attack, shouts erupted over the valley. Aracir sank into stinking Kru'ul flesh as Skálda turned her head.

Swooping in from the direction of wyrm country, above the Eldruna Pass, were dragons. Many dragons.

The Kru'ul surrounding her forced her attention on their flailing blades, but she cared little for them; they were all brute force with little strategy behind their swings. Her chest hammered faster. An entire dragonflight streamed over the Eldruna Valley in arrowhead formation. Eyrek's surviving riders. Their true enemy had arrived.

Eleven chethems and one eldragon soared for Solhall, the only section of the Eldruna Valley that the enemy had not penetrated. Her neck tendons clenched so tight—until the first of the dragon slayers fired. Twenty-three more bolts discharged from the battlements. Skálda pulled her axe out of a Kru'ul's ribs, following the volley with the turn of her head. The awesome sight of colossal missiles overhead sickened her. The chethems shrieked and slammed into each other, but the devastating rain took them down. The only one that emerged alive from the volley was the eldragon, the flight that must have belonged to the Primarch she battled above the Nifvinter Mountains.

So, she thought, this was how Soren's followers had destroyed Tera Beren. His marksmen were utter beasts. She shoved through more Kru'ul, grateful all over again she was fighting on the Vigardian side.

Instead of continuing its path to Solhall, the eldragon pulled up sharply. More bolts sailed past. The eld was far lither than the smaller, three-fingered chethems. With stronger wings of four fingers, the High Dragon ascended in an upward spiral that would have been impossible for Nornsir or Feorya. The bolts kept missing. Then, as if realizing they were wasting missiles, the Vigardians stopped firing altogether. The elvish rider guided his dragon into a full, upside-down loop high in the sky. This would throw most Builders in Aranor Elondris from the saddle, belts and stirrups or not. Before them was an advanced rider. Once the eld finished its loop, with its newly accumulated momentum, it burst forth toward Solhall. That dragon would be the first to penetrate the city's airspace. It bayed in triumph.

A bolt exploded its neck.

Skálda widened her eyes, watching everything over a Kru'ul's shoulder. Without even a death scream, the eldragon dropped like a stone out of the sky. She did not envy its rider the bone-crunch of his fall.

"Good shot, Rulf," she muttered, and kneed a Kru'ul in the groin.

She kept moving steadily toward Lord Rystendal, but with a swarm of skirmishing Kru'ul and Vigardians in her way, the High Elf might destroy all of Eldruna before she ever made it to him. Skálda clenched her jaws in frustration. Ducking a spiked club, she smashed her axe into a Kru'ul's eyeless face. "Get out of my way!" she yelled.

An unnatural shadow fell over the field. Impulsive dread washed over her. At the next opportunity she could, Skálda glanced up.

"Eyrek..."

It was not Eyrek. This new dragon was only a little bigger than the dead Primarch's eldragon, though it was moving at razor speed. She was of slim build, with a long, narrow head that reminded Skálda of a heron's bill. Her scales were a stunning purple-gray; her head was white but for two black streaks striping the scales around her eyes.

Skálda forgot herself to that dragon. It was a cranewing, an endangered species that Dragonsteel exclusively held in the High Eyrie. That was according to Anders's bestiary. When she was younger, he let her play with his warboard and simulate campaigns with dragons of her choice. More than once, she had pretended to Build with cranewings. They were far from the strongest, but they were swifter than elds, and one of the fastest flights on the continent. Seeing this rare dragon in real life surged back in her a strong, child-like wonder.

The *Lhaer'thri* read 2,009 chapters. This one had to belong to the she-bane, Detherys.

The cranewing covered the length of the valley in a third of the time as the eldragon. Seeing the she-dragon approach, Solhall's battlements blasted another wave of missiles.

The cranewing veered to the right. Tucking in her claws, she whirled round and round, so quickly, the sight of it made Skálda dizzy. The bolts sailed past her narrow, slender body. How Detherys did not plummet from the saddle, Skálda did not know. She surmised not even Eyrek, with all his flight experience, would have been able to pull off such a feat. It took a very different kind of rider to own a cranewing, which likely was why, like other rare breeds, the Order restricted who could Bind with it.

When the cranewing next unfolded her wings, Solhall fired a second wave at her. But the dragon contracted herself again, whirling and whirling, transforming into a gyre of smeared grays and whites that streaked like a return missile over the skirmishing hordes.

The Vigardian reserves shouted, horrified, as the cranewing made it to the rear of Soren's ground forces. What Detherys Lorathari shouted from dragonback echoed over the entire valley.

"*M'ethil!*"

Burning light spilled out of the cranewing's maw. The reserves detonated into flames. Skálda bellowed as she evaded a flail to the head, but the cacophony of war drowned her out. The Dragonlord's flight spewed more glowing yellow over the rear cohorts. Although the cranewing's fire-breathing was a fraction compared to what Skálda had seen of Tythandrell's in Dellfast, it would be enough to skew the battle in the Order's favor.

Within minutes, they lost at least one thousand men, about a fourth of the men they had left. The cranewing was scorching Prince Vharyn's Kru'ul just as much as Soren's Vigardians. The way the elf goaded her dragon to sustain the *m'ethil* told Skálda that, like the elf's post leader, she had no qualms about committing war crimes for her own purpose.

Skálda kicked aside a Kru'ul, elbowed another in the nose. She fought harder. Eyrek might never appear on the battlefield. Between Detherys and Rystendal, they would fall within the hour.

Another uncoordinated wave of ballistae forced Detherys to retract back into a defensive position. Her cranewing bolted away from the blazing ranks directly outside Solhall's main gate. But after three more sequences of whirling, the she-dragon did not return to her fiery rampaging.

With a temporary gap in between the skirmishing, Skálda turned her head. The cranewing was diving low, her maw parting. Not far from Skálda, six Kru'ul caught a bloodied Soren inside their circle. He drove his axe into them, but he was fighting alone, his back turned to Detherys.

"Soren!" she shouted, abandoning this section of the skirmish to sprint to him. He did not hear her.

The cranewing's shadow fell over him. The Kru'ul were now dead at his feet. Soren turned around, but it was too late. He raised his axe, his only miniscule defense against a diving adult dragon.

Skálda made it to one hundred paces from Soren when a second airborne giant faded out of the sky. It appeared in piecemeal brushstrokes; first its head, then its neck and wings, and the rest of his body, like it was ink forming a painting out of the air.

She staggered to a halt. The dark dragon slammed against the smaller cranewing. His mold was majestic as an eld's, though he reminded Skálda of a winged lion. A black mane lashed against his neck in place of spikes, and his tail ended in a dark tuft. He pinned the she-dragon's wings and slammed her against the ground. With no time to deaccelerate from her dive, she made a crushing impact, bouncing thrice, as she skidded over the grass. There came a sickening, gravelly pop of a spine breaking. The cranewing lifted her neck weakly to bite him, but he crunched down on her throat.

Though Skálda could not see Detherys, the she-elf's bloody screams perforated the air.

Skálda sprinted the rest of the way to Soren and seized his arm. The Vigardian king was in such a stupor, he turned to her without seeming to see.

"You have a *dragon*?" she hollered, as more bones crunched behind her.

"Skálda? You have returned—"

"You are the Draughammr. The *Dragonslayer*." She emphasized that last word in her accented Elondrian. "And you have a dragon? What in Finngolfa's ravens!"

"He... is not my dragon."

"Then what would you call that?" She gestured at the midnight-blue beast behind them that was tearing through dragon flesh. With one victorious claw pinning his dead prize, he turned his neck and roared at the approaching Kru'ul. A riptide of flame blasted out from behind his monstrous rows of teeth.

Soren stood taller with pride. "Saarhekhu is a wild dragon of the North. He Binded with me before I became the Draughammr. He does not belong to me."

"You are Binded, but he is not yours? That makes no sense."

Skálda squinted up at the howling mammoth's spine, searching for a saddle. There was none.

Soren seemed to understand her intent. "I do not ride him. It's a long story."

"I have time."

"No, Kvael-Akar, I do not think so. We are on a flaming battlefi—ah."

Detherys crawled out of the shadows between Saarhekhu's legs. Her eyes were wild with shock. The *saer'ammath* had not settled in yet.

Seeing the madness in those eyes, it dawned on Skálda the life of a rider was far from glorious. On the battlefield, Bindings were severed. Dragons died. Their riders were burdened with dreadful deaths. She could not fathom what it would be like to live her last moment trapped in a saddle, on her dead dragon, in freefall two thousand feet in the air as she waited to die in the fall. She could much less fathom seeing the dragon she had Realm-Built to 2,000 chapters perish in a blink. And yet the Order declared the Realm-Building Enterprise was all glory, no gore.

Waggling her eyes, Detherys's unsteady gaze fell on Soren. She drew her longsword. Her shock was blistering into rage. She took a running charge at the Draugh—

Saarhekhu turned his neck and snapped her up. Her head and upper half vanished between his jaws.

Skálda screamed, toppling onto her backside in terror. Paying her and Soren no heed, the wild dragon gorged down the rest of the elf in one bite. His gullet bulged as the remains of Detherys Lorathari tumbled into his belly. Then he turned and planted his wing talons on either side of them. He stretched his jaws wide again as he loomed from above, trapping his next prey. The weight of the dragon's shadow flattened them on their backs.

Skálda prepared to kiss Finngolfa's ravens goodbye.

A deafening dragon belch, and a bit of hot slaver, torrented over them. Skálda held her nose against the rancid air. The beast was grinning.

"What the Hel?" Soren sat up. "Where are your manners?" He waved away the noxious cloud. "You don't stink any less than when we first met."

The Draugh wrested her to her feet with one powerful tug. Dragon slaver and bits of Detherys stained Skálda's leather jerkin. "I don't understand."

"He came because I entreated him with the *arendùr ilenion.* The Dragoncall. I did not know if he would listen and could not factor him into my battle plans."

With the flames walling them off from oncoming Kru'ul, they found a temporary respite. The wild giant drew his nose closer to Soren, waiting for a pet. Smiling, the Draugh rubbed his scales and an old scar running down the ridge of his right eye.

"Saarhekhu the Nightborn. He says he did hear my call and was delayed by the distance." As Soren stroked the length of his head, the dragon lazily closed his eyes, rumbling as if smitten by a girl. "He is an old friend I met in exile. In return for his Binding, I slay Morghûl thralls. He is the entire reason I was able to advance to my *kvael-akar* rank." His eyes glinted. "Rank of Draughammr."

That explained how his body was dragon-enhanced and as physically formidable as Eyrek's. She read 6,555 chapters in this beast. No wonder he had demolished Detherys's flight of 2,009 chapters. For a wild dragon to be so far advanced, Saarhekhu must be many centuries old. Certainly, besides for Bale, he had to be the last free remnant beyond the Order's control.

Soren winked at her. "Now you know my secret. Don't tell anyone."

"I would like to make up ranks in the wild," she muttered.

The nightborn shifted his glowing blue eyes to her. His affection turned to wariness.

Before Soren could reassure him, a Great Dragon's roar trembled the heavens. The entire battlefield gave pause. That roar alone awakened a fear so ancient, it stilled even the Kru'ul. The northerners were the palest of all. The setting seemed to fade away into an age past as they remembered again the Dragon Wars. Scarred into their soulscripts were memories of their ancestors falling to the winged beasts, and above all, the Greats that had obliterated Elondria's mightiest empire. Dragons, not elves, were a Vigardian's primordial enemy.

As the Day King appeared over the southern horizon, all the Deep North seemed to hold its breath. No noise existed besides the terrifying cadence of beating leather. A gargantuan shadow passed over the fighting hosts. No one moved. The eerie freeze stopped time on the field.

For all Skálda's oaths to annul Eyrek, seeing him again atop his golden titan curdled her blood. She would never forget the way he looked atop Emberglade, nor the insanity in his eyes. The sweet memories of embracing him in the Skonkauld, and stroking Tythandrell outside Bregan Island, seemed like a lifetime away.

"I tell myself again and again that I will kill him," she murmured, "but I don't think I ever could..."

"Because the Skitr King is mine." Coldness curtained Soren's face, draining the love and wonder for Saarhekhu that was there just a beat earlier. Skálda stepped away to give them space.

"You need to get to a dragon slayer." She glanced about the valley's devastation, particularly at the mushrooms of smoke rising from the rear ranks. "Do you have any left?"

"I have plenty more in Solhall."

"Then get to Solhall."

"I will not abandon my people—"

"Proud skit, enough of the theatrics. You are their best shot!"

Soren looked at her wryly. "You sound like my Light-blessed father."

"Shut your mouth and run, Draugh! I will take care of the Kru'ul."

"Our Kvael-Akar, here to break the continent as usual." He chuckled under his breath. They started their separate ways inside their ring of fire, but sharp horns in Solhall's direction made them pause.

Soren widened his eyes. It was a distress horn. Man-sized silhouettes were scaling down the Lupines, inching toward the settlement. The mountains fell at a near ninety degrees and served as Solhall's natural fortification from north, east, and west, yet whoever was coming seemed to have little difficulty maneuvering the slopes. The enemy numbers were few; perhaps two hundred. That should not be enough to overwhelm the five hundred Vigardians left to defend the settlement, yet Skálda smelled foulness in the air.

"What do you see?" Soren murmured to his dragon. The slits in those blue eyes narrowed, and his throat contracted with a low shriek. The Draughammr exhaled sharply.

"What?" said Skálda.

Suddenly, the urgency to return to Solhall consumed his bearing. "I must go."

"Go. I will find—"

"My father." Soren was already fallen to a sprint. "Find my father, Skálda! Protect him!"

Saarhekhu suddenly went quiet, watching his Binded recede into the distance. With the fire ring and the nightborn's presence safeguarding Skálda, the Kru'ul streamed past her. More horns were blowing, different Were signals she did not recognize. Detherys's dragonfire had weakened the flanks. The Kru'ul were now nearly to the rear, penetrating ever more deeply into the Vigardian host. Most of the Weremen were dead, but many more Kru'ul kept spilling out of the pass. Before nightfall, they would penetrate the rear, surround the last of Soren's host, and reach

Solhall's gates. That historical landmark had not been built to withstand a siege.

We have lost, she thought.

The realization should have terrified her, but she was too numbed. How could she have expected anything more than this, when they had been so outnumbered?

More horns, blowing in a new sequence and range of notes, blasted across the field. She barely heard them. The last surviving Svennish fled to the eastward slopes that marked the beginning of the Völundr Reach. It was a retreat of defeat. The voracious Kru'ul, encouraged, resumed their charge to Solhall.

It was the touch of a prodigious shadow, and the faraway call of a *luinor linnari* that woke Skálda.

She looked up. A golden colossus passed overhead. Tythandrell was so close, she could have reached up and touched his spiked tail. The barbed, impenetrable plates of his underbelly streamed past her. Eyrek was not flying for Solhall. His Dragonsighted eyes were set on someone else.

"Soren," she murmured.

The Draugh was in a sprint to Solhall's gate. There was still so much distance between it and himself. He would never make it in time.

Saarhekhu parted his jaws. Silent as the shadows, he launched himself in the air

Skálda left the fiery ring and kept pressing on to Lord Rystendal. The elf was close to her now. His spells had stopped. He was slowly advancing toward an isolated circle of Svennish—King Leondran and a bulky house guard. The king's back was turned. He had lost his helmet, and his left arm was bleeding from a deep gash. His face twisted as he fought an oncoming tide of Kru'ul.

As Tythandrell loomed closer to the Lupines, Solhall discharged a tide of ballistae. The Great Dragon banked. He was hardly as swift as the cranewing, and one nearly grazed his thorn-crowned head. The rest were out of range. The Great Dragon dove lower, closing the distance between himself and Soren.

Up on the saddle, Eyrek drew his greatsword. He appeared tiny astride Tythandrell's colossal back. The Dragonlord's intention was clear. He would not let Soren die by fire. Skálda had a feeling her brother would drag Soren back to Exar'forda, and kill him slowly on a torture rack.

Just before Tythandrell could clamp the Draugh into his claws, Saarhekhu faded out of invisibility and pinned the larger dragon from above. Tythandrell roared. He wavered in flight, swerving away from Soren. The nightborn spat a fireball at Eyrek, but the Second Rider shouted the *ciryamor,* shielding them. Then, on Eyrek's orders, Tythandrell rolled over in the air and landed back-first, skidding across the valley. At 6,554 chapters, Tythandrell's scales were too hardened for the low fall to damage him. Neither did the dragon's weight nor the booming crash pulverize Eyrek's bones, for the Dragonshield formed a barrier between him and the ground that protected him. Now Saarhekhu was pinioned beneath.

Eyrek held the shield and called a command in Elvynnöthe. Before he slid to a complete halt, the Great Dragon twisted his neck around and clamped the nightborn's shoulder. The smaller dragon wailed.

Lapsing the shield, Eyrek leapt onto the field, entirely unharmed by his adroitly maneuvered fall. Saarhekhu wrestled himself free from Tythandrell's jaws, taking off a chunk of his shoulder flesh. Blood poured down his neck and breastplate. Hastening for a defense, he expelled flames at the Day King's head.

Eyrek rolled in front of his dragon, swiftly raising the Dragonshield again. Tythandrell and Saarhekhu's chapters were a match, and the Dragonshield's borrowed strength repelled the nightborn's attack. A vociferous torrent of fire washed off the translucent gold dome. Skálda knew if Detherys, at her 2,009 chapters, had tried to do the same thing, Saarhekhu's flames would have shattered the shield.

Saarhekhu's neck tendons strained as he fought to sustain his flame and break the Dragonshield. But the superheat would not touch Eyrek. Tythandrell roared, enraged that the wild dragon was trying to kill his rider. He padded around the shield and snapped at the nightborn from his left flank. Saarhekhu evaded. The attack forced him to let go of his dragonfire. Panting out clouds of vapor, Saarhekhu withdrew and hurtled himself back into the skies.

The much larger Great bellowed above the valley, a male's call of victory and royal dominance. Tythandrell started to give chase, but Eyrek ordered him to stay grounded. The dragon slayers were on his mind. If they flew any closer to the settlement, the marksmen would not miss.

As Skálda fought on the other side of the valley, she watched Soren's dragon labor to ascend. The gaping wound on his shoulder sprayed blood over the battlefield. Hanging his neck, Saarhekhu opened his maw in pain, but the brave beast never even uttered a cry of suffering. Like a gust of stardust, he camouflaged into the skies and vanished over the Völundr's eastern hills.

Skálda tore her axe out of a Kru'ul's belly, taking out intestines, all. Bile spattered over her face. She must have looked like a fiend, Kru'ul guts soaking her scalp and dripping off her axe.

Lord Rystendal was so close now, less than twenty paces, but more flaming Kru'ul kept getting in her way.

The High Elf pulled his destrier to a halt before the Fjorlanders and murmured in Elvynnöthe. A fallen Kru'ul club levitated off the ground. Following the direction of Rystendal's steepled fingers, it flew at a royal guard and caved in the bulky Fjorlander's skull.

King Leon extricated himself from a Kru'ul and cried, "Hal!"

Skálda narrowed her eyes, reading the High Elf's lips. "*Quenar-*

isíl," he had said. She repeated the elvish word over and over in her mind.

All the Weremen out here were dead. The king was alone, trapped between a horde of Kru'ul and a High Elf. Skálda hurled off a clawing ghoul and tried to race to him, but another caught her axe with its flail, trapping her into a new skirmish.

Leon girded his sword and turned to face the elf on his own. His breaths shallowed in fear. Even a man as mighty as him on the battlefield stood no chance against an elvish mage.

"*Malhdrith nizyldor*," Rystendal said.

King Leon dropped his sword suddenly, his face twisting in distress. His left hand hovered in the air. He was powerless to put it down, no matter how much he fought against the magic.

"*Galh ilun kadir!*" Lord Rystendal formed a crushing fist.

The little bones in Leon's fingers and knuckles flailed as if in a madness, and imploded. Leon screamed with pain, crashing onto his knees. All the bones in his hand were ground to dust, and what remained of it appeared like shriveled clay.

The screams would not stop. Dismounting, the elf drew his curved eldersword. The Anárion blade coruscated in the smoking daylight; rare, enchanted steel that was unbreakable except by elvish magic. It marked him as a sworn member of the Imperial Dragonguard. Leon had not the mental resolve to back away. He shuddered in agony, gazing up at the elf with glistening eyes.

"Your flesh will satiate the Kru'ul, human," he said. "But you would be more profitable without your ability to resist. You will lie on your belly..." The dragon-shaped bone of his sword's pommel crashed against the king's skull. "Unable to move, as they feast on your intestines..."

Skálda removed the screeching head of the Kru'ul in front of her. Wresting herself from the tide, she resumed her sprint to Soren's father. He lay on his stomach, in too much shock to move or even breathe. Lord Rystendal had his right arm pinned beneath his boot. The eldersword lifted above the king's remaining hand, his sword hand.

At ten paces away, Skálda raised Aracir, preparing for a toss into the wretched elf's neck—but someone yanked her back.

"*Mahlenn*," a she-elf sang.

The sword came down over Leon's hand.

"No!" Skálda screamed.

His cries distorted into shrieks. Rystendal hefted the decapitated hand like a war prize. He roared in triumph, a sound too bestial for an elf. For a dizzying moment, an ice-blue holograph of Crixalas—his Binded's lingering dragonscript—warped over his body. Even from the grave, shards of that baneful soul still dwelt inside Rystendal's.

A metallic reek rose above the ichor and smoke. Her throat stone gagged from rising bile. She was smelling human blood, King Leondran's blood, pouring out of ruptured nerves and arteries. Vigardian legions may have perished, but seeing the king crippled by this elf left her shoulders feeling crushed. Soren would break when he found out.

Fjorland had fallen.

A flurry of Rangers blocked anymore of her view of him and the Judge. Directly in front of her was Xandria Kirylith, armored in black-dyed dragonhide. Two more Rangers circled Skálda. The she-elf gripped her mirksword. It was a slender, curved elvish blade that was rather short, meant for cutting down a foe at close combat. She expanded her arms, grinning through her gleaming rows of teeth. "Well? Aren't you going to try to kill me?"

Rage powered Skálda's pivot. In one swift arc, she whipped her axe out for a side cut into the Ranger's neck. Kirylith ducked. The elf's sword came in to impale Skálda's exposed side, but she sidestepped. Skálda attempted another straight thrust into elvish flesh while the Ranger's back was turned, but Kirylith whirled around so quickly and caught Aracir's beard beneath the mirksword's flat.

With one shove, she hurled Skálda back. It was only Skálda's proficiency with her footwork, and the lightness of her weight, that kept her from tumbling onto her backside.

Skálda snarled through her fury. All the training sessions with Soren could not help her. Against an elf, she would always be only half as swift or strong.

"Where is the *maddha*?" Kirylith made a show of glancing around as she evaded Skálda's savage swings with ease. "Or was he too much of a coward to fight on a battlefield?"

Skálda's angled thrusts seemed to amuse the elf. Kirylith allowed the next jab to come at her face, only to catch the axe with her sword at the last moment, this time hooking it at the sword's cross guard. Skálda was forced to look into the elf's smirking eyes. That face was one spit away. Skálda attempted a hard kick in the thigh, but the elf, who always seemed to anticipate her move, let go and sashayed aside. Ducking Skálda's next thrust, Kirylith dashed her elbow against her head. The force crashed Skálda onto her hands. Aracir thudded several paces away from reach.

"Oh," the she-elf said, advancing closer. "Perhaps he found wisdom in abandoning his allegiance to a *kvael-akar*. He has left you to this human demise, hasn't he?"

Skálda clambered off the grasses, snatched her axe, and launched herself back at the elf, but another Ranger clipped her over the shoulder with a sword. Hissing, she pulled back. Blood seeped through her padded leather. Skálda lashed at the gangling bald Ranger, a jab meant to keep him back, then turned back to Kirylith—but she was not fast enough. The she-elf sliced her across her other shoulder, tearing open her jerkin.

Pain stung her eyes. Skálda staggered backwards, pressing a hand to her fresh wound.

"Don't worry," said Kirylith. "The Order will bring the *maddha* to justice, nonetheless. Just..." She swept aside Skálda's axe with the flat of her mirksword. With her defenses open, the elf dashed

Skálda's face with her pommel at a speed impossible to stop. "Like..." Another cut slashed open the skin between Skálda's ribs. "You."

Skálda careened onto the balls of her feet, battling for a focus point as three Rangers circled her. None of her cuts were deep; they were toying with her. They did not mean to kill her here. She imagined them strapping her down to the torture rack next to Soren's. The last thing she saw in this world would be the Lord Prince and Second Rider's faces looking down at her in Exar'forda's darkness.

Kirylith called to her companion, the bald Ranger. He tossed her a set of manacles. Catching them, she said, "How does it feel to actually fight when you are not running like a coward? Not easy to fight elves, hmm, *mahlenn*?"

Skálda whirled back to evade a slash at her hamstrings and swung Aracir at her assailant, but the bald Ranger was too quick. He stepped out of range. Flaming ravens, it was like swatting at flies. They only came close when her back was turned, but when she was forced to leave the skirmish with Kirylith and jab, they danced away again.

Kirylith caught Skálda while she faced the bald Ranger and raked her mirksword's wicked edge down her back, tearing open leather, linen, and flesh.

Skálda screamed.

Before she ever had time to stop her fall, Kirylith booted her between the shoulders, plunging Skálda onto her belly. A flash of pain watered Skálda's eyes. Instinct made her try to immediately rise again, but Kirylith pinioned her between the shoulder blades with her knee. Skálda was immobilized. The bleeding sting from all her various cuts made it feel as if she were being drowned in a salt bath.

The Rangers yanked Aracir out of her grip. Shackles closed over both her wrists. The chain was so short, she could not spread her wrists apart more than a nail's length. Skálda screamed and tried to pull her arms away from them, but Kirylith kept her down. A sword hilt slammed against the side of her head.

The world flashed from red to a blinding, faded white that lingered over her vision. Horns kept blowing over the field, a distant echo that sounded an entire continent away.

Kirylith turned Skálda face up on her back with her boot. "Come up, *kvael-akar*," she twittered. "It's long overdue you meet our Lord Prince..." The grinning elf hauled her back to her feet by the short chain. Reeling her around, the elf made it so that Skálda's back was pressed against her breast. Kirylith clenched her chin and turned it in Lord Rystendal's direction.

"But first, His Lordship would like a little word with you. I fear it is regarding his dragon."

The she-elf marched her toward the Judge.

28

THE ELF IN BLACK ARMOR

Mat Brynhild of Bregan Island gaped as ever more dark-clad elves scaled down the Lupines' sheer slopes. Advanced ropes and pulley systems he had never seen before lowered them into the city.

"Solhall is breached!"

The shout echoed over the settlement's thatched cityscape. Vigardians abandoned the battlements, rushing out to meet the elves.

These were nothing like the Rangers that had set Mat's home to fire. As soon as their boots touched against grass, they loped into formation, moving as one. Each was young and very fair, an individual work of artistry. Their satin faces glowed with beauty; their molded bodies suggested nothing but a lifetime of the most elite military training. Straight, glossy locks washed down their backs, not a single braid out of place.

Mat felt right like an Elondrian stain before them.

Marching from out of their ranks was a male elf in dragonhide armor dyed black. Solhall's burning winds swept the burnished onyx hair from his face. His every movement sang of excellence and discipline. Where he passed, even the huskiest, most toughened elves dipped their heads.

"You know our purpose," he told them.

The Vigardian charge now reached Solhall's highest slopes. Bellowing war cries, the Weremen rushed at them in a wave, slamming their axes down at elvish flesh. No blade ever landed. The elves cut them down in fluid pivots and thrusts. Not even hauberks and thick gambesons could stop the Rhaennörians from opening their throats like they were sculpting art from wood. None broke a sweat. To Mat, it looked more like a dance of entertainment than killing moves in battle.

The Vigardians crashed before their boots, groaning as the dirt streets ran with rivers of their blood. The elves stepped around them with equanimity and resumed their disciplined marching.

Mat was stunned. "Who by the ravens can kill Vigardians like that?" he cried to Faelan, who was watching beside him in the yard. "They acted like the Vigardians were little sheep..."

"They are Khethar Vael."

"Is that supposed to be elvish for something important?"

"That is the most elite military unit in Rhaennöria. They serve the Highmark."

"Bollocks," said Mat. The Highmark was the Imperial Seat of the Morghûl Empire. He rubbed his eyes, sure that he was dreaming, but the elves were still skirmishing below.

"I go my entire life never seeing an elf," he muttered, "and now they just start sprouting up all around me like nettles..."

"Something is wrong," said the Primarch. "They would know the Were King and Elder Leondran are on the field, not here..." He nodded to their leader. "That elf is searching for something."

"Not someone?"

Solhall housed a hundred thousand commons, yet small as the Khetherae numbers were, where they marched, screams tore into the late afternoon skies. More skirmishes with the Vigardians spread in a fan over the city.

"They look younger than us," Mat mumbled.

"They're students," said Faelan. The elves passed in and out of sight, but he kept his narrowed gaze on them. He was probably pondering a defensive campaign, Primarch to the core the man was. But bands of Vigardians were already dead, and not a single elf had fallen.

Many of the Dellfast thralls housed below the slopes were rushing past the low palisade and into the small court where Mat and Faelan now lived.

"There!" a woman cried. "Those are the riders. Hurry along, Reva, they will protect us!"

Faelan glanced over his shoulder, to the longhouse in the rider court where Liv was taking sanctuary. The moment the Were King had left the city for battle, he had hastened to bring her up here. Ever Livana, she came out to direct and batch her people into the surrounding longhouses.

"Ah," Mat grunted, as commons jostled past him. Several praised him for being a courageous Builder and suggested he tell his dragon to kill the elves quickly.

"Yeah, yeah, come in, we'll keep you safe," he said. "No problem. You know, my dragon has 23 chapters and those elves are slaughtering the Vigardians like lambs..." Sweating, he glanced at Faelan and whispered, "Got a plan yet, Primarch?"

"We fight."

Mat laughed. "We fight *elves*?"

A storm of hooves pounded on the road. Faelan shouted at the Dellfasters, his people, to bar themselves inside the longhouses. One of the Were King's shield-brothers, the young one they called Raldefur, pulled up at the entrance of the rider's court. Three more mounted Vigardians accompanied him.

"Defend the city," he hollered. "Defend yourselves!"

This isn't good, Mat thought. If the Vigardians were exhorting even the thralls to fight, Solhall was fallen.

"Defend with what?" said Faelan.

"There is an armory on Ljósa, the alley intersecting the thingstead and Himmel Marketplace. The big market." He gestured over his shoulder. "Bear arms. Lord Jarmon has ordered that none of the Wereguild harm you."

"Free our dragons," Faelan said. "I don't need your rusted axes."

"The elves are coming, dragon man."

"You're sentencing those commons to die. They can't fight Khetherae, but Incendra and I could."

Rulf's fist turned white as he squeezed the reins. He looked like he was fighting for words. "...I can't. Wish I could. Any beast that flies over the city will be shot down. Draugh's orders."

A small squadron of elves was rushing to the manse. Seeing Rulf and his Vigardians, they halted outside the rider's court. One stepped out of the cohort to meet them. All the elves here were beautiful, but the authority and grace radiating off his broad shoulders convinced Mat he was of the most highborn lineage.

It was the elf in black armor.

The touch of his shadow was terrifying enough, but worse were his ears—sharp, long ears the length of an elvish dagger. It was one thing to fight a Fair Elf that could not draw magic, but no human could defeat a High Elf with more than twice a man's endurance and strength.

"Get behind me," Rulf hissed to them.

Mat glanced at Faelan. The Primarch did not move, but Rulf and his Weremen reined their horses in front of the gate protectively.

"I can't free your dragons," Rulf murmured, "but I can defend commons." He untucked the axe at his belt.

With a nod from their cohort leader, two Khetherae at the front marched for Rulf's companions. Human blood dripped off the points of their curved swords. In only a few parries and thrusts, the students tore the Vigardians off their saddles and slammed them to the ground. The men choked on their blood, their bellies spilling gall. With the utmost grace, the Khetherae flicked the human stain off their slender blades and straightened back into a latent stance, standing by for more orders.

The Dellfast thralls in the longhouses screamed. They were watching everything through the windows.

"Skálda should be back by now," Mat whispered to Faelan in a frenzy. "And Anders. Why aren't they back yet?" When the Primarch ignored his question, Mat said, "We need to plan our escape!"

He glanced back at the she-dragons. Feorya and Incendra did not get along—not that Feorya got along with any dragon but the Skoll flights—yet the spotted pica was hiding right behind the larger dragon. Her clipped wings hugged her body tight. The eld barely noticed. Incendra snapped her tail, anxious to protect her rider.

"Hey!" Mat hissed to Faelan. "Did you hear?"

The commons could not all be saved. It could not be helped. But if he and Faelan combined their dragon-enhanced strength, he was certain they could yank the nails out of the ground and free their flights. Feorya could not fly, but they could climb the Lupines and escape north.

Tension bunched in Rulf's shoulders. The Wereman was thinking similar thoughts. He still had time to flee and abandon them all.

Rulf tightened his grip on his axe. Shouting a Svennish war cry, he heeled his mare into a charge. He lowered his axe at the High Elf for a death swing. The cohort leader ducked, rolled aside, and arced his sword upward, burying it effortlessly between the Vigardian's shoulder blades.

Mat impulsively rushed at him. The Were King's youngest

shield-brother crashed to the dirt. With his polished boot, the cohort leader flipped him onto his back. The Wereman was still alive, but his face was paling in shock. He reached blindly over the dirt for his axe. The cohort leader angled his sword point above Rulf's heart, and thrust down for the kill.

"No!" Mat cried.

The young Wereman rolled his eyes to the sky. The smoke of war spread ever more over Solhall. His lips moved with a murmur.

"*Við erum... Vigardians.*"

The breath left Rulf, and his head slumped. Mat pressed his hands to his face in despair. His heart felt quartered. Skálda always said he was too sentimental, that it would be the death of him one day. But raven skit on her. How had it all come to this? What were they all killing for?

Faelan did not look away from the elves. *That* man was never sentimental, except with his wife. While the Khetherae leader wrenched his sword out of Rulf's heart, Faelan picked up a fallen Vigardian's axe. The elves waiting on the road noticed.

"Your Grace," one murmured.

The cohort leader turned around, glancing at Faelan, then Mat. The dark-haired elf must have spotted the dragons in the background, for he said, "*Lhaer'thri.*"

Mat swallowed. The elf was reading them, and indeed he nodded slowly, as if coming to an understanding. He turned to Faelan and extended his stained sword in an invitation. "Primarch."

Faelan took a running leap, meeting the elf's sword with the axe. The rider slashed with a bestial ferocity. Mat saw the burn in his eyes to protect Liv and Incendra. He had lost all his riders, everyone he loved in Dellfast, but he would not lose the two left in his heart. The elf saw this, too, and took a step back.

"*Ciryamor!*" Faelan charged at the Khetherae leader with his translucent crimson shield. The elf evaded. In two pivots, he swung himself around Faelan, to his unshielded left flank, and thrashed his back with the sword's pommel. The rider crumpled to his knees in pain.

"Skit!" Gasping, Mat glanced around and snatched up Rulf's axe.

Several paces ahead, Faelan attempted a weak swing, but the cohort leader caught the haft and yanked it out of his grip, tossing the axe to his colleague. "I would have him. Leave his dragon."

More elves marched in, blocking the court's only exit. They jerked Faelan's arms behind him. He attempted a fistfight, but they bound his wrists with rope. He shouted and wrestled. Those callous elves gagged him next, keeping him from speaking anymore Dragonspells.

"Faelan!" Liv burst out of her longhouse, screaming for him. Two common women held her back. He writhed helplessly, shouting to her through his gag, as the elites marched him out. In the background, Incendra roared, pulling against her chain and slamming her wings against the ground.

At last, the dread moment came, and the cohort leader turned to Mat. He noticed Mat holding the axe, standing above Rulf's corpse. Mat's heart was torn. The logical thing was to drop the weapon and flee for the mountains, flee even without Feorya... but he was no coward.

He positioned himself between the elves and the commons, taking Faelan's former place, and Rulf's before him. His breaths quickened. He was going to die. This was utter stupidity. He knew it.

The cohort leader slowly advanced, until the tip of his shadow touched Mat's frayed shoes. "Vaeritas!" Mat wanted to cry to the sky. He felt like underfed offal before this clean-cut, wholesome elf. Even so, war had a way of cornering a man and bringing out his truest self. Mat found he did not have the heart to run, but he had the courage to fight.

He bent his knees, and clenched the axe harder. "Skit," he whispered under his breath. Sweat poured down his neck. "Skit, skit, *skit*..."

The cohort leader stopped two paces from him, eyeing him like the easy prey he was. He was certain that elf could smell his fear.

After a long moment, the High Elf said, "If you wish to escape, this is your opportune moment."

Mat dropped his jaws. The broad Khetherae withdrew, sheathing his sword and rejoining his ranks. More elves rushed past him. None of it made sense. As a High Elf, he ought to be the cruelest of them all. Mat remembered Lord Rystendal's carnage against the Skonkauld islanders. But this elf was not like that. He was ruthless... and perhaps a sliver compassionate.

"Wait!"

Mat rushed after the cohort leader. To his elves, the leader shouted, "Our enemy is upon us!"

Panting, Mat fell to his knees. "Who by the Sun *are* you?"

The elf turned to him. The flaming swatches of the sky blazed against his burnished pauldrons, shaped like dragon heads.

"I am Rhysaeran Velandrion, the one who never fails."

He seemed to speak those ominous words for the continent. Mat almost collapsed on his hands. Velandrion. That was the same house name of Aeogorath the Great, and the only highborn family the Morghûls intermarried with. He was before the continent's ruling family.

Solhall was lost, and none of them on the battlefield even knew it.

The cohort leader pulled away to join his rushing contingent to the manse, leaving Mat wide-eyed on his knees. Prince Rhysaeran's last shout faded into the distance.

Prepare me a dragon slayer!

29

REMEMBER THE HORN

SKÁLDA FELT an onset of fever as Kirylith marched her to Lord Rystendal. Every spot on her body stung and her own blood soaked her leathers. Every three steps, her knees collided against fletches stuck in the ground.

Waves of panic smothered her. Never in her life had she worn manacles. Never in her life had someone subjugated her to themselves. This was worse than death. Skálda thrashed to pull apart her shackles.

Kirylith drew a curved dagger and pressed it against her throat. "Behave yourself now, *mahlenn*."

Across the rush of Kru'ul, the Judge stood over the king, reveling in his suffering. Skálda tossed her gaze over her shoulder, willing desperately for someone to come. Help, she thought. Help. No Vigardian on this side of the battlefield was in sight.

She could fight any battle, she could die in battle, but she could not abide capture.

Kirylith shoved her again in the back. Skálda tripped over more arrows. The Rangers laughed. They were almost to the Judge when a shadow fell over them. The she-elf only had time to look up before an acrid musk crashed into her.

A flurry of leathery wings blinded Skálda. The impact thrust her onto her elbows. Behind her, Kirylith drowned the valley in screams. The tortured noise congealed Skálda's blood. It was a noise she never imagined hearing from this particular she-elf. The two Rangers left guarding her went agog at whatever was behind them, too immobilized to do anything.

Exhaustion weighed her down, but with the last of her willpower, she lifted herself back on her knees and pulled herself around.

An adolescent dragon kept Kirylith pinned with his bulky talons. His teeth were stained red. He kept yanking out more of her small intestines. Already, her ripped stomach was pouring bile over the grass. Ravens have mercy, Skálda thought, the she-elf was still alive. Kirylith was too weak to fight him, but she let out dying shrieks that raked Skálda with fear. Snarling, the dragon lunged at her head. He tore it from her and hurled it in Lord Rystendal's direction. Then he bent down and dug into her raw offal.

"Bale?" Skálda whispered.

Hearing her, his neck snapped upright. But his livid red eyes fixed on the last two Rangers at her side. They fled in terror. His snarl burgeoned into a roar. Leaving Kirylith's carcass, he galloped after them, the power of his beating wings flattening the grass blades. The ground rocked from his weight. Skálda shut her eyes, petrified.

He charged past her and caught the bald Ranger in his fangs. Shaking the elf a few times, Bale catapulted him away into the distance. Seeing the last Ranger still in flight, the dragon launched himself at the elf. In a few strides, he caught up and clamped down hard over the elf's torso. The Ranger went limp. Only then did Bale let go.

Skálda stayed on her knees, lost for words.

Bale slowly turned around to face her. This snarling beast was nothing like the little hatchling she had saved in the Skonkauld. His four horns were a terrible spiked mass that crowned his head. Set deep inside his eye hollows, his red eyes were like demons scorching her soul. Nothing in all the world should love such a monstrous creature... yet she did.

Her eyes welled with tears. Skálda was not sure he would recognize her anymore.

But he did. He padded over and laid his jagged chin against her shoulder, cradling her. His gentle rocking thickened her tears. Skálda clasped him tighter, as best she could with her shackled wrists.

"Bale," she whispered.

"My wolf. I am sorry."

Skálda tried to open her eyes, but flaming ravens, she was a mess. She wiped away the blur. "In the forests... why didn't you let go?"

"I didn't know how."

"It... it's alright."

"It is not. The spoiled meat was right. I know what I am."

She stroked his scaled cheek. "I know what you are, and that changes nothing."

Bale nuzzled her head. *"I left because I cannot stay with you, Wolf. I am growing too strong for humans. Even being in the presence of my mind and script will soon be too much for you."*

"Then I will become stronger." She wiped her eyes, and rose shakily to her feet. "Don't ever leave again." She gazed up into the malignant glow of his eyes. "You understand? We will find a way to control this. It is not your burden, but ours together."

Skálda embraced him with her arms curled against his shoulder, tighter this time. It felt so good to hold her dragon again.

A growl rumbled in his throat, suddenly. He spread a protective wing over her. She turned around.

Lord Rystendal was ten paces away, looking up at Bale. How long he had stood there watching them? Skálda glanced over his shoulder. The king lay on his side, his eyes closed. He was dead. The old fires she bore for elfkind burned in her.

"Look..." Skálda gestured with her shackled wrists up at the scaled black monster. "Now you have your answer, Rystendal. What fell into my home was a Bael. That is why I defied the Order, why I took things this far. We are Binded."

"The Order will find out, *kvael-akar*."

Skálda laughed and glanced up at Bale. "He says the Order will find out."

"No one can Bind with a Bael, human filth. What have you done? You are a fool to have let it grow to this!"

The inhospitable glow of Bale's eyes brightened. Skálda shrugged and left Bale's side. She kept marching until she was a dozen paces from them, well out of their way.

"Very well," said Skálda. "Finish what you came for."

Rystendal glanced at her in disbelief, then turned his wavering gaze up to Bale.

"But I will warn you..." She studied the pair. Bale's thorny head now towered over the Judge. His fell snarling paled the elf's face. "He remembers what you tried to do to him when he was a baby."

"You ignorant fool," the elf rasped. "We must tell His Grace before it is too late. This will destroy Elondria!"

"No, but I think he will destroy you."

Bale poised on his haunches to lunge. The Judge hastened for a spell. Skálda murmured one of her own under her breath.

"*Quenarisíl.*"

A distance away, Aracir quivered over the grasses. The cool rush in her blood vitalized her. This was not anything tethered to Bale, but a wellspring of power that washed away her fears of powerlessness and surged her with a renewed, breathtaking freedom. It was a little larger than when she had first drawn from it in the Isendal River Valley in the late spring.

Skálda steepled her fingers together, as she had seen Rystendal do, and directed it at him. Before he finished his spell against Bale, her blade smashed through the soft flesh of his nape. He crumpled to the ground.

It took almost a full minute before either of them would move. Atrocious as Bale looked, she felt his tiny sigh of relief through their Binding.

"It's over," she said.

The Battle for Solhall was not over, and their flight as *kvael* from the Order was far from over, but he knew what she meant. Seeing this elf's death was a monumental closure for them both.

It was Bale who moved first. Hanging his head, he trudged over and wrapped his tail around her waist. Skálda held onto him. For the first time since the battle began, or perhaps since Bale had fallen into the continent, she was lucidly present. She gazed across the field, to the scattered fires blazing outside Solhall. Endless Kru'ul bounded toward the city, their silhouettes misshappen from the clubs and war hammers they held. She and Bale were the only ones left on this side of Eldruna. Smoke from Detherys's dragon now blackened the evening, obscuring the bedazzling white sphere so many Realms above.

One Bael caused this, she thought. ...I caused this.

She turned her gaze askance at King Leon's carcass through the smoke, and narrowed her eyes.

"Bale... he's alive."

The tail around her loosened. There was no mistaking it. The king's shoulders were rising and falling shallowly.

"Your Majesty!" She hurried to Kirylith's corpse, searching for the lockpick that would free her from her shackles. After groping through intestines and a bit of spilled spleen, she found them and freed herself. Bale followed as she raced to the king.

A horseman appeared in the distance, moving toward her in a gallop. Smoke burned her eyes. It was difficult to see at first. Asveig was waving at them.

Skálda ignored him and knelt beside the king. Leon was unconscious. The sight of his shriveled left hand pulled her stomach. His right stump was bleeding horrendously. Rystendal had utterly ravaged him. Bale stopped beside her, rumbling through a grimace. It was a wonder the King of Fjorland was not dead.

In the background, Asveig galloped closer, his charger spraying dirt behind its hooves. He bellowed something at her, though she could not hear.

"I need to borrow your chapters," she told Bale. "He has lost more blood than what I will have the affinity to heal. May I?"

Bale touched his nose to her hand, then rested it on the king's shoulder. A quick *Lhaer'thri* showed her 96 chapters. They were so close to an Ealdorman rank. All the skirmishing this solstice had grown him. But now was not the time to celebrate.

Skálda submerged her mind into their Binding's river of energy, becoming aware of their shared power running along each individual rung of his chapters. She bade the dragonscript's tendrils to creep over her, and enclose her, until the scorch of Bale's soul fused with the icy burn of hers.

"*Anora'thil.*"

Beneath her outstretch palm, tiny embers, the same shade as the cinderlight glistening over Bale's wings, glowed beneath her skin. As she channeled, they formed threads that caught onto the king's stub. Glowing flesh weaved itself together and closed. Skálda held on with all of her strength. Sweat trickled down her temple as she willed even a hand to reform, but that was too far beyond her strength. Already, exhaustion battered her mind.

Asveig pulled up so sharply beside them, his horse spunning once in a circle to decelerate.

"What are you doing?" he roared. For some reason, he was enraged. "Did you not hear me calling?"

"What does it look like I'm doing?"

"We must leave."

"I haven't finished healing him yet—"

"Remember the horn!"

"What horn?"

"Ah!" Asveig waved at the air like he was beating Kru'ul. Seeing Soren's father near dead on the field seemed to heighten the man's already hysterical mood. "Never mind. Now, we run."

Skálda looked around for a Kru'ul. "From what?"

"On the saddle, *now*!"

With that much choler in the Vigardian's eyes, she dared not argue. Skálda had no choice but to stop the spell. Most of the king's stump had closed, but pores continued to bleed. She glanced back at Bale. "Can you carry him?"

"I'm not strong enough yet to carry two."

"Just him. I will ride with Asveig."

Bale did not look pleased about this, but he knelt onto his forelegs and lowered himself to make it easier for her to haul the king onto his back. She rubbed his neck. "Good Bael."

She grabbed onto Leondran's slumped body and hollered at Asveig, "Don't just sit there. Help me!"

The Vigardian looked like he would skit himself. She could not fathom what was throwing him into such a fluster. Cursing under his breath, Asveig slid off the saddle and took the king's other arm. Together, they dragged him onto Bale's back. She fit Leondran's crumpled bulk in the cleft between his wings as best she could.

"Don't let him fall."

"No need to tell me, Wolf. I will keep him."

She opened her mouth to reassure Bale they would reunite again soon, but Asveig yanked her onto his mount. Spurring the gelding, he hissed in her ear, "We run like we are running from Helgaard."

The charger indeed took off like it was running from Tythandrell's diving maw, though she saw no Kru'ul directly around them. Not even Eyrek appeared in the skies. But hooves beat like a frantic drum against the field. Bale soared overhead, his shadow touching her, then passing her.

It was rare Skálda rode a horse in a gallop, and the violent jerking made her suddenly aware that the smoking field was strangely silent. Not a single Vigardian horn was blowing anymore. Even the distant peal of charging Kru'ul masses looked off... because no one was stopping them. She realized what was wrong. The Vigardian host still stood, yet not one Svennish was present on the field.

"...never understand how you allowed yourselves to be lured so far out on the battlefield," Asveig ranted. "Told you to remember the horn. Remember the horn. *Remember the horn...*"

When his mumbling annoyed her past her breaking point, she snapped, "What about your Sun-blessed horn?"

The rumbling started. It was faint at first, like discontentment or ill-ease in a dragon's belly. But then she felt its growing power under the saddle's leather. All the Eldruna Valley was swaying.

Asveig heeled the gelding harder, though it could go no faster. The wretched beast panted through its nostrils and mouth, discharging a spray. The swaying turned into a voluminous groan, like Eldruna was in its final birth pangs. Rising above the roaring tumult was something else—the ethereal song of a thousand Thomdrim. As they sang, the tree roots beneath loosened their great lattice. Beginning at the Eldruna Pass, a mighty fissure split the earth open.

"Mercy Finngólfa," Skálda said, suddenly understanding.

They were galloping over a tree-root tunnel, except this was nothing like what she saw in the Prannon, or even Dellfast. The entire boundless valley was *one* hollow cavern.

The splitting started slowly, but once the rear of the valley caved, the ripple that followed accelerated like a breaking tidal wave. Asveig was taking them to Völundr's eastern slopes overlooking the valley. As the smoke cleared ahead, Skálda squinted. The remaining Vigardian ranks were on those knolls—that was where they had retreated. Seeing her and Asveig racing against earth's pursuit, thousands of them bellowed or waved their hands. She heard none of them above the roar.

The gap between the gelding and the divine shockwave closed to less than one hundred paces. The intensity of the massive grinding power was an earthshake in her own chest. Whatever this tunnel, it was far, far deeper than Dellfast's.

Everything along their flanks was breaking. Gravel flew into her eyes and mouth. The fissures caught up with them, until their charger was galloping over falling earth.

That was when Skálda saw what was below. Eldruna's tree roots opened into a terrifying, dark labyrinth as unfathomable as a fall from Atallgaard. Even with the day's cadaverous light, she saw no bottom to it. The gelding screamed above the breaking uproar. Its hooves were airborne.

They were falling.

The strangeness of the moment slowed down time. Skálda traced her eyes across the titanic chaos around them, to the gravel suspended everywhere like dust motes caught in blossoms of firelight; the blasting stench of wet loam; cascades of Kru'ul tumbling upside down, in freefall, on the other side of the valley. Tree roots pulled free and braided together, all at once. Braids. The braids reminded her of Aesir's braided metal ring. All that he said about *Mhir il'Feannor*, the Eternal Circle of Traust, suddenly came back to her.

"Everything we do is connected across space and time," the elf had warned. "Every time the braids merge like this, it symbolizes the impact of a significant event. A summation of our works, the good and evil..."

Skálda wondered how much of her own singular actions had steered the continent's fate to this.

Everything was suspended on marionette strings, merging into the scene that could be no less than the beginning of a Second Breaking. She was certain of it now. This was a great Merging of the Braids Aesir had foretold.

I dreamt of falling, she thought in a dazed wonder. And now I am.

It was her last thought—and the gelding's leap ended. It landed at the base of the knolls. The roaring cheers of the Vigardians above could not drown out the racing of her heart.

They finished the last stretch of their gallop to the top of the hills. She and Asveig were sweating as hard as the horse. Before Asveig even pulled to a halt, the Vigardians dragged them down. Warriors and shieldmaidens she did not know embraced her in a fervor. Their emotion overwhelmed Skálda. Many were weeping. They were doing the same wretched thing to Asveig. To think, these sentimental Svennish were the same murderous Wereguild that masterminded the downfall of the Ivarion's realm.

Through all the jostling, she somehow found Bale. The Vigardians had already spread Leondran's body over the grass. Asveig shouted at his men to give the king space. With the Battle of Eldruna Valley over, Skálda was lucid enough again to loop her arm over Bale's lowered neck. Together, they gazed past the overlook to the remains of Solhall's lands.

The devastation was unfathomable. The breaking halted some twenty paces from Solhall's closed gate. All the valley, from that gate to the pass several span away, was gone. Remnants of earth continued to chip off and tumble into the darkness. All was still and quiet now.

At this angle, Skálda had a better view of the tree-root cavern. The Thomdrim had built it half a span deep. Hordes of Kru'ul lay dead at the stony bottom. It looked like a necropolis, the way stray rays of sunlight passed in and out through the smoke.

She had thought seeing cranewings, nightborns, and Baels was a sight to behold, but this was something different altogether; the end to a battle that not even the greatest High Elf could capture in a ballad.

"The Thomdrim must have built this over centuries..."

"Solhall was more to the eye," he agreed.

Indeed, Thorgest Vigarda's capital seemed a shamble compared to even small cities like Dellfast. She had not understood what made it so legendary and foreboding to the Vigardians. But her ancestor's secret never lay above earth to be seen by the common eye; its treasure was hidden beneath. Eight hundred solstices ago, Thorgest planned for a day like this... and it had arrived in Soren's time.

The distant clangor of swords stole her attention. A battle was still raging inside Solhall's gates. Neither the Draughammr nor the Ivarion were in sight... but that did not mean they had fallen with the Kru'ul.

"The battle isn't over yet." She turned to Bale, clenching Aracir tight. "It won't be over until one of them is dead."

30
THE WOLF AND THE DRAGON

UP ON BALE'S BACK, Skálda streamed over Solhall's thatched skyline. They flew low enough for her to search the streets for Soren. An outbreak of skirmishes blighted every corner of the settlement. By now, most Vigardians defending the city lay dead in the alleys. Uniformed elves advanced deeper into the streets, cutting down any Wereman in their way. Every dragon slayer stationed on the walls was burning.

"*Wolf*," Bale called.

Their Binding throbbed with his worry. She turned to follow his gaze. Below them, hordes of thralls twisted into the rider courtyard. Mat waved his arms, directing them as best he could, but too many were pouring in, desperate for rider protection. Livana was on her knees, hands pressed to her face in violent weeping. Faelan was nowhere in sight. Near the entrance, a corpse bled over the dirt. Rulf was dead.

"Ravens," Skálda murmured.

Bale descended, intending to land by the riders. She inhaled and gathered herself back to the present. She had to stay present. Eyrek was alive, and no doubt close.

"Not there," she said. "The manse, Bale. If Soren were anywhere, it would be there."

As his spiked tail skimmed the rooftops, his passing shadow drew pauses from the skirmishers. He beat his wings harder, taking them up to the pinnacle of Solhall's northern slopes. More elves were swarming up the road toward Soren's stronghold. If the Draugh was inside, it would only be a matter of time before he was surrounded. Bale circled the manse once before they found him—he was caught in single combat in the private yard outside the mead hall.

"There!" she shouted.

Bale folded in his wings for a dive. Frit and Evynd crouched beneath the dining table on the patio as their father dueled. The wide-eyed princess clenched her toddler brother's wrist. In her other hand, she squeezed Fjella's old axe.

Before Bale's claws touched the dirt, Skálda leapt off his back, drawing Aracir. She pulled up short.

Soren's scalp was soaked. His bun had come loose, and his short braids battered his flushed cheeks with his every pivot. Bearing a skáldwolf shield with one arm, he swung his axe with a carnal ferocity, never straying more than several paces from the children. His limbs bled from various cuts. Soot blackened his face. For all his savagery, Skálda tasted visceral fear in the mist of sweat warming the courtyard's air. This was a wolf desperately defending his cornered pups.

The Draugh fought like he was wounded, though she saw no debilitating gashes on him. Every time he ducked a swing, he contracted his shoulder and winced in agony. Then it dawned on her. His Binding. He was feeling Saarhekhu's shoulder injury like it was his own.

Skálda's belly knotted. This was the moment she expected to see Eyrek within touching distance. But on second glance, it was not the Ivarion he fought, but an elf in dragonhide armor dyed black. She narrowed her eyes. He had the long, dagger-pointed ears of a High Elf that curved elegantly to the crown of his head. This was a Rhaennörian highborn.

She might have felt relieved it was not her brother, except this elf was a bred killer. He jabbed at Soren with complex sword combinations Skálda had never seen before. Every precise swing displayed the highest of military discipline. Dragon-enhanced as Soren was, his shared pain through Saarhekhu's Binding made him struggle to hold the elf at bay. His axe could barely even penetrate the elf's defenses. If he was not summoning any Dragonspell, Saarhekhu must be too far out of range.

"Who is he?" she murmured.

This High Elf was radiant with virility, and the most comely of any she had ever encountered. He beheld none of the lunatic bloodthirst that had consumed Lord Rystendal's eyes. His erect, self-confident carriage was like one born to rule.

Bale curled back his lip. "*I smell the poison of Morghûl blood in this one.*"

Skálda glanced at him, stunned. *One of the Lord Prince's brothers?*

"Can't say... I don't recognize this script."

She jogged to the children. Soren never took his eyes off his foe, but the elvish prince glanced at her in between his ripostes. Frit caught sight of them and cried, "Skálda! Bale!"

She charged straight into Skálda's arms. Skálda bent down and accepted a tight squeeze. Evynd waddled over to follow her example. The children were shaken. Frit was quailing with terror. She must have never seen an enemy fight this close to home. It appeared to be a copperbit flip on whether her father would pull through alive.

Clasping their hands, Skálda pulled them behind the table.

"If the Draugh does not kill that elf," she said, "I will." I will kill that Morghûl spawn, she thought. He would be a warmup for the

Lord Prince. Though Soren barely gave her a glance, her presence made his shoulders loosen, and a greater reassurance strengthened his lunges.

The toddler pointed at Bale. "Dragon hungry, I feed?"

"Not now, Evynd."

"Why?"

Skálda ignored him.

"WHY?"

"Be quiet, Ev!" Frit hissed.

Evynd burst into tears, the same time Soren's axe landed a cut over the elf's shoulder. Their foe pulled back, grimacing in pain. Frit gasped, her head perking. It looked like Soren had the upper hand.

The Draugh bent his knees, preparing for what all of them hoped would be a final thrust. Frit cheered and shouted at her father to finish him. Evynd, observing his sister, forgot his tears and clapped enthusiastically—until Eyrekvald Ivarion sauntered into the yard.

Frit screamed in hysteria. Terror bolted down Skálda's spine. The thing she most dreaded over this past solstice was finally happening... and she was not ready for it.

Soren slowly straightened. For all that Eyrek had changed, his thunderous bearing was still no less a king's. The elf felt it, too, and stopped fighting. He stepped aside for the Dragonlord to pass.

"My Lord," the elf murmured, "all the dragon slayers are destroyed. The city is—"

"Leave."

The elf, no doubt in pain, held himself with dignity and nodded. Just before he retreated, a strange look passed over his eyes. Skálda saw something portentous there. Not long after, his orders to his cohorts echoed over the manse.

Eyrekvald Ivarion traced the courtyard—the Draughammr first, then Bale, then Skálda, standing behind the long table, holding the children. In this manner, he was a true Builder, absorbing every detail of his battleground before executing his precise killing campaign. Suddenly, she was not sure anyone here could defeat him.

The tip of his giant man-reaver rested against the dirt. The way he tilted the corner of his mouth made Soren tighten his grip on his axe.

"Were King."

"King Skitr."

The Second Rider took his first step. His vengeful gaze was not on Soren, but on the children.

Alarm made Soren jerk backwards. "Frit!" he shouted in the Svenning. "What are you lingering there for? Take your brother out!"

Seeing Elondria's greatest Dragonlord draw closer was paralyzing the little doe. Soren backed another two steps, holding out his axe protectively. Skálda felt his terror. His greatest fear was playing out before his eyes.

Frit screamed through her tears. "I'm not leaving! I'm not leaving. I'm not leaving you..."

Eyrek's smile chilled Skálda's bones.

Soren murmured over his shoulder, "Please, Skálda."

"Come on." She tucked her axe to her belt and tugged the children through the doorway. They made it halfway through the vast mead hall before clanging steel erupted outside. Frit shuddered into helpless sobs, but Skálda hissed, "Your da will be alright. Hurry up!"

The manse splintered into more noise. The Khethar Vael were breaking in from the north side. Lady Sibbe and a cluster of handmaidens screamed as Skálda streamed past them. She rushed the children to their quarters and stowed them under Frit's bed.

"Don't leave this room for anyone, you understand?" Skálda's whispers came out harsher than she intended. Evynd was already sniffling. "I will be back for you—"

"No, you can't leave us!" Frit screamed.

"Quiet! Your da needs Bale and me."

"No, no, no..." Frit clawed Skálda's arm. "You don't see it. Ev and I are going to turn out like Rik, and Sylv, and our big cousin Keldara. The Skitr King took them all away and beheaded their father. Our uncle." Skálda tried to pull away, but she clamped on. "I command you to stay—"

"*Princess Fritjolf*," Skálda snarled. "If you don't quiet, you *will* turn out like them. The Ivarion will hogtie you all the way to Exar'-forda, and after he's done plucking off your cute little fingers and toes, the Lord Prince will throw your bones to Lumaerrax. You think Bale is a 'mean dragon'? Do you know what Lumaerrax does to Svennish children?"

They quieted their sobs at once, their eyes stretching wide.

Oh, Skálda thought. I went too far. She patted them on the heads. "Good children."

Drawing Aracir, she rushed back out. This time, they did not scream for her.

The moment she burst back outside, Bale raised his head and stomped his front talons over the dirt. She caught him by the horns and rubbed his headplate for comfort. His neck was quivering.

The Draughammr and the Ivarion were engaged in the blazing fires of combat now. The former had thrown aside his shield to rid himself of the extra weight. Eyrek's plated armor and padded pauldrons bulked his already broad frame, yet he was so dragon-enhanced, he moved at *more* than thrice the speed of an ordinary man. His blood-red mantle gusted with his every pivot. Soren's axe paled in size compared to Storm's Fury, his legendary greatsword. The blade itself was a voracious beast that roared as it thrusted. Every time its double edges swung violently at Soren, the very air seemed to keen.

Palpable rivulets of sweat deluged Soren's neck. The Wolf of Old Svenn was the swifter of the two, moving lighter on his feet. His footwork was more maneuverable, the way Saarhekhu was in the air. Yet Skálda noticed one wrong angle made him wince. His dragon's shoulder wound was ebbing at his strength.

A malicious glint brightened Eyrek's eyes. He seemed to feel something none of them did. He withdrew several steps, lowering his sword. Panting, Soren paused to catch his breath. Unlike the Ivarion, he had been battling for days, and his exhaustion showed.

Eyrek raised his fist. "*Ruthra'ruín*!"

Skálda went aghast, and searched the skies. Tythandrell was nowhere in sight, but Skálda remembered the elvish prince's words. *All the dragon slayers are destroyed.* The Great must be close—close enough for a Dragonspell.

Dread weighed Soren's shoulders. No man on the continent would be a match for the Ivarion when he invoked Tythandrell's 6,554 chapters of Dragonstrength.

A gilt hologram flared over Eyrek, like perfectly fitted armor hovering over his outline. A beat later, it seeped over him, and vanished. He clenched Storm's Fury tighter, and charged back into combat.

"Soren," she whispered to Bale. "He won't live through this..."

Skálda saw traces of fear on the Draugh's face, but he was too proud to flee his nemesis. He met the Ivarion's raised sword with a feint, then pivoted to the right. His axe came up in the air, past Eyrek's defenses, for a clean cut on the side of his neck. But Eyrek had feinted, too. He spun away from Soren's thrust. With both hands gripping his sword hilt, he slammed down onto Soren's weapon.

The Anárion blade shattered the axe into a starburst of thick steel pieces. The momentous impact thew Soren off balance. He crashed onto his wounded shoulder and skidded over the dirt.

Skálda dug her nails into her flesh. Soren reached over for a weapon he knew was not there. Before he ever had time to rise, the Second Rider hauled him up like a babe and slammed him against the courtyard wall. Wood burst apart. Forming a mace with his fist, the Dragonlord struck Soren's jaw with all his enhanced strength.

She glanced away, letting out a quiet breath.

Blood spattered over Eyrek's chin. He did not even blink. With a shout, he flung Soren's muscled bulk across the entire length of the yard.

"Ravens," she whispered. "I don't think the Svennish gods fight like that..."

"We should go," Bale said nervously.

"We can't leave him." But even as she said this, her grip on Aracir slackened.

Soren shut his eyes. His face was turning white. He pressed a hand tight to his side. A rib must have broken, or perhaps several. Heaving like a beast, the Second Rider chucked aside his greatsword. He reeled in Soren by the ankle and smeared his foe's blood over his face.

"Is this it, Were King? Is this all you have?"

The Ivarion's laughter thundered into her bones. Soren was right all along. This was not her brother. She had lost her older brother twelve solstices ago. This was a self-made villain of the warzones a villain the Lord Prince had forged.

The greatest of Dragonlords yanked Soren upright and landed another dragon-strengthened fist at his broken ribs. Soren jerked his neck, biting down a cry of agony. Tears rushed down his sharp cheekbones.

"You are nothing." The Ivarion caught a handful of dirt and viciously kneaded it into Soren's hair like a crown of dust. "*Nothing* beyond the shelter of your savage forests and little tree tunnels. You are a parasite to the Order, the rot kindling we burn!"

He impaled his fingers between Soren's ribs, breaking open

flesh. The Ivarion caught a cracked rib and tore it out, puncturing through more skin.

Soren burst into screams.

They were endless, so macabre, it drew even the elves to the yard's outer limits. As soon as they saw the Second Rider, fear shadowed their eyes, and they retreated as quickly as they came. Soren kept screaming.

"Eyrek!" Skálda shouted. "Stop!"

"Do you know how you will die, Were King?" he said, ignoring her.

Tears of agony rushed down Soren's face.

"I will take you back to the ruins of Tera Beren. I am going to suspend you in the room that used to be Leofraen Amanoor's office. I am going to skin your hide, just a little bit at a time, and break every bone in your body from your toes upward. And as you slowly die, you will look upon all the heads you spiked at my gate." Eyrek took hold of another rib. "At the front of Helgaard's pile will be your children. I will behead them after we are done here, hmm?"

The Ivarion snapped another rib. Skálda thought it impossible that Soren's screams could become any worse, but they did. They drowned all the skies above the manse from inhumane suffering.

"If we don't run, then we must do something," Bale urged.

Under her breath, she said, "*Quenarisíl.*" The greatsword quivered over the dirt. She steepled her pointers. It followed the direction of wherever she dragged them in the air. She thrust her palms out. Storm's Fury discharged at the Dragonlord's back.

"*Ciryamor!*"

His bellow was terrifying. The blade struck the Dragonshield, rebounding high in the air. Without so much as a twitch, the Ivarion raised an arm and caught it. He stood, and turned to her.

Skálda backed away by impulse. "Skit," she whispered.

The shadows of vengeance darkened his eyes.

"Sister," he said. "Do you not know I am the Enterprise? Do you not know how many chapters I bear?"

He tightened his grip on the hilt, and advanced on her. Her dread turned into terror. Bale rumbled, but she felt his shared fear through their Binding. They were fodder against the Ivarion.

"I know how many chapters you bear, Brother." Keeping to the yard's edges, Skálda carefully moved toward Soren. Bale rotated with her, a low growl caught in his throat. "You advanced by thieving lands from the Vigardians. You became the Ivarion by murdering kingdoms of commons and Thomdrim. To think we all hailed you. The lies you spoke to us in the Skonkauld, it was glorious." She bellowed, "Hero of Elondria, a king of blood and bones!"

He trailed behind her, baring his bloody teeth. "Yes, I knowingly attacked weldin and country kingdoms. But they were dogs that would not bend their knee to our Republic. The Order promised protection from the Betrayer in return for their cooperation. If I did not bring wealth to this wilderness, and build military on it, who then would stop the Betrayer when he invaded?"

"You would sooner kill Svennish commons who refused to cede their heritage to the elves," she spat. "And we all would have heaped lays on your name until you unleashed your *m'ethil* on us all!"

"Commons?" he said. "You think commons will stop the Betrayer?" He nodded at Soren's broken shape. "Vigardians? Or Thomdrim? When the Morghûls could not even surmount him forty solstices ago?"

"You were one of us, Eyrek." She was nearly to Soren. "You grew up on Skuller's Row."

"Do not presume I do not keep account of the things I've done. But it has always been necessary—"

"For the Enterprise? With you, it is always for the Enterprise, even if you massacre an entire city for it!"

"No. For Elondria. For my defense of *you*, and all the beloved commons and flat-nosed beasts you mourn over," he snarled. "For even the Were filth you defile yourself with."

"You and your Lord Prince talked of invasions for years..." She stopped beside Soren. "But I think there is no invasion. The southern continent was never mobilizing. This is all a ruse so you can Build for the Morghûls."

Eyrek laughed in disbelief. "Is that what your Were King tells you? That is what made you kill my riders?"

She climbed onto Bale, taking hold of his neck spikes. "*Hethrîth in'loeg mírael,*" she murmured.

Soren's body lifted into the air. She held onto the spell until he hovered above Bale and out of the Ivarion's sword range. The Dragonlord looked up at her. The predatory coldness in his eyes prickled her spine.

"I asked you to Build," he said quietly. "You promised me, Skálda. Instead, you have betrayed me."

"*Éad'hel!*"

Bale launched himself off his claws, catching Soren on his neck. Skálda held onto him tightly in front of her, between her chest and the spikes. He was still conscious; his shield-brothers would have been hysterical if they saw him in this condition. Two broken ribs stuck out of his flesh. Finngólfa knew how many more were broken beneath. She clasped tightly onto his hand.

As they soared away from the manse, the Ivarion's eyes trailed her.

31
I WON'T LET YOU FALL

"I can't hold on, Wolf," Bale pleaded. *"It's too heavy..."*

They had just crossed over the Völundr Reach's eastern border. Solhall and the wasted Eldruna Valley receded behind them, but he could ascend no higher. With every pump of his wings, he was straining himself. Two adults on his back were too much for a young adolescent.

"Hang on, Bale!" she called above the winds. *We need to find a place to hide Soren. We are too close to Solhall. Can you go for a little longer?*

The young dragon bared his teeth. Already, they were falling in altitude. They were not high in the air as it was, but the conifers below rushed closer.

"Can't, Wolf..."

Land! Land, we will make do. She stroked his sweating neck for comfort, tormented as she felt. Eyrek was coming. Eyrek would hunt them at any moment. But Anders had chewed out Mat and Egil more than once for trying to ride their dragons before they were old enough. If a youngling carried more weight than he could hold, he could crash and even kill himself. It was more than enough that Soren was dying over Bale's back; she would not entertain her dragon's death as well.

Even so, Bale shattered the canopy. Branches splintered, leaves exploded everywhere. Skálda shielded her eyes. Blinded by the uproar, all she could think of was holding on tightly to Soren. The sharp plummet turned her insides over. After more knocking against her limbs and head, they landed on the forest floor. The impact hurled her and Soren off Bale's back. She plummeted hard onto her elbows, scraping off a good amount of skin.

"Bale!"

Paying no heed to her stinging pain, she raced to him. He lay on his side, his wings crumpled over the needle carpet. Panic rushed into her. Circling around him, she cupped his heavy, spiked chin.

"Bale," she panted. "Bale, are you alright? What is broken?"

He lifted himself off his shoulder suddenly, shaking off the dust and leaves. The young dragon looked shaken. *"No breaks, Wolf. Alright..."*

She touched her head to his briefly, then glanced over his neck spikes. Soren was sprawled over the forest detritus, his eyes closed. Viscous blood soaked his torn gambeson. She limped to him, unable to think. Eyrek was coming. Soren's wounds were horrendous. Eyrek was coming...

Ahead of them were the rushing roars of water. She had been here before. This was the same waterfall they passed during their campaign against Garreck Kingsley. She glanced over her shoulder.

"Bale! Will you help me bring him behind those falls?"

Together, they hauled him past the tree line, over the pool of rocks, and into the small cavern behind the cascade. She sat him upright against the uneven wall. Vapor drenched her face, flattening the lank strings of her hair. He choked on blood, suddenly, though his eyes stayed closed.

"Skálda," he murmured, as she surveyed the natural defenses of the cave. "Skálda..."

When he would not stop calling to her, she stopped her flustered pacing and crouched by him. His lips were moving, but she could barely hear him over the roar.

"My axe..."

"It's gone," she said.

"Put me out."

"No, Draugh."

"Please..."

Skálda hovered her hand over his broken ribs, and said, "*Anora'thil.*"

Threads of her soul energy coursed through her arm, passing out of her and into him. Soren sighed as his flesh wove itself together. Losing every additional thread felt like a tug of her heart, a draining and weakening of her soulscript. Her head slumped. She would need tens of Skáldas to heal the extent of his wounds, but she would not let go.

"Wolf, stop!"

Bale butted himself between her and the Draugh, pushing her away with his horns.

I need to—

"You are already battle-weary! Silly wolf, your soulscript is too small! You'll kill yourself."

He was right. It was impossible to overdraw from a dragon's soul reserves. A dragonscript had chapters and was far larger and more complex in structure than a human's soulscript. Aesir once told her that drawing to the last ten percentage of a dragon's chapters would black out rider and flight. But a human's script had no natural limit to prevent overdrawing. If she pressed on with the *anora'thil*, and left herself no energy in her physical body, she would expunge her own life.

I can't borrow from your chapters, she said. *It won't be enough anyway, and we need the strength to fight.*

He jerked his head. *"You want to battle the Great One?"*

We have no choice.

"The Great has many, many chapters."

I know.

"We'll never win."

I know, Bale.

He lowered his head with a dragonish frown and padded away. *"Very well. We fight tonight."*

After a long moment, she told Soren, "I will come back after I face the Ivarion. He won't find you."

Soren groaned as he shifted against the wall. She had sealed his flesh at least, though the ribs remained broken. "Frit and Evynd..."

"He won't find them either."

As she marched out, he whispered, "'One greater than you is coming.' That is what the hjarta told me."

Skálda pulled to a halt. The fall's thunderous roar enveloped her. She glanced over her shoulder. His eyes were open now, and on her.

"When we first met," he said, "I recognized you from the Vidarskog Stones. I thought you, not the Ivarion, would be the one to slay me and destroy the guild. But I see now what she meant."

Bale glanced at her. He, too, understood the foreboding implication of this.

"You must lead the Wereguild in my stead," he said.

In the distance, a Great Dragon roared.

"You will live, Draugh." Skálda forced herself to march on. She refused to accept the burden of his words, and neither would she say farewell. This would not be the end.

Once she was back in the air, Bale rumbled quietly. A winged leviathan hovered over the eastern wealds, its scales shimmering like smelting gold. Skálda wondered how she had ever found Tythandrell beautiful. In the backdrop, the smoking twilight was fading straight into a deep indigo. It would be a fell night.

"Ready?" said Bale.

No, she wanted to say. Eyrek's last words plagued her soul. *I asked you to Build. You promised me, Skálda. Instead, you have betrayed me.*

Eyrek had given her everything—a purse of talents, an invitation to join his posts, his protection, and patronage. The axe she now fought him with. A brother's love. In the Skonkauld, he had suffused her with his love, yet she had assaulted his riders and allied with his nemesis. Eyrek was right. She had betrayed him—betrayed the man she loved most in the world.

"I can't do this, Bale."

"It was an illusion," he urged. *"Remember? Out there, that is not Eyrek Branwright. He is gone. That is the Ivarion."*

"I have to believe my brother is still there."

Bale rumbled again.

He was waiting for her. The Ivarion would not stop hunting Soren until he was dead. She reminded herself of Dellfast, and the oath she swore to break the Order. Dragonsteel meant to eliminate anyone who refused to yield to the script of its rules, and all its accompanying definitions of who an Elondrian could be. But like a flight's dragonscript, a man's soulscript was his story. The free Vigardians, the beating Story of Old Svenn, were depending on her and Bale. For that fading story to live on, a soul story that was also her own, she would inevitably have to remove the Enterprise's head.

Skálda closed her eyes. For a minute, she listened to the rhythmic beat of Bale's wings.

"Wolf?"

"Yes, Bale?"

He gave pause. *"They call me a Breaker. But I want to be better than that. I want to be remembered for something more. I don't want to Break, but I want to help Elondria."* He craned his neck to glance back at her. *"I know a Bael must die. But I will be the Bael that dies doing good."*

Skálda stroked his neck's black armor in wonder. How had she ever landed with a Bael so pure? He was so good, this Bael, the light of them both, and the heart of Elondria. Once more, she reaffirmed her vow to protect him with her life.

"They call me Kvael-Akar," she said, nodding with understanding. "In Elondria, to Build is to Break, and to Break is to Build. We go, Bale, and this time, we do not run."

"We die well."

Extending his neck, Bale tucked in his claws and pounded his wings. They accelerated until the winds of the heights scourged her face. The Völundr Reach blurred beneath them like a tapestry of dragonfire. Bale roared out a challenge. The dormant megalith gliding in the distance wakened. He returned the roar with thrice the power more. The petrifying avowal of death blasted over Vingulmark's wilderness, silencing every lesser beast. Soon, it was as if the North itself was holding its breath, waiting for the clash of dragons.

"Now, he comes," Skálda murmured.

Every beat of Tythandrell's wings were thunderclaps of power exerting his dominance over the continent. A turbulent backdrop of clouds rolled in from the east. A gust of leaves swirled over it like embers lighting in the dark. The Great Dragon was not swift as Detherys's cranewing, but he was so large, within just a few wing-beats, he was sailing above at a much higher altitude. Merely the weight of his shadow could have been Soren's royal longship crashing onto them. Skálda glanced up. Her brother's adult flight was easily five times her own.

An elvish command echoed across the cloud-streaked welkin.

"Bale, duck!" she bellowed.

A wroth tide of cacophony blasted at them. Bale swerved aside, but an acrid stench beleaguered her ability to think. She was smelling pythorum. It secreted from a dragon's activated fire glands; bile that sustained and superheated its breath, and improved its range. The reek was unfathomable, the smell of night terrors. As a mature Great, Tythandrell was producing so much of it. Neither could Skálda see, for dragonfire bathed the world into sharp contrasts of blinding light and saturated shadow. She shielded her eyes as Bale battled to fly fast enough to escape the fiery onslaught.

Crixalas could only sustain a skinny but nefarious column for ten beats. This monolithic *m'ethil* lasted for so long, too long. Skálda began to despair that it would never end—but it did, abruptly, an entire *minute* later.

By the time she could see again, she gasped quietly. The Völundr Reach was shrieking in bright yellows. The trees had been reforged into torches that absorbed the charring smell of Tythandrell's glands. Sections of the forest were collapsing, molten rain raging toward the understory. She pitied the forest animals trapped below.

The Day King roared in pride, reminding the continent of his sovereignty over all living creation. Bale recoiled. The Great's visage had turned into a shadow against the now boundless red kiln that was the sky; it shimmered everywhere from the aftershocks of his dragonfire, like the muscle twitches of a killed animal.

Skálda had known dragons were capable of destruction, but she could not fathom how her brother—ultimately, how the Lord Prince—could control this unrivaled weapon. She imagined, if the Second Rider so wished, he could burn a megalopolis like Elenntar, the capital of the Republic.

Bale retreated south, away from Solhall and toward wyrm country. The Eldruna Valley and the besieged Hammerfest Dike streamed below them. Tythandrell gave chase. Out here, the autumn squalls brought early flurries. At the onset of nightfall, the giant vanished into the gusts of oak leaves. The silence that followed was eerie. Bale breathed hard through his lathered nostrils. The only noise out here was the comforting whoosh of his wing membranes.

The next blistering column that blasted out of the darkness sent Bale shrieking.

He deflected so sharply, Skálda would have fallen off his back if not for an impulsive grab on another neck spike. The young Bael was so harried, he did not wait for her commands, but soared straight for a mighty mountain range. She recognized it as the Álfvindor Alps, the border between the free Deep North and her old home of Aranor Elondris.

Even the mountains trembled from the approaching tempest of Tythandrell's wings. Bale soared along a sheer mountain face, until they were parallel with it. Tythandrell was in close pursuit, every flap effortlessly ascending him higher. The plated musculature of his tail skimmed the mountain, spraying an earthstorm of scree below them.

The squall thickened as they ascended higher. It was not long before Skálda felt like she could reach up and catch the cold stars. The Deep North rolled below them in strange, ethereal patches. Bale had never taken her this high. Tythandrell temporarily faded from sight again. She sensed the Ivarion was pulling him back for his next calculated attack.

Skálda shivered in her shredded battle leathers. It was only a matter of time before the Great Dragon unexpectedly reappeared and crushed them whole between his jaws. She glanced down at the mountain, seeing memories of Hrafjenfall and her ritefest again, and forced herself to think. That they were flying right on the edge of the Republic, on the border of two worlds, disquieted her. It seemed a portentous omen.

Think, she told herself. This was one more ritefest. She had not won ritefest, or any other campaign, by strength alone. Neither could she expect to against the Ivarion. As Bale soared ever higher to the summit, the answer came to her.

I have an idea.

"Feed him to the wyrms?" Bale said grimly.

I need you to take control of my mind.

The Binding rocked from his cringe. *"Never, Wolf! I haven't mastered the power. I could kill you like before."*

You are a Bael, she said. *The master of all minds. Can you channel between minds?*

Since he hesitated, she ran through her plan. He did not immediately answer. They were almost at the summit. She could not see Tythandrell, but the huge vibrations of his wingbeats blasted the air along her neck. She smelled his fire glands powering up. The sovereign terror was fast approaching.

"I can't do it, Wolf," Bale insisted.

Skálda drew in a deep breath, to keep herself from succumbing to hysteria.

"When you left," said Skálda, "Anders said something meant for us. He told me, 'Be not *kvael-akar* and Bael, nor rider and dragon, but stun the world. Show them something they have no name for.' That's what you wanted, isn't it?"

She felt Bale's frown through the Binding. The summit appeared above them, fading in and out through the flurries.

"What I am asking is what Anders would have wanted of us. The good we can do for Elondria." She exhaled. "I trust you, Bale."

Something in that whisper made the fortifications in his heart shift.

"Very well," he said.

Skálda did not know if she would live through her plan, but it was a sacrifice she was willing to make. Perhaps the old rider had given his life for her because he had known she and Bale were the hope of the continent.

Bale made it to the peak. The pythorum stench was overpowering her again. He stopped ascending, but simply suspended them over the pinnacle. The vantage stole her breath.

She saw what Soren must have seen before he took his charge as Draughammr so many solstices before—her ancestral home in all its beautiful entirety, the sum of the mountains, woodlands, and valleys, converged in one story called Old Svenn. She understood evermore in her soul what he had fought to protect, and why she and Bale had to succeed now.

It was the perfect last view before her death.

She closed her eyes, reaching deep into herself. When she at last found what she was searching for, she bade Bale to take her.

Tythandrell burst out of the darkness. Through the Binding, she saw as Bale did. His gaping jaws were open. The back of his throat glowed like a forge in Helgaard, the final *m'ethil* that would turn their bones to ash.

Bale started his channeling—and her mind filled again with his tranquil assurance. Skálda let go and gave control of herself entirely to him, trusting her soul to her Bael.

The Ivarion roared. He clenched his head with both hands. Blinded by his rider's incapacitation, Tythandrell thundered with him. His armored chest collided against the mountainside. The peak quaked, and boundless earth and stones deluged below.

Bale was channeling Skálda's childhood memories, everything she remembered when Eyrek Branwright still lived with her in the Skonkauld. In those days, as a little girl, she had looked up to him, loved and trusted him with her whole heart. He was the big brother that was her whole world. Those were the days long before she knew Kael and even Anders, who would become her protectors in Eyrek's place. In those early days, she and Eyrek had oft gone to bed on empty tummies. Anything he foraged, he always gave to her first, no matter his own hunger. When he was not hunting, he labored for Herser Bjerke at the fisheries, from predawn to midnight, earning what little copperbits the island headman could give him. With those scraps, he bought wools he wove with his own hands into coats that would keep her warm enough from the glaciers.

One night, she lay in the barn, beset by the coldlung fever that had claimed many Skonkauld lives. He said by her bedside, holding her little hand tight.

"It won't take you," he whispered. "Not *you*, Skáld."

For twelve nights, she battled for her life. He refused to leave her even to eat or rest.

"I won't let you go," he kept reminding her, every dawn and night. Yet the fever only worsened. Every night, neither of them knew if she would make it to morning. But there was not a moment when Skálda opened her fluttering eyes that her brother was not there. Tears streamed down his face.

"I won't let you fall," he promised fiercely. "I won't let you fall..."

While their mother wallowed in her madness, Eyrek had lain by her in the barn, giving her freezing body his warmth. On the thirteenth day, she woke with enough strength to clutch his big, scarred hands, and whisper, "I won't let you fall either, Brother."

Hearing her conscious again, her big brother had taken hold of her little shape and wept into her wools. She had first learned the true meaning of love not from Anders, but from him.

"That is the Eyrek I know," she whispered presently into the gusts.

The same tears he had spilt for her now streamed down her own chin. As the high emotions of those memories left her, the Binding with Bale magnified, until what surged into Eyrek utterly blinded him.

"Enough!" the Ivarion bellowed in a terrified fury. "Skal—Skálda—stop!"

But she could not let go. There was no escaping Bale's hold. The vengeance, rage, and unforgiveness the Ivarion would not let go of looped back to her through the channel. But her Bael-Binding forged her memories into a greater power. The poison of the Ivarion's emotions entered her and washed away like purified water. As the loop continued, the emotional intensity of their shared memories swelled mightier, mightier, until neither of them could think or feel anything else. Skálda's human flesh became a husk to the roaring blaze of their *aracir*, their forsaken sibling love.

Tythandrell plunged down the mountain, as blinded as Eyrek. Only Bale, the conduit, was unaffected, though she felt something like tears through their Binding.

Bale dove after the Day King. Tythandrell crashed onto an overhang close to the peak, trembling the entire range. His thick belly armor protected him from the fall, but he writhed, his wings snapping as he fought for lucidity. The Ivarion attempted to climb down the saddle and draw his sword. Instead, he crashed onto his knees. Tears rushed down his face. His shouts turned into pleas to stop. Any longer, and the intensity of the memories would shatter their human minds.

Bale held on for a little longer so that Skálda's reminder would dent the Ivarion's mind and soul forever. Then, when he felt they were ready, Bale gently released them.

Her vision was terribly blurred, but she managed to stay upright. Skálda touched his neck for balance, wrestling Aracir from her belt. Bale looked on as she trudged over to the Ivarion's crumpled body.

"You once promised you would never let me fall," Skálda whispered. "But I have."

He stayed on all fours, heaving with sobs.

"Do you recognize this blade?" She turned the axe, so he could see the lines in Elvynnöthe, and recited them back in the Svenning:

"Though distance leaves your bickering forgone,
We shall meet as one blood anon,
To resume your squabbling up on dragonback,

O loving sister, in a most beauteous dawn."

"Dawn is upon us," she said. "Perhaps you foresaw this day would come, for we have faithfully brought these elvish words to life."

She tossed Aracir into the snow. He kept his eyes closed.

"I promised you once that I would never let you fall," she said. "But you have."

He opened his mouth, struggling to speak, but nothing came out. He could not stop weeping.

"We forgot our promises to each other," said Skálda. "But we have taken things far enough. I will not strike you again, Eyrek. I remember who we were. You will always be my brother... A dying child's whole world."

Skálda nodded to the elvish axe. "Take that blade, and do what you must to me. I won't run anymore. For I still see Eyrek Branwright before me..." Her voice fell to a quieter whisper. "And that man is a hundred times the Ivarion."

He wept harder. These were the final words that broke him. He would not take the axe.

"You do not understand," he finally said.

The dragons quieted as gusts enveloped the two siblings.

"'I need you,' he said. 'This...'" Eyrek formed a fist against the snow. "'This is your purpose. You must never forget.'"

Skálda's pale hair whipped against her face. He looked up to meet her burning eyes.

"That is what the Lord Prince told me. He was speaking of the Enterprise... and he was right."

"No, Eyrek—"

"It started as a dream. Ours is a wretched world for a common, you know that. I wanted to be earthbound no longer. Since the beginning of time, mankind dreamed of flying. The Enterprise made those dreams possible—far beyond what any of us could imagine."

"Do you not see what the Lord Prince is?"

"How do you still not understand?" He tightened his ringed fist. "You remember who I was. You say that boy is a hundred times the Ivarion, but what truth is that?" He laughed bitterly. "The only worth I ever felt was in Realm-Building. The only recognition the continent ever gave me was when I succeeded, and by the Light, I was so good at it. The greater I Built, the more the elves stopped treating me like the skit of the earth. I Built so high, the highest of them accepted me as his own."

He exhaled, and planted his knuckles into the ground to steady himself. Skálda shook her head.

"You still see yourself as a poor common," she whispered. "Even now. Even after all you've Built."

"I am the one that destroys mediocrity and weakness." He glanced at her desperately. "But I have become the very thing I fear."

Skálda knelt beside him, astonished. "You're afraid they will see what I saw in the Skonkauld..." She took his arm. "Eyrek, you have nothing more to prove, and what do you have to prove to *elves*?"

He tried to pick himself up, but fell to his knees again. Skálda caught him.

"I never meant to take things this far," he admitted. "I never imagined it would turn into this."

The whorls of flurries and leaves abated.

"I was never supposed to become Second Rider, or Bind with the Day King," he whispered. "I was never good enough for it. But I wanted to do something great for the people."

"I know."

"I wanted to show commons like us that they could be more. That they could be *free*. Free from the shackles of being a human.

On the day I must go to the grave, I wanted Elondria to see me off as their hero."

"I know." Skálda cupped him by the jaws. "You are good," she said. "I know your heart, Eyrek. You had a vision for the Enterprise. You care deeply about people. Not like me. I would let the Kru'ul trample them all."

He laughed quietly.

"You meant to use the Enterprise for good. But the Lord of the Order is not." He looked away. "Vharyn Morghûl twisted you to see the world through his eyes. But you are not him, or his war instrument. You are my brother."

He returned his gaze to the snow. The winds gnawed at their sweating necks.

"Old Svenn will never stop defending her freedom," she said. "But tell Vharyn the Vigardians will stop attacking his dragonposts. In return, the Order will expand no more into the Deep North, nor in any other land that belongs to another free peoples. What posts you have left, you will disassemble."

"You still forget about the Betrayer."

"If the Betrayer invades, the Vigardians will fight with you."

Eyrek shook his head. "We have not enough posts or Dragonlords. He will overcome us."

"He may try."

Abruptly, he pulled himself away and stopped below his dragon's saddle. For a long time, his mantled back faced her. The Second Rider was thinking, considering everything that had just occurred. Skálda steadied her breaths. This was the moment of final decision—the moment when he would either take to heart what she had shown him, and return to the Republic forever; or turn around to plunge his sword into her belly.

The Dragonlord climbed onto Tythandrell's back, sheathing Storm's Fury. Skálda let go of the breath she had been holding in. The Day King was watching his rider curiously.

"You have grown much," Eyrek said. "I hardly recognize you, Sister."

She met his gaze with her resting glare.

"But you are right. We have lost too much. I..." He slowly nodded as understanding passed over his eyes. "I choose to let go."

They were simple words, yet the weight of them shifted his entire countenance. This mighty rider was releasing his path of hate. Skálda sensed all the Deep North breathing a sigh of relief.

"I made a promise to my riders long ago," he said. "I do not know what the Order will do from here, but I vowed to resign... and I intend to keep that oath."

He wrested the Second Rider's brooch off his chest, looking down at it. His gaze swelled with heavy emotion. He clenched it tight, then tossed it to her. Skálda caught it by reflex.

"I choose to let go," he whispered again. "For Vhenna... and for my child, I must. *Éad'hel!*"

The Great Dragon grumbled at Bale to move out of the way, evidently peeved he would not get to blast apart the younger male after all. Skálda slipped Aracir back to her belt and ran toward them, waving her arm. "Hold on! Eyrek, did you say *child*?"

Tythandrell leapt off the overhang. Skálda glanced at the sheer drop below them. A few beats later, they were soaring forth into the air, in a northeastward direction. He was going to bring the last of his riders home.

"Eyrek!" she called again, clutching the brooch.

He glanced back at her from the saddle.

After a moment, she said, "I won't let you fall."

He smiled, and repeated those words to her. They were simple, but they held a boundless depth of emotion. Trouble was in his countenance. Even now, she saw how much he was warring with himself not to ask for the brooch back. He was battling to let go of the Ivarion. It would not be easy for him—or any of them—to fully forgive what had happened. Today, their emotions were at their peak; but when they woke tomorrow in their beds, the pain and anger would be there, certainly, and perhaps the regret of what they had decided here. They would have to face the terrifying prospect of who they would be without the Enterprise. Who would Eyrek be without the Ivarion? Who would Skálda be without dragonposts to defend the Wereguild from?

If Soren were here, he would berate her for letting him go. There was no telling if the Ivarion would ever return. A little voice warned her it was too likely. But that was a battle for tomorrow. Today, at least, they had won.

Eyrek made it several leagues north from the Álfvindors when a dragon slayer bolt soared out of the woodlands and burst open Tythandrell's neck.

32
VAERITAS IN THE FLESH

"EYREK!" Skálda screamed.

Blood sprayed over the skies, so much of it. The shriek that came out of the Great Dragon's jaws seized her with gooseflesh. Bale screeched with him. Tythandrell spiraled in the air, taking his dying roars downward.

Skálda was in too much shock to move. Bale jostled her onto his back and took off.

A red fog enshrouded the Great Dragon. The bolt was entrenched deep where his shoulder met the neck, but it seemed that with even the slightest movement of his flight muscles, it tore more of his neck open. His wingbeats weakened, and his leathery sails leveled out.

Skálda could not think, or comprehend what was happening. The Day King was dying. After the peerless invincibility she had seen of him this night, it was not possible. Bale strained his neck, slapping the air with his wings as he struggled to reach them.

Tythandrell was falling from the clouds now. The Great Dragon turned upside down, his neck slackening, his belly splayed against the rising sun. He was beyond saving, but she could catch

Eyrek. She could repay all the good he had done for her, and prove her avowal of forgiveness.

A bolt suddenly shot at her, whooshing past her ear. Bale shrilled and pulled up in the air.

Skálda exhaled in confusion. It had come from the forests, away from the lingering fires. It was the same dragon slayer that shot Tythandrell. Why would Soren's men shoot at her?

A third bolt forced Bale to whirl away sharply, away from Völundr's eastern sprawl. In the distance, the Day King vanished over the Lupines.

As she watched, the blur of disbelief returned to her eyes.

She never heard the crash, but the dragon's screams stopped. Eyrek would have never survived that fall.

It took her a long moment to become aware that Bale was keeping them aloft. He gently called to her, but she could not hear. Her eyes stayed frozen on the horizon. The rise and fall of her chest were shallow, too shallow.

"Wolf?" Bale urged. *"Wolf, we have to go home, alright?"*

She never answered. She could not.

"I won't let you fall..."

Tears trickled down to her chin. Her own failed promise crushed her chest. She had failed him for a second time—and there would be no third.

Another Anárion-tipped bolt shot at them from the understory. Skálda felt nothing, did not move, but it awakened a roar of fury out of Bale. He swerved away and took them back to the knolls east of Solhall, where the Vigardian hosts camped.

THE MOMENT they landed outside the woodlands, to the hill where Asveig tended to King Leondran, the senior Vigardian rushed out to approach her. Jarmon was at his side. The crowd of

Weremen and shieldmaidens behind them appeared just as consternated.

"We saw you fly out of the city with the Draugh," said Asveig. "The Ivarion pursued you on his beast..." His intonation ended with a question.

"My brother is dead."

This drew hisses of astonishment from the commanders. But soon after, the crowds roared in elation, chest-bumping each other or clapping each other's backs. Asveig saw no smile on her and, sensing something was wrong, did not join them. She turned her back, but he caught her shoulder and kept her in place.

"Someone shot him," she said. "And they shot at Bale."

Asveig glanced back at Jarmon, but the stout Vigardian shook his head. "Rulf is dead," he said. "The rest of the marksmen are in the city, or they are also dead, thanks to the elves. Couldn't be Wereguild."

Bale suggested, *"The Dragon Chainer?"*

Perhaps. Perhaps the Lord Prince had hidden in the woods and decided to punish his Second Rider for a change in heart. But that was a ludicrous stretch. It seemed unlikely that someone of the Lord Prince's rank would make use of Wereguild ballistae in place of a Great Dragon.

I don't think so, she said.

In the end, she supposed it did not matter. She had tried to save her brother, but he was dead. The only thing keeping her upright was the hand resting on Bale's spiked neck for balance. The commanders peered at her with a question on their tongues, but no one wanted to be the first to ask.

"The Draugh is alive," she affirmed.

They let out audible sighs.

"I can take you to him."

Asveig gave her a nod, and glanced back at the crowds. "Ulfrin, stay with the king. Danheim, with me. My horse!"

Skálda led a small contingent from dragonback into the evergreens. Bale flew low, just above the trees. Though he was in a mellow glide, even the horses in gallop struggled to keep pace.

After Bale landed, and they were back in the cavern behind the falls, Skálda pulled up short. It was empty.

"He was here," she said.

They followed the trail of blood out to the other side of the falls. Lord Jarmon shoved past them and squatted over the loam, studying the tracks.

"Only one pair, from what I can see," he called to them. "It looks like the Draugh left of his own accord." The warrior stood. "If our dragon girl here did not exaggerate the measure of his wounds, he could not have gone far."

They began a search that lasted into the predawn hours. When they returned to the knolls, neither was King Leondran where they had left him. Asveig looked like he would axe someone, but Ulfrin, the Vigardian in charge, spread his hands.

"The king insisted he needed the privacy."

"Privacy for what?"

Ulfrin blinked. "You did not hear?" The warrior pointed southward at a nearby knoll. "He's speaking with his son."

All of them turned. In the distance, two silhouettes stood at the hill's edge, overlooking Solhall's remains together. Asveig sighed. It was a noise between profound relief and annoyance. But even he could not pull back the smile tugging at his beard.

It was over. The Battle for Solhall was truly over.

"I'll make sure they are alright," Skálda said. She urged Bale back into the air for a short flight.

The shadows of the Deep North assumed a dramatic black in these early hours. Contrasted against them, the sky was bedazzling, bright as the strike of sunlight against a dragon's scales. She imagined the shared, living *m'ethil* from a thousand dragons birthing this new, blazing firmament.

They landed just outside the tree line. Bale stayed in the umbrage, insisting she not bother them.

"Father wants privacy with his babe, rude wolf," he said.

Skálda, however, was too impatient. They had just won a war against the Order, and she needed to clasp their arms like a true Vigardian. It would help keep her mind off Eyrek.

Soren isn't a babe, and I did not know a Bael was so mannered. She trudged out to meet them. Bale shook his head in disapproval.

But he was right. As she approached from the trees, the deep emotion running between the two kings weighed the air. In the end, she kept a respectable distance.

Fine. I'll wait. She felt the dragon chuckling at her.

Several paces ahead, the rising dawn silhouetted father and son. She marveled that Soren was standing upright. Then again, her healing spell must have helped, and Saarhekhu must still be alive if his rider's physical strength remained supremely dragon-enhanced. At his excess of 6,000 chapters, it was the only explanation for it. Any other normal mortal with torn ribs would be unconscious or halfway to death.

Someone, Asveig perhaps, had lent King Leondran a Wereman's tattered cloak. His ravaged hands were not visible under it, for he wrapped it tight around him. This man, too, ought to be unconscious. Like Soren, he had sustained gruesome wounds from the battlefield.

Then again, they were Astoraines.

Soren finally lifted his gaze. "Vaeritas has left our family."

"Nay, Vaeritas has blessed us."

"You think what happened to your hands is a blessing?"

"I am still alive, no? Well, I suppose that might not be a blessing to you." Leon chuckled. "It's all about choosing your vantage."

"What will Mother's vantage be when she sees you?"

"Oh, we'll worry about your mother tomorrow."

The Draugh pressed a hand against his forehead, turning away.

"You've lost too much for me." His voice thickened. "I told you not to come. You should have listened."

"Soren—"

"How will Fjorland take this? The Elenntarien? Your enemies will call you the cripple king! The Eldari will scorn your voice and call you a traitor for fighting here!"

"Soren..."

He shook his head. "I should not have joined that hunt. I should have never left home. Not if you were the cost."

"Son," Leon said gently.

Soren would not look at him.

"I have made many decisions in favor of the Republic, but I came here to show you that you have always been most important. You are my *son*. No matter the times, no matter the difficult decisions we make, that never changed. If the cost for you was my hands, then it was a good cost."

The Draugh's jaw was shaking. "Flames on you." Turning back around, he withheld himself no more and clasped the elder king's shoulders tight.

"I've missed you, Father," Soren whispered.

Leon smiled, making no attempt to wipe away his tears. "It feels good hearing you call me that again."

The reverberant affection in their eyes reflected the living dawn. It reminded Skálda of her last precious moments with Eyrek. She took another step back, then another.

When they let go, Soren grunted, wiping his face with his sleeve. "You should know, if you are returning to the Republic. Why Aeogorath tried to kill me."

"Son, let's speak of the past no more—"

"You must know," he pressed. "On our last visit to Elenntar City, all those solstices ago, I saw..." He let out a short breath. "I saw His Eminence and the Morghûl queen. They..." He leaned closer and whispered in Leon's ear. Tight creases formed on the older king's forehead. Skálda could only hear bits of what Soren was saying.

"...after Conclave... house in Brindlemoor Bay... tried to conceal..."

The next time Soren pulled away, he said, "They know that I saw. That's why the queen sent Aeogorath to kill me."

Blistering fury beset King Leon's face.

"You must tell the Elenntarien and have them removed from power," Soren said. "Save the Republic, Father. Become the High Eldari we need. If you don't find a way to indict them, I foresee the Morghûls and their Dragonsteel will take over the continent. They will use an invasion from the Betrayer as their vindication. It is already beginning."

"They will regret ever touching my family." Leon gnashed his teeth. "When the Elenntarien finds out about this, you have my word it will bring them down." He glanced southward. "This cannot stay hidden any longer, Soren. I must make haste for a return..."

While they murmured between themselves, the larks stopped singing. The distant forest to the south silenced in a wave that rushed toward Skálda. Her smile faded.

Bale reared in the darkness, shrieking through flared nostrils. *"Get back, Wolf!"* His terrors quaked their Binding, impregnating her mind with his thoughts.

By the time the two kings noticed, it was too late. They parted from each other, gazing eastward with their mouths open.

If Tythandrell was a colossus, what soared over the southern skies dwarfed even him. This dragon's wingspan could easily have been three hundred paces across. Where it flew, it left a violent trail of displaced air behind it that put out Tythandrell's fires and forced the trees to bow. It was entirely a luminous white, though it caught all the swatches of dawn and scintillated like the sun itself.

It struck Skálda that she was looking upon Lumaerrax, the highest-ranking dragon in the Order.

She lost all feeling in her chest.

Where the white mountain landed, it eclipsed even the dawn-light. The entire overlook trembled in a boom. The Astoraines backed away, dumfounded. Lumaerrax's glowing eyes, a fired purple, burned from high above.

"Finngólfa's ravens," Skálda whispered. One might think Bale a monster, but this was an abomination. It should be an impossibility of nature that so tiny a rider could command her like a tame beast.

Yet someone did. The one who sat below her neck was cloaked in fulgent white silks. An ample hood swathed the face in shadow. Unlike all other Builders in Elondria, he did not ride with a saddle. Before the Astoraine kings, he slowly pulled back his hood.

"Vharyn Morghûl," they said together, their eyes lurid with fear.

Leon's voice came out hoarse. "What... what are you doing out here?"

Skálda was frozen. There before her was her nemesis, yet she could not fathom it. The *Lord Prince,* a legendary rider that existed only in old, forgotten stories, was here. Under her breath, she spoke the *Lhaer'thri*... and wished she had not.

Lumaerrax had 9,998 chapters.

"Something's wrong with her, Wolf," Bale whispered.

She felt it, too. A fell energy cloaked the queen, like she was shrouded in a plague Skálda was only partially seeing. It made her feel bodily ill, though she could not put to words exactly what it was.

At this angle, she saw only one half of the Lord Prince's face. His jawline was sharp as unhewn gypsum. His varnished hair snagged itself in half-done braids. Disheveled as he was, the elf glowed with a lustrous beauty, like being beautiful was effortless; albeit the arch of his brow was cruel. And if she had ever seen the ears of a High Elf, his were sharper, more taloned than any other; the proud mark of the highest elvish royalty.

Soren drew the longsword at his father's hip, though he winced, and his face twisted with pain. It was his broken ribs. Even at his mind-boggling dragon rank, he looked like a broken plaything in the High Elf's shadow.

The Lord Prince never acknowledged them, nor left dragonback. He switched his gaze between them with bloodcurdling calm. Leon's shoulders tightened. It was obvious the Lord Prince had come for one purpose only—to kill the Were King.

The words that passed through his lips were neither Elvynnöthe, nor Elondrian, nor any tongue she had ever heard. These were a combination of letters impossible to pronounce or replicate. It dawned on her, in growing uneasiness, that he was speaking Nhorssn. The lost language of the Rhún, the original source of all magical power.

Smoldering runes faded into the air before them. They were diabolical, like embers fallen out of Helgaard, bleeding through the Middle Realm's visible plane.

A heatwave shimmered the air. It mesmerized Skálda. The power that awakened levitated the threads of her soul. She swore she was standing in a slow-burning kiln, floating on the balls of her feet. The sheer energy inebriated her. This was ponderously more than the strength Eyrek wielded, even with his *ruthra'ruín* or *m'ethil*.

All the gods have mercy, she thought. Every Builder on the continent was an unborn fetus compared to this elf.

The runes rippled mightier, mightier, sedating the air. Their malignant light strobed the Astoraine faces. All sound muffled, until Skálda felt like she was standing underwater, on an ocean floor where everything was heavy, slow, and muted. This was no Dragonspell, nor anything of the natural Magia. It could not be.

Vharyn raised his palm and unleashed the runic power at Leon.

A trail of translucent, shimmering energy pulsed toward the king. Everything was slow, even her ability to breathe. Soren saw it coming. His mouth tore open in a cry. *"Father!"*

The Were King threw himself in front of Leon.

He was a pace too late. The achromatic column struck Leondran Astoraine square. On impact, a new blast of soundless energy hurled Skálda against a tree. Soren was far too proximate to it; its outer diffusions struck him alike. No one could say how close Saarhekhu was, for even if Soren had invoked the *ciryamor*, the end would have been the same. The Dragonshield would have shattered like old glass before the Lord Prince's power.

Soren's cry turned into a scream as he caught his father's arm. He clasped onto it tight. The Lord Prince's Deathspell blasted the Astoraine kings off the overlook. The light dimmed in Leon's eyes, and his neck fell limp. It was the last thing Skálda saw before father and son vanished into Eldruna Valley's abyss below.

The Nhorssn runes faded, and with it, the heady swell of energy.

Skálda remained paralyzed. Her mind could not comprehend what she just saw.

The Lord Prince gazed off into the distance, retreating into thought. He seemed in no hurry to return to Rhaennöria. As Skálda stared at him under the tree, the dawn's rising light drew back the forest's shadows. Lumaerrax rumbled. She was calling to her rider. He shifted, and his superior elf-eyes found Skálda in the umbrage.

Looking into those eyes was like impaling her own on broken glass. She did not understand how Eyrek had ever called him "friend."

The Lord Prince cocked his head. His gaze flickered to Aracir tucked at her belt. "*Kvael-akar.*" He smiled. "I forged that blade for you."

Skálda found herself too tongue-tied for words.

"I had my family smith forge it," he said. "It is a Morghûl blade. Strange, how the Sun's threads of fate work, no? We were supposed to shake hands in Exar'forda, simply because of who your brother is. You were supposed to become my Builder. Perhaps a Dragonlord as great as the Ivarion. Certainly, my loyal human friend."

Finding her voice, she sneered. "Your loyal slave. Dragonlord? I have become something far better."

The Lord Prince laughed. "Riddle me this, *kvael-akar*. I still cannot understand. Why..." His brow arched into a sharper descent. "Would you even fathom to oppose me?"

She drew Aracir from her belt.

"I annul dragonposts. I command Judges and Dragonlords and every manner of Builder. I do not Build realms..." Against the shifting dawnlight, his long shadow extended to her. "For I kill Eldari and *acquire* realms."

Skálda started toward him.

"You see," he said, "all Elondria is merely a game on my warboard. I move, create, and destroy pieces however it suits me. You are just one more of those little pieces. And I..." High on his white throne, Vharyn Morghûl turned to her in full. "*I* am Vaeritas."

The dawn blazed in a storm flare behind him. The mutilation she saw on the right half of his face wrenched her gut. It was manifold more hideous than any Kru'ul she had killed on the battlefield.

But it did not stop her from taking a running leap.

Bale sank his teeth into her leathers and wrenched her back. Skálda crashed onto her hands.

The aloofness in the Lord Prince's eyes drained. Lumaerrax's snarl deepened into a malignant rumble. She, too, recognized what the shade of Bale's scales meant. It was an ancient memory, a primal fear branded into the minds of all races.

"That is why," the Lord Prince whispered. "A Bael. Vaeritas, a living *Bael* on Elondria..."

"Don't fight Morghûl, stupid wolf!" Bale stopped her second attempt at a lunge with another tug. *"No wits can win!"*

He all but shoved her onto his back. Perhaps he was the wiser of them both. She knew what Vharyn Morghûl was; she had witnessed it, yet her all-consuming purpose was to annul him. Bale raced into the forest's darkness on all fours, away from the scintillating Lord Prince. Skálda glanced over her shoulder. His receding shape faced her in harrowing starlight. A new set of runes shimmered into the air.

Seeing them plunged her back into the present moment. "Bale," she whispered. "He's going to—"

And the breaking came.

Roots tore out of the ground. Entire trees, ancient sentinels of the Deep North, exploded in front of them. Bale snarled in fear. Splinters flew into her eyes. The Völundr Reach was rocking and pulverizing. The space between the evergreens made it too narrow for flight, and in his attempt to ascend, his wings slammed against the trunks. In the pandemonium, leather membrane ripped. Bale spun over his heels. The fallout of the runic spell tore her off his back. The Lord Prince was recreating—annihilating—the very terrain to his own purpose. Skálda screamed Bale's name. He had been right. The Lord Prince was impossible for her to kill... because he was Vaeritas in the flesh.

They were lost to the unending starbursts of chaos, and into the nether they vanished.

33

THE CRUCIBLE OF DESTINY

SKÁLDA WOKE on the shores of a fjord, to cerulean daylight.

She lay supine on the dirt, in the same shredded, filthy leathers she had worn for a fortnight. Shading her face against the sun, she sat upright.

The land was tranquil out here. Warm breezes carried the sough of crystal waters. A stray zephyr tickled her hairs here and there. One would not have believed it was autumn. But something was not right. The dragonfires from her duel with Tythandrell were no more, yet not a single bird sang.

A thick layer of blood and grime crusted her scalp. She rubbed her head, to a spot at the base of her skull where it throbbed most. All of her was stinging and achy, as if a monstrous fever had hit her overnight.

Squinting, she croaked, "Bale?"

No answer came. Skálda labored to twist her body around and glance behind her. On the slopes overlooking the fjord, the conifers were completely gone. The earth was charred—and the unbidden memory of Nhorssn runes cut through her eyes like a sun glint against a blade. She hissed. The Lord Prince had left the Völundr Reach a burnt wasteland at least one league in diameter.

"Bale!" she screamed, her throat tightening.

She searched for the Binding, but she could not feel it. Her chest heaved faster, but she reminded herself that did not mean he was dead. Their bond worked differently, and it only meant he was not proximate.

Someone shouted back from somewhere in the forest. She staggered around. Aracir was still tucked in her belt. She drew it, readying herself for a skirmish.

"Aesir?" she whispered, not entirely lucid.

Mat burst out of the trees and pulled up short. "Skáld!" His eyes were wet. The oversized tunic he wore was so stained with grime and sweat that she could not say what its original color had been. His shoulders were taut with hysteria.

The moment they met eyes, he bounded to her and squeezed his arms around her. Tears dampened the crook of her neck.

"I know you don't like hugs," he whispered, "but please, just... just give me this."

Skálda returned his embrace. They closed their eyes and wept quietly together.

"I thought you were dead." Mat let go and wiped his eyes. "I... Light, Skálda. I saw what happened. I saw... *him.* We all did, those of us left in Solhall. I couldn't believe it. I never imagined I would ever..."

"Have you seen Bale?"

Mat slowly shook his head. "I'm sorry."

She turned her back, steeling all emotion from her face. Her eyes were pooling, but that infuriated her, and she fought it back. She was in control of her emotions. It would be alright. This was the end she had promised Soren, the end she promised Aesir. She remembered the way Bale had cradled her on the battlefield, what he had said to her. Bale would have wanted this, too.

Tears streamed down her face. She said nothing of it, kept staring blankly at the fjord. Mat edged closer and wrapped his shoulder around her. Together, on that stunning morning, they sat in the sunlight, watching the shores.

"Looks kind of like home, doesn't it?" he said.

She gazed out over the bend in the river. A mountain slope obscured whatever terrain was behind it.

"The Norfjord," he went on. "By the Kyrjá River." He scratched his overgrown beard. "Maybe home would have looked like this if the Naüthe melted, eh?"

"It's not as beautiful."

"No," Mat agreed.

"I miss it," she said. "I miss smelling the pine cones in the Krigsgaald. I miss seeing Breck and Dringed's lights at night. I miss Herser's shouts at the fishing holes. Whenever I heard it, I knew I had woken too late."

"Kael and I wouldn't ever let you sleep in late."

"Especially on the morning of my own ritefest."

Mat laughed softly. "Good thing that eld never hatched for you, or we wouldn't have had *this* fun, yeah?"

She pulled her skinny knees to her chest and hugged herself. "I miss the deathly cold. The hunger. That constant hope of a better future. The *battle* of it all. Waking up every day accepting the Skonkauld's challenge to live, and survive. I miss the fear of taking Snoga into the Krigsgaald and wondering if I would walk out alive." She dropped her voice. "I used to hate Bregan, Mum, the islanders, all of it. I put all of my dreams in the Enterprise..."

Mat glanced at her.

"But sometimes, I think," she said, "the best things are right where we are. Right at home."

Her childhood friend reached over and looped an arm over her shoulder. In another time, Skálda might not have let him, but she did not fight now. He returned his gaze to the crystal distance.

"I miss seeing Skoll Tower from every horizon," Mat said. "I miss having to clean up the dust heap of Anders's hall, and getting to sleep in after ritefests like a vagrant."

"You're still a vagrant." She nodded at his shredded tunic, his unshorn face and wild bed of hair. "Always were."

Mat laughed. "And you look any better?"

She smiled wistfully. "I miss Anders."

After another long pause, he nodded. "I miss him, too."

The dazzling sun, mild as it was, scorched her pale flesh. As a Skonkaulder, she was not used to such brightness or warmth.

"They took Faelan prisoner," Mat said. "The Khetherae elves left before the rest of the Vigardians could return to the city. We freed Incendra, but she's gone after him. They'll probably kill her, or some Ranger will. The battle is over, but... it doesn't feel like it ever ended."

"It hasn't," she said. "The Lord Prince isn't dead."

Mat furrowed his brows. She thought back to the black-armored elf that had battled Soren in the yard. Something about him, and that last portentous look he had given Eyrek, lingered in her mind.

"I'm going to stay in Vingulmark, I think," said Mat. "Or wherever the Wereguild goes now. I've no future in Aranor Elondris. The Order will keep hunting us, and someone needs to take care of Liv and Feorya."

He glanced at her, a question in his eyes. Skálda pulled her knees tighter to her chest. She did not know where her place was. The Draughammr was dead. He had wanted her to lead the Wereguild, yet... the Deep North did not entirely feel like her home either. Not while the Lord Prince was alive.

The sun rose higher in the sky.

That was when she felt someone watching them from the shadows of the trees. Skálda turned around. Noticing, Mat turned with her.

The common eye might have seen nothing, but she was a bred hunter. She knew when even the skáldwolves were watching her. But it was not a wolf that stood between the trees. It was something that blended with the darkness, imperceptible but for two crimson eyes...

Skálda jerked to her feet. "Bale?"

Mat stood with her, his eyes widening.

She sprinted over the dirt to reach him, crashing once on her knees. Her body was so weak with exhaustion. The moment her sinewy arms looped around his neck, she shuddered, though she was long dried of tears.

"LET IT GO," Bale said, as she labored to heal him with the *anora'thil*.

He was cut everywhere, and both wings had a plethora of little punctures. A particularly large one on his rear leg was hurting him; he would not stand on it, but kept the knuckles of his muscled talons balanced against the ground.

Skálda ignored him and said, "*Anora'thil.*"

"*Wolf.*" He nudged her with his muzzle. "*We are tired. There will be time for laboring, but now we rest.*"

"He broke the land. He almost broke us. He can Break—"

"*No, silly wolf. The Morghûl is no Bael. He can break the land, but he cannot Break worlds.*"

In the distance, Mat lounged on the shores to give them space, gazing up at the sky. She had never seen Anders's animated post second look so lost.

"That may be," she said, "but if he can break the land, he can break what's left of Midgaard. Isn't that our entire world?" When he did not answer, she added, "I've given this much thought, Bale.

A Second Breaking is already here, and it's not coming from you, or above."

He shook his spiked head with deep worry. *"Morghûl is no Realm-Breaker..."*

"You heard what Soren wanted. He needs us to defend the Vigardians. To do that, we have no choice but to annul the Lord Prince—"

"Good wolf." The dreadful crimson lights in his eye hollows radiated a warmth only she could feel. *"I cannot."*

"If we allow him to live, all of Elondria—"

"I cannot, because I want to keep going to Traust."

Astonishment suppressed the words on her tongue.

"I have thought very much, too..." He sank onto his chin and claws. *"The truth is, Wolf... I never wanted to hatch. I saw the mind-memories of my father in my egg. I saw what Baelaeryx did to the upper Realms."*

"Baelaeryx was your father...?"

He sighed glumly through his nostrils. *"This new war on Elondria is all my fault. I brought it when I fell."*

"It is my fault, not yours. I made the decision to defy the Order."

"It is bad, isn't it? Everything we have seen."

"Bale—"

"But it will still be nothing compared to a Breaking. Only Baels can Break, Wolf, and all Baels do. It is in our nature, eventually. I cannot control my powers, and I will only grow stronger. The Morghûl knows I am here now. He searches. Always, the Vile One searches... and he will not stop until I am dead." Bale looked at her. *"Will you take me to Traust, for me?"*

Skálda realized that since the day she met Bale, everything had been about her, what she had wanted. *She* had wanted to take him to Traust, only because of guilt and the judgment she could not bear from Aesir. And she had lured Bale into the crossfire of her war against the Order. Even now, she wanted to use him to overturn the Lord Prince and the Realm-Building Enterprise.

But it was time to let go and allow Bale to decide his fate.

"I... am ready to go home."

Even as he said this, his voice quavered. Skálda brushed his neck. "I don't know the way to Traust... but we will find our path together."

The young Bael kissed her with his nose. Skálda smiled, rubbing his armored cheek with a hunter's fondness.

They might have spoken more, but Mat shouted from the shores and waved his arms. Skálda looked to the fjord. Around the river bend, a longship sailed their way. As its eighty oars rowed, the vessel's bow bobbed like a horse in a canter. The mainsail had a white skáldhead imprinted on blue wool.

She hobbled onto her feet. It was Soren's royal ship.

"Stay in the trees," she urged Bale. Now that the Lord Prince knew about him, the fewer eyes that saw him, the better.

Skálda emerged out of the shade, glaring against the blaze of autumn daylight. Mat waited for her, worry growing in his countenance. She touched his shoulder briefly and came out to meet the Vigardians.

Asveig leapt out first. Something hung over his back. Skálda squinted behind him. Frit and Evynd were on the boat, barricaded between bulky Weremen. They looked so small and vulnerable; seeing them alive heartened Skálda. Frit waved at her enthusiastically. Jarmon followed Asveig, blocking anymore of her view of the princess. The heavy crash of his boots sprayed water. The two hulking reavers waded toward her. Anyone else would have fled for the trees.

They stopped several paces away, as begrimed and foul-smelling as she probably was. Skálda crossed her arms. "What is this, a parley?"

Jarmon laughed, but Asveig stayed stone faced. Skálda nodded at the horned helmet hanging behind him.

"Well met, Draughammr."

Asveig said nothing of her comment. "We have been searching for you. My thanks to the Light that you are alive."

"That is as close as you'll ever come to admitting you love me, hmm?"

Even that did not elicit a twitch out of his face. Skálda glanced at Lord Jarmon. "What will make that man smile?"

The braid-bearded Vigardian sneered. "Don't you know by now that he does not smile?"

Ignoring their quips, Asveig dove straight into his business. "We must speak."

"Here I am."

"The Astoraines are fallen."

"Yes, I know—"

"I speak of them all. We received a transmission from our Republic contact. Prince Calabran is stepping down from the throne. No other Astoraine is in line to take it."

Skálda frowned. "Stepped down to go where?"

"He has accepted a position as a Builder of the Order. An egg hatched for him. Under the royal seal, he has..." Asveig struggled to speak. Emotion was bottled in the old warrior's eyes. "He has bequeathed it to another."

"Hold on," said Skálda. "He bequeathed *Fjorland* to another? The entire kingdom?"

Since Asveig could not bear to voice it, Lord Jarmon said, "To the leader of the Lightcloaks."

She uncrossed her arms. "The Lightcloaks...?"

"Our enemies, thrall."

"Call her that no more," Asveig snapped. "She is not our thrall."

"False Sun warriors of the desert." Jarmon's snarl deepened. "Fell Vigardians in the east."

"They are not Vigardians." Asveig, the Republic one of them both, interrupted to explain. "The Order of True Light reigns from the wastes of Fel Tirion. Their members are militant fanatics, no true Vaeritians." He spat in disgust. "They hunt free men with affinities, believing it to be their duty to the Lord of Light. Should that happen, their inquisitors will offer you two choices—serve their vision of Vaeritas, or die a slow death by their Illumination." He nodded to her intently. "They must not find you."

"I am still not following—"

"We knew they were formidable," Jarmon prattled on. "But not by how much. The Kru'ul they deployed against us was nothing to them. Twenty thousand Kru'ul—*nothing*! But..." He took a menacing step forward. "They are coming. Oh, they are coming. Fjorland's demise is just the beginning. Another continental war comes, a bigger one perchance..."

Skálda glanced between the men in disbelief. Asveig was not a man to smile, certainly, but it looked like he was holding back tears.

Rogue fanatics taking over a *Republic* realm? she thought. The Astoraine's ancestral inheritance passed to them? She wondered how the Elenntarien could ever allow it.

Even a common would know that was as impossible as a Bael falling from the sky.

"Just the beginning, just the beginning," Jarmon cried. "No one has ever seen such an abomination in all our lifetime!" Asveig glared at him. "Fjorland turned into desert Vigardian land! Mark me, it will be like Old Svenn. All the continent will fall to dragonfire and—"

"Shut up, Danheim." Asveig shoved the Wereman behind him. "Not another word out of you."

"This is Vharyn's doing," she said. "He gave Fjorland to them."

"Of course it is his doing, foolish girl!" said Jarmon. "Or is it my mother's doing?"

"Skálda." Asveig interrupted before his stocky shield-brother could say anymore. "What Fjorland and the Wereguild have lost... is immeasurable. It cannot be explained in words. Leondran Astoraine..." She swore then he was going to break.

"I understand," she said. "He was your friend."

Jarmon sneered. "You aren't telling her everything."

Asveig inhaled quietly. "The Lord Prince framed Elder Leondran's death on you. It has been transmitted across the Republic. He was a very influential man, very beloved. All Aranor Elondris is wroth. The continent is hunting you and your Bael."

The blood drained from her face. She almost glanced back at Bale. They were twenty-five hundred span to Traust. More, since the Deep North had taken her even further from where she had started her journey in northern Fjorland with Aesir.

Slipping the helmet off his back, Asveig knelt low before her.

"We would have you lead the Wereguild... Draughammr." He offered Soren's helmet.

She had known this was coming. Yet the shock of it impacted her no less. Everything Asveig was telling her was too much to take in on these shores.

"He wanted this. He told me this, before our battle began." His eyes were welling. "And from what I have seen... I support him entirely in the matter."

Discomforted by his emotion, Skálda glanced at Lord Jarmon. "You want this too, dear shield-brother?"

"Hah! Fjella's killer commanding me?" He shrugged. "I don't like you. I never will. But you slayed Skitr, so perhaps I will consider offering you an old, rusted Wereshield to start."

She bit back from reminding him she had not killed Eyrek.

"Gracious, brother. Perhaps I will consider if I like your beard."

"Skálda." Asveig lifted his head, annoyed that she was not indulging in the emotional intensity of the moment.

"I cannot," she said.

Both men jerked in astonishment.

"I do like your beard," she told Jarmon, clasping his beefy shoulder, "and I cannot become the Draughammr."

Deep creases appeared on Asveig's forehead. "But—"

"Not yet." Skálda paused, and nodded to the trees. "I have a promise to fulfill first."

"What promise?"

"My Bael would have me take him to Traust. The Draugh would have wanted this also."

They sobered.

"After it is done," she said, "I will study with the Brother Mages. The elf told me I have an immense affinity." She avoided speaking Aesir's name. "I won't keep letting it sit untapped in me, but I must master elvish magic. Above all, I must learn the Lord Prince's power—"

"It was an illegal spell worthy of a Kar'thuul-dur sentence," Asveig said sharply. "I served an Eldari. I know the laws of the high courts. It was black magic. If the Elenntarien knew he cast it, or that he even knows it—"

"What?" she said. "He is awakened, although now I believe he wasn't ever dormant. He's negotiating with militants. He has proven himself too powerful for even the Elenntarien to arrest." She brushed Aracir's haft. "But I will study the Nhorssn runes, learn everything he knows. When I return, I will be ready to face him again... for only when he dies, the Vigardians will live free."

The Weremen did not speak. Even Lord Jarmon's sneer had fallen off to morose disappointment. They were afraid. Without her and Bale, they were lost. No one else was strong enough to defend them from the Order.

Skálda took Asveig's arm, then Jarmon's, and stepped closer. "It is as you said, my brothers." She glanced between them. "It is not an end, but a beginning. I will return. You have my oath."

After a long moment, Asveig pulled the helmet back to his chest. He nodded at Jarmon. Before he left, the braid-bearded Vigardian gripped her arm firmly. "May the wolves be with you."

Asveig waited for Jarmon to return to the ship. Once they had their privacy, he lowered his voice. "The Draughammr said something in his final days, something I will never forget."

Skálda waited.

"'The breaking of realms is the crucible of destiny.'"

She thought on those words.

"A common man sees that the continent is breaking, one realm at a time," Asveig said, "and he despairs. But I venture to think the greatest legends of Elondria will rise out of whatever is coming."

Skálda slowly nodded. "Tribulation is strength," she whispered. Her brother's slogan reminded her of what Asveig was telling her now.

"In all honesty, it did not feel entirely right to offer you this helmet." The Vigardian caressed the dragon horns. "In my head, I agreed with the Draugh. But in my heart, I see something else in you, Skálda. I saw it the day he confided in me the hjarta's warnings. I saw it even that day we struck blades in the Prannon. After that day... I never forgot your eyes."

She frowned. Asveig leaned into her ear for a whisper. "I see the first Baelrider... I see a Breaker of Enterprises."

His words should have shaken her to the bones, yet she felt a calm assurance settle in her heart. It was confirmation of all the restlessness she had ever felt, the secret hungering that bloomed in her soul the day she rescued a hatchling from the Krigsgaald. With a Bael, her strongest desire was possible.

The desire to Build on Elondria something even greater than the Morghûl Empire.

"Choose your path carefully," Asveig said, stepping back. "One misstep, and a Building could become a Breaking."

Skálda gripped his hauberk's sleeve before he could pull away anymore. "Asveig..." She dropped her voice to a whisper. "If I endeavored to Build an empire with a Bael, if I could make it happen on this continent... would the North fight with me?"

He looked at her for a long moment. Her heart was hammering like a war drum. She had never disclosed this dream to anyone, not even to Bale, out of fear and guilt. She could already hear Aesir's voice in her head. It was treasonous. Above all, it was utterly laughable to even consider challenging the House of Morghûl, High Elves that had countless times her affinity. She never should have said anything. Asveig would disperse her silly secret across the Wereguild. All the reverence she had bled to earn, even her right to rule them, would be lost.

The Draughammr's advisor inclined his head, and whispered something she would never forget. Skálda let go of him. The racing of her heart returned to a glacial, settled calm.

The new Wereguild leader trudged back to the ship. He called over his shoulder, "Boy! Are you coming?"

Mat jolted, and rushed to follow in gratitude. Passing Skálda, he squeezed her arm.

"Fey and I will see you again one day, yeah?"

A few minutes later, Asveig was helping Mat's skinny shape crawl into the boat. With a drumbeat, and a yell from Jarmon, the oarsmen resumed rowing in time. Bale came out of the woods to take his place by her.

They stood on those shores, watching, until the prancing skáldwolf on the mainsail vanished over the river bend. Skálda kept rolling in her mind Asveig's last words to her.

"Sovereign Queen," he had said.

THE REAVE AT OSMENDELL

EPILOGUE

"I DREAM OF FALLING."

"I dream of falling."

They spoke those words at the same time, waking from their afternoon nap. Skálda gazed up at the deep green canopy, her head pillowed in her crossed arms. The pair were as vitalized as they could be to begin their long journey south. But the remnants of Skálda's dreams troubled her. Bale's falling terrors had long become her own, braided permanently into her soulscript. That ubiquitous terror of something she could not name was only growing heavier in her flesh, like night falling over her.

Now that the Lord Prince was gone, the Völundr's blackbirds had at last returned to their autumn ballads. The music brought her a relief. She could not help but think about Soren on their last morning together. She wondered if he and his father had arrived yet in the halls of Aethragaard, the highest of the Realms, and found a dawn even more beautiful than that last one.

Neither she nor Bale wanted to rise, so they continued to lie there together.

Skálda absently brushed his neck scales with the back of her fingers. They were evening out, no longer the mottled, chaotic pattern she remembered when he was a hatchling. Her quiet humming and stroking settled him into a deep peace. It helped her forget about her own grief.

"Wolf?"

Yes, beloved?

"I wish I were not a Bael."

"Bale," she said reproachfully.

He kept his chin resting on the ground, unwilling to look at her. She might have admonished him, but stopped. Since Dellfast, and perhaps her entire life, she, too, had longed to be anything other than herself. She had always wanted to be *more.* A better rank. Always, the rider of a dragon at the highest, *best* rank. Anything but what she was. But Mat's words to her that night beneath the stars suddenly made sense.

Gently, she said, "Why apologize for what you are?"

"How can I not?"

Skálda climbed upright and cupped his big head with both hands.

"The Realm-Building Enterprise defines everything we are," she said, looking into his eyes. "You are either a Builder, or a civilian. You are dragon and rider, or you are nothing at all. You are an Ealdorman, or Baron, or Primarch, or some other elf-forged rank. There is always a name for your rank. We know each other by rank and post only. If you have none, then you are a *kvael,* or something lesser they already have a name for." She rubbed him along his thorned jaws. "But if we refuse to be defined by them, then what are we?"

"I don't know."

He looked at her expectantly. Though she had not spoken of it aloud, he knew this was the very question she had sought an answer for since leaving Aranor Elondris.

"We are none of those things," she said. "I say we are not even *kvael-draek* or *kvael-akar*." At his skeptical look, she said, "Soren made up his rank. Draughammr, he called himself. Asveig called me a queen."

"Oh?"

"And you are no Breaker that fits any narrative of Elondrian history. You have the biggest heart I know."

His eyes flickered with hope.

"Before I met you, I dreamt of finding my place in a world contained inside the Enterprise. But you and I, we have slipped past the bars. We do not fit the definitions the Order places on us, which makes us free to choose who we will be."

"But I am still a Bael..."

"Yes, you were *born* a Bael. You have the sovereign power to recreate us and the continent."

She rested her head against his.

"And by that, we will do more good than what the Realm-Building Enterprise ever defines possible, hmm?"

"If we are not just Bael or kvael-akar*, then who are we, Wolf?"*

"I am Skálda. Just Skálda. And you are Bale. Isn't that enough?"

She smiled.

He closed his eyes, and rumbled. Their Binding flushed with a power greater than anything Skálda had ever felt from any man, elf, or dragon. It was the pure love of a Bael.

THAT AUTUMN DAYS ahead remained picturesque. It was never too frigid during the nights, but the air was a pleasant crisp against the hearth of Bale's belly. The sun continued to pour over Skálda, though with winter on the horizon, she decided she would not mind what sunlight she could soak in now. Before starting their journey, they had washed in the fjord. Already, she was feeling much lighter and ready for a new adventure.

Since Bale's wings needed time to heal from the Lord Prince's spell, they hiked the northern slopes on foot. At the end of the fortnight, they crossed out of the Álfvindor Alps and entered back into Aranor Elondris.

Seeing the free North recede behind her gave her a resounding ache. Every time she looked into that pass, the mighty echo of its majesty reverberated in her soul. She had gone into it a thrall, and come out a Vigardian with a destiny. Perhaps not unlike Soren.

But Bale reminded her through the Binding that she would one day return. She had promised her people.

They stayed on the slopes. Enlivened by the sun, Bale chomped lazily at yellow butterflies. Being on elevation always gave Skálda a reassuring sense of control, and it was no different now. The familiar landscapes made her miss Aesir's banters dearly, but she spoke nothing of it. They would find their way south by the sun and stars. Neither of them knew where the Freeholds were, but making it to Elondria's southern shores was a start.

After another fortnight, they reached the end of the Prannon Stretch. This was the farthest Skálda had ever travelled from home. Out here, the slope they hiked turned bare on one side, levelling sharply into a grassy gorge. On the other side were more mountains. A sparkling stream meandered its way through the valley.

"You know," Skálda said, as she climbed along, "it hasn't failed to pass my notice that you officially broke your 100 chapters."

Ahead of her, Bale gave what appeared to be a dragonish shrug. He was more interested in the cabbage butterflies.

"*106* chapters, to be exact." Skálda held onto an overhanging branch for balance. "That makes *me* an Ealdorman. 'Ealdorman Skálda, milord,' how does that sound?"

She felt him rolling his eyes through the Binding.

"My ravens, I am eligible to start a post. But where? Maybe we ought to return to the Skonkauld and finish what Anders started?"

"My wolf can do much better."

"Or perhaps I should beg the Lord Prince for a ring, do you think?"

Her dragon snorted. *"Ealdormans don't get rings, silly wolf. No calling you 'lord' either. Not till Baron rank. A* real *grownup rank."*

"Oh, pardon me. You seem to know more about the Enterprise rules than I do."

He arched his neck loftily. *"I pay attention, maybe."*

"Because you *do* want to Build."

That drew a snarl out of him. Skálda chuckled.

The slope ascended them even higher into the air. Bale, still ahead of her, jolted to a stop. Sensing an energy shift in their Binding, Skálda marched over, resting her hand on his shoulder. "Bale? What is it?"

He did not answer. He was gazing into the dell below. Skálda quieted.

A thousand paces below appeared the first sign of life since Solhall. It appeared to be a village ruin nestled at the river's bend. Rubble was strewn over the weedy grasses. Vines of honeysuckle strangled the huts, and every window with shutters had been blown out. From the looks of it, it had been abandoned for many solstices.

Troubled memories flickered in and out over Bale's eyes.

"You remember this," she said. "You know what happened here?"

"This place is called Osmendell."

Skálda narrowed her eyes. That was the same village Eyrek said their father, Jorn Branwright, had retired to. Eyrek had claimed by the time he found it, the retired platoon leader had already passed from age and the elements.

"Do you know who did this?" she urged. "Was it Eyrek? The Order?"

Bale turned his head until she could no longer see his expression. His strange mood discomforted her, but it was not until she felt a tug on their Binding that she hurried closer to the edge. His falling terrors were returning, but he was fighting to keep them from overpowering her.

On the opposite side of the village, on the open dells to the north, was the world wonder she most dreaded—*faolrún*. These were just as monolithic as the runic scrollwork in the Naüthe's glaciers, and no less terrifying. Their individual swirls grooved the earth like steppes. The longer she stared at them, the more she heard an otherworldly howling in her head, though the dells stayed tranquil.

Skálda was completely certain now that they were following her.

And something else. With the Binding ever strengthening, something between them was different. If she focused, she could see faintly through his mind. A red film overlaid her vision... and she suddenly understood the *faolrún*. She could read the unnatural formations, a Nhorssn message written from no race in Elondria. The same ciphers repeated themselves on end.

Skálda glanced at the sky, to the invisible Break in Midgaard's veiling that Bale had fallen through. Somewhere up there was Atallgaard, the desolate Realm of the Breakers... but the glyphs suggested it might not be lifeless.

"'Find the thief,'" she whispered. "What thief?"

"I know what you desire, Wolf. I wish I could give it to you. But I should have told you sooner."

"Told me what?"

"It's why I ran from Atallgaard... He forced me to hatch for him."

"Bale, what are you talking about?"

He slowly turned to her. *"My rider, my real rider, is hunting for me."*

AUTHOR'S NOTE

Thank you for reading through!

I hope you enjoyed *A Banishing of Kings*. This was originally Part Two of *A Breaking of Realms*. It had to be split or you would have a series debut at 900 pages! Believe it or not, this concludes just the opening act of *Realm Breaker*. From here, things get even more epic as higher powers clash against Skálda's morally gray desire to Build an empire. And of course, Bale grows ever more into a Golath destined to Break the last habitable Realm. I'm so excited for what's in store—and I hope you are too.

If the story connected with you and you'd like to see more, will you *please* consider leaving a review, or even a quick rating, on Amazon?

Reviews are crucial in helping other readers find the book. They also convince Amazon's algorithms that the book is worth promoting. If you're unable to spare a quick few minutes at this time, please consider taking 10 seconds to post a rating on Amazon.

Alternatively, if you scroll all the way to the end of this book, your Kindle app will also prompt you to leave a rating. All you have to do is tap on the stars. Thank you so much!

Until the next adventure,
Jasmine Young

Visit the
Dragonfyre
Bookstore
Signed
Jasmine Young
Breaking of Realms
She was born to be
Queen
Reign of Dragons
A Fantasy Anthology
A Breaking of Realms
Realm Breaker
A Bond of Brothers
For limited &
special collector's
books!

DRAMATIS PERSONAE

Non-Dragons:

Aeogorath Velandrion

The late elvish future king consort and the older brother of Rhysaeran Velandrion.

Aesir Luthonder

An elvish ranger and the personal advisor of Queen Lhyestrae Morghûl.

Asveig Torfiner

A free northern warrior.

Calabran Astoraine

The young crown prince of Fjorland.

Detherys Lorathari

An elvish rider and post second of Skygate post.

Eveillan Astorvalden
The last emperor of the fallen Svenn Empire.

Evynd Astoraine
A prince of Vingulmark and the son of Soren Astoraine.

Eyrekvald "Eyrek" Ivarion
A prominent dragon rider.

Faelan Pranathor
A dragon rider and post second of Dellfast post.

Fjella Wulfgar
A princess of Isgardia and the daughter of Inaric Wulfgar.

Fritjolf "Frit" Astoraine
A princess of Vingulmark and the eldest daughter of Soren Astoraine.

Garreck Kingsley
An elvish rider of Dragon's Helm post.

Gwynevere "Gwynne" Aelfwyn
The queen of Fjorland.

Inaric Wulgar
The king of Isgardia.

Jaccorias Vikarie
The warden of Kar'thuul-dur Keep and the Illuminator Exarch (High Mage of True Light).

Jarmon Danheim

A free northern warrior.

Jofreid Anders

A dragon rider and post leader of Skoll Post.

Jorikvald "Jory" Skard

An advisor to King Leondran of Fjorland.

Kaelan "Kael" Vetura

An orphaned woodcutter and student apprentice of academics.

Leofraen Amanoor

An elvish rider and post second of Tera Bera Post.

Leondran "Leon" Astoraine

The king of Fjorland and an Eldari (a supreme theocratic leader in the Republic).

Lhyestrae "Lhyra" Morghûl

The elvish high queen and an Eldari (a supreme theocratic leader in the Republic).

Livana "Liv" Tamarath

A dragon rider of Dellfast post and Faelan Pranathor's wife.

Matleif "Mat" Brynhild

A dragon rider and post second of Skoll Post.

Raldefur "Rulf" Ilfsson

A free northern warrior.

Rhysaeran Velandrion

The elvish future king consort and the betrothed of Vhalentae Morghûl.

Rystendal Vacerys

An elvish Judge.

Sigrede Branwright

A widow and the mother of Skálda Branwright.

Skálda Branwright

A young hunter of wolves.

Sorenthor "Soren" Astoraine

The Were King and the ruler of Vingulmark.

Staunnton Berethor

The High Eldari (executive theocratic ruler of the Republic).

Torsten Ulvrik

A dragon rider and post second of Dragon's Helm post.

Vhalentae "Vhenna" Morghûl

The elvish crown princess of the Rhaennörian Empire.

Vharyn Morghûl:

An elvish prince and the Lord Prince of the Order.

Xandria Kirylith

An elvish ranger.

Dragons:

Aeyrinth

The silver-green dragon of Garreck Kingsley; an eldragon.

Bale (Baelaeryx)

The black dragon of Skalda Branwright; a Bael.

Crixalas

The ice dragon of Rystendal Vacerys; an icescourge.

Elda

The gray dragon of Torsten Ulvrik; a mood dragon.

Feorya

The spotted dragon of Mat Brynhild; a picadragon.

Incendra

The red dragon of Faelan Pranathor; an eldragon.

Lumaerrax

The white dragon of Vharyn Morghûl; a Great Dragon.

Nornsir

The gray dragon of Jofreid Anders; a picadragon.

Saarhekhu

A wild indigo nightborn.

Tythandrell (Thane)

The golden dragon of Eyrekvald Ivarion; a Great Dragon.

***Dragonposts*:**

Dellfast

Post Leader: Alarek Tamarath
Post Second: Faelan Pranathor
Riders: Brennwald "Brenn" Matheson, Livana Tamarath

Dragon's Helm

Post Leader: Eyrekvald Ivarion
Post Second: Torsten Ulvrik
Riders: Garreck Kingsley

Skygate

Post Leader: Eyrekvald Ivarion
Post Second: Detherys Lorathari

ABOUT THE AUTHOR

Jasmine was thirteen when she first dreamed of becoming published after devouring Eragon in a few days on Grandma's couch. As a nerdy introvert, her exposure to fantasy started with hiding out in the library with a great book.

Thirteen years later, her tomboy dreams came true.

Today, she is known worldwide as a part time beach hermit and a full time rebel. She is also the proud mother of two young children, Bubble and Mochi. Both happen to be baby parrots who reside with her in her dream state of Florida.

When she's not reminiscing about her gaming days or getting lost in old epics like LOTR, she writes epic fantasy to entertain and empower, especially the underdogs.